ON THE
RAZOR'S
EDGE

ON THE RAZOR'S EDGE

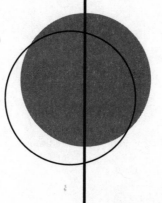

MICHAEL FLYNN

A TOM DOHERTY ASSOCIATES BOOK
NEW YORK

ON THE RAZOR'S EDGE

Copyright © 2013 by Michael Flynn

All rights reserved.

Maps by Jon Lansberg

A Tor Book
Published by Tom Doherty Associates, LLC
175 Fifth Avenue
New York, NY 10010

www.tor-forge.com

Tor® is a registered trademark of Tom Doherty Associates, LLC.

Library of Congress Cataloging-in-Publication Data

Flynn, Michael (Michael F.)
    On the razor's edge / Michael Flynn.—First edition
        p. cm.
    "A Tom Doherty Associates book."
    ISBN 978-0-7653-3480-0 (hardcover)
    ISBN 978-1-4668-1553-7 (e-book)
    I. Title.
    PS3556.L89O5 2013
    813'.54—dc23
                                        2013006328

Tor books may be purchased for educational, business, or promotional use. For information on bulk purchases, please contact Macmillan Corporate and Premium Sales Department at 1-800-221-7945 extension 5442 or write specialmarkets@macmillan.com.

First Edition: July 2013

Printed in the United States of America

0 9 8 7 6 5 4 3 2 1

CONTENTS

MAIN CHARACTERS

Francine Thompson	d.b.a. Bridget ban, a Hound of the Ardry
Graceful Bintsaif	a junior Hound, deputy to Bridget ban
Lucia D. Thompson	d.b.a. Méarana, a harper, daughter of Bridget ban
Ravn Olafsdottr	a Shadow of the Confederation of Central Worlds
Donovan (the scarred man)	d.b.a. the Fudir, sometime agent of the CCW
Gidula	Counselor to the rebellion (black, a white comet)
Swoswai Mashdasan	Commander, 423rd Fleet (Qien-tuq Borderers)

Hounds of the Ardry

Greystroke	longtime companion to Donovan and Bridget ban
Little Hugh O Carroll	Pup to Greystroke, d.b.a. Rinty
Gwillgi	League observer in the Confederation

Black Shuck, Cŵn Annwn, Grimpen, Matilda of the Night, Obligado, et al.

Rebel Shadows

Khembold Darling	Gidula's ship-captain (yellow, a daffodil; comet canton)
Eglay Portion	Gidula's seneschal (tan, a rose; comet canton)
Domino Tight	a young Shadow (tawny, a lyre proper)
Oschous Dee Karnatika	"the Fox," field marshal of the rebellion (scarlet, a black horse)
Dawshoo Yishohrann	leader of the rebellion (black, white diagonals)

Big Jacques Delamond (white, a blue trident), Little Jacques (swallowtail, red), Manlius Metataxis (sky blue, a white dove), et al.

Loyal Shadows

Shadow Prime	Father of the Abattoir (black)
Ekadrina Sèanmazy	field marshal of the loyal Shadows (black, a taiji)

Aynia Farer (lime, a lion), Phoythaw Bhatvik (yellow, two black crows), Epri Gunjinshow (forest-green, a lily), et al.

Those of Name

Tina Zhi	the Technical Name, the Gayshot Bo
Paul Feeley	the Radiant Name, the Nangling Bo
Hayzoos Peter	the Powerful Name, the Sing Song Bo
Ari Zin	the Militant Name, the Woqfun Bo
xxxxxxxx	the Secret Name, the Bo'an Ghincat

Magpies, boots, sheep, foo-doctors, archivists, villagers, Terrans, Names, Protectors, et al.

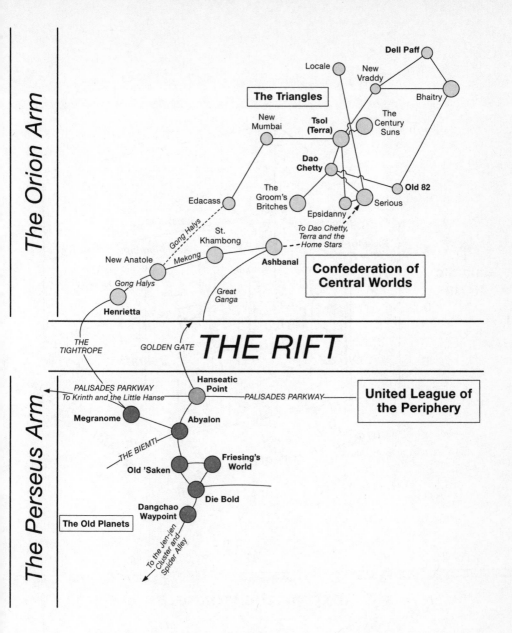

MAP OF THE BORDERLANDS AND THE OLD HOME WORLDS

Planar projection of the Confederal Borderlands and the Triangles. View is from Galactic North. Not all worlds or roads are shown. Worlds are not all on the same plane.

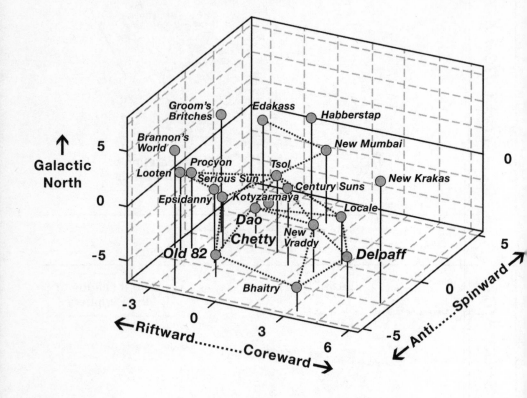

Groom's
Britches
Edakass
Habberstap
Brannon's
World
New Mumbai
Procyon
Tsol
Looten
Serious Sun
Century Suns
New Krakas
Epsidanny
Kotyzarmaya
Dao
Locale
Chetty
New
Vraddy
Old 82
Delpaff
Bhaitry

Galactic
North

5

0

-5

-3

0

3

6

←Riftward..........

Coreward→

-5

0

5

←Anti.......Spinward↗

0

0

5

ΜΑΡ OF ThE ΤRIANGLES

Oblique projection of the Triangle District. The view is outward from the Core and slightly north of Sol. The Rift and the Periphery lie far to the left. Roads are not shown. Stars connected are roughly equidistant. "A dozen lights from star to star."

Data from a marvelous site: http://astronexus.com/node/34.
To see what the sky looks like from other stars, see here:
http://astronexus.com/node/69.

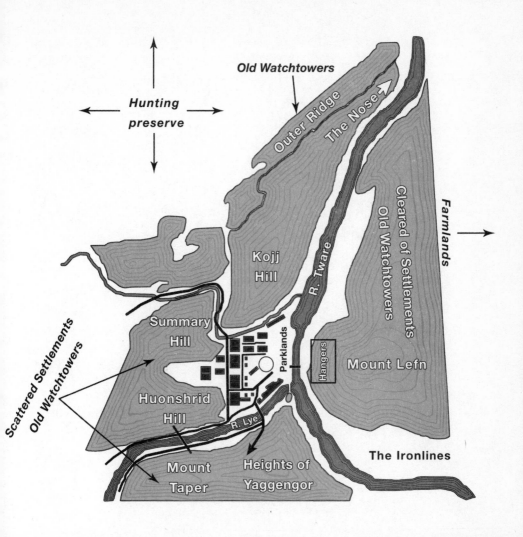

MAP OF GIDULA'S STRONGHOLD

Thus the peoples of the world foresee a time when their land with its rivers and mountains still lies under heaven as it does today, but other people dwell there; when their language is entombed in books, and their laws and customs have lost their living power.

—Franz Rosenzweig

ON THE
RAZOR'S
EDGE

AN RÉAMHRÁ

In the beginning, there were three, because in these matters there are always three. One was a harper and one was a Hound and one was nine.

There were others, because in these matters there are always others. There were other Hounds. There was a Shadow, and other Shadows. There was a Name, and other Names. And had any of them done other than they had, matters would not have tumbled quite as they did.

But a man is the master of his acts, provided he acts with virtue; and the chief of these virtues is courage. Children lack courage because they see all fears as things to be removed by their parents. But a man may regard fearsome evil and see the outcome as dependent upon his own actions, and so he may become master of them. This is true even if he ultimately fails, perhaps especially if he fails.

There was a treasure, because in these matters there is always a treasure. And there was a far quest, and an ancient tyranny; and longing and greed and ambition and treachery. There was courage and cowardice, as one often finds when something very small stands against something very large. One man had let his fears become the master of his acts, and so men died and cities burned.

But at the heart of it there was a shining kernel, something hard and bright and unbreakable that had been hidden away and all but forgotten by its hiders. At the heart of every treasure, as always in these matters, there was another treasure beyond all price.

And so in the beginning there were three; but in the end, there was only one.

I. DOGGEDNESS

First, the Hound.

Francine Thompson was a Hound of the Ardry, and this was no small thing to be. Hounds enforce the law when the law has failed. They lead when leadership has failed. They rescue when hope has failed, and will assassinate when all else has failed. It was a fearsome thing to have a Hound on one's tail, and many a desperado has surrendered on no more than the rumor of such pursuit.

Among their number, Francine Thompson was accounted not the least. Breezy, and confident to the point of arrogance, she carried herself as if she were the Queen of High Tara. It was in her stride and in her voice, which crashed like the bursting sea; and when she tossed her head, her hair was a breaking crimson wave. Her skin was a deep gold, and her eyes the green of flint. She operated under the office-name of Bridget ban; and she was at this point in her life the one thing that a Hound never is, and that is dreadfully afraid.

Afraid enough, in any event, that she had issued a Call to

Hounds. It was not often, and never for matters trivial, that more than one Hound was needed on a quest; but Bridget ban had such a need and the Call had gone out over the Ourobouros Circuit. An even score of her colleagues heard the summons and a dozen were close enough to reach Dangchao Waypoint in time for the facemeet on her estate.

That estate, Clanthompson Hall, stood lonely sentinel on the endless prairie called the Out-in-back. The Hounds fore-gathered in the arboretum of the Old Keep, a high-ceilinged room whose dark wood half paneling and heavy roof beams bespoke a ruder age. Ancient banners hung from the joists—some torn, some faded, one whose bloodstain must never be laundered. Oh, the day was long past when the Thompson lev-ies had marched forth under them. Recovered technologies had made of such banners little more than convenient markers for standoff weapons. But they would do for pomp, and they complemented the ancestral portraits on the corbels beneath them: grim and gay, wild visaged and thoughtful, and all bear-ing that Thompson cast of eye that was something more than confidence and a pennyweight shy of arrogance.

The arboretum flourished in the sunlight piercing the clerestory windows, and lent the indoors an outdoor ambience. Her staff had laid out a table of impressive variety, with cheeses imported from Gehpari and pondi-cherries and other fruits and melons from New Chennai. The other foods were from local estates: marble-case from Kurland, bright-mix milled at Dalport, fish-rolls from Honig's Beach, and—this being Dangchao—thin-sliced haunch of Nolan Beast. The wine had aged in Clanthompson cellars, and the spirits had dripped from the coils of the family distillery in Glennamor.

Of the Hounds, some had come from affection for Bridget ban, some because they expected an intriguing quest, some per-haps to gloat over whatever matter had impelled her cry for help. The men and women of the Kennel were a varied lot, and rivaly for status was not unknown among them.

The ancient Hound na Fir Li had sent his regrets and his senior Pup, a thin, hawk-faced young man of olive complexion who bore the name Obligado. The Pup moved with an economy of motion, and gave the impression that he skimmed a half thumb above the floorboards. He spoke little, but listened much; and Bridget ban marked that a point in his favor.

Grimpen arrived, too. He had just completed a small matter involving the pirates of the Hadramoo, having toppled the government of New Constancy on Abyalon, captured an agent of the People of Foreganger, and assassinated both the Molnar and his chief of auguries over the old business of the *Merry v Starinu*.

"A man in his cups," Grimpen rumbled while the gathered Hounds enjoyed drinks and stories, "should take care which crimes he confesses, and to whom, for his boon companion may prove not merely judge, but executioner as well." Grimpen had a laugh like an earthquake just before the rocks shear.

His glass was nearly lost in his massive fist, while that of Graceful Bintsaif seemed almost too large for hers. Tall, and lean as a whippet, the junior Hound seemed constantly to strain against an unseen leash. "Do you know what sort of killing machine the People sent?" she asked.

Grimpen's head tolled. "No. I know only that it never arrived, so the Molnar had the pleasure to deal with me instead of the People. One day, the Ardry will need to take a fleet into the Cynthia Cluster and root them out, tooth-and-toenail. And maybe deal with Foreganger, too."

Graceful Bintsaif glanced toward Bridget ban, who held the other end of her metaphorical leash, and gave a slight nod. Grimpen's story confirmed part of a tale they had already heard.

"So what is such mysterious mission you propose us?" asked Anubis. His facial hair was very dark brown and his nose and mouth thrust prominently forward. The gene-wrights of the long ago, when knowledge had passed for wisdom, had engineered his ancestors for cleverness; but a tangling of genes had carried with it a distinctive, foxlike countenance, so that all men noted that here was a clever one and so responded with heightened wariness. His parents had come to the Periphery as refugees and he spoke still with a Confederal accent.

Bridget ban swirled and patted him on the cheek. "Oh, a grand quest, darling, but we are not all here yet." The numbing fear had turned her heart to ice and her stomach to knots, but she would not show her colleagues any but blithe assurance.

Black Shuck scanned the room. "Grand enough," he said, "to call so many." His words came out flour fine: a sweet voice for so rough visaged a man. He was not so large as Grimpen, nor so clever as Anubis. Neither could he match Bridget ban for seduction. He was second-best at everything. But he was second-best at *everything* and even his most jealous rivals admitted that he was Top Dog.

"Gideon's band, darlin'," Cŵn Annŵn told him. She was a robust thing, even standing before the broad-shouldered Shuck as she did. There was Jugurthan in her genes, so that while she appeared wide and dumpy, it was muscle-firm down to the bone. "Gideon's band," she said again, this time herself looking about the room. "Our hostess rounded up a passel in hope of brandin' a few. She don't 'spect everyone here to join her." Her voice drawled in the lazy accents of Great Wally on Megranome.

"Perhaps she expects only me," declared a silvered throat from the doorway. Conversation ceased abruptly across the room, and one or two of the gathered Hounds visibly shivered.

It was a sweet voice that chilled the heart. Even Black Shuck shifted from foot to foot before facing the newcomer.

The woman wore black diaphanous robes girt at a high waist with a silver cincture. A silver-and-turquoise scapular hung from her neck. Her black hair was clipped short and lacquered so that it formed a sort of helmet for her otherwise-uncrowned head. Her lips blossomed scarlet; her fingers rang with drizzle-jewels. Altogether, a striking presence, and not merely because of her cobralike poise. It was a look to die for, and many had.

Matilda of the Night.

When she stepped into the room, her robes billowed in her wake, as if she dragged that night behind her. Other Hounds drew back as she passed, lest she pass too close and (as they told themselves) spoil the effect.

Bridget ban was not immune to the impact that Matilda so often had, but she was the first to shake it off. She herself often made a striking entrance, though she more usually turned heads toward her than away. She crossed the room with arms stretched in embrace. "Tilly!" she cried. "How de*light*ful to see you!"

An *abrazzo,* two quick pecks on the cheeks, and the spell was broken. *Tilly?* That was not quite so daunting. Conversations resumed, laughter rose, though both were more subdued than before.

"Delight, my dear," said Matilda to Bridget ban in a low, throaty voice, "is not in it. And . . ." Turning. ". . . *This* must be Graceful Bintsaif!" She extended a hand to the junior Hound, who barely hesitated before taking it. "Na Fir Li has told me *so* much about you. How can such a limited man raise such fine Pups?"

"Perhaps," murmured Graceful Bintsaif, "because my old master is not so limited as some suppose."

Matilda stiffened fractionally, but a server in household livery distracted her with a tray of drinks, and she fussed over them long enough that when she finally straightened with a colorfully layered beverage in a tall, thin glass the moment for taking offense had passed. Cleverly done, Bridget ban thought, and no one lost face. She did not very much care for Matilda of the Night, but Bridget ban counted such temperance a point in her favor.

"Are we all here, now?" Matilda asked. "Cafall, Yeth, Barghest . . . Kirkonväki? The Gytrash . . . My, my! A mixed bag, darling. Some top cuts, but also some ends. But . . . I suppose one takes what the net hauls in."

"I expect one or two others," Bridget ban said.

"Who? That young man sitting behind the juniper ferns?"

Bridget ban stepped back and peered through some of the foliage. "Ah. Come join us, Hugh," she said.

Little Hugh O Carroll rose from his casual concealment with a pot of ale in his fist. He was solidly built, with a square jaw and dusty-red hair. His left cheek bore the memory of a scar, and he smiled in that half-shy, half-sly manner that had seen him safely through the guerilla on New Eireann, many years before. It was then that he had learned the art of concealment. If there was a cover, he was beneath it. If there was a hole, he was in it. If there was a corner, he was around it. He went now by the office-name of Rinty, but to Bridget ban he would always be Little Hugh, that hard young man with the soft affections who had heighed off hunting the Dancer with her.

Bridget ban introduced him to Matilda, and the Dark Hound took his hand. "A bit old for a Pup, aren't you?" There was a subtext there not hard to read.

"Oh, I started late," Hugh said cheerfully. "I'd been a planetary vice-manager and a guerilla leader before."

Matilda acknowledged that with a bob of her head. "And who is your master?"

"I am," said Greystroke, who stood at her side sipping a tall iced tea. "Greystroke," he added. "And we *have* met. I was the baggage handler at Port Kitchener a few hours ago. You warned me away from your satchels."

"I was the hackie," Little Hugh volunteered helpfully, "who drove you to your hotel."

"Well," said Matilda of the Night, looking from one to the other, "aren't you the dynamic duo."

"Greystroke and I hung about Kitchener a few days," Hugh said. "We wanted to see who was coming. Met most of the Hounds at Inbound Processing. 'Och, aye, m'laird,'" he said in a broad Dangchao accent. "'Mought I help ye wi' yon wee baggie.' Except Black Shuck, who would have recognized me from that business on Uobigon, and Cŵn Annwn, who somehow eluded us. Oh, and the Gytrash, who arrived before we did."

"It was just to keep in practice," Greystroke added. "Rinty here has a talent for disguise—they used to call him the Ghost of Ardow—and I have a talent for going unnoticed. Who looks twice at a baggage handler or an unremarkable dough-face in a crowd?"

They broke up and moved off to greet other colleagues. Greystroke lingered. "We're with you, Frannie," he murmured to Bridget ban.

"Greystroke, darling. Ye've not yet heard my proposal."

"Does that matter?"

Graceful Bintsaif sidled up after he had gone. "I don't like it," she said. "The way they all try to get one up on one another. I don't like it when I get drawn into it."

"Oh, they may bicker and play games—and strut before the Little One if it means moving up the pyramid. But when what matters matters, you can depend on each and every one of them to the very limits of his skill."

"Though first," said Graceful Bintsaif, raising her drink to her lips, "you have to get to what matters."

It was a hard winnowing that the Red Hound made of her guests. She must harvest the volunteers she wanted without insulting the others. In the end, she was successful enough, though she endured a disappointment or two.

"I need your help to find my daughter," she told the assembled Hounds when once the buffet had been cleared and the musician dismissed and they had adjourned with sherry and port to the long table in the banquet hall.

"Ah," Greystroke murmured to Hugh. "I had wondered why it was not Méarana who played for us."

"I wonder what she's gotten into now," Hugh sighed.

"What is this, Red Hound?" cried Garm. "A Call to Hounds for a mere family contretemps?"

"And is she not of age?" added Barghest. "She may go and come as she wist."

Black Shuck stood. "Hold your gobs!" he said; and, he being who he was, they held them. "Our colleague would not have summoned us for no better cause than a runaway daughter. Daughters have run away since the dawn of time, and for the same reasons. There is something darker yet to come." He turned and bowed to his hostess and resumed his seat.

"Points off for Barghest and Garm," Hugh whispered to Greystroke. "Too quick with the quip."

"A case of days ago," Bridget ban announced when silence had been restored, "my daughter was kidnapped by a Shadow of the Names."

Would the Red Hound ever speak more than one sentence

without a hubbub of interruption? This was just as well, for the memory of it closed her throat and filled her heart with ice.

"A Shadow!" "How?" they wanted to know. "Why?" "Where?" "We'll scour the Periphery!" "Is she taken across the Rift?" A Shadow was not so easily laughed off as a runaway daughter. If there were aught in the Spiral Arm undaunted by pursuing Hounds—who might even welcome them for the sport—it was a Shadow of the Names, their opposite numbers in the Long Game between the League and the Confederation.

"Why did you not tell us so straight off?" demanded Garm, retrospectively embarrassed by his earlier jape.

Hugh spoke behind his hand. "Easily answered," he told Greystroke. "She wanted to know who would go for the sake of the daughter, and only then who would go for the sake of the Shadow."

"Where is the Fudir in all this?" Greystroke complained. "The harper is his daughter, too. Why is *he* not here?" That had always been a stumbling block between Greystroke and the scarred man: that the harper was the daughter of the one and not of the other.

"Syne twa metric weeks an' more," Bridget ban said, lapsing momentarily into the local dialect, "Ravn Shadow Olafsdottr plucked her from within these very halls."

Black Shuck grew serious. "A grave breach of security." The rebuke was sharper given the sweet, judicious tone in which it was couched.

"The de'il wi' yer fashin', all of ye," she said. "We tracked her coming in. Not even a Shadow can cross yon heath and escape my eyes. And the Bintsaif and I held her fast the while as she spun her tale and laid out her petition. She desired that I cross the Rift with her on a quest of her own, and failing in that she—"

"—took your daughter," guessed Black Shuck.

"Why snatch the daughter," said Kirkonväki, "if the task wants the mother?"

"The Ravn did nae trade my skills for harp-speil," the Red Hound told him. "My daughter's the drag to lure the hound."

"Drag success," Anubis noted. "You go. Red Hound pride pricked. Shadow enter your very stronghold, you hold close watch, yet allow her slip away—with your daughter—as easily as eel slip through fingers."

"Too much Schadenfreude," Greystroke whispered to Hugh. "Cross Anubis off. What is it?"

"Sure, and I'm waiting to hear what the Ravn's proposal was."

"Even if all of us here were free to go with you," said Garm, "we would be few enough to scour an empire."

The Gytrash stood. "Your daughter's fate sorrows me, Red Hound," he said. "And my heart is yours to weep into, but there be no hope to this quest. The Confederation be big and broad, and a slip of a girl a hard finding in all those bright stars. 'Tis a just quest, a worthy quest, and a cause must be just before its undertaking is just; but it must also have a chance of success, and alas 'tis ill-starred to succeed. She is more vanished than a grain of sand on a beach. Meanwhile, a massacre pends on Harpaloon that I must see to." He bowed, and after courteous farewells and expressions of good fortune he strode to the door. A few others stood with him, but only Garm, Barghest, and Anubis followed him out. The others lingered, and one— Black Shuck—sat back down and something of a smile crossed his face.

"First cut," said Greystroke.

"You'll notice who have held peace till now," Hugh answered. "Grimpen, Matilda, Cŵn . . . Mark young Bintsaif, how grim she looks. She is frightened sick, but she will go."

Grimpen rumbled, and it took the others a moment to recognize the sound as laughter.

"What is it, Large Hound?" Cafall asked.

"Our departed colleagues do not grasp the meaning of 'hopeless.' If success is sure, what need is there for hope? A quest like this cannot be hopeless, for there is nothing to it but hope."

"All right, Frannie," Black Shuck said. "The pessimists have gone, and don't hold it too hard against them. There is another war brewing between Ramage and Valency, which Garm and Barghest must attend to; and there is Harpaloon for the Gytrash to handle. Your daughter's taking is a tragedy; but it's a big Spiral Arm, and not the only tragedy in it. Now, where has Ravn taken your daughter?"

Matilda of the Night spoke up. "Don't look so surprised, Kirkonväki. The Ravn wanted our Bridget ban to aid her in a quest, and took the daughter to lure her to it. What point the drag if the hound cannot follow?"

"Aye," said Bridget ban. "And 'tis Terra."

"Deep in the Triangles," Cafall observed. "Hard by Dao Chetty."

"I put out a Stop Traffic order as soon as I learned they were gone—and, aye, finding one needle among thousands of ships queuing up for the roads is a hard finding indeed. She slipped the net, and only later, reviewing the video records, did Graceful Bintsaif and I pluck her out—artfully disguised—in the queue for Megranome via Die Bold."

Greystroke rubbed his chin. "She's taking the Tightrope. The long way around . . . I wonder why?"

"Why, to give me time to catch up! Ravn does not want to arrive at Terra too far ahead of help." There was a modest comfort in that. No harm would come to Méarana as long as Ravn needed Bridget ban. About the afterward she was less sanguine.

Kirkonväki said, "Then it is a matter only of heading her off."

Black Shuck sighed and glanced at the door, then at the remaining Hounds. "A complication, Red Hound. There is a struggle in the Lion's Mouth. Shadow wars on Shadow, some to uphold the Names, others to bring them down. Gwillgi is observing matters for us over there, and some of his dispatches have reached the Kennel. Shadows operating in the League have been going home one by one."

"Aye," said Bridget ban, "and among them was one that some of you know: Donovan buigh of Jehovah, who calls himself the Fudir."

"And half a dozen other names beside," murmured Hugh.

"Donovan is at the root of it all . . ."

"And why am I not surprised," said Greystroke.

"Ravn drugged Donovan on Jehovah," Bridget ban told them, "and took him across the Rift, where the leaders of the rebellion coaxed his allegiance. In the course of affairs, Ravn and Donovan became what they call gozhiinyaw—blood brothers. That displeased her patron, Gidula, who had her tortured and imprisoned. She escaped and besought my aid in an act of vengeance and rescue. From Gidula's hands, she would pluck Donovan buigh; from Gidula life, she would pluck her vengeance."

"Ah," said Hugh, "that explains why the Fudir is not here for his daughter."

"It may also explain," guessed Greystroke, "why his daughter was so easily taken."

"I knew Gidula in the long ago," mused Black Shuck, "when he and I alike were young. A rebel, you say? Yet he was as staunch a Shadow as the Names could ask."

"And perhaps even still. He was working inside the rebellion to subvert it. It was on this point that Ravn finally broke with him, for she was won over to the cause by Donovan."

Yeth folded his arms. "So, to find your daughter, you must find the Ravn. And to find the Ravn, you must find Donovan. And to find Donovan, you must find Gidula. That is a great deal of finding."

"But one may find the arrow by watching the bull's-eye," said Cafall. "On Terra, you say?"

"Aye. The rebels courted Donovan because in an earlier rebellion he had learned a way out of the Secret City. The rebels want to use this as a way in, for they have planned an attack on the city. But Donovan had forgotten the key when his mind was shuffled and dealt."

Kirkonväki slumped back in his chair and drummed the table with his stylus. "It would be one thing to slip over there and winkle your daughter out if she were merely lost in the Confederation, but she is a prisoner of a Shadow. But even that might be done, save that the condition is to free Donovan buigh from Gidula's stronghold. But even that might be done—Gidula is old, and Donovan himself might give aid from the inside— save that the Confederation is at war with itself and Terra is in the heart of the Confederation. And Donovan himself is in the very center of the maelstrom. The Shadows will be more alert to intrusions."

"Say rather they would be more distracted," Bridget ban said. "The maelstrom swirls below the surface. Outwardly— for merchants, tourists, officials, even their military—the waters stay glassy calm. For the most part, the war is waged by stealth. And while Shadows' eyes are drawn to the Secret City, we might slip onto Terra and be done and be gone."

Greystroke leaned over to Little Hugh as they broke for an intermission. "'For the most part,'" he quoted.

Hugh shrugged. "She is still holding something back. But why?"

"Because," Greystroke said, as he watched Cafall, Yeth, and Kirkonväki thank Bridget ban and take their leave, "she has a lagniappe for those of us who stayed."

Bridget ban was disappointed at losing Yeth and the Gytrash and uneasy at keeping Cŵn Annwn. A very good practitioner, but close observation would note her Jugurthan ancestry; and Jugurthans were as rare across the Rift as foxies were on this side. Nonetheless, she had kept Greystroke and Little Hugh, as she had known she would, and Grimpen, who was methodical but thorough. Matilda she did not care for, and would have traded her for the Gytrash, but her skill was undoubted. Graceful Bintsaif, Bridget ban's aide, was proven, but of the Pup, Obligado, she was unsure.

Black Shuck stood by the door.

"Top Dog!" said Bridget ban. "Ochone! Will ye abandon me, too?"

He wagged a finger at her. "Your wily ways don't work on me, Briddy. All that—what do you call it? Cozening and sweet talk. I'm too old for the flattery to work. I'm half out the door, *but I'm not there yet*. I have heard much that tugs at the heart. Your own daughter, ochone! The shame of a Shadow eluding you in your own stronghold. What is their term? *Sīdáo zhwì*, 'to escape stealthily from detention.' Even that this former lover of yours has been kidnapped and may be tortured to reveal what he knows. Sorrow upon sorrow! But do you not see a pattern? For I surely do. They *want* you to cross over. They are waiting for you. The entire story may have been naught but a lure to draw you deep into the Confederation."

"An' that was why I refused Ravn's plea to go with her.

But, Top Dog, my bairn is stolen awa', and that is an argument wi'out rebuttal."

Black Shuck grunted and shoved his hands in the deep pockets of his coverall. "But there is yet one thing missing. This quest you propose will require the Kennel's chop. Entering the Confederation, the very Triangles; infiltrating a Shadow's stronghold; *assisting in his assassination* . . . Should you be discovered, the Shadow-factions may unite once more, to the League's sorrow. So the Little One will approve *your* chasing after Méarana, for the excellent reason that he could by no means known to man stop you. But to take others with you . . . ? Give me a reason why I should not walk out that door. Tell me what the *League* stands to gain, not what aches in Francine Thompson's soul."

"She's 'bout to tell us, Top Hound," said Cŵn Annwn. "But first she had to thin the herd, like. Ain't that so, darlin'."

Bridget ban had seated herself at the head of the table, and leaned forward now with her fists balled together. "Let me tell you *how* Ravn Olafsdottr escaped."

II. AND DID SHE TEACH YOU THREE THINGS?

O Harper, *know what treachery abides*
In hearts of those who once you thought as friend.
How like a fang, a serpent's tooth, they wound!
  O Shadow! Think on what you say,
    For how can enemies betray?
O Harper! Think you that it is but pride
Affronted by Gidula's dire deed,
To find myself by my own trust impugned?
  O Shadow! Think howe'er you must.
    Who ever in a foe did trust?
O Harper! Know that foes do constant bide.
And on their constancy one may depend.
Oh heart and mind to whom I was attuned!
  O Shadow! Think you any would
    Inflict the pain a comrade could?
O Harper! Do not seek to shift the point
Of my arrow from the heart that it intends,
Or stay my shears from that which it must prune.

O Shadow! Prune as you decide,
For in our joint affairs we are allied.

Second, the harper.

When resolution follows shortly on resolve, doubt has little time to gnaw at purpose and success is either gratified—or moot. But when the clock drags on, imagination conjures possibilities from the vasty deep, not all of them cheerful. And so a warrior leaping upon a chance-met foe does not pause to consider the possibility of failure, while one advancing at the double quick across an open field might halfway there long for the cozy comforts of his trench.

So, to Méarana Harper, as Ravn bore her into the Confederation, what seemed a good idea on the spur of the moment appeared less grand during the canter the spur induced. She had thought that by going with the Shadow she would draw her mother in her wake, and so secure her father. A clever scheme, she had thought; but perhaps less clever in fact than in thought.

In appearance, Méarana was much as her mother limned at an earlier age, though with sharper corners. There was a hardness to her, but not her mother's hardness. The latter was annealed from the abuse of her affections, the former from receipt of too few of them. It was fairly said that Bridget ban had used love; while Méarana was unused to it. She knew it only as sentiments left in the wake of her mother's hasty notes.

There were certain corners of Méarana's face—her chin was one—that bespoke her father. And if anyone in life had been more absent than her mother, it was Donovan buigh. She was a master harper—an ollamh of the *clairseach*: a lap harp of the old style, strung with metal cords. Sometimes when she played, they drew blood.

The cloak of invisibility, a wonder of unknown provenance, had slipped them past her mother and her aide, past Mr. Wladislaw and the household staff, past Hang Tenbottles and the security detail on the perimeter. In some fashion no longer known to men, the "metafabric" bent light in all its forms and created "blind spots" in space and time, masking those events enshrouded by it. Secret even in the Confederation, used only by the Names, the cloak and other wonders, collectively styled "the Seven Vestiges," were closely guarded by an oath-bound college in the Gayshot Bo. But enamored of his charms, the Technical Name herself had given cloaks to Domino Tight, who had in turn given them to Ravn Olafsdottr. Thus does love—or perhaps lust—erode like acid even the oldest of tabus.

But it had not escaped Méarana's attention that Ravn had brought *two* cloaks to Clanthompson Hall. So while it had been the harper's idea to go with the Shadow, it appeared to have been the Shadow's idea that it should be the harper's idea.

They had departed Dangchao Waypoint in a monoship that the Shadow had weeks earlier leased on Peacock Junction under the name of Jin-ho Kisanaluva. She had stopped on Die Bold, done the usual touristy things, and managed to get her picture in the *En Courant:* cowering in the background while two business travelers in a Port Èlfiuji lounge broke each other's noses in her dubious honor. In the stereograph, "Kisanaluva" did not much resemble Olafsdottr. The skin tone was lighter than its wonted coal-black. The build appeared thicker than her serpentine slenderness. The nose seemed broader, the hair, dark and shoulder length rather than the usual yellow stubble.

"It seems a lot of trouble to go through," Méarana suggested when she had learned all this, "simply to prepare a false identity."

"When diligently sought," the Shadow advised her, "it is best to be someone else."

A Stop Traffic order was out by the time they had reached Dangchao Roads, but after 2,452 outbound vessels the customs officials no longer checked documentation with the same sprightly verve and enthusiasm as they had the first few hundred. A cursory visual examination confirmed that "Jin-ho" did not match the description of the sought-for Confederal; and a database search unearthed the account in the *En Courant* and receipts from Port Kitchener and a "dude ranch" near Casa Dio, nowhere near Clanthompson Hall. If the official ever considered that a Shadow would find little difficulty embedding false records into a system, he was not so impolitic as to say so. He may even have considered that the greatest risk in searching for Shadows lay in finding one.

In any case, "Jin-ho Kisanaluva" got the wave-on to continue acceleration behind a departing Hadley liner, maintaining such-and-so separation and, "Have fun on Megranome."

Méarana was determined to pry her father from Gidula's stronghold, and if Ravn thought she needed help the harper was disinclined to argue the point. That Bridget ban had been equally disinclined to provide that help distressed Méarana beyond measure, and she had hit on this idea—of sneaking off with Ravn—as a way to force the issue. "The idea," she told Ravn one day as they crawled through the high coopers of Abyalon, "is that Mother will come after me."

She said this not because she supposed Ravn had forgotten but because she had grown ever more conscious of the Shadow qua Shadow, and thought the gentle reminder of a vengeful Hound in hot pursuit would calibrate Ravn's behavior. Not that the Shadow had evidenced any threat—although the mere presence of a Shadow was quite enough threat—but their common goal was to free Donovan buigh from the hands of Gidula. Ravn, however, had a second goal: to murder the man who had tortured her; and the harper could not help but wonder, should it come down to the one or the other, which goal Ravn would score.

A woman betrayed, tortured, and abused by her erstwhile benefactor might be expected to harbor some degree of resentment, but Ravn Olafsdottr was remarkably cheerful as they wound their way through the streams of space. Méarana did not know whether this was fugue, masochism, or simply putting up a face. She had thought hate a prerequisite for murder, and was surprised to learn that her companion rather liked Gidula.

"He dreams the old dreams," she told Méarana one afternoon in the monoship's small lounge, "and what dream can endure the daylight? It shrivels at the first touch of sun. Gidula feels the cold kiss of morning."

"'The old passes away,'" Méarana quoted, "'the new is always born.'"

Ravn switched to Confederal Manjrin. "Most profound. Wise thinker, or fool."

"It was Raisha Lu, a novelist on Friesing's World about three lifetimes ago. She wrote—"

"Wrote nonsense. What can new ever be but newborn? A heartbeat later—no more new. What your Lu say be said long time, ten thousand lips, ten thousand ages. Sentiment old—but not yet pass away." She turned and seemed for a time to listen to the music she had chosen for that evening: a composer and a style from some bygone era of the Confederation's history. The harper did not find it pleasing, and wondered if the nature of the Confederals could be found in their preferences for such stringent measures.

"Detestable to gods and men," sang a mournful voice,
"Are lies and treason dark.
Yet across the broad millennia
Is Jason ever sung,
Who to take the Golden Fleece
Betrayed with perjury."

The music resumed the strange a-harmonic plonking and Ravn faced the harper once more. "It was Gidula and his like-minded friends—men who met on old estates, who bore names ancient and bold—who alone stood firm against the Names, when the likes of Dawshoo and Oschous dipped their heads and tugged their locks and did as they were told. Against his treatment of me, throw that in the other balance pan."

"Is it an account, then? A toting of assets and liabilities? I don't believe it. A man's character is seamless. What he does for good or for ill springs from the same soil. If Gidula is a traditionalist . . . Oh."

"Yayss. When Power o'ersteps His bounds, He violates traditions first of all. It is those who seek change who excuse power's extension, and they swear they will put it by when once they have succeeded. But whene'er did a man seize power and walk away after?"

"There are stories," Méarana said. "Cincinnatus. Washington. Venagar. Apaloram."

"Four!" exclaimed the Shadow. "Faith in humanity restored!"

"Mock if you like. There were certainly others. Less famous precisely *because* they let go of power."

"Oh, be not so truculent, sweet." Ravn patted her on the cheek. "At least there were four."

"But if Gidula is on the right side . . ."

Ravn laughed. "Too many sides. Maybe none of them right."

———

Ravn brought the monoship across the bar from the superluminal tube called the Tightrope and arrived once more in
Henrietta Roads, broadcasting her fu, her authorization. (The
fu was faux, but that was a small matter for a Shadow.) She
opened negotiations immediately for the return of *Sèan Beta,*
the smuggler's ship that she had donated to the Fleet the year
before.

"These be ticklish talk," she warned Méarana in the Alabaster accent she sometimes affected, "boot noo tickle during
dicker."

Discussion escalated slowly, corkscrewing up a level at a
time through the hierarchy, while Ravn descended toward the
impound orbit, where such vessels were kept. Rather than repeat herself with each new flunky, Ravn played a recording in
which she gave the required information and pleaded her
case, ready to flip to real time if she achieved breakthrough.
They started with interface clerks, worked up to the Gamzöng-
zhy, the Superintendent of Prize Vessels, who deferred to the
Shivegun Vayshun Madlow Gunly, or Commander, Fleet Logistics. Ravn maintained a degree of patience during this peeling of the bureaucratic onion that would have reduced the
harper to tears.

"Behoold, fate of peacetime navy," Ravn announced during one interlude while the comm. unit played insipid music.
"With noo enemy to fight, they create oobstacle courses to
clamber through." She sat before an oval screen on which colors flowed and blended in synch with the music. Méarana
stood nearby but outside the ambit of the Eye. No point adver-
tising her presence.

"Then perhaps 'tis just as well they have no one to fight,"
she suggested.

"Be not deceived, sweet harper," Ravn answered. "All this

miigimoos stop when enemy appear. Well, perhaps not *all miigi-moos*."

"Do we need this smuggler's ship that badly?"

"Ooh, yayss. When we rescue your father, we need bigger ship. Accoommodate Doonovan's egoo. And . . . ," slipping into the Manjrin, ". . . he appreciate art."

"Art?"

"Full circle. Kidnap him in that ship, so rescue him in same. Also: sentimental value. Doonovan and I fight Frog Prince in *Sèan Beta*. Reminder bring tear to his aged eye."

"What will you do if the Fleet won't give permission?"

Ravn flashed a broad smile. "Silly harper. I take it."

"Take it. From the Fleet."

Ravn snatched at her own shadow, cast by the running lamps, and made as if to peel it off the wall of the comm. station. "Shadows slip through such thumb-fingers as they."

"Then why dicker at all?"

A shrug. "So they not shoot at us as we scamper off. Hush now, sweet." A nod to the screen. "Next act of Kabuki."

By the time they were connected with the office of Swoswai Mashdasan himself, Ravn and Méarana were deep in the sun's gravity well, approaching co-orbit with the impound vessels, and the time lag between message and response was minimal.

The garrison commander sat behind a broad desk flanked by the starry black banner of the Confederation and that of the 423rd Fleet (Qien-tuq Borderers, "Ever Vigilant"). He wore undress grays with his badge of office on a chain around his neck and a string of decorations on his breast. Méarana wondered how a military that had not fought an actual war in more than a generation could award so many medals. But she supposed the Fleet no different from other professional organizations, which existed largely to bestow awards upon their members. Perhaps the medals represented rebellions crushed, or exceptionally good table manners.

The swoswai greeted Ravn with no great joy. He appeared ill at ease and his eyes wandered. At times, he fingered his medallion as if to assure himself that it was still there.

Here was a man, Méarana marveled, who commanded ships sufficient to reduce a planet to rubble and troops enough to subdue a continental rebellion—and a solitary Shadow in an unarmed monoship could bring an ooze of sweat to his brow.

"And why should I return the ship to the Lion's Mouth?" said the swoswai after Ravn had explained her request. "Especially when that mouth now roars with two tongues."

Ravn blinked, then smiled, and her eyes became razor thin. "Ooh!" she said. "You have learned mooch, swooswai! But is this soomething you *ought* to have learned?"

The garrison commander scowled and his eyes danced. "We're not stupid, you know. MILINT received dispatches from Yuts'ga. You Shadows burned down half a city there."

"It was not soo beeg a city."

"Yes? Well, I swore an oath to uphold the Confederation. What did you swear?"

Ravn looked on him with pity. "To kill her enemies." The smile with which she delivered this chilled even Méarana. But then Ravn added with unusual gentleness: "Do not choose sides in the Shadow War, oh master-of-ships-and-men, for all your ships and all your men would not avail you, whichever side you took. In these degenerate times, it is dangerous to have an opinion, any opinion."

Mashdasan ran a hand across his cheek and chin. "Don't be too certain, Deadly One. My loyalty is to the Confederation and to the Names."

"Good. So be mine. Hooray for Confederation! Huzzah

for Names! We do secret handshake later. Will you give me back my ship?"

"So you can use it for this illegal rebellion of yours?"

"When is rebellion legal? Love doos not mean you nayver spank the little rascal. No, let us say, swooswai my sweet, that I be on sabbatical from Shadow War and my poorpose for now be harmless, moore or layss."

Mashdasan shook his head, as if brushing off flies. "I'm a blunt man, a simple soldier, and I grow impatient with the antique wordplay your kind enjoys. Speak plainly."

Ravn sighed and leaned forward into the comm. screen. "I greatly fear, sweet, I can say nothing that will improve your situation. Life is color of your uniform; but rebels and loyalists not see matters so, and those caught between may find themselves ground to powder. What is monoship *Sèan Beta* to mighty Four-twenty-third Fleet? A mosquito among eagles. We swap. You give me *Sèan Beta* and I give you *this* ship. Very fast; good for courier work. Smaller, true, but what you lose in cubic you gain in delta-V. I give you word of honor our Confederation not suffer."

"Your word of honor . . . And what is honor worth?"

"A great deal, for is very rare coommodity these days."

The swoswai's lips curled. "And hence that much harder to recognize." He looked to the side and something flashed briefly in his eye. "Very well," he said. "I'll notify Fleet Logistics. They will send you the necessary orbital parameters." He reached out and blanked the screen.

Ravn sat back in the comm. chair. "The fool!" she said, yanking off the headset.

Méarana arched her brows. "Why do you say that? He gave you what you wanted."

"But too quickly," the Shadow answered. "Boots like pack rats. Never give up bauble unless forced."

"So . . ."

"*So who force him?*" Ravn tilted her head back and to the side. "How did he learn of the Shadow War? *And why tell me he knew?* And why tell us how loyal he be, if he think us rebels?"

"Us?"

"Who was he telling?" Ravn tapped a finger on the console . . . Then she leaned suddenly forward and called up a recording of the conversation. She stepped it forward to the moment near the end when the swoswai had glanced to the side. "Eyes may not be window to soul," she murmured, "but sometime make splendid mirror." She boxed in on Mashdasan's eyes, expanded, boxed again, enhanced. Then she grunted. "So."

Méarana leaned across her shoulder to see what the enhancement had revealed: a sleeve of dark but indeterminate color was reflected in the cornea.

"Shenmat," said Ravn in a flat voice. "Rest follow by deduction. Who, in all the worlds of all the suns, wears the body stocking? Shadows and their magpies. And loyalist, or he not so shy of Ravn's eye."

"But you're a loyalist, too," the harper pointed out.

The Shadow put a finger to her lips. "Shh. Is secret. Always problem with undercover. Better job you do, more your friends shoot at you." She stood from the console.

"What now?" said Méarana. "Surely the Shadow in Mashdasan's office wasn't there waiting on the chance you might show up!"

"No. Shadow come to Henrietta to question swoswai. Word of last year's facemeet is leaked. You and I . . . ? Phrase is 'target of opportunity.' Problem with tiptoe through minefield is sometime you step on mine."

They received the orbital parameters from SVMG. There were six, relative to Henrietta's sun and the plane of her planetary family. "Longitude of ascending node . . . ," Ravn sang as she worked from the pilot's saddle. "Argument of perihelion . . . Inclination to planetary plane . . . Where are you, my sweet? Ah! Stationary Station, I see you. Mark! Two more now . . . Hah! Mark, and . . . mark! Triangulating and locking on."

"What if the Shadow told him to send phony parameters and put us into the wrong orbit?" Méarana asked when the Shadow emerged.

"Oh, sweet Mashdasan nayver do that to darling Ravn! Boots nayver take orders from Lion's Mouth. Late swoswai correct. Boots not stupid. Maybe not broad-minded like Shadows, but inside box?—think very deep. Mashdasan knows he is dead man. Cannot be less dead by fooling Ravn, but fine vengeance on his killer to help his killer's enemy. No, we may rely on parameters. We may also rely on Shadow."

"How so?"

"He too know our destination but no time to climb up, catch us. So he use smartie or wave cannon . . . Subvert instructions no very large matter. Imitate swoswai voice; manipulate swoswai ymago in tank. A piffle." She sanpped fingers. "Give orders destroy us. Boots nayver obey Shadow—likely much vexed when learn he kill commander—but boots obey words on comm. link, no questions; and a little kaowèn harvests all access codes."

Destroy us . . . Méarana's heart went cold, and she wondered what she had gotten herself into. "So this unknown Shadow could pot us at any time?"

Ravn sat at the astrogation tank and began tapping commands. "Likely not any time. Mooch traffic in these orbit, and we be small rental ship. Better if wait until we match with target. Then . . ." She made frying sounds with her tongue and Méarana flinched.

"Why not wait until we board *Sèan Beta*? That is more certain still."

"That is also Fleet property. Fry intruder one thing, but even wave cannonier scratch butt and wonder what the *xing jiao* is going on if asked to fry impound ship, maybe ask for confirmation back up corkscrew of command. So . . ." She touched the tank in several places, reaching into the hologram to toggle certain commands. The tank turned gray and dots of various colors blinked their way through it.

Méarana said, "Ravn?"

"Hoosh, sweet. Thinking very hard . . . Ah. We blend in with traffic here . . . to . . . here. Then . . . Is asteroid going our way. We ride with it to . . . here. Natural object in free trajectory. STC brain subtract those, so make us invisible. Bad time, *here* to *Sèan Beta*. Must leave friendly asteroid and make matching transfer to rendezvous. Curse upon Holy Newton's hemorrhoids! Longer trip time, but . . ." She engaged the alfvens and the little rental grabbed the corduroy of space and yanked. Somewhere aft there was a loud and unpleasant sound, and Méarana smelled an electrical odor.

"Second reason we want smooggler ship. Survey class alfvens. Grab strings of space deep in gravity well but not burn out like these poor ship." She patted the control board fondly.

"Ravn? Why do you think the Shadow will kill the general?"

"Do not *think*—*know*. Fool try to warn us. That was very nice, and I kiss his lips, but not very wise. He knows Shadow War, stresses his loyalty for benefit of interrogator, but looks sidewise to warn us. Wink-wink, nudge-nudge. 'Someone in room with me.' But sooch body language and sly allusion subtle oonly to man of 'bloont' character. Shadow not fooled.

So Mashdasan suffer fate of all who place generative organ between hammer and anvil."

"So the Shadow did not go there *intending* to assassinate him."

Ravn swung her seat around. "Likely noot. Oonly to torture him and learn what he could of the facemeet Dawshoo held there last year. Why do you ask this?"

"Mother taught me a thing or two. The Lion's Mouth sends you out in pairs, don't they?"

Ravn nodded. "Usually. Second kills first if first falters. Nice system. Encourages job commitment."

"How sweet. But that suggests that while the first does not know how to contact the second, the second keeps tabs on the first."

"Yayss . . . ?"

"Then the Shadow in the swoswai's office . . ."

Ravn grinned broadly and smacked the console desk with the flat of her hand. ". . . exceeded his instructions!"

"But the second would not know why. So if 'Dawshoo' sent a congratulatory message to the first in care of the swoswai's office, the second . . ."

". . . would intercept it, find it but moodestly difficult to decrypt, and perhaps woonder if his first is playing a traitor's game. Young harper, I like the way you think."

Méarana touched her forefinger to the tip of her nose. "Confusion to the enemy."

"And perplexity upon our foes."

"I wonder," said Méarana, "why Mashdasan tried to warn you. It's not as though he was on your side."

"Perhaps he had something to prove to himself. Dawshoo humiliate him last year. Two such affronts he would not accept. Fool. But sometimes fools do brave things."

"Are we going to make it?" The harper tried to ask with an air of nonchalance.

"All in hands of Fate. Tell me this, harper. Your mother taught you a thing or two. But did she teach you three?"

Space Traffic Control watched the monoship emerge from the detection-shadow of Asteroid Laatmui 27 and make a dash for the ships in the impound orbit. Grabbing space, she moved in quantum jerks, building velocity. STC noted, too, from the shell design that the ship was Peripheral built. This information spread across the surveillance web, downloaded into cognizant systems, was picked up picoseconds later by Midsystem Sector Defense. The field control officer noted the orbit and checked against the fire order sent from Siling Bo Henrietta. Burn the vessel matching orbit with the designated reference. Obvious now, the reason: an attempt by Peripheral agents to hijack a Fleet vessel. An earlier search had flagged the reference vessel as one promised to the Lion's Mouth, and the officer shuddered to contemplate the consequence if he allowed it to be stolen. After verifying that no other ships were matching orbits with the reference vessel, he sent the release-to-fire message to the wave cannon Stout Defender, *which was best positioned to take it out.*

The range officer of Stout Defender *pinged the target, obtained range and velocity, and computed azimuth and bearings and fed this to the gunner.*

"Charging," the gunner's mate called from the bowels of the capacitor banks. "Flux nominal." Then, "Charged ninety-five percent."

"Locked on," said the gunner. He studied the data on the monoship, decided it was unarmored, and computed the kill burst. Then he doubled that just for luck, what gunners called the "200% Kill" level. "One-bar-nine," he ordered.

"One-bar-nine," the gunner's mate concurred, having carried out an alternative computation.

"Burn it."

There was, of course, no bright streak of light of the sort entertainments liked to pretend. Nor was there anything so dramatic as a fireball when the target absorbed the gravity wave. But the monoship began to break up.

"Debris field confirmed," the range officer announced. "Spreading. Talker, alert Range Safety Office at STC. Parameters follow. The pings show multiple large fragments following the original orbit, a few others tumbling off to the sides on daughter orbits." Some were approaching the craft promised to the Deadly Ones. She hoped they wouldn't hole the vessel. Shadows could be quite prickly when it came to their rides.

"Scratch one," said the gunner.

The range officer continued to monitor the debris field while the gunner's mate wound down systems and toggled them to safety mode. "I hope," said the gunner, "this wasn't just another drill."

III. UNLEASHED

Invisibility cloaks?" rumbled Grimpen. "The Seven Vestiges?"

"The Vestiges appear to be a sort of trove," Bridget ban said, "that their Tech Control Ministry, the Gayshot Bo, sequesters and manages."

"Vestiges . . . ," wondered Greystroke. "'Leftovers.' Old Commonwealth tech? The Confederation inherited most of the Terran Commonwealth of Suns."

"What else could it be?" said Obligado.

"Prehuman," suggested Little Hugh, "like the Ourobouros Circuit."

"*Seven* Vestiges," said Cŵn Annwn. "You've named the cloak and the quondam leap."

"Leaping from world to world," said Black Shuck, "sounds impossible."

Matilda of the Night somehow caught their attention without saying a single word or making the smallest gesture. A secretive smile played across the scarlet of her lips. "Keep in mind," she said, "that one 'widow' might birth more than one daughter. It is premature to tally them. The Gayshot Bo broods upon many wonders."

"Why do they do that," wondered Little Hugh, "when they could use them in the Long Game? It seems contrary to their own interests."

Matilda smiled more broadly, "Darling, have you ever been *Across?*"

"But, Briddy, 'tis all hearsay," Black Shuck reminded them. "It's what Ravn told you, or what she told you that Domino Tight told her—or what she told you that Tight told her that the Technical Name told *him*. Hearsay, double and triple hearsay."

Bridget ban leaned back in her chair. "And yet . . ."

"And yet," Top Dog acknowledged, "why tell *that* tale and not another? Yes, it would slide down smooth should the Little One be willing to swallow. It is worth the sniffing out. But, Briddy . . ." His arm swept and encompassed the remaining Hounds at the table. "Had you mentioned these Vestiges before, the others might have stayed."

But Bridget ban shook her head. "If they would nae stay for Méarana," she said, "they should nae stay for *tarnhelm*."

Black Shuck nodded, as if she had confirmed a matter already known. "Aye, you dangle these baubles to sweeten the Kennel's disposition so that you may take a pack to rescue your daughter. You see? I understand your seductions. But it also changes the complexion of the quest. This is not a mere swoop-and-snatch off Terra, a feat difficult enough. These 'Vestiges' are held by the Names themselves, and to seize them wants penetration of the Secret City."

"The rebels are planning an attack within the Secret City," Bridget ban reminded him. "They intend to finish the Shadow War with a single bold stroke. In that confusion, a small band might slip into the Gayshot Bo and, while all eyes lie else-where, record the treasures."

She gathered the eyes of all those present. "Are ye with me?" And this gathered the ayes of all those present. All but Black Shuck.

"And where do you stand, darlin'?" warbled Cŵn Annwn.

"Yes," said Matilda of the Night, "are you with us?"

"It would mean a great deal if you would come," Bridget ban urged him.

Black Shuck moved away from the doorjamb on which he had been leaning and, in straightening, seemed to grow taller. He thrust his hands into his coverall pockets and lowered his head. The tink of glasses stilled to form a silence into which his words might fall.

"I've been hounding most my lifetime," he said quietly. "Valency, Orsini's World, Foreganger, Gehpari. A litany of crimes and disasters. But I like to think there were small, mean people—killers, tyrants, thieves—who watched nervously over their shoulders for thought of me; and refugees, prisoners un-just, and the helpless caught between two fires who knew some ray of hope when my name was whispered among them. I have fed the hungry when famines struck, clothed the naked after earthquake or flood, led the distressed to safety, and removed hobnailed boots from unnumbered faces; and never, I hope to tell myself at the end of days, did I do any mean or unworthy thing. But, Briddy ban, I am seven-score years, and my youth is behind me. I have been three times across the Rift, and from a fourth such journey I would not return."

Bridget ban tried to speak, but Black Shuck raised a palm. "No, hear me. Your quest is worthy. Not for the Vestiges—although if found they may soothe the nerves of the Little One—but for your daughter. For her—and aye, for your Don-ovan, however little you've mentioned him—I would approve the quest. I will go—but I will go to High Tara for you. I will be your champion in the Kennel, secure you resources, deliver you what information might smooth your path. You will need identities, comm. channels, transportations. But none of this will I do unless . . ." And he turned his eyes on the seven other Hounds and Pups who sat at the table. "Unless you go in for Méarana Harper. If it is merely for the glory of it, or for the chance to snap up ancient baubles, it is not worth the going. So, tell me that this is so."

Over the next two weeks, they reviewed the recordings Bridget ban had made of Ravn Olafsdottr and her tale, studied gazetteers of the Confederation, digested Gwillgi's intelligence reports, planned their entries, their points of rendezvous, studied clothing styles, loaded earwigs with Confederal dialects, established passwords, and learned the identities they would assume. Black Shuck supplied them with contact information for agents-in-place—and for Gwillgi, too, should they find themselves in position to make contact.

"Though if Gwillgi ain't wishful o' being found," joked Cŵn Annwn, "it ain't likely that we'd be a-findin' him."

They split into two teams and worked tactical plans at opposite ends of the hall. Bridget ban naturally took the lead in planning the extraction of her daughter from Gidula's stronghold on Terra. This proved remarkably difficult, since they knew almost nothing of its layout and facilities. It stood somewhere west of Ketchell, on the Northern Mark, but intelligence was scant and uncertain. They would need tactics flexible enough to conform to situational details as encountered.

Black Shuck took the lead in planning the extraction of the Seven Vestiges from the Secret City. But because he was often on the Circuit with the Kennel, the task more often fell to Matilda of the Night. Obligado's master, na Fir Li, who had once walked the streets of the Secret City, also sent information, though of older vintage. Little by little, a simulacrum of the Secret City rose from the holotable.

"For such a secret city," joked Little Hugh during a break, "we have more information on it than on Gidula's station."

Matilda smiled coldly. "Don't suppose that streets and buildings constitute its secrets." She regarded the ghostly structures on the holotable—simple blocks, since architectural details were lacking. "This one," she said, pointing to a long oblong hard by the Red Gate. "That is the Gayshot Bo. The Vestiges will be in a vault somewhere in that building."

"Do we enter by the Red Gate, then?" asked Obligado.

Matilda laughed. Cŵn Annwn studied the layout. "I don't s'pose they open the Gates to any poke comes along. How'd yuh get in, Tilly? Or na Fir Li or Black Shuck?"

The Dark Hound had long changed her black robes for an equally black coverall. "Through patience," she said, "establishing identities, securing migration chops, obtaining licenses and work permits. Na Fir Li was a licensed beggar and sweeper. I was a courtesan. Black Shuck . . ."

"I went in as a day laborer," said Top Hound. "It took three years to become a Known Man in the San Jösing slums, a drinking companion to those who knew those who had passes. Three years to build the ID up. And it took the Protectors three weeks to tear it down. But I was in and out in two."

Bridget ban had been listening to everything. "We dinnae hae years!" she cried. "Once we snatch my bairn from Ravn's talons, we must enter the city quickly and be done."

"You could," Matilda pointed out, "return your daughter to the Periphery while the rest of us complete the quest for the Vestiges."

But Red Hound tossed her head. "I'll nae lead ye in if I dinna lead ye out."

"Then," said Black Shuck, "you will need to learn from your Donovan the secret passage by which he once escaped the compound."

"He is nae *my* Donovan," insisted Bridget ban, "but aye, we must needs free him from Gidula. His rescue is why Ravn snatched my daughter in the first place." Méarana had gone willingly, even obstinately, but Bridget ban had not shared that deduction with her colleagues.

One of Tenbottles' men entered the hall, looked from table to table, and strode up to Obligado with a message packet off the Circuit. The Pup broke it open and extracted the flimsy. "Ah!" he said after a moment's reading. "My master has de-tached a cutter from the Sapphire Point Squadron for our use, the advantage of which is that it was Confederal built and pressed some years back into the Service as a prize. It is already en route."

Grimpen grunted, and the sound was as of a quake deep within the earth. "Transport and logistics solved."

"No," said Black Shuck. "You'll not put yourselves in one basket. Too much is at stake. We may lose some of you on this venture. It is no lackaday stroll. But a fell swoop ought not net *all* of you."

An uncomfortable silence fell over the Hounds at both tables. Cŵn Annwn made a sign to avert the evil. Death was always a possibility, but they preferred that it remain only a possibility. Only Matilda of the Night smiled, and her lips were the color of blood.

They decided to go in as four teams, led by Bridget ban, Greystroke, Grimpen, and Matilda. Obligado would go with Grimpen and Cŵn Annwn with Matilda of the Night. Hugh, of course, would go with his master and Graceful Bintsaif with Bridget ban. They would take different routes and rendezvous on Terra.

On the last night, after everyone had taken leave, Graceful Bintsaif found Bridget ban in the library under the glitter of night. All the lamps had been extinguished and the room was lit only by the starlight that sifted like flour through the bay window. It was bright enough to see by but not so bright as to pluck out details. Bridget ban sat on the stool that her daughter had occupied during that fateful interrogation. She was merely a shape within the shadowed room, starshine highlighting her hair, accenting her profile. Graceful Bintsaif stepped within and closed the door behind her.

"Grimpen and Obligado have gone," she announced. "They'll nestle the cutter on the hull of *Kethwick Harpy* and pretend to be a navigation submodule. The border is open to trade ships. They'll detach at Epsidanny. There's a ship's fu they can use for authorization within the . . ." She fell silent as Bridget ban failed to respond. "We received a message from Greystroke," she continued. "He was about to enter the Roads. They'll board *Chettinad Rover* as crew when they reach Abyalon, then jump ship once across the Rift and make their way as spacehands."

The Red Hound might as well have been one with the furniture.

The junior Hound sighed and sat herself in the seat she had occupied while Ravn had spun her tale. Reflexively her eyes flicked toward the sofa, as if she expected to find Olafsdottr still in it. "It will all work out," she said. "You'll see."

Bridget ban stirred. "Will it? Of the five Hounds who have infiltrated the Secret City, only three returned. So by the odds, I am leading three colleagues to their deaths."

Graceful Bintsaif swallowed, said nothing for a moment. "The odds are there to be defied. We may not need to enter . . ."

The older woman put hands to knees and pushed herself upright. "Of course we will."

"Perhaps it was only a story."

Bridget ban went to the bay window and stood within its ambit. She threw open the casements, and the soft sounds and cool breeze of the prairie night swept in. A sheet of paper on the side table fluttered and the resinous odors of sunflowers and the more pungent milkweeds filled the room. A soft, distant hoot broke the night, and she shivered.

"Owl," she said. "A poor omen."

"Owls aren't good," Graceful Bintsaif agreed, "but we'll find her."

Bridget ban stared at the silhouette of Firstblest Mountain, the tallest of the Dōngodair Hills, backlit by the distant gleam of Port Kitchener. God, it was so lonely Out-in-back, lonelier still with but one soul missing from it. Had Méarana felt this way when her mother had been out among the bright stars?

"She is my life, Graceful Bintsaif. She is all I have, the one good thing I've done that might outlast me. And it's been *weeks* already. They'll be past Henrietta by now. My God, how I wanted to fly after her! But I knew that only fools rush in. I had to plan. I had to . . . bide my time. And every day that dies, she is a day farther from me."

"There is a positive side to that," ventured her aide.

Bridget ban turned away from the window and Graceful Bintsaif could just make out the quizzical twist of her features. But she did not ask what the positive side was. So the junior Hound took a deep breath.

"Ravn is going after Gidula, right? We're certain she spoke sooth on that score. And Gidula holds Donovan buigh. So every day that passes, she is a day closer to him."

The Red Hound sighed. "I'm not sure that's a positive side."

IV. THE SYNTHESIS

And third, there was the scarred man . . .

The scarred man had wearied of waking in strange ships, although he did not see how until now he had had much say in the matter. This time, he lay immobile on his back while an autoclinic caressed him, fed him, evacuated him, and numbed him where the pain grew too great. Soothing medications dripped into him; burned skin sloughed snakelike from his arms; cells were cultured, regressed, grafted. New skin grew. Bones knit. He wondered at one point how much of the original him might be left.

Perhaps he would get a better body out of this. One with skin not so parchment tight across his bones, with eyes less sunken, with the scalp free of the crisscross scars that parted the tufts of snow-white hair. Perhaps he would be restored to the vigor of his youth.

But probably not. He was not sure he had had a youth, or that it had been filled with vigor. The scars that parted his hair had parted his mind, as well. Years ago, the Names had divided it into sundry and diverse shards, each an expert in some facet of the espionage art. The intent had been a team; the consequence, a committee; the price, a loss of memories.

So while his body thus healed itself of its wounds, his minds were free to consider how he had come by them.

At first it was difficult. The mind recoils from injury, and Donovan's mind had recoiled in multiple directions and it took awhile for them to find one another. It was not exactly amnesia; it was more like fugue. But parts of him remembered different things: sights or sounds; strategies and tactics; thoughts and words. From these fragments he sought to assemble the thing entire.

How long recollection took he could not say, nor how reliable the result. Pollyanna was prone to burnish his memories with the polish of best construal, and the Sleuth sometimes spanned the gaps with bridges of logical interpolation. Yet events were not always logical and their meanings seldom rosy.

We been in a fight, the Brute concluded. He could name the blows by the wounds they had left behind. The melted skin implied the penumbra of a dazer burst. The snapped rib entailed the shod foot that had cracked it. The holes in his leg intimated shrapnel; the slice, a sharpened edge.

But we're alive, the Sleuth submitted. *That means we won.* "Although if this were victory," the Fudir countered, "we would just as soon not taste defeat." Besides, other events than victory might end with the scarred man bundled in an autoclinic. Rescue, for instance. Preparation for torture, for another.

Consciousness was a sometime thing. Sleep was a blessing.

In sleep, the Silky Voice took over, metering out soothing enzymes, working in concert with the autoclinic. Donovan worried, as was his nature, over in whose custody they lay and for what purpose; but as no one in the ship's crew had made an appearance and as his present state precluded effective response in any case, there was little point to the bother save to upset the enzymatic balance. So the Silky Voice sedated him as well.

Only the Brute seemed unaffected. But that was because the Brute was immersed always in his senses, keenly aware of his surroundings at all times. He knew how his knee bent *just so.* He knew the curl of each finger, and the lay of his head. Kinesthesia was his, and proprioception. He knew the drape of each tube across his body, the warmth of the osmotic infusers and the limaceous slime of the gels in which they nestled. He felt the rush of the richly scented air that coursed through his nostrils and into his lungs.

Like a tiger, the Brute was a smooth stimulus-response machine, his reflexes unencumbered by reflection—yet, for all that, he was not severed entirely from his more cerebral compatriots in the small principality of Donovan's brain.

It was a hell of a fight, the Brute told them one morning. **But you shoulda seen the other guy.**

He remembered the combat now. The old ruined warehouse. The loyalist Shadows led by Ekadrina Sèanmazy and the rebels led by Oschous Dee Karnatika, locked in the mad embrace of mutual and escalating ambuscade. The abrupt appearance of the late Domino Tight; the sudden and fearful manifestation of several Names; Ravn Olafsdottr and her wild and fatal play wearing Padaborn's colors that had finally induced him to take up arms himself. And his own death struggle with Ekadrina.

<And then Gidula swooped in.> That was Inner Child, the wary and watchful one.

"Maybe," said Donovan. "But if he rescued us from Sèanmazy, he rescued her from us."

Gidula is a rebel, said the young man in the chlamys, but he is also a traditionalist. For everyone, the world is as it was when we came of age. Gidula soaked up *djibry* with his mother's milk. He can no more act in a non-*djibrous* manner than he could wear motley to a pasdarm.

A few days later, two magpies in black shenmats with Gidula's comet on their sleeve brassards entered the dispensary.

"How we feeling?" the junior magpie asked. He wore the skull-and-crossbones breast-badge that marked him as a medic. He glanced over the readouts on the autoclinic, waved a slug across the infoports, and spoke a few words into it. His was not an idle question. Readouts could tally only quantities. *These* neurons were firing; *those* areas of the brain lit under resonance; *such* were the blood pressure and heart rate—but none of it could capture the *quality* of pain. There was no gauge for suffering.

"We've felt better," Donovan allowed.

"How many fingers am I holding up?"

"Two. How many fingers am *I* holding up?"

The medic smiled. "One. What is the square root of seventeen?"

"Four point one-two-three."

The medic looked up and Donovan added, "Metric. Four point two-nine-two, in dodeka."

"Name the Crossings."

"Including the Tightrope? Point Pleasant, Krinthic Junction, Hanseatic Point, Sapphire Point . . ."

The smile vanished. "Those are the Peripheral names."

"Well, we lived most our life over there—as *myan zhan shebang,* a sleeping agent—later as a discarded wreck of a man." He cackled to show how wrecked he was.

"You were ill-used," said the older magpie, speaking for the first time. The medic glanced at him but said nothing.

"I've prepared a schedule for your physical therapy," the medic told Donovan. "Ready to get out of the box?"

Donovan agreed that they were ready and, with a little assistance from the two comets, was soon disconnected from the support systems and lowered to the floor, where he stood in momentary unsteadiness. The medic spoke another verbal note into his slug. Donovan glanced at the other three autoclinics in the room. Empty, but he had a phantom recollection that one of them had been occupied. He stretched, touched his toes, inspected those wounds visible from his perspective. He wondered if he should pretend to a lesser vigor than he felt. One of a man's sharpest weapons was underestimation by his foes.

"What of the others?" he asked. "Ekadrina, Oschous, Big Jacques . . . Ravn?"

The medic glanced up from powering down the autoclinic. "Master will discuss that with you."

Donovan turned to the older magpie. "You don't talk much."

"Don't need to."

"And you are . . . ?"

"Your sparring partner. Physical therapy."

"We had enough sparring with Ekadrina. We were hoping to relax."

The older magpie nodded toward the autoclinic. "You have been."

"I think we like you . . ." Donovan looked at the brassard. "Should we call you Five, or do you have a nicknumber?"

A smile very nearly cracked the man's face. "I will have to you soon a schedule sent of our sessions." And he bowed a fractional amount from the waist. From the man's careful pronunciation the Fudir judged him not a native speaker of Confederal Manjrin, but he did not recognize the home-world from which the man's consonants sprang.

"If you'll follow me," the medic said, "I'll take you to Gidula. He was anxious for your recovery and wanted to see you as soon as you were ambulatory."

Donovan could think of several reasons for that anxiety, not all of them a comfort. Gidula had snatched him away from Ekadrina, but he was not especially certain it had been a rescue.

Don't worry, said the young woman in the chiton. Like the Brute always says, we've got him outnumbered.

"Pollyanna," Donovan chided his optimism, "you've forgotten his magpies."

We may have a handle there, said the young man, if I've read the body language aright.

The medic led Donovan down a carpeted hallway lined with paintings composed of intersecting geometric figures in various bright colors. Hand painted, the Pedant noted, and not drafted by machine. 𝕿𝖍𝖊 𝖘𝖚𝖇𝖙𝖑𝖊 𝖎𝖒𝖕𝖊𝖗𝖋𝖊𝖈𝖙𝖎𝖔𝖓𝖘 𝖎𝖓 𝖙𝖍𝖊 𝖆𝖗𝖙—𝖔𝖗 𝖘𝖍𝖔𝖚𝖑𝖉 𝕴 𝖘𝖆𝖞 "𝖈𝖗𝖆𝖋𝖙"—

You shouldn't say anything, the Sleuth suggested.

—𝖆𝖉𝖉 𝖒𝖆𝖗𝖐𝖊𝖙 𝖛𝖆𝖑𝖚𝖊 𝖙𝖔 𝖙𝖍𝖊 𝖜𝖔𝖗𝖐. 𝕿𝖍𝖊𝖞 𝖌𝖗𝖆𝖓𝖙 𝖆𝖓 𝖆𝖘𝖘𝖚𝖗𝖆𝖓𝖈𝖊 𝖔𝖋 𝖊𝖝𝖈𝖑𝖚𝖘𝖎𝖛𝖎𝖙𝖞 𝖙𝖍𝖆𝖙 𝖒𝖆𝖈𝖍𝖎𝖓𝖊-𝖈𝖗𝖆𝖋𝖙 𝖉𝖔𝖊𝖘 𝖓𝖔𝖙. 𝕻𝖊𝖗𝖋𝖊𝖈𝖙𝖎𝖔𝖓 𝖎𝖘 𝖙𝖔𝖔 𝖊𝖆𝖘𝖎𝖑𝖞 𝖎𝖒𝖎𝖙𝖆𝖙𝖊𝖉; 𝖋𝖑𝖆𝖜𝖘 𝖆𝖗𝖊 𝖚𝖓𝖎𝖖𝖚𝖊.

The Fudir's previous life as a thief in the Terran Corner of Jehovah had given him an appreciation for art that a mere connoisseur did not possess. "We could make a shiny ducat from these pretties," he murmured.

They give insight into Gidula, said the young man, both their hand-crafted nature and their subject matter.

Subject matter? said the Brute. **They're just shapes.**

Yes. Exactly.

The hallway led around an S-curve and ended at an open archway, on the other side of which lay a vestibule. A young magpie sat behind a minimal desk, engaged in a multitude of tasks. One hand wrote on a light-pad with a stylus; the other hand entered data on a touch screen. Her throat worked as she subvocalized into a pickup. Her goggles, which lent her an insectlike appearance, flickered with disparate information on each lens. Earwigs undoubtedly whispered independently in each ear. A paraperceptic. Donovan regarded her as he might an evolutionary ancestor, and not without a little envy. *Her* channels were merely sensory and motor. Her intellect and will had not been fragmented into independent personalities.

"Ah, don't fret, Donovan buigh," the Fudir told himself. "You'd be lonely without us."

Two other magpies sat in the vestibule along one wall, talking to each other in low voices. When Donovan and the medic entered, they glanced up and fell silent. One of them favored Donovan with a barely perceptible nod.

The office manager appeared not to notice, but that was the way of paraperceptics. They took a certain pride in what they called "multitasking" and delighted in disregard. Donovan was certain that she had seen him, studied him, and informed Gidula immediately of his arrival. The other two magpies returned to their conversation.

The medic had handed his slug to the office manager and departed. The Fudir looked about the room, and saw two open seats on opposite sides of the room. He started toward one, stopped, and turned toward the other, stopped again, and scratched his head. This attracted the attention not only of the two magpies but also of the office manager, which the scarred man counted as a signal accomplishment.

"What are you up to, Fudir?" he muttered.

In a whisper: "Let's maintain the charade that we're still fragmented."

After that display of prowess with Ekadrina?

"How many of Gidula's people actually witnessed that fight? As far as they're concerned, their boss rescued us from certain death."

"Maybe so, but I don't think the Old One will be fooled."

Perhaps not, but the manner in which he is not fooled may tell us much.

Did you notice the body language of the three magpies? said the young man. Number Two, the paraperceptic, seemed suspicious—but Twenty-three smirked while his friend Seventeen stifled genuine distress.

"Conclusions?"

The manager suspects the Fudir was playing Buridan's Ass. In her position, she'd be privy to most of what Gidula knows. Twenty-three holds us in contempt. He knows we were supposed to be broken and doesn't yet know we fought Ekadrina to a draw. But Seventeen . . .

". . . is a genuine partisan of Geshler Padaborn."

Who is supposedly us. The scarred man would not mind so much being a great hero from the past if he could remember any of the heroics. When the Names had diced and sliced his mind, they had buried his memories under a pile of shavings and debris.

Our therapist, Five, is also a Padabornian, the young man added.

The scarred man considered this. He had decided long before that Gidula was attempting to subvert the Revolution from within. Why bring Padaborn back if you truly believed him a ruined man? To raise the rebels' spirits with the *idea* that Padaborn had returned, then crush them with the *reality* of the scarred man.

On the other hand—if anything as twisted as the politics of the Confederation had only two hands—broken or not, Geshler Padaborn knew some way into the Secret City; and whatever Gidula's original purpose in peeling the scarred man from his uisce, he had other purposes now.

Yet Donovan understood that Ravn had been sent to snatch him more than two metric years ago and the rebels had determined to attack the Secret City a little over a year ago. Their curiosity regarding Padaborn's escape was more recent than their desire to secure his person.

Unless, said the young man in the chlamys, *we have been misreading them all along.*

"That's your job," Donovan murmured. "You're supposed to get inside the heads of our enemies and figure out what makes them tick."

"Without," the Fudir warned, "empathizing too much."

Several of the Shadows now in rebellion had fought to suppress Padaborn's Rising. One obvious reason for the contradiction was that the Rising had been premature and in the interim minds had changed, enthusiasms had shifted, and the doubtful had grown convinced. Perhaps the Names had overreacted in the aftermath. Such measures could trigger the very revolutions they meant to crush. Lucky Nanduri, the fifteenth maxraj of New Chennai, had put down the Mylapore riots with exquisite cruelty. His tontons had burned entire neighborhoods, blown up family compounds, executed citizens rounded up in sweeps regardless of whether they had participated in the riots or not. *"Fear begets obedience,"* the maxraj had declared. What it begat was twelve weeks of quiet. Then rebellion erupted across the continent, from Royapuram to Coromandel. When royal troops were ordered decimated as punishment for allowing the sack of the Coromandel Taj, the Palace Guard itself had turned on the maxraj, slaughtered him, and offered the Golden Tuban to a surprised—and rather unwilling—second maternal cousin.

Something similar may have happened in the wake of Padaborn's Rising.

Watch the magpies, the young man advised them. *They dream "the great game of the beautiful life." There is ever romance in the heart of cruelty.*

Aye, thought Donovan. *The grand gesture, the emotion*

that tugs at the heart, the sheer drama of *Padaborn on the Roof-tops* might lure Shadows into rebellion for no better reason than the tears of a pasdarm.

On the Rooftops . . . ? There was a vague recollection there, but it would not come clear.

There was another answer, less obvious. The Shadow War was not in fact a resumption of Padaborn's Rising. "The lamp that was lit" had not been lit again but was another struggle entirely, with different goals and only coincidentally similar objectives.

"Who fights for anything so abstract as 'liberty' or 'tradition' anyway?" Donovan grumbled. "The Shadows fight for injury or revenge or ambition, and because they have reached the point where nothing else is left. The fine words they make up later to justify themselves. An ambitious man like Oschous Dee might prate about oppression, but *he* was not oppressed, and had the paths of his ambition wound the other way, he would be defending the Names as loyally as Ekadrina."

"You're too cynical," the Fudir told him. "Méarana always said so. Ambitious Oschous may be, but there are safer ambitions than raising the red banner."

And would Ekadrina fight so doggedly were she not equally fervent in her loyalty? asked the Silky Voice.

"The drivers of doggedness and bravery needn't be devotion and conviction. Ekadrina and Epri are Korpsbrüder, trained together by Shadow Prime himself. She's in it because Epri is in it, and Epri stayed loyal because Manlius did not . . . "

"And Dawshoo rebelled because Manlius did . . . Never mind. We get the picture." Motives were complex and seldom known, even to the actor. Purposes were easier, and often could be teased out. Two men might conspire to murder a third: but one to protect himself, the other merely to rob him.

The inner door opened and a fourth magpie emerged. This one betrayed no emotion on noticing Donovan, and the young man tagged him as "enthusiasm unknown." The other two magpies rose and the three left the room together, murmuring in low voices.

The paraperceptic did not look away from her work. Hands danced across touch screens, eyes scanned scrolling images on her goggles, information whispered in her ears. She spared a moment of her mouth. "He see you now," she said with admirable concision.

The scarred man hesitated and waited for Two's reaction to the hesitation.

"He wait."

Donovan grinned at her. "What are you doing after work, *babe*?"

The term of endearment was Terran, and unfamiliar to her; the essence of the question was not. "No 'after work,' me," she told him. "You wish enter 'jade gate pond,' I multitask." The face she turned to him was rendered beetlelike by the flickering data goggles, and she seemed suddenly a strange and alien thing.

Donovan recoiled, his joke gone sour in his mouth. He could imagine her busily manipulating multiple information streams even while she beat her chosen lover wet, and the pleasures of the latter would in no wise interfere with the efficiencies of the former. There was something in that which repelled him. One ought to take pleasure in one's pleasures.

Gidula sat in a high-backed black padded chair at the far end of a long room. The carpeting was hard and durable, and woven in a tapestry of interlocking brightly colored lines against a sable background. The pattern reminded the Fudir of vines and creepers; the Sleuth, of mazes. The sable was shot through with silver threads, which lent it an odd sense of depth, as if the pattern comprised a catwalk above a deep and dimly lit cavern.

Crossing the room, Donovan made a play of walking carefully on the tapestry, as if he feared falling into the illusory sable pit.

"Really, Gesh," Gidula said. "We know better, don't we?" He gestured broadly with his left arm. "Please, sit."

Gidula had no desk, as such. He sat within a nest of shelves and surfaces and glowing screens, some of which seemed permanent, some mobile, and some of which recessed into floor or ceiling as needed. At his word, a chair slid up from the floor, locking itself in place. Donovan made himselves comfortable and waited.

Gidula gestured with his right hand and a door slid open on the back wall to admit an androgynous servant bearing hot drinks on a wooden tray. The fey offered the drinks first to Donovan, who selected one at random, then to Gidula, who raised the second to his lips.

Donovan sipped from the steaming mug. If Gidula had wanted to poison him, he would have been poisoned while lying helpless in the autoclinic. The beverage was an infusion of some sort, with a hint of licorice. He blew on it to cool it.

"Why play the scatterbrain?" the Old One asked. "We brought you back to lead us, to lend your legendary name to our cause."

"You brought me back to learn the entry into the Secret City."

How better to lead us, Gidula's shrug proclaimed, *than to lead us to victory?* But Donovan had long decided that the last thing a triumvirate wanted was a fourth man.

"Naturally, your infirmity dismayed us and we had almost given up hope you would recover your wits. Oschous promised to revive you, and Olafsdottr went with him to assist. And it is clear from your actions at the Battle of the Warehouse that they succeeded. Surely," and here Gidula's voice took on a note of disapproval, "surely the continued pretense does not mean that Geshler Padaborn has gone shy!"

The scarred man pondered his reply. If Gidula had hoped for a broken Padaborn, what would he do when faced with a whole? Ravn Olafsdottr had advised him to act disintegrated, and it was clear now that in doing so she had betrayed her master. "You know you get scatterwit," he said in the Terran patois. "Billy Chins tell him so."

Gidula sighed. "Billy turned his coat and threw in with the loyalists. We thought he meant to dissuade us from recalling you. But no man can be impaired in the mind and still be standing after a battle with Ekadrina Sèanmazy."

"What man unimpaired would engage her in first place? Besides, we were *barely* standing."

"Barely is more than her other opponents have stood."

"Ravn slain," he said, "we see red; go berserk, fight like madman. Which," he added in a different voice, "is appropriate, seeing as we *are* a madman. Perhaps facing prospect of certain death focus our minds most wondrously."

Gidula said nothing for a moment. Then he crooked a finger and summoned the fey once more to his side to refresh his mug. This time, he took a deeper draft and set it on the waiting tray with a satisfied sigh. "You've hardly touched your drink," he pointed out.

"I just woke up," the Fudir said.

"It's a stimulant. Tell me, Gesh: why will you not join us? It's not for lack of inducements. Vengeance for what the Names did to you. The glory and honor of your name. Not even for Terra! I'm certain Oschous Dee took you to the mountaintop and showed you Terra. I'm disappointed."

He really did sound disappointed—but the nature of that

disappointment remained elusive. "True Terry-fella, me. But Oschous no Terry-man."

Gidula invited details with his silence. So the Fudir recited the Terran rhyme:

"Pallid and ebony, dun and sallow,
Thus the colors of Earth do follow."

"There be no fur-face foxes among the races of Terra."

"Did Oschous claim to be a Terran? That surprises me. Dee Karnatika is generally more careful in his lies."

The Pedant mulled over the conversation in the fox's shipboard sanctum. No, Donovan decided, Oschous never had made that specific claim. The best lie is the one you induce your hearer to tell himself. "His promise was smoke. Terra can never be truly free," Donovan said. "Not in the Triangles. She stands too near to Dao Chetty and Delpaff, to Old Eighty-two.

"A dozen lights from star to star,
Thusly arranged the Triangles are."

"Too close for one to escape domination by another. It requires only a would-be conqueror with enough swagger in his step—or enough steps in his swagger."

"Would you rather it be Terra dominating the others, as in the 'golden age'? I'm sure the Delpaffonis or the Eighty-seconds have other perspectives."

Donovan sat forward in his chair. "Those with a stake in the status quo might feel some disquiet at the thought of change."

"A great deal depends on the nature of the change, does it not? Most change is for the worse. Delpaff and Old Eighty-two—and a dozen other worlds beside—may chafe under Dao

Chetty's thumb, but they'd not exchange it for Terra's. As for those worlds far from the centers of power—Henrietta, for example—they find the yoke endurable and the checkreins lightly held."

"The worst sort of slavery is when the slave does not feel the collar."

"Is it? I would have thought that the best sort." Gidula raised a hand *just so* and the fey scurried over without the carafe.

"Yes, Law Gidula? How may I serve you?" The contralto would have served either man or woman. It was drawled, halting, uncertain. The face was ageless; the eyes were old.

Gidula smiled at him, patted his cheek, groomed his hair. "Tell me, Podiin. How long have you been in my service?"

"Sir? Aw my life. Seven years an' fawty, each basking in the sun of my law's ray-dee-ents."

Gidula gathered both the fey's hands and clasped them between his own. "You have served me well, Podiin. I have thought of freeing you."

The fey's mouth gaped open. He fell to his knees, grabbed Gidula's left hand, and bestowed kisses on the back of it. "Please, Law Gidula! Do no do tha' to me!" Tears coursed down his cheek, and he moaned. "Please, my law, have I naw serve' you well? Don' sen' me 'way!"

"But you would be *free,* boy!"

The fey sobbed. "No, my law! Will freedom feed me? Will it care for me? Will it ensure me again' sickness? No, Law Gidula, only your gen'rous and open han' cares for me—as I care for you."

Donovan noted to his own astonishment the tears wetting Gidula's cheeks. "Ah, no, my boy, no," the Old One said stroking the servant's head. "I'll not do such a thing to you. You will stay at my side; and when the gods call me, you alone will scatter my ashes."

That sent the fey into further paroxysms, only the tears now were those of joy. He bubbled his thanks, covered Gidula's hand with kisses. Gidula with his free hand produced a kerchief from a sleeve and dried first his own eyes, then the servant's. "Here, now," Gidula said, "stand up, boy."

When the servant was once more erect, Gidula twisted a ring off his right hand and gave it to the servant. "Here, Podiin. Wear this with pride." The fey might have collapsed once more into weak-kneed delight, but Gidula held him up. "With pride, I said." And the fey nodded and visibly braced his shoulders.

"Now bring the Donovan and me a selection of fruits and light-meats. Hurry along."

When the servant had vanished, Gidula sniffled, turned to Donovan, and spread his hands as if to say, *There. You see?*

"Trained from birth, was he?" Donovan said. "Small wonder freedom terrifies him. He's known no-but else."

"It's not a bad life for his ilk. They are suited by nature to serve others."

"His ilk . . . The feys?"

"What? No. Feys are no more servile than foxies or clappers or any other race of men. But they have their share of the mentally slow. Podiin can follow simple instructions, act on his own in familiar, structured environments, but he would be lost without the direction of others. What do you do with them out in the Periphery? Kill them at birth? Toss them on the street to fend for themselves?"

"It was a nice performance. I noticed he got a black pearl ring out of you."

Gidula shrugged. "A man may be slow but nonetheless reach his destination. He is retarded, not stupid. But enough. I take it my point is made. You might not find Terra so eager to be 'free.' Our society is a tightly woven network of obligations." He interlocked his fingers and tugged. "I am as much in Podiin's service as he in mine. No, do not sneer, Gesh. You have lived too long among the Peripherals and their anarchies. A tightly woven web, I say, of beliefs, customs, tales, fealties, and the like. Our law books are thinner than the Peripheral's because we are led by living words and not by dead legalities. When right action is needed, a parable is a surer guide than a statute. It is what gives us stability. It is why the Confederation is still what it always was, while the Periphery is constantly stumbling about."

"'Still what it always was . . . ,'" said the Fudir. "But there was a Commonwealth, once."

"Ah, the fabled Commonwealth of Suns. You Terrans look back at it misty-eyed, and I grant you it scaled greater heights than either the Confederation or the League has attained. But the Commonwealth was arrogance at the center, with the reins held loose. That is not a happy formula. If you value the lightly held leash, modest fellowship is best advised. But if you would strut your boots on other men's faces, clench the reins tight and never relax."

"The Commonwealth was not like that!"

"Were you there? Well, perhaps you are right—about her early days. But the Triangles did not rise up on a whim."

Donovan tracked the fey as he returned with the refreshments. He hated servility in all its forms, and the Kabuki that Gidula had played with the fey sickened him; yet even he had to admit that there were gradations to the thing. Obedience need not be servile—and Gidula had wept true tears. The philosopher R. V. Ambigeshwari had spoken rightly in the autumn of the Commonwealth when she wrote: *Every system works—after its own fashion; and every system fails—in its own way.* Maybe so, but he didn't have to like it.

Podiin proffered the tray first to Donovan, who saw that

"light-meats" meant thin slices of fish or meat wrapped around vegetables and caked in rice. The scarred man let the Silky Voice make the selection. Inner Child noted that the boy now wore Gidula's ring on a chain around his neck. Podiin favored Donovan with a smirk, as if this small boon had marked him a man among men. Donovan did not know whether to rejoice with him on this small victory or pity him for his larger defeat.

"A stable system, you say. Yet, you want to overthrow it." Gidula was supposed to be a leader of the Revolution. There was a limit to how far he might plausibly go in defense of the status quo.

Gidula made his own selection, then waved the boy aside, to stand by the wall out of earshot. "A dead man is stable," Gidula said. "Only living men stumble. But that our social fabric has frayed at the top does not mean that the tapestry must be burned entire. Poor Ravn understood that. You see, *Those* do not command our customs the way they command our laws—and custom is king of all. If it is our part to obey *Those*, it is *their* part to be worthy of obedience."

Donovan, the Sleuth, and the Fudir considered this while the Silky Voice and the young man carefully studied Gidula. "And some of Those are not."

"It is the part of a good shepherd to shear his flock, not to skin it. I believe you Terrans have a saying. '*Numpollyarky*' something, something."

"*Numpollyarky ysceala tattoo.* 'The act is unworthy of the person.'"

"You Terrans . . . ." Gidula laughed and shook his head. "You always have a great mouthful of words."

"It gives us something to chew on."

"Clever, too. I suppose with every man's hand against you, the Fates have sharpened your wits, or you'd not have survived.

Well, it's been a long, hard time since the Commonwealth fell," he continued. "Those were other days, and they worshiped other gods. The histories of the Late Commonwealth, while it was in power, were falsified through terror and sycophancy, and after its fall through the distortion of hatred. But the heat has gone out of it now; the coals are grown cold."

Donovan looked at him oddly. "And so you enjoy," he quoted, "'the rare happiness of times, when you may think what you please, and express what you think.'"

Gidula shrugged and sipped from his drink. "When have there ever been such times? It is never too wise to express what you think. But our scholars now look back on the Commonwealth with neither the servility nor the enmity that once consumed men. We can begin, a little, to regard the age with dispassion."

"I wonder if dispassion is an improvement."

Gidula leaned forward. "Listen, Gesh. We must kill men in this struggle—our brothers in the Abbatoir, even some Names. Best if we don't hate them in the bargain. Hate makes personal what should be detached. *Those* have done, as you Terrans say, acts unworthy of their status, and so must be expunged, some of them. But the act is no more a matter of hate than would be the stomping of a cockroach."

The Fudir swallowed a spiced tuna roll wrapped in a banana leaf. "I'm no cockroach," he said. "I'd rather be hated."

Gidula grunted. "You may get your wish. The Names have been aroused from their delicate slumbers and have begun to meddle in affairs not proper to their offices."

"Oschous told me about the business at the pasdarm on Ashbanal. And two or three intervened on Yuts'ga."

"And that was only overtly," the Old One agreed. "There have been covert moves, as well. And *Those* have shown . . . disturbing capabilities."

"They did seem to come and go rather abruptly," the Fudir said dryly.

"And given what *Those* have revealed, what might yet remain occulted?" Gidula leaned forward, forearms on his knees. "That is why I urged an infiltration of the Secret City itself. Do you see why we must *end* this, Gesh? And end it soon? Before the real revolutionaries, like Oschous or Domino Tight, burn the whole tapestry and we lose the good with the bad—and before Those of Name escalate the struggle with their meddling and we lose . . . everything."

Donovan took over from the Fudir and laughed. "One more enticement, eh? 'Help us prevent a worse conflict!' *Those* did *this* to me . . ." He ran a hand through the furrows of his head, over the headlands and ridges and tufts of woodland-hair where the plows of his tormenters had broken the soil of his mind. "Why should I care how badly your Confederation suffers? *How can it suffer too much?*"

Gidula evinced no reaction. "Because," he said in reasoned tones, "what has a shopkeeper on Henrietta or a schoolteacher on Delpaff done to merit slaughter? Ask yourself, who would suffer first and most of all should our cities burn? Why do you think we've labored these twice-ten years to keep the conflict tightly controlled? Why do you think we put *boundaries* to it?"

"Boundaries of straw," Donovan retorted. "Why suppose they will stand one moment beyond the first hard blow?"

Gidula sucked in his breath and leaned back suddenly in his chair. "Ah. So. Wisdom dawns. You *do* remember—or some hidden part of you does."

The response was unlooked for, and Donovan retreated in confusion. "Remember what?" He growled. And the Silky Voice, deep within, said, *Some hidden part?*

"How Padaborn's Rising spun out of control. How whole city blocks were smashed in San Jösing and people whose only

crime was rising early to go to work were scythed down because Padaborn rose too early for another purpose. You want
to believe that the violence was inevitable, and not a misjudg-
ment on your part."

"Are you done telling me what I believe?"

"But Gesh, Gesh. A tumor can be carefully excised. There
are medicines that invade the body and touch nothing but the
malignancy. We can remove the malignant Names and not touch
the benign ones, not touch the honorable neutrals, not touch the
sheep."

Donovan said nothing. His inner voices were silent. He bit
into another light-meat and found the taste sour and the texture glutinous. "You almost had me, up to the 'sheep.'"

Gidula lifted a hand, as if helpless. "Delicacy of nomencla-
ture will not alter the facts. The great mass of men must be
led—or driven. We propose they be led."

"Are they to have no say in how they are governed?"

"Does it matter how they are governed, so long as they are
governed well?"

"It matters a great deal. If it belongs to the people to choose
a king, then it belongs to the people, if the king is become a
tyrant, to remove and replace him."

The Old One pressed his hands together and touched them
to his chin, just below his lips. "That has the flavor of some
ancient Terran sage. But tyranny travels with the fastest ship.
Your League will feel the hand of the Ardry and his Grand
Sèannad heavier on her shoulder now that your Ourobouros
Circuit inserts its tentacles into each man's world."

"Enough," said Donovan, rising. He started to turn, checked
himself, faced the question he had been avoiding. "What happened to Ravn . . . and the rest?"

Sadness overcame the face of Gidula. "Alas, the Ravn is no
longer with us."

Donovan knew bleakness in his heart. He was not sure he had come to like his kidnapper, but he had certainly grown used to her sassy presence. There had been a mischievousness to her that he had found appealing. "She was always cheerful," he said.

"Yes," said the Old One, "but she was working on that and making great improvement. As for Oschous, he fled to Old Eighty-two, along with Big Jacques. Manlius and Dawshoo had already gone to the Century Suns by prearrangement. They intend to . . . What do you Terrans say?"

"Lie low."

"Yes. Such a colorful 'lingo.' "

"It's a patois. A synthesis of a dozen different tongues. The ancient tongues—"

"Is it." Gidula was not really interested. "Oschous told me that Domino Tight survived the assassination attempt—he was not clear how—and has agreed to enter San Jösing and set up safe houses. Everyone is recruiting new magpies. So the team we agreed would infiltrate the Secret City remains nearly intact. Like you, Big Jacques must recover from his wounds. We are going to make contact with Little Jacques, who will meet us on Terra."

"On Terra." The name went through Donovan like the slice of a sword and cut short all his thoughts.

"Why, yes," said Gidula. "I thought I had told you. My offices are on Terra."

"The Taj . . . ," whispered the Fudir, slowly sinking back into his seat. Oh, to see the green hills, to walk the holy soil of Vraddy and bathe in the sacred Ganga . . . To see Zhõgwó. And Vrandja, where the Yurpans lived; and Murka—and walk the fabled streets of Pree and Mumble, Vayshink and Ũãva-jorque.

And Iracatanam Antapakirantamthe, the Capital of All the Worlds.

The Fudir fought to keep the emotion from his voice. "When," he said, "do we arrive?"

"In four standard days. Ekadrina used you ill, and it wanted all this time to restore you. Work with Five. Get your strength and endurance back up." He rose and took Donovan by the elbow and bowed him toward the door. "The time has come to bury all pretenses. You really *must* remember the way into the Secret City. It is essential to our plans, and I propose to do all in my power to aid your recollection."

Somehow, that last was not a comfort to Donovan buigh.

V. THE PASDARM AT THE IRON BRIDGE

Terra. The world from which once set forth the great star-captains of old: Yang huang-ti, Chettiwan Mahadevan, and all the rest—to conquer worlds and write their names in glory. Later generations, lacking their vigor, mocked their outsized exuberance. *Glory? They could not have been serious!* But mockery has always rung false and uncertain from the lips of those to whom no statues would ever rise.

The ships had gone out at first looking for life, confident that they would find it in abundance. They recited a mantra called the Prayer of Drake. But they found no answer to their prayer save the lichens of Dao Chetty or the worms of Yuts'ga, and some torpid seas soupy with eukaryotes. On a few scattered worlds, they discovered the indecipherable evidence that Others had once walked there in times forgotten. Where are they? Where are they?

Nowhere, it seemed. And so, deprived of true aliens, the men of Terra had fashioned their own. The great science-wallahs of old who had touched the genes of plants and of animals touched even those of men themselves, transforming disappointments to joy and shaping each new world to their partiality. New kinds of men arose and dreamed new kinds of dreams. They scattered Arks before them like dandelion seeds to quicken worlds they themselves would never live to tread.

For a time, great fleets of suspension ships sought to relieve population pressures at home by carting off the excess. That did not work. A vigorous age reproduces with vigor; as those whose cradles are barren are also barren in other ways. Elsetime did people search out nooks where they would be free to live as they wished. That did not work, either, for men bring oppression with them wherever they go and those who find their dreams will press them upon their children. At still other times, they had been forced out against their will for reasons economic, political, or judicial.

In the end it was sheer osmosis that populated the Spiral Arm, a complex stew of curiosity, greed, displacement, persecution, and deliberate exploitation. It was a thin gruel. A random sampling of stars would find nothing, not even death, for a thing must live before it can die. Not every star is caressed by the tendrils of Electric Avenue, and so their worlds spin forever beyond reach, no matter how close they might lie as the crow does fly. And even within the network are worlds untouched by the Arks: worlds in eddies and cul-de-sacs and whorls or up blind alleys, worlds so unpromising, so meanly endowed with even the inanimate, that there was little point to sprinkling the animate upon them: superjovians whirling like dervishes about a fire; marsbodies too weak to retain their warming blankets; worlds wrapped so tightly that their very air pressed and crushed and incinerated even the hope of life. But here and there: oases that could be nurtured and cultivated into suitable—sometimes barely suitable—homes. Out into this vast, untouched, and untouchable desert, mankind spread through the creases of

space. They went sometimes with heads cocked high, sometimes in shackles. Sometimes because they had everything to
gain, sometimes because they had nothing to lose.

But they went.

All his life—to the extent he remembered a life—the scarred
man had dreamed of Terra. It was the grail of all those huddled
in the Terran Corners of the Periphery; those who had not
forgotten the days of old, who preserved the languages and
lore in their Terran Schools when everyone else had forgotten,
who loved the memory of a world they had never seen. Man
was at home on a thousand planets, but only one was the home
of man.

Every Terran yearned to make the hajj, and "Next year on
Terra" was a common valediction among them. The Brotherhood schemed and plotted to return all Terrans to the home-
world. Some few thought to reignite past glories in the face of
the Names, but more simply desired to nestle in the mother
world's arms: to see "the Taj and the Wall and the Mount of
Many Faces," to visit the Monument of the Lions in the pass of
Jelep La, or the wreckage of the Beanstalks brutally scythed by
the conquering Names of Dao Chetty. "Twelve-gated Terra,"
she had been called, for a dozen of these massive elevators had
girdled the globe and had perceptibly slowed the world's rota-
tion. Most of all: to visit Iracatanam Antapakirantamthe, the
Capital of All the Worlds.

As Gidula's ship crossed the orbits of High Wonsing and
Tin Wonsing and passed within distant sight of the glorious
rings of Tousing and the somber-striped king of planets, Muk-
sing, the scarred man found his breath growing shorter and his
heart beating stronger. He knew these worlds by older names—
Ketu and Raku, Cani and Viyazan—and the Pedant mulled
names older still, bestowed by cultures near forgotten. At

times, the feelings welled up uncontrollably and he would break into tears.

His companions, far from laughing, often wept with him. He had found them easily moved, as often by others' emotions as by their own. Just as a play in shaHmat might inspire them to sudden rage, so a homecoming could induce sudden tears. And so a mood at once festive and romantic suffused the staff and crew of *White Comet*. Five recalled a woman he had known in Ketchell; Twelve spoke longingly of sailboats on Lake Montang. Twenty-four remembered hang gliding in the Angies. Even Gidula grew wistful and from time to time pulled a small box from the recesses of his clothing and inspected within it a lock of hair.

But she was called Zăddigah now, was Terra, a name bestowed long ago by her Dao Chettian masters. It meant something like "dirt-ball renewed." And, as if world had changed with word, she little resembled those meticulously labeled ancient maps copied and recopied in Terran Corners across the Periphery. She seemed to wear a powdered wig.

"Clouds?" Donovan guessed.

"Ice," Gidula told him.

Oceans had receded, and freshwater lakes had appeared in unlikely places. Deserts and taiga and scrubland dominated the terrain and the cities huddled against rivers, lakefronts, estuaries. Gidula's shuttles coasted northeastward high over the Megan desert, across the open waters of a circular, nearly enclosed sea, skirting the edge of the Fladda scrublands, before entering the substratospheric traffic corridors and turning north-northeast along the open boreal woodlands that lined the eastern edge of the north-south landmass.

The city of Ketchell formed a crescent around a large, natural harbor where the land turned east. Towering larches and spruce, interspersed with birch and ash and broken by pale-green meadows, dominated the mainland behind her. Beyond that: a glimpse of taiga and, on the far horizon, a gleaming white rime of glaciers. Then the shuttles swooped in low for their final approaches and the northlands dipped beneath the horizon. Tubeways ran off south and southwest.

None of the roads from Ketchell ran north.

Gidula's headquarters lay some leagues west of the city, nestled in a bowl dominated on all sides by abrupt heights. A south-bound river, the Tware, ran through it along its eastern marge, entering and leaving through gaps in the encircling hills. A second river, called the Lye, ran the gantlet between a pair of sheer limestone cliffs on the southern edge of the bowl before tumbling into the Tware.

"It does not seem very defensible," Donovan told Gidula as they watched the approach on a screen in the lounge.

The magpies who surrounded the party chuckled and Gidula arched an eyebrow. "That depends on who is playing defense."

"It's dominated by high ground on all sides." Inner Child, of course, had noted that right off.

"Ah, but first an enemy would have to seize that high ground. Those farmlands may not be as open as they appear. Really, Gesh, who is there to attack my compound? There has not been a war on Zãddigah since time unremembered. This is not the Periphery. We keep a tighter rein on anarchy here than they do across the Rift."

Donovan was unruly enough himself not to relish the thoughts of leashes. But he admitted that things might look different to a man whose home has been smashed and plundered by raiders. Tyrants were often welcomed with open arms.

"Other Shadows," he suggested. "I've heard there is a war on."

The Old One smiled. "But against a Shadow attack what possible fortress might matter?"

A small, flat area on the eastern bank of the River Tware provided a landing apron for the shuttles. As each one grounded, tugs moved her into hangars excavated under the cliffs of Mount Lefn. The planetfallmen handled things smoothly, and soon Gidula, his servants, his magpies, and his opportune guest had forgathered in a broad lounge within the cliff, where the servants broke open wardrobes and pulled out a variety of festive clothing with which to drape their master and his people.

Gidula wore black, of course, accented with white trim and bearing the comet on breast and back. A round brimless cap sporting feathers of the black swan graced his head. On his hands, elbow-length leather gloves in dark gray; on his feet, matching felt shoes with black ankle stripes.

His magpies were variously accoutered. The most junior wore white, sleeveless surplices atop larch-green hose. Their comet badges were set in black squares on breast and back. Senior magpies wore black shenmats with Gidula's mark patterned throughout in white. Donovan was surprised to note a full Shadow, who wore a blue shenmat adorned with daffodils and sporting Gidula's comet on a brassard. Donovan guessed him the captain of Gidula's ship. He had his own cloud of magpies— likely the bridge and engine crew—and these bore bouquets of daffodils stuck jauntily in wedge-shaped caps.

Donovan found himself outfitted in Geshler Padaborn's colors by aggressively servile valets. A blouse of sky-blue with puffed and slit sleeves over tubular trousers of forest-green, topped with a white snap-brimmed hat called a fedora, which he was told meant "faith of gold" in the ancient Murkan tongue. A half dozen of Gidula's magpies had been brevetted in Padaborn's colors to provide him with an appropriate entourage.

The large and dolorous Five looked especially incongruous in such gay garb, but he wore it with genuine pride.

"It is to me honor," he told Donovan amidst the bustle. A single tear made its way through the bristles of Five's cheek. Succumbing to an impulse whose origin he did not know, Donovan touched his forefinger to the tear and crossed his heart with it. "I think I will call you 'Pyati,'" he said. At that, his physical therapist broke down entirely and the other five magpies clamored to touch Pyati as well.

Donovan looked to see if Gidula had noticed the interplay, and of course he had. But the Old One's face had never revealed very much, and did not do so now.

Servants from across the river joined those from the ship and began to play on panpipes and tambourines, dancing in curious jerky steps as they did, swaying their upper bodies. The music never settled into anything Donovan thought tuneful, though it seemed always on the verge of doing so. The servants wore motley with comets on their sleeves. They hoisted banner poles with flags for Gidula, Geshler Padaborn, and Khembold Darling, the other Shadow.

Then the Shadows mounted peculiar one-man autogyros called *siggies* that raised them up above head level. These vehicles were controlled by motions of the knees and feet, and by body balance. Some of the senior magpies had similar, though less lofty, vehicles. Everyone else walked.

Or danced.

It was a peculiar assembly that exited the hangars under the cliffs of Mount Lefn: half procession, half parade, half dance, arranged in no particular order, save that the magpies always contrived to place Gidula foremost behind the musicians and Geshler and Khembold right behind him. Pyati pressed some metal tokens into Donovan's hands before they exited.

Outside, a modest crowd greeted them with cheers and

waves. Many wept. Some wagged little hand-flags of the three Shadows, as well as that of a fourth. Donovan heard cries of "Welcome back, Lord Gidula!" Gidula, for his part, smiled, raised his gloved hand in greeting, and tossed tokens to the crowd. These were eagerly snatched in the air, scrabbled for on the ground. None of it seemed orchestrated, all of it seemed sincere; and yet at the same time it all seemed very much routine.

"Silky," whispered Donovan. "What was that business with Pyati's tear?"

That was not I, said the Silky Voice.

I did it, said the young man in the chlamys. Our Pedant found some old memories of Shadow culture, and . . . It seemed the right thing to do. With that one sentimental gesture, we captured his loyalty. And probably that of our other magpies, as well.

"Crap," said the Fudir.

Yah, said the Sleuth. *If we are starting to remember stuff like that . . .*

. . . 𝔱𝔥𝔢𝔫 𝔴𝔢 𝔭𝔯𝔬𝔟𝔞𝔟𝔩𝔶 𝔞𝔯𝔢 𝔊𝔢𝔰𝔥𝔩𝔢𝔯 𝔓𝔞𝔡𝔞𝔟𝔬𝔯𝔫.

Following Khembold's lead, the scarred man joined in the token tossing. At first he worried that flinging his arm would throw him off balance, perhaps topple him from his high perch on the *siggy* he rode. But the gyros easily compensated for his motions and the Brute quickly learned to master its controls.

"Padaborn!" shouted a woman in the crowd, and when Donovan looked her way she opened her blouse for him. The Fudir leered, but the Silky Voice turned it to a polite smile and a wave.

"I could get used to this," said the Fudir.

"So," Donovan mused, "this is how Shadows comport themselves at home."

The other side of the plaza funneled onto an ancient iron

bridge across the River Tware. It was a cantilever bridge, the Pedant noted, but fashioned to resemble a suspension bridge for some long-forgotten reason. There was a plaque beside the entrance reading: *She still stands!* in the ancient Murkanglais and attributed to one Mayor Donna Sanjezz, otherwise unknown to history. As each member of the procession stepped on the bridge, he paused and touched the first right-hand suspender—a steel beam that had been polished smooth by the custom. Parts of the bridge had been quite evidently repaired or replaced over the centuries, and Donovan wondered sardonically whether any part of the original relic really did still stand.

The structure was unimpeachably ancient, and even the newer parts were old. It very likely dated from Commonwealth times, if not earlier. The piers were built of granite blocks, black with age. Plast-seal protected metal and stone from the elements, and the stresses were likely relieved by strategically placed gravity grids.

A juggler came up beside Donovan, entertaining the people lining the bridge. When Donovan tossed a token at the crowd, the juggler nimbly snatched it from the air and added it to the balls he kept cycling, to the applause of everyone, including Donovan himself.

"Nimbly done!" Pyati called up to him.

"I'm glad someone here knows what he's doing," Donovan answered.

"Oh ho!" said Pyati with a nod toward the right bank of the river. "A pasdarm!"

From the second pylon a deep-purple banner unrolled above the bridge deck. It bore a single teardrop in its charge. Beyond, on a grassy sward on the western bank, a pavilion had been erected and pennons flapped from its poles. The pennons bore a rose in a tan field with a comet in the canton. A Shadow in a black-and-tan shenmat stood akimbo at the far edge of the bridge.

"Eglay Portion," Pyati told Donovan. "Who is for Gidula the seneschal. He runs the headquarters, like Khembold runs the ship."

"And he stands in our way because . . . ?"

Pyati shrugged. "That is depending on ground rules. Our earwigs will catch the narrowcast when closer."

But another of Geshler's magpies had trotted ahead and returned now excited. "Eglay will fight man-to-man with each of due rank—Shadows or senior magpies—until someone has defeated him. First fall. No bones or blood. Until then, none may exit the bridge."

Pyati smiled. "May magpie fight magpie?"

"No side bouts. And Gidula doesn't fight."

"What! Is he then the Lady of Secret Isle?" The other magpies guffawed broadly. But Donovan already saw Gidula leading his paraperceptic office manager toward a pair of thrones mounted to the side of the bridge.

"Two is the Queen," he told the others from his vantage point. "And the whole of her court, beside."

Pyati looked at him for a moment before sputtering into laughter. Seventeen had a servant run back to the baggage train and dig into the wardrobe, returning with a coat of tears: the purple shenmat. "Here ya go, Geshler," Seventeen said, holding it out. "Best ya not fight in them puffy sleeves. Too much for an edge to catch on."

But Donovan waved him off. "It won't be a long fight."

Seventeen scowled. "Ya ain't gonna throw it, are ya?"

Donovan watched from his high-seated *siggy*. The first challenger was Magpie Four Gidula, who stepped forward confidently and touched Eglay's banner with a staff. Khembold Darling steered over beside him and extended a hand.

"I had no chance earlier," he said. "I hight Khembold Darling. It is an honor to meet you at last, Deadly One." Then, dropping his voice, he murmured, "My father was with you in the Rising."

Donovan allowed as he was pleased to meet him, but he wondered quietly how, if Khmebold's father had been a rebel, Khembold himself was still among the quick. But then it was not impossible for some to have escaped notice in the aftermath.

"Eglay is a good 'un," the ship's captain went on in a normal tone, and he settled his *siggy* to face the contestants. "Not much for him to do here but spar and practice. Staff does all the drudge. Two times in three, he'll knock me down. Don't underestimate his youth and vigor. You and I are both older men, and just off a long and wearying journey. And you have sparred with Ekadrina."

"It was more than sparring. We should both be dead."

"What a man should be and what a man is often depends on the man."

Donovan grunted. "Well, Eglay may have youth and vigor on his side, but we have old age and treachery."

Number Four was already down. The crowd cheered and Eglay strode in a circle with his arms stretched upward. Then he reached down and helped the magpie to his feet and they embraced briefly. A medic ran forth to tend to the magpie's wounds. Number Two, as Queen of the pasdarm, graced Eglay and his opponent with an absent smile. Donovan wondered if the paraperceptic were even capable of giving her full attention to anything.

Gidula's Number Three magpie had stepped forward.

Khembold sighed. "My turn next. After months sitting in the pilothouse of a starslider." They watched Three spar gracefully with the seneschal. He was fast and agile and landed a few good blows that in context could have been telling, but he was betrayed by the boundaries of the ring and the Judge blew him offsides. Cornered, he ran out of wiggle room and fell as if poleaxed. The medics carried him off on a floater.

Khembold sighed. "Eglay could be taken down a peg. Well, I can put on a decent show." He *siggied* to the end of the bridge, touched the banner with his staff, and leapt off his scooter. He and his colleague bowed to each other and Khembold launched a whirling side-kick as they rose from the bow.

But Eglay had been ready for just such a play and danced away from it.

Donovan stopped watching. Silky, he thought, give us plenty of juice. Brute, are we up to this? Our body, I mean.

Ya want we should fight, or take a dive?

Donovan considered the matter. "Fudir?" he muttered.

The Fudir rubbed their hands on their pants. "I don't think Gidula set this up so we could take a dive."

Ya think Gidula set it up, then, not this Eglay?

Gidula's conflicted, the young man said. He wants what he thinks we know, but he doesn't want Geshler Padaborn hale and whole and idolized. He can't have us killed. Too many people know we're in his jurisdiction and some of his own magpies might turn on him. He wants to cripple and humiliate us without obvious assault, so a nice, friendly bout to lull us and an "accidental" rabbit punch that the other rebels can believe.

"Sir?" Pyati tugged his sleeve. "Are you all right?"

Donovan shrugged him off. "Any more senior magpies?"

Five tried to look modest and failed. "Eglay's good. Last time, he beat Khembold and went through eight top magpies before he went down. He's not unbeatable. Last year, Khembold and he wrangled for a good quarter clock before Khembold won, and another time Number One got him with a surprise move."

"I'd wondered if there were a Magpie One Gidula."

"Detached assignment, I was told," Pyati said. "He's about ready for his own name. I could soften Eglay up before you take him."

"No. I'm hungry."

Pyati looked at him. "Meaning . . . ?"

"I have to get past Eglay to reach the buffet table."

His magpie chuckled. "Oh, well said! Oop. You sooner get your chance than later. Khembold twisted a little too much on that right, and left himself open. Fare well, master."

The last remark was called out as Donovan coasted forward on his *siggy* to the edge of the bridge, where he dismounted. The festive crowd gathered there cheered his appearance, though the Brute's keen ear picked out a hubbub of questions about his identity and even more questions on the odds. Gidula sat upon his ebony throne, leaned forward with his arms resting on his knees and a look of curious indifference on his face. As King of the pasdarm, he could show no favoritism. Number Two, on a lesser throne beside him, was as usual preoccupied with a half-dozen different matters, but with one slice of her attention she watched him approach Eglay Portion.

Eglay was slightly the worse for wear. As good as he was in the arts martial, a certain amount of damage was inevitable. What sort of honor was it, Donovan wondered, that drove these people to make such gorgeous spectacles of themselves for no other purpose than to inflict mutual injury? Eglay's right eye was puffed and he favored his left leg.

Gidula spoke. "You have not dressed to honor the occasion, Geshler Padaborn."

"What?" Donovan replied. "These are my dining clothes. Is there no banquet following?"

Eglay sucked in his breath. "Bow the honors, then, so the Lady may wave her kerchief."

"Let the gods wave the kerchief," the Fudir told him. "When the breeze next snaps the pasdarm banner, that will be our signal."

The idea was novel, but Donovan saw its immediate appeal in the brightening eye of Eglay Portion, and heard it in the sighs of the magpies gathered round. "Nobly said," Donovan heard one comment. "Place it in Fate's hand."

Eglay nodded and faced the pasdarm banner, but Donovan watched the spruces on the side of Mount Lefn. The wind was from the south this day, and he awaited the ripple in the needles that signaled a breeze coming toward the bridge. With the other eye, he watched the banner.

"Hit the juice, Silky," the Fudir murmured, and the Silky Voice, back in the hypothalamus, sent adrenaline coursing through him. The chattering crowd, the rippling river, the birds in flight seemed to slow. He caught a motion in the trees to the right, where the river made a slight bend and ancient and vine-grown stone pillars rose from the water. The shiver crawled through the trees and the Sleuth gauged its speed and said, *Three, two, one, take it, Brute.*

And Donovan lashed out just as the pasdarm banner snapped. When he completed his turn, he found Eglay prostrate on the ground.

The crowd fell momentarily silent, as if they too had been stunned by the move. Then the voices began. "Geshler struck prematurely." But another said, "No, but it was on the very spur of the moment." "I hardly saw the kick." "Did his hand move?" And then a great roar of approval parted their lips. It was not that they enjoyed seeing Eglay brought down, but that he had been brought down so smartly. It had been, in its own way, a work of art.

Donovan stood over Eglay and extended a hand. "At a later time," he told his opponent quietly, "we will meet when you have not been wearied beforehand by so many others."

Eglay took the hand and Donovan pulled him to his feet. A very short moment then lasted a very long time as the seneschal evaluated the man who had beaten him.

Perhaps Gidula had told Eglay to break Padaborn, had told him of his terrible injuries and long recovery, and intimated that a victory would be simple. Perhaps, as the Fudir and the Inner Child suspected, he had even been told to land blows beyond the bylaws of the pasdarm. But the fight had been to the first fall and he could not now move against Padaborn without seeming small in the eyes of his colleagues. Finally he said, "Teach me how you did that."

He reached to embrace Donovan, and Khembold, seeing this, limped forward so that the three of them joined in a fraternal embrace. This brought the crowd to a fever pitch of ecstasy, and Donovan knew he had made another friend on Gidula's staff.

From the look on Gidula's face, he knew it, too.

VI. ONE OF THE PLEASANTEST THINGS IN LIFE

Gidula's compound—the Forks—was a quiet campus consisting of a hundred buildings clustered on the flat space in the fork of the rivers. These included private dwellings, barracks, commercial buildings, an athletic complex, administrative offices, as well as koi ponds and water-channels and tree-shaded garden-parks. The buildings wore soft autumnal shades that blended with the terrain. Once every twelve-day, trucks with fresh produce choppered down from the villages on the surrounding heights to a farmers' market. Anything not provided locally came from Ketchell, the nearest city. While not entirely self-sufficient, the compound did produce most of her own basics. Maintenance sheds, machine shops, a forming shop for plastics and another for ceramics, and various other workshops lined the small creek that wound through the gap between Summary and Kojj Hills to empty into the Tware upstream of the Lye. All of this was carried out by a remarkably small staff, nominally directed by Eglay Portion.

Gidula gave Donovan the liberties of the Forks, and the scarred man spent the better part of two months in nature hikes, faux hunting, and research in the Administration building library before he made his move.

The Old One, for his part, caught up on his correspondences, and couriers exchanged cryptic messages with Oschous and Big Jacques at Old Eighty-two, with Manlius and Dawshoo in the Century Suns, and with Domino Tight in a safe house in San Jösing. The worlds of the Triangles were close spaced, no more than a few days apart by superluminal tube, so it was practical for messengers to speed back and forth among them.

The other conspirators were under deep cover, yet Gidula lounged openly at his main stronghold. The Fudir wondered about that for a while, until Eglay told him that Gidula's reputation was one of meddlesome neutrality. Even at the Battle of the Warehouse, he had acted to *break up the fight,* not to support either side. Ekadrina could testify that he had rescued her as well as Padaborn. Past his fighting prime, he gave quiet advice to the Revolution, but this was not known to anyone save the inner circle who had met at Henrietta. Even so, his magpies kept wary watch—on approaching air traffic, on ground-cars, and on peddlars and others who arrived by shank's mare. There was a surprising amount of traffic, but it was a lonely outpost, Eglay said, and traveling companies of players and other entertainers were always welcome. As were deliveries of simulations and other games. To guard against "system twisters," nothing was ever sipped off the stream but must be delivered and tested in cartridge form.

There was a continual round of exercises, both physical and mental, by which the Deadly Ones maintained their acumen. Donovan discovered that he could manage his fights in such a way as to make his opponents look good. He even contrived to lose a bout or two on occasions when he thought he might do so in safety. He also nurtured his relationships with the staff. The Fudir could be an engaging personality when he turned on the charm, and both the Silky Voice and the young man could empathize with cooks and gardeners every bit as well as with magpies, couriers, and Shadows.

The scarred man sought to win magpies and others in key positions, changing black stones for white, surrounding Gidula with his own people. He was not so foolish as to suppose that, should a break come with Gidula, most of his newfound friends would go anywhere than with their first loyalties, but some of them he judged as fairly won over, and he knew that Gidula must worry on it some. Pyati was his for a certainty, and so also Seventeen and several others.

By the same token, Two would never be his, never be anyone's but Gidula's. And Two, he had begun to think, was the single most dangerous magpie on Gidula's staff, with the possible exception of the still-absent Number One. Possibly more dangerous than Eglay and Khembold, who were full-ranked Shadows. Donovan sometimes watched the others work out, and had sat in the bleachers of the *pleshra* while Two had defeated four midranked magpies in rapid order, including two in a single bout. And the whole time, Inner Child knew, a part of Two's multifacted attention had been kept on him, where he sat in an upper tier. He began to wonder if there was more to Number Two than simple paraperception. He had gotten hints last year from Oschous that there were others who had undergone the operation that had formed his inner multitude.

She might be one of us, the Sleuth hazarded.

"For some values of the term 'us,'" Donovan responded.

The weather was brisk: frosty in the morning, but warming up toward the afternoon. On several occasions, Gidula took him out on faux hunts on the reserve atop the northern heights. They were driven in a quadwheeler up Kojj Hill to the Nose and then over the Outer Ridge. From there, the hunting reserve rolled flat to the distant blue ridge that marked the northern marge of a great valley. Here and there, coppices of spruce and larch and bushy thickets along the streams broke the monotony. The game was primarily beeshun and elk on the plain, and moose in the thickets.

At the crest of the Nose, Gidula halted the hunting party and, while his magpies stood about pointedly looking elsewhere for imaginary threats, he stumped heavily to where the hill fell off abruptly to the waters of the Tware. Gidula removed his hunting cap and held it in both hands while he gazed northward up the mist-shrouded river and the wind through the funnel of the gap whipped his clothing. After a few moments of this, he made a hidden sign with his right hand, knelt, and, gathering up a bit of gravel from the ground, tossed it chattering over the side.

Gidula returned to the vehicle and, closing the door, tapped the driver on the shoulder, and they continued over the Outer Ridge. Gidula did not explain why they had stopped and by this signal Donovan knew better than to ask.

Soon enough, the outriders located a moose, and Gidula, as host, graciously deferred to his guest. The scarred man passed on an offer to implant a *niplip,* a locator beacon, in the creature. What was the point of hunting if you did not actually have to hunt? Instead, he gave the Sleuth his head and let him cut for sign while the Pedant compared footprints and scat with sundry memories of catalogs, lists, and databases. They followed the moose into a stand of tall, cathedral trees, through whose needle leaves the sunlight was sifted like flour. The floor was clear of underbrush and the morning birds scolded his approach. Moss and tiny yellow and violet flowers carpeted the rocks, and a chill mist hugged the ground. Every outline seemed softened by the morn.

He came across a human footprint and studied it for some seconds before scuffing it out with his boot. Later, he reached a break in the trees and found a meadow of short, dark grasses and large, mossy boulders enclosed by spruce on three sides. Overhead, branches wove a canopy. A stream trickled through the meadow, accumulating in small pools that promised, when the spring rains came, to soak the meadow into swamp. He saw the ski-marks of a lander in the mud near one of the pools and filed the information away.

He spied the moose near the opening at the farther end of the meadow and crept closer, going to his belly and wriggling behind a deadfall of trees. He tested the wind (he was down-wind) and raised himself up to the edge of the fallen trunk and painted the moose with his spot rifle and—

—and he peers above the parapet of a ruined building, his hands choking his spot rifle. Stone lion heads gape from the cornices beside him. Bolt tanks flank the triton fountain in the rubble-littered plaza below. Bullets sing off the plasteel and he ducks back down. The assault has failed. The Protector's flag still flies over Coronation House.

He rolls to another position, estimates where the closest tank must be, then pops up and "paints" the tank with his spot rifle and ducks back down before the chatterguns walk in on him. He waits, but nothing happens.

"The Protectors must have sanded the satellite," he says. "Our submunitions didn't lock on to the painter!"

There is no answer. He looks around. The parapet is empty save for the dead.

The sky turns white and the building shudders. He feels a tingling even through the insulation of his shenmat. The bolt tank has fired. It will be several minutes while it recharges. But of course there are four tanks, one at each intersection, and they will take turns. Across the plaza the Chancellery flashes and the walls fall in upon themselves as the building comes down. Another post lost. How much longer can he hold the Education Ministry?

A young woman touches him on the shoulder. She is young, hardly more than a girl, unarmored, uninsulated, barefoot amidst the broken glass and masonry that litter the rooftop. She wears a Doric chiton and seems too delicate even to live on this world, let alone in the hell it has become.

There is a way out of this, she tells him, and her voice is like a melody.

Donovan rolled back panting behind the fallen tree trunk.

A memory, said the Sleuth. But when and where?

"And whose?" the Fudir added.

"Pollyanna?" Donovan said. "You were there, on the rooftop. What was that?"

I don't know, the girl in the chiton answered. It was muscle memory. It was the heft of the rifle, the motions of our body, that evoked it. Ask the Brute.

But the Brute only shrugged.

"A genuine memory?" Donovan proposed. "Or a false one, implanted by suggestion after all those interrogations, the recordings played while we slept?"

𝔚𝔥𝔢𝔫 𝔱𝔥𝔢 𝔭𝔢𝔬𝔭𝔩𝔢 𝔞𝔯𝔬𝔲𝔫𝔡 𝔶𝔬𝔲 𝔠𝔬𝔫𝔱𝔦𝔫𝔲𝔞𝔩𝔩𝔶 𝔱𝔢𝔩𝔩 𝔶𝔬𝔲 𝔱𝔥𝔦𝔫𝔤𝔰 𝔞𝔟𝔬𝔲𝔱 𝔶𝔬𝔲𝔯𝔰𝔢𝔩𝔣, 𝔶𝔬𝔲 𝔢𝔳𝔢𝔫𝔱𝔲𝔞𝔩𝔩𝔶 𝔟𝔢𝔤𝔦𝔫 𝔱𝔬 "𝔯𝔢𝔪𝔢𝔪𝔟𝔢𝔯" 𝔱𝔥𝔢𝔪.

And thank you for that tidbit, Pedant. I think the memory was real. We were in the Secret City during Padaborn's Rising.

"But false memory or real," demanded the Fudir, "which of us had it?"

Who cares? said the Brute, and he whipped his spot rifle over the deadfall, ran his sights up the middle of the foreleg, and painted the moose just about one-third of the way into the body. The anatomist watching remotely through the sights ruled both shoulders broken, with a high probability that the heart had been pierced as well. The moose would have buckled and fallen.

"Good shot, sir," Pyati told Donovan over the link. "Those beasts like to go die in hard places. Always best to drop them where they stand."

Donovan reflected that that was good advice for more than moose.

He and Gidula painted five "kills" between them that day, according to the anatomist and the armorer. Gidula announced the sixth a kill-in-fact and brought down what he called a lazarus elk, bearing an enormous spread of antlers. Apparently, the creature had once been extinct and the science-wallahs of the Old Commonwealth had somehow rebooted it. The beast wanted three high-velocity rounds to topple, and Gidula erected a cairn on the spot and burned thereon the offal as an offering to Jana Wogawi, the Goddess of the Hunt. The remainder of the carcass they field-dressed and sent back to the Forks by airtruck, to be butchered and sold at the twelveday market. The head and rack Gidula kept, as a trophy for the Gun Room.

Betweentimes, Donovan endured multiple interrogations with Gidula. The Old One tried all the same tactics that Oschous had tried, and with all the same results. Yet he must have known those methods had proven futile. So why the Kabuki?

He can't simply pith us, the Sleuth said. *If the memories are truly inaccessible, he will not find them by drilling. And afterward, all hope of obtaining them would be lost.*

Beside which, the young man in the chlamys said, you've made too many friends. Oschous—and by now Dawshoo—knows Gidula has you, and he's not ready for an open break with the other two triumvirs. Some of his own people might now turn against him if he pressed kaowèn on "the great Geshler Padaborn." I could name the magpies that would flock to your side in such a division.

But there were others who hated the Names deeply enough that they would tolerate any means, including kaowèn, to obtain the key to the Secret City. This struck Donovan as odd, even ironic. What was the point of revolution if matters did not revolve and men just as cruel seized the reins?

The question arose obliquely one afternoon when he and Pyati had been sparring in the *pleshra*. "I don't mind at the helm a strong arm," the magpie said while they showered off the grime of combat, "or in the saddle a keen pilot. But when authoritarianism is with decadence tainted, our liberties fade."

"Can there be liberties under authoritarianism," said Donovan, "however undecadent they might be?"

Pyati paused while soaping up. "Of course. When the leash is slackly held, and tugged only now and then and for good cause."

"I'm inclined," the Fudir replied, "to regard the existence of the leash as sufficient irritant."

The other nodded, considering the words. "You saw in the League the anarchy that follows when there are no leashes. The Old One names two oppressions of sheep. The first, when power is arbitrary; the second, when there is no power at all. When no man holds the leash, all men hold leashes, and tyranny is petty and irksome and everywhere. Instead of the great laws, we have the niggling nettles of many small laws. The leash is always there, master. What matters is who holds it."

Donovan rinsed off, ducking his head under the cascade. "Then why," he said when he emerged, "have you joined the Revolution?"

Pyati seemed surprised by the question. "Why? Because my

master has told me. Because wise managers have become petty tyrants. Because they push and prod, but do not lead. Because they have trampled our traditions *and have dropped the leash*. Revolution is coming, whether we Shadows lead it or not. Better us than chaos."

Donovan studied his own naked body in the mirror, considered how frail he seemed. He did not attempt to count the scars, for chaos seemed embodied in their very number and placement. One day, he knew, there would be no autoclinic handy to knit them up afterward.

A Shadow was expected to use his mind as well as his hands, feet, and happenstance bric-a-brac. And so the scarred man's exercises were more than merely physical. There were simulations, puzzles, scenarios, war games—in which the race went not to the fleet, but to deceit.

And so he had learned—or relearned—a number of plays. Some he had never forgotten. He had used The Little Birdie in the Terran Corner on Jehovah, igniting a rumor-storm with a series of well-placed and well-timed whispers that had culminated in the dismissal of the Jehovan Inspector of the Starport market. Other plays had the quality of the newly remembered. When he finally made his move, he chose The Missing Man, which required the cooperation of several collaborators and the subversion of the compound's information system.

The essence of The Missing Man was to create the illusion of a presence from the fact of an absence. Donovan knew people who could appear to be absent even when present. Greystroke Hound was a past master of that art. But the real trick was to appear to be present even when not. To accomplish that feat, Donovan chose Pyati and Eglay Portion.

As Magpie One Padaborn, Pyati had to be in on it. He

controlled Donovan's calendar, could cancel appointments, tell people that they "just missed" the boss, and give Donovan's residence the appearance of being lived in. Beds would be mussed. Meals would be cooked (and consumed). Spools and bubbles would be left about. Eglay Portion was seneschal of the Forks and could game the system in ways that Pyati could not. He could set up exercises, bouts, exits from and reentries to the compound, and create evidence that Padaborn had been in this or that building. That would be tricky because Magpie Two Gidula monitored the system and she was remorselessly attentive.

Donovan could not expect to fool Gidula for very long. At some point, Two would compare visual surveillance data to the building entry logs. But the scarred man did not desire a long tomfoolery. It need only be long enough for him to drop out of sight. The Fudir had chummed the understaff and crossed certain palms with silver. This had secured him a great deal of useful information on places to go in Ketchell.

"I need to get away," Donovan told his coconspirators by the koi pond. "I need to be by myself, relax, see the sights. If I can get my mind off everything that has happened these past few months, maybe I can remember what the Revolution needs me to remember." He needed, of course, to give them a reason they could agree with.

Pyati nodded. "A fight with Ekadrina would fuddle any man."

And it had killed Ravn, Donovan recalled. He remembered his quondam kidnapper capering past him through Oschous's command post, running out through the burning warehouse to her doom at the hands of the loyalist champion. Suddenly weak in his legs, Donovan lowered himself to the bench. Fish, attracted by his shade, clustered for the expected treats.

"What is it?" Eglay asked him.

"I was thinking on poor Ravn," the scarred man told him.

Eglay nodded. "A bold colleague," he agreed.

"You miss her," said Pyati, sitting beside him.

"I never thought I would. My first thought after she snatched me was how I might slay her and escape. But she died for my sake."

"I'm sure that was not her plan," said Eglay.

"Is no big deal, dying," said Pyati. "It's something we all do, at least once."

Donovan grimaced. "At least," he said.

"Well, you did, no? Technically, you were in the tank for one, two days dead. And here are you, good as new. And Ravn, when we dropped her at Delpaff, was hearty as a kitten."

Donovan grabbed the magpie's sleeve. "What? She's alive?"

Pyati disengaged from the clutching hand. "When last I saw her. Why? Did Gidula say otherwise?"

"That son of a . . ." But the Pedant recalled that Gidula had said only, *Alas, the Ravn is no longer with us* and when Donovan had mentioned Ravn's death the Old One had not corrected him. Oh, Gidula was an exquisite liar! He could spin a fantasy by telling the stone-cold truth.

Eglay too was surprised. "Ravn's not dead? Gidula has said nothing."

Pyati shrugged. "She offended him over some matter, and he is not speaking her name until she brings him a present."

Donovan knew what the offense must have been. When she had rushed forth wearing Padaborn's colors, Ravn had joined the Revolution wholeheartedly—and Gidula was inside the Revolution in order to subvert it.

"Well," Donovan said, placing a hand on each knee and pushing himself erect. "Perhaps I will have a present for him, too."

The three of them departed by aircar the next day, ostensibly to show Donovan the wonders of Ketchell. Pyati assured him that these wonders were not so numerous as to require the entire day, and the fact proved as true as the word. Ketchell was a crescent of low buildings, none more than ten stories high, around a circular harbor formed, according to local folklore by a stone dropped by the god who built the sky-vault. Donovan supposed it a remnant of the Cleansing and spent long moments on the quayside watching the waters break along its rim.

"What was Ketchell called before it was Ketchell?" he asked his companions.

Eglay Portion shrugged. "As far as I know, it was always Ketchell. There are traces of buried ruins farther inland, though, where the shoreline used to be before the ice sucked up all the water. There are supposed to be layers of successive cities there going back to ancient times."

Donovan wanted very much to visit those ruins, which he took to be those of Ũãvajorque, but he could not spare the time for it now. He and Eglay and Pyati retired to a quayside restaurant where they huddled with other diners around a radiant fireplace and consumed large steaks of a fatty meat and root vegetables cooked nearly to sludge. "City's not noted for its chefs," Eglay commented superfluously.

Donovan looked around the dim-lit room. It reminded him a little of Gatmander: cold and lonesome, and despair coating everything like a fine dusting of grit. "This must be some happening place during the winter," he said.

Eglay shrugged. "We usually bunker up at the Forks. And there isn't much that is more cheerful than evergreen boughs and hot-rod wine and a roaring fire come Midwinter Eve and a visit from Sīgyawn Yowshã. But I hear down here in the city the suicide rate always spikes that time of year."

Donovan wondered that they had not used everyone up by now.

Pyati shrugged. "Usually off-planet, me."

"They say the ice came on sudden," Eglay volunteered. He raised a fatty slice of beeshun to his lips and chewed thoughtfully. "Something like," he said, then swallowed. "Something like the ice caps—you'd think they'd always been there. But the locals tell me it was only a century or two from a nice, pleasant, temperate world to . . . a wall of white along the north."

Pyati said, "When did it happen?"

Eglay waved his now-empty fork in spirals and intoned, " 'In the time before my grandfather's grandfather.' "

Donovan grunted. "Back then, was it? Surely there are records in archives somewhere. This world was civilized longer than any other in the Spiral Arm."

"Sure, but only the mountains last forever. There's a town over the other side of the world has a clay brick with writing on it that goes back to prehistoric times. I seen it myself, but it looks like chicken tracks to me, and no one knows how to read it. But there was war and fire and mice and all what have you. There was a long Dark Age when almost nothing was recorded."

"Nothing at all?"

"Gidula told me that things had been 'written in the sand.' He said that meant 'in silicon.' It was all digital bits and you needed special machines to read them, and—"

"I can guess the rest," Donovan said. "New technology. New machines. Pretty soon they couldn't read the old storage devices, and the media eventually decayed."

"Crazy people. The sign by the Iron Bridge is about the only thing left from that era. We got the better idea: something works, don't change it."

"And if it doesn't work?"

Eglay Portion laughed. "Don't change that, either. Might get worse."

After dinner, Eglay and Pyati flew back to the Forks where, using this stratagem or that, they would create the illusion that Donovan had returned with them. Donovan for his part shook the dust from his feet and went off in search of a foo-doctor whose name he had extracted from the Assistant Un-dercook of the Common Mess. (He had been surprised at the extent to which the kitchen staff emulated the manners of the Shadows. The Chief of the Cuisine cooked nothing himself but sat in a great chair much like a throne set in the center of the kitchen while others in strict hierarchy cooked, baked, washed, and served—and brought things to him for taste and approval.)

The search took Donovan to a part of town that the touris-tas would have shunned, had there been any tourists desperate enough to visit Ketchell. Construction standards across the Confederation were unimaginative but solid, yet even plasteel and metaloceramic could take on a decrepit appearance when too little attention was paid to their upkeep. Façades became darker from grime and neglect. Here and there, a splash of color around some doorframe or window or a brightly pol-ished god only served to heighten the general drabness.

The people with whom he mingled were a close and soli-tary lot, each intent on his or her own personal mission, lifting no eye for a passing stranger but giving the Fudir as if by in-stinct a wider berth. Not even the body over which they stepped engaged their attentions.

In a few places, the buildings were coming down. A couple were demolition sites with large machines idling on rubble-strewn lots, but most were a more spontaneous and involuntary dismemberment. Where the foundations were exposed, Donovan noted older foundations buried deeper in the ground.

This was a city with a long past, he thought, but a short future.

He found the promised *daforni*—what he would have called a "pub"—along the northeast end of the waterfront, where the ground-car wires ended and only walkways penetrated the warren of tumbledown shanties. It was called "The Severed Arm" and above its entrance a well-muscled arm, clench fisted and flexed, extended toward the street. It had once been painted in lifelike colors, something between bronze and tan, but the years of dirt and sea-brine had tarnished it and it seemed now as if gangrene had set in.

When Donovan entered, all activity within ceased and eyes turned toward him. No one came to The Severed Arm by happenstance, and the patrons paused to assess his significance. After allowing time for a sufficient appraisal, Donovan stepped up to the bar, taking a position from which he could watch the entire room. The bartender ignored Donovan until he slapped a five-*bayzho* coin on the bar. This was a part of Ketchell that preferred its transactions manual and untraceable.

"*Ē grizhdahl o'uizhgy, borva.*" He employed the Late Murkan dialect still used in parts of the Northern Mark continent. The "please" seemed to amuse the bartender, but he feigned a lack of understanding, so the Fudir ordered the whiskey in Manjrin. "In clean glass," he added.

The bartender set a tumbler down, and the amber fluid sloshed over the rim and spattered the bar top. "It's alcohol," he said. "Sanitizes the glass."

The Fudir lifted the glass and, as he sipped, mentioned a name.

The bartender shook his head. "Never heard 'f him."

Before he could turn away, the Fudir said, in the accents and rhythms of Old Eighty-two, "He should be grieved to hear so."

It was an unlooked-for retort and surprise stayed the bartender's motion. "How so?"

"The thing that he does, he must do. Else they will come here on the seek, to this very place, disturbing the peace of mind of many."

The bartender laid a thick forearm on the table and leaned upon it. "And if he does do it?"

"Then those whom they will seek will be gone from this place, never to brighten its precincts again, never to trouble you the more."

"That end may be reached," the bartender suggested, "with less effort and greater profit." He smiled, but his teeth were like the line of northern ice astride the far horizon.

No, said the Brute, **it could not.**

The bartender looked into his eyes for a moment, then shrugged. "Ah. The *Terran* Foo-lin! Him I may know."

"There are many Foo-lins," the Fudir allowed. "A man might not know them all."

The bartender reached under the bar. "Art thou a Terran, also?" he asked in the Tongue.

The Fudir might have happily assented to this, but Inner Child seized control. <I don't understand.>

The bartender relaxed infinitesimally. "I asked if you was a Terran."

"This is Terra, no? Are not all here Terrans?"

"This world is called Zãddigah."

"That only means 'New Earth' in the old Cant."

"If it does, then new it is. I will explain because you are an Eighty-second and so, ignorant. The Old Terrans left this world to wander off among the stars. Our ancestors came from worlds nearby, and we inherited the earth. A remnant of the

Terrans also remained who preserved old ways—as if they were still the lords of all creation—until they learned their new place on the New Earth. Across the Rift are some who style themselves Terrans, and they would come here if they could and seize our homes, save that our faithful boots prevent them." He reached into a pocket and produced a flat, dull metallic disk. "Here. This sigil will direct you to the man called Foo-lin. But go wary of him."

"He is a Terran, you say."

"He is. He worships the vanished Commonwealth like all his tribe, but he at least knows it has vanished. Go now, before you draw your pursuers to this place."

The disk lighted with an arrow that directed Donovan toward the storied Foo-lin. Much of the scarred man followed it, while his remainder kept watch on shadows and alleys. The expected ambush came less than five blocks from The Severed Arm.

Three men whom Inner Child had noticed earlier slipping out the rear of the *daforni* leapt dagger drawn upon him. Surely, a man who sought the service of Foo-lin would carry much portable money on his person, for Foo-lin was among those who shunned the traceable sort.

But the Brute had been waiting for the moment and at the first squeak from Inner Child—as a shadow moved within a shadow—he swung into a kick, disarming the first and breaking his arm. The second man he dispatched with a backhand fist and the third by driving his bunched knuckles into the man's solar plexus.

It was the work of a moment, and the three were lying on the brickwork adding their vomit to the dried blood of past attacks. Donovan bent over them.

"Tell your master that he gave you too much time with his

story of Old Earth, and that you grew restless in your concealment, thus betraying your position. Tell him that those who
will betime notice my absence are not mere policemen, but
Shadows of the Names. They *will* know I passed through The
Severed Arm. It may be a matter of some few days before they
come, but come they will. Tell the taverner to take what measures he sees fit."

The moans of his three attackers increased in pitch and
Donovan left them there. He did not know if any of them
would return to warn The Severed Arm, nor did he care.

He followed the sigil deeper into the warren, but at a certain shop, a late-night *daga,* he heard men speaking in the
Tongue. He paused and dropped the name of Foo-lin in their
ears and received in return flat-faced stares and, from one man,
a slight nod toward the right.

Outside the shop, armed now with a warmed peach pastry,
he checked the sigil. It too directed him to the right. He
shrugged. Perhaps the directions were genuine after all. Undoubtedly, the bartender received a portion of Foo-lin's fee
and, while deprived of the whole of Donovan's purse by the
failure of his cutthroats, he would at least garner his commis-
sion. Wise is the man who profits from either side of a wager.

Foo-lin was located in the basement of an abandoned apartment house. Perhaps it had once held supplies or boilers or
comm.junctions. What it held now was the equipment that
Foo-lin required to practice his trade: scalpels, anesthetics,
stitchers, a white ring that was no longer quite white.

"What you want?" was his friendly greeting.

"I seek that for which thou art justly famed," the scarred man
answered in the Tongue.

That did not elicit the response the Fudir had looked for.

The wizened old black man scowled. "You accent funny. Where you from?"

"I hight a Terran, seeking help of Terra. By the Taj and the Wall and the Mount of—"

"Ayii! *Thou art a Peripheral Terran!* Go 'way! You bring trouble." He made fending motions with his hands but continued in the Tongue. "This be Holy Terra. Profane her not!"

"What I seek is simplicity itself: the removal of *niplips*—locators—from my body."

"Ayii. That be against the *fiqh* of the Northern Mark. Shall I place my head on the block merely because thine ancestors once lived here?"

"No," said the Fudir. "Because I have coin to give." He handed over the sigil he had been given.

Foo-lin laughed. "If thou comest from The Severed Arm, few are the coins remaining thee."

"Yet fewer still are the patrons remaining to The Arm."

The foo-doctor paused and looked at the scarred man, as if for the first time. "Where are these coins of which thou braggest?"

He handed Foo-lin a leather bag the size of his palm. The other glanced within and hefted its weight. "And the brothers of these few lonely orphans?"

"Safely concealed. But when thou hast finished thy work, the remainder shallt be thine."

"Thou art a man of care. Remove thy clothing, then, down unto thy skivvies. And please to be lying on this table where I will perform the ritual called 'the scanning of the cat.'"

Donovan stripped, and the scars on his body gave the doctor pause. Then the old man shrugged. "I must cut thee open to remove any *niplips* my cat may find. But what would mean another scar among so many? I see that thou art not a man of such care as to avoid injury."

"I fought a Shadow."

The foo-doctor scoffed. "Who can walk away from such a fight, save only a . . ."

He fell silent as answers suggested themselves. "There are rumors," he ventured, not looking directly at the scarred man.

"Believe them all. They may not be true, but they make thy life more interesting."

Donovan expected the ritual to involve the sacrifice of a cat, but there was no more involved than his passage through the white ring. The foo-doctor uttered certain prayers and incantations while he did so. *"Step one,"* he recited in the ancient Murkanglais. *"Turn the red power switch to ready . . ."*

Foo-lin located two *niplips*. They had been implanted, Donovan was certain, during his long sleep in the autoclinic aboard *White Comet*. Once they were found, it was the work of a few moments to remove them, requiring little beside a local anesthetic and some deep cuts. So far as pain went, it was the sort that the Silky Voice could easily handle.

"Those who would track thee," Foo-lin said, handing over the *niplips*, "will know when and where they are destroyed."

"I know this thing, and for thy sake and the sake of all our common ancestors I will not destroy them here. But those who would track me will know the path these traveled and will follow their spoor to this place. Thou needst not know who they be."

"Though one may hazard guesses." He spat on the floor. "This place . . ." The foo-doctor looked about the dilapidated basement. "I spread my tents where I wist. This *keller* will be empty when they come."

"Thou hast no love for the Names."

"It is Terra of Old that I love alone. To the Names, I am

indifferent. They are now; one day they are not. But Earth alone abideth."

"And yet thou scornest the Terrans of the Diaspora."

"They have fallen from the Faith, even as they have fled from the Earth. They would erect a secular Terra on the soil of the holy Commonwealth. 'What's done is done and what's gone is gone, and what's lost is lost and gone forever.' What might they hope to revive but a corpse—a zombie Commonwealth, with Men of Brass aping the deeds of the Men of Gold. Beside which, it would arouse my neighbors against all Terrans and bring the boots upon our faces."

The Fudir made a sign with his right hand. "Dream thy dreams of old, O venerable one. No such ill shall come of my visit. I am but a lonely fugitive."

"May thy heels be swift, thy breaths drawn sweet, and thine end swift and painless. Now, about my fee . . ."

The Fudir laughed. "Know that there is ever a place for you in the Corner of Jehovah. Mention to the Seven the name of the Fudir, and if they do not slit thy throat from mere exasperation at the reminder they will welcome thee. The remainder of thy fee sits 'on deposit.' There is a loose brick on the face of this very building, in the cavity behind which I placed the coins. I will touch the brick casually—so—as I depart. Thou mayest then, at thy leisure, collect the remainder of thy fee."

"Few are the men I would trust on such a promise."

The Fudir wondered how much was trust and how much prudence in the face of a man who had beaten the thugs of The Severed Arm and (putatively) a Shadow. "I crave one further boon of thee. It is on me to make the hajj. I am given to understand that the Mount of Many Faces is close by this place."

The foo-doctor laughed. "Aye, if by 'close' thou meanest 'on the selfsame continent'! What drollery! Thou wishest coordinates for your flier? It is but the labor of a moment." The old man busied himself at his console and shortly returned with a small disk. "Insert this in thy navigation system and straightaway thou shallt be taken to the legendary Mount." He smiled as if at some secret joke.

Donovan understood the foo-doctor's wit early the next morning when the flier he had rented under the name Tjoslina Tuk went into a tight circle above the specified coordinates.

The land below him was capped under milk-white ice a mile thick.

The wind howled unobstructed across the northern ice-plains, buffeting the small craft and challenging its autopilot to impressive feats of stability. Tiny ice particles rattled off the windshield.

The Fudir sighed. So much for the legendary heads: for Washington and Abe; for Jeff and Teddy; for Miwel II and Kgonzdan the Oppressed. *They were not even buried,* he thought—or the Sleuth thought. *They were ground to powder by unimaginable pressure against the mortar of the earth.*

It comes on suddenly, the Fudir remembered. A century or two from grassy plains to ice desert. But it wants thousands of years to melt.

𝕴𝖙'𝖘 𝖙𝖍𝖊 𝖆𝖑𝖇𝖊𝖉𝖔. 𝕺𝖓𝖈𝖊 𝖙𝖍𝖊 𝖑𝖆𝖓𝖉 𝖜𝖍𝖎𝖙𝖊𝖓𝖘, 𝖎𝖙 𝖗𝖊𝖋𝖑𝖊𝖈𝖙𝖘 𝖒𝖔𝖗𝖊 𝖘𝖚𝖓𝖑𝖎𝖌𝖍𝖙.

Donovan sighed. He had planned to tuck the two *niplips* up the nostril of Miwel II, whose copious nasal passages were said to have led into vast and secret chambers, full of pre-Commonwealth treasure. A suitable place for Donovan to search out; a reasonable place to have become trapped.

Instead, he tossed the two devices from his flier and let them fall to the ice, to be buried by the drifting powder. Then he turned his vehicle to the west and sought the fabled city of Prizga.

VII. MANY ARROWS LOOSÈD SEVERAL WAYS

You love your comrade so in war.
When you see your quarrel is just
And your blood is fighting well,
Tears engulf your eyes.
A great sweet swell of truth and pity
Fills your heart on seeing friends so valiant.
And you go to die or live with them,
And for love to ne'er abandon them.
And from that arises such a joy
That he who has not tasted it
Knows nary joy at all. Think you
That a man who does that
Fears mere death?

An ancient sage once wrote that all things happen by chance or by design, but that chance was only the intersection of two designs. Consider the man who is struck on the head by a hammer while walking to his lunch.

Everything about his perambulation is designed, which is to say intended. He is hungry—it is that time of day for it—and he habitually takes his lunch at a café two blocks distant from his workplace. It is a sunny day, so he wears no cap. None of this is by chance.

Likewise, the workman atop the roof of the building half a block along. He too ceases work for lunch and, habitually, leaves his tools unattended. Because of the geometric arrangement of his tools, his foot nudges the hammer as he arises, the which, in obedience to the inexorable laws of action and reaction, nudges back and so begins to slide. The god Newton teases it down the slanted roof tiles until it tips into his clutches and is pulled to the street below, even as the unfortunate lunch bound is passing beneath.

"Ah, what ill luck," say the street sweepers as they cleanse the blood and brains from the duroplast walkway. Yet everything that has happened is the consequence of the actors' intentions or of nature's laws—and some say those laws are but the intentions of a greater Actor.

We call it "chance" and we marvel because our superstitions desire that concatenation be as meaningful as causality. The man was brained by a hammer! It must mean *something*. There must be a connection! And so poor Fate is made the scapegoat of intersecting world-lines. Having become all tangled up in the threads, we incline to blame the weaver.

Which is to say that if two travelers intend the same destination, it is no great thing that their threads might cross along the way.

A third thing that Méarana's mother had taught her was how to handle herself in free fall wearing a skinsuit. This was a fortunate skill, as Méarana's mother well knew, for it enabled the harper to step out of a doomed ship wrapped in nothing much more than a leotard, helmet, and cloak of invisibility, and to coast until coming to rest on the side of the smuggler's mono-ship.

"We must match our mootions while still blocked from view," Ravn Olafsdottr had warned her before closing the skinsuit seals. "It would noot do to touch the vessel with too great a delta-V."

"Bug on a windshield," Méarana had agreed, a Terran phrase her father had once taught her.

And so they had launched themselves into the void. Ravn had waited until the last possible moment, when the external sensors had detected molecular jangling and an exponential increase in surface temperatures. "Wave cannon," she said, and they had jumped with their baggage in tow even as behind them their ship began to disintegrate. After which, their cloaks made them invisible to GEM detectors and their luggage drifted like so much debris.

The entry locks of ships are never sealed because no pilot wishes to face the air lock and pat her pockets wondering where she put her keys. But operating keys are another matter. No pilot wishes another to saunter on board and fly off with her ship. The former owner, the late Rigardo-ji Edelwasser, had been a bonded smuggler, and Ravn, before she had turned the vessel over to Fleet, had squirreled a duplicate set of hard keys inside one of his many hidey-holes. The soft keys she had memorized. It was a matter of minutes to retrieve them, insert them into their proper ports, enter them at apposite terminals, or speak them into appropriate pickups and thereby complete the circuits for command and control.

The ship's departure occasioned no comment from Space Traffic Control beyond the granting of clearance and the as-signment of a departure orbit toward the New Anatole entrance of the Gong Halys. STC had been informed earlier by SVMG that the Lion's Mouth was repossessing the *Sèan Beta*. Best it depart quickly before another unauthorized ship should attempt to seize it. One fewer Shadow in Henrietta system would make everyone happier.

Including the Shadow.

A monoship had little room for song and dance, but Méarana and Ravn managed. Life seldom tastes so sweet as it does when stolen back at the very brink from those who would take it. Méarana finally understood, a little, a phrase favored by the Ravn: "life along the razor's edge." She was rushed. She was high. She was giddy. They drank toasts to themselves, each other, the dead swoswai, and the live Shadow they had manipulated into avenging him. Méarana extemporized a rollicking geantraí while her companion danced a staccato of footwork known to the high-up hills she had once called home. In the end, laughing, they fell into each other's arms.

"On to Terra!" Méarana declared to the grinning face above her.

"Noot quite yet, sweet. First, we stoop at Dao Chetty."

Méarana pushed the Shadow off her and sat up on the couch. "Dao Chetty?" she said with sudden apprehension. The capital world of the Confederation. The center of all iniquity. A world whose very name fell leaden from the lips.

"I moost meet soomeone there," Ravn said.

"Oh no, we must heigh for Terra, to rescue my father!"

"Oh, my sweet, yes. All in good time do I bring Gidula his praysent." The Shadow leaned forward to pat her cheek, but Méarana ducked it. "Listen to me, yngling," the Shadow said in a voice with more iron and less play. "Your father is like a toothache. To pull him from the mouth of Gidula is more than my strength. So I must persuade Domino Tight to join us. It will not be easy to divert him from his duty, but like a frog, I will capture him with my tongue. Haha." Then, more seriously, she added, "To rescue your father wants more than to reach Terra quickly—but impotently."

The harper leapt to her feet and turned away from her companion, folding her arms. "But you don't need this Domino Tight. Mother is—"

"Following us? You meant her to when you joined me." Ravn nodded slowly, as if to herself. "That is why your companionship was worth the wager. But I have no assurance that the wager is won, and 'one sure ally on hand is worth two that might lurk in the bushes.' It is best to copper the bet. And a second Shadow may dissuade your mother from foolish decisions if she does follow."

"But what if Gidula should kill Father before we get there, because we delayed to fetch this Domino?"

"A large 'if,' and large because it contains two," said the Shadow. "The first *if* is Gidula's. He may have *already* killed your father, months ago. He may kill him five minutes before we land, however fast we scurry. Or he may have melted butter on Donovan's head, put melons under his arms, and seated him at the right hand of power. Until we *know* Schrödinger has cut the thread, all possibilities remain open. Ignorance is hope. Beside," she continued, "the second *if* belongs to Donovan. Gidula will not kill him until he cracks his memory. But I spend many months with your father, and I know, a little, how his mind works. Well, some of his minds. The scarred man's egg is not so easily cracked."

"You don't think he'd cooperate with Gidula? I mean, if he thinks Gidula plans to overthrow the Names, and he knows the way into the Secret City . . ."

A shrug. "That secrecy is his life insurance. Once revealed, of what use then, Donovan buigh? He think long and hard which of us he lead inside. If he does start remembering, he will . . . his phrase, 'take a hike.'"

"You sound as if you and he planned this all out ahead of time."

"Ooh, you grant poor Ravn too mooch foorsight. But Donovan is my brother-in-blood. I have died for him, and he put on the shenmat for me. That is . . ." She waved with her hand as if swatting flies. "You cannot understand such things. I will save him if I can. This I vow on the blood of the Abattoir. But never forget, young harper, this war has larger goals, and the prices for them are higher than his life—or mine." Her voice had progressively hardened as she spoke. Then the sprightly smile returned. "Now, coome. I shoow you where your father and poor Ravn battle Froog Prince togayther."

Méarana followed the Shadow down the long hall from the control room. All this time, all these many weeks of travel, and she had forgotten that her companion was a Shadow and had her own objectives. Méarana remembered another thing. Ravn had said in the sitting room at Clanthompson Hall that in the Shadow War she had already killed her brother.

The harper did not care for being manipulated. She did not like it from her mother, she had not liked it from Donovan, and she certainly did not like it from this strange, charming coral snake of a Shadow. The Shadow had wanted the help of Bridget ban and, failing that, had taken Méarana to force her mother's play. And the Shadow had managed all this while allowing Méarana to suggest and lead the escapade!

And so a little reserve grew in her resolve. She was no longer quite so intimate with the Ravn, did not follow her around as before or hang over her shoulder. Perhaps Ravn was relieved by this, though nothing showed in her demeanor. It would not be accurate to say that Méarana acceded to the stopover at Dao

Chetty. Her consent was neither requested nor required. But she did agree, if only to maintain the fiction that she and Ravn were partners in this enterprise and she was not simply a stage prop. Ravn, whether she saw the need for the charade or simply did not care, accepted Méarana's agreement with grave thanks.

And so Méarana spent the next two months composing goltraí in the lounge where Ravn had once so fruitlessly imprisoned her father. In the hidden room where the smuggler had died, Méarana found traces of the blood that had splashed there: stains painted in difficult corners and angles. She thought how easily her father could have died. She thought how easily the Ravn could have bought herself time by slamming the door and shutting Father and Froggie together. The laments played without a title in Méarana's mind and ran from there down to her fingers and so out to the strings.

She tried as well to compose a tune to depict her mother hastening after her, but it would not cohere. In the night, when the strings were stilled, a thin sliver of doubt would stab Méarana: There was no pursuit. Bridget ban had weighed the costs and the benefits and had written her daughter off as lost. It was a relic of her childhood, was this cold fear, a piece of an age when her mother would disappear for weeks or months at a time and the daughter would wonder if she would ever come back.

And that led to a fresh, new thought. Had Méarana initiated the play with Ravn as much to test her mother as to rescue her father?

In the Triangles, space had so configured itself that a cluster of priceless sunlike stars lay cheek to jowl, each a mere dozen light-years or so from the other. This had once mattered a great deal, as the first starships had gone the Hard Way, across the Newtonian flats. The Hard Way was a long way, though longer for those left behind than for those setting out, but it was doable at the margins. First steps are larrikin steps, and these suns lay where a child might stumble eagerly toward them. As the old song ran:

> *A dozen lights from star to star.*
> *Thusly arranged the Triangles are:*
> *From Sol to Dao Chetty*
> *To Vraddy to Sol.*
> *Dao Chetty to Old 82,*
> *From Delpaff to Bhaitry*
> *And thence to New Vraddy*
> *'Tis only a short way to go.*

Oh, it might be more than a dozen, or less, but "fourteen-point-three lights from Bhaitry to New Vraddy" does not scan. Afterward, the discovery of the tubes had made flatland distances irrelevant. It might be 14.3 light-years "as the crow flies," but who flies with the crows anymore? Distances were measured in days, now, not in years. And sometimes, at long, long intervals, ships drifted in from the Newtonian flats, bearing their cargos of ancient spooks, after journeys far longer than their crews.

The old home-stars from which we once set forth.

That line resonated with poets of a certain bent, those for whom the glamour of forgotten pasts conjured emotions of loss and regret, of faint distant bells and twilight languor and ruins seen by moonlight. But Méarana gazed upon the skies of Dao Chetty not because she was seized with nostalgia but because somewhere in that firmament her father sat seized. Ravn flagged the star for her on the view screen while they lazed into co-orbit with the way station: Tsol. An undistinguished star—bright, but no brighter than others nearby—sixteen degrees north of the equatorial line, and just south and east of a brilliant marker star called Arctors. It was not even the closest sun to Dao Chetty. That honor belonged to Epsidanny, which lay farther east near a trio of markers called Reckless, Nan Ho, and Denrō, the last named of which was also known as the Serious Star because it was the brightest in all the sky.

Méarana regarded Terra's sun with the same affection and longing that the ancients had felt on contemplating Ur of the Chaldees, which is to say none at all. Her father, she knew, felt different. Once upon a time, everyone had lived there. But that was a fact, not a feeling, and she knew it only as a place from which she must rescue him. Once upon a time, everyone swung in trees in some African valley. No point getting all choked up over it.

Ravn docked at Tungshen Waising, a vast habitat built into and around a dwarf planet situated sunward of the primary ramps off the superluminal tubes. It could barely handle the traffic, and the throngs that moved through it were a focused lot, rushing to make the bumboats, or other liners bound elsewhere, or to arrange layovers while they awaited connections.

Dao Chetty was the capital of the Confederation and like any center of power she attracted a multitude of people eager to wet their beaks in her nectar. From harmless touristas to would-be bureaucrats; peddlers and purchasers of influence; messengers, merchants begging relief, immigrants and visitors, emissaries of sector and planetary governors, Shadows, rebels, boots, assassins, spies and saboteurs. This was the honeypot of the Confederation, the thunder-mug of the Central Worlds. Here docked the great liners and humble yachts, the ominous warships of the Fleet, the stealthy ships of the Lion's Mouth, and the bristling survey vessels of the *Kazhey Guk-guk* bringing word of worlds at the farther edge of settled space.

Tungshen herself boasted docks and maintenance yards, freight transshipment and passenger transfer, residence quarters for the staff, and—to maintain the ever-percolating transients— hosted entire cities of hotels and gardens and restaurants and theaters within her bosom. Ravn and Méarana put up at a hotel in the Seventeenth Sector called the Four Great Heavenly Kings. It would take several days to find Domino Tight, keepers of safe houses being by design not easily found, and he would need several days thereafter to climb up to the coopers, so they had might as well be comfortable in the interim.

Méarana was surprised at Tungshen's dowdy appearance. Little enough had she glimpsed of the Confederation during her slide through it, and she supposed its age ought not have surprised her. The Triangles had been the heart of the old Commonwealth of Suns, but it seemed as if little had been refurbished since then.

It was less the antique feel—the red and gold lacquer, or the translucent panels and low ceilings, styles and skins—than it was the general air of dishevelment. Dirt snuggled in corners, rust peppered surfaces, ad hoc repairs had become permanent by the sanction of passing time. On the way from the customs clearance to the hotel she noticed a crew of technicians consulting small pocket-sized manuals and arguing over the precise meaning of the text, so it did not surprise her to learn that some subsectors of the habitat had been sealed off and abandoned in place.

"It wants *shwee* to keep these things up," Ravn commented when Méarana mentioned the matter.

Méarana's earwig told her that *shwee* meant "liquid, water, juice," which seemed less than informative, but Ravn explained it was slang for *chin-chin,* or money.

"Money like tourist," she said while they waited in queue to check into the hotel. "Come to Dao Chetty. But unlike tourist, money never leave Dao Chetty. Names build new palace, not maintain old habitat. Tungshen always muddle through—Commonwealth tech down in the bone—so each cycle, squeeze budget more. Someday . . . Who knows. Maybe, squirt *shwee* where *needed*, not where *wanted*."

That was dangerous talk. Méarana looked around the lobby, where hundreds were lined up in front of the kiosks. "Should you be talking like this?"

Ravn laughed. "Too much talk-talk in lobby. No one over-hears anything. But do not talk so when we stand near kiosk." She glanced at her identity card. Méarana had learned that Shadows kept caches of documents, credits, equipment—called "spookers"—secreted about the Confederation. When she had worried about being detected here at the capital system, Ravn had laughed at her fears. It was the boast of the Deadly Ones that their false documents were finer even than the official ones.

"We move like leaves bloowing through autumn forest. We are coolorful, yays, but there are too many leaves. Even with clayver machines, the Names and their minions cannoot sieve every datastream for the whisper of us. Even when I coontact my sweet Dominoo, what is one more call-worm amoong all the rayst?" Then, dropping the accent, "Merchants with secrets, families with secrets, agents with secrets . . . All messages sent in code. How they find pea under so many mat-tresses? Hush, now, while I speak with this infernal device." She glanced again at her identification card to remind herself of which regional accent to affect and began to jabber with the kiosk in a patois too fast for Méarana to follow.

They were ahead of the standard clock and wide awake in early sector morn. Not that it mattered. The spectrum lamps might brighten and dim to the spin of the capital far below, but the habitat never really slept. Ships arrived at all hours, and there must always be someone ready to welcome them, service them, kiss up to the powerful among them, and separate the rest from their wages. Ravn went to find the nearest message center.

"There is only slight risk," she told Méarana. "Poor Ravn must use code known to both Domino and me, and what is known to two is known to too many. But even if intercepted, decoding yield only allegory. Sweet Domino kens the sooth of the allegory. We are high up here, and even light wants seven hours to creep down to capital and another seven to haul sorry-ass answer back up. Slow conversation, yes? Much nicer have Ourobouros Circuit like you have in League. Oh, well. Someday we have. Not to worry, sweetling. Ravn returns soon."

And with that, the harper was abandoned in a semisumptuous suite in the middle of a strange and hostile realm. She wandered through rooms whose tatterdemalion furnishings even when new would have seemed spare. Holopictures on the wall displayed alien people and scenes: a hard-faced woman striking an absurdly formal pose, Shadows riotously caparisoned facing off in a pasdarm. Even the landscapes appeared subtly foreign, as if there were nationalities of flowers and races of trees.

She tried some audiobooks. (The earwig was no help in reading text.) But the style of the recitations struck her as bombastic and strident. Statements sounded like questions. Tonal cadences gave narrative the stridency of argument.

The music was not much better. She had left her harp concealed aboard *Sèan Beta* lest it mark her as alien. But the modalities of the Confederation seemed wanting in subtlety and listening to them soon palled. Like their clocks and their rods, they divided their scales into twelve increments, and the ratios of their tones sounded irrational.

And so, after an impatient time, she took herself to the café restaurant on the primary mezzanine. There she ordered a green tea and sat on the open patio to watch the passing stream of humanity on the concourse outside the hotel.

She saw foxes and sharpies and feys; skin tones from coal-black to pasty-white; eyes and noses of sundry shapes and in virtually all combinations. She even saw a few like herself: golden skinned and red of hair. She couldn't tell if their eyes were green. Absurdly, the sight made her feel less alone, even though such folk were found on a great many worlds. The mix was different: more foxes, fewer sharpies, no Jugurthans at all—and once she saw a close-clustered group in veiled, ankle-length gowns who *clacked* as they scurried by.

But the bustling masses seemed somehow different from a similar crowd of Leaguesmen. At first, she could not say why and thought it was the styles of clothing—drabber and more uniform than that to which she was accustomed—but it eventually came to her that they had the gait of a beaten people. They shuffled more than strode. They walked with heads more nearly bowed. These were a people thoroughly domesticated. *The sheep,* Méarana remembered.

Exceptions stood out. Men and women in baggy suits, moving with purpose and puffed with importance. She guessed them functionaries coming to or going from the capital. A plumpish, pale woman with head erect and searching eyes, who locked gazes for a moment with Méarana. A squad of boots tramping across the public square in cadence. A tall, black woman in resplendent red and black robes adorned with the yin and yang. This one strode with a thick quarterstaff in her hand, and was accompanied by several younger men and women wearing her livery on black body stockings. Others quickly stepped aside to clear her path. Many bowed, though she deigned no notice.

A Shadow of the old school.

Méarana was suddenly thankful that Ravn Olafsdottr was not sitting with her on the patio café, for Ravn was at least overtly with the rebellious Shadows and this one, to all appearances, was not. The harper ducked her head to her tea. The tall woman was just passing through Tungshen like everyone else. She was not searching for Ravn, nor would she recognize the harper as an outlander. But even so, it was best not to catch her eye.

When Méarana raised her head to peek, the Shadow was gone. But there was a man sitting at the table with her.

Méarana started, but he only smiled and raised a glass. "Hard night? You should drink something stronger to get your juices flowing." He spoke Manjrin with an odd accent: vowels clipped and final consonants bitten off as if by his large, even teeth. His *t*'s seemed to come from the middle of his mouth.

"This serves well enough," the harper told him, and sipped again at her tea. Was this an intrusion, or did strangers share breakfast tables here?

"I'm outward bound," he said, "toward Habberstap. I have a Confederal legacy for the tax farm at Bowling Brook. I'm to be the Shearer of the Postdown Flock."

Méarana did not understand what that meant, only that it meant that he was trying to impress her with his minor importance.

"How nice for you."

"Where are you heading to?"

The harper searched for an answer, wondered at the intent of the question. Was he really a minor official heading to his posting? Or was he a secret policeman grilling a suspicious stranger? "Henrietta," she said on impulse.

The man nodded. "I thought I heard a frontier accent in

your voice," he said, to show how clever he was. "First time to the capital?"

"Ah, yes."

"Pretty impressive sights."

"I . . . haven't been down yet."

"Booked on a later shuttle, hey? I'm waiting for my out-bound flight, so we've both got a couple of hours to kill." He laid his hand on her arm. "What say we gang up on those hours and kill them together?"

Méarana did not understand what he meant until his hand moved to her thigh. "I'd say there are some pretty impressive sights to see up here," he added.

Nearby boulevardiers smiled over their cups and croissants. A few made signs with their hands wishing her copulatory success. Evidently, this sort of cold accosting was not unusual here, which eliminated the gelding knife as an appropriate re-sponse.

"No," she said in a low voice, so only the man could hear.

"What? But . . ."

Méarana used her sky-voice, throwing it so that it seemed to come from over the man's left shoulder. "She said no!"

He turned to look, saw nothing, and the harper tried to bolt, but the man held tight. He squeezed, hard. "You gene-tampered tease!"

Another voice interrupted. "Excuse me, but that is my seat."

Fool me twice, shame on me. The man ignored the new voice—until a thick finger tapped him authoritatively on the shoulder. Méarana saw the plumpish woman she had noticed earlier among the passersby. Not plump at all, now that she could see closer up, but simply wide and solid of body. Her hair was a wool cap of tight black curls; her cheeks, a rose-red. But there was something in her eye that seemed familiar.

The importunate man tossed off the last of his drink.

"Sorry, ladies," he said. Rising, he muttered, "All the good ones are taken."

The strange woman sat herself down and took one of Méarana's hands in her own. "Work my play, darlin'," she said. "Smile a little."

"That man—"

"—saw you sitting alone. Round hereabouts, unless you wear the veil, that means you're available. Easily available. It's the way they think out here. Not a one of them can imagine a solitary reason not to indulge their pleasures at any opportunity. They eat when they're hungry, the drink when they're dry, they—"

"I get the picture."

"I don't know if you do. Because they can't imagine a refusal, either. Easy indulgence of the senses impairs the reason. It's how they keep the sheep sheepish."

"Who are you?" demanded Méarana.

"Just the kindness of strangers, ma'am."

"No. Strangers don't do kindness, not in the Confederation, not in the Triangles, and certainly not this close to Dao Chetty." She stopped.

The plumpish woman raised her eyebrows. "What is it?"

"Your Manjrin has an accent. It's faint, but it's definitely there."

"Oh, for pity's sake."

"And you're letting it show on purpose, aren't you? It's Megra—"

"Oh, I don't think one should speculate overmuch . . ." She cocked her head as if listening to something, then said, "Best I be going. Listen to Auntie Gwen: You will be visited tonight by a spirit of things to come. Say nothing to anyone."

With that, "Auntie Gwen" rose from the table and, with unhurried steps, left the patio. Though there was no rush to her movements, she vanished in moments among the surging crowd.

Ravn Olafsdottr sat at the table. "Ooh, you nooty girl!" she scolded. "I said to stay poot. You should not be a wooman aloone."

"Oh," said Méarana offhandedly, still thinking about her strange visitor. "I have a guardian angel."

Guardian angel. Why not say *Hound,* for that was surely "Gwen's" profession. The League maintained agents within the Confederation, and Méarana's mother must have somehow gotten word to them to intercept her at points near Terra. She marveled for a time over the coincidence before she realized that coincidence was not in it. Mother knew Ravn was taking her to Terra. Why pursue when the destination is known? Agents were likely watching at the transfer points at New Vraddy, Bhaitry, and Old Eighty-two as well as at Terra herself.

Méarana sat on her bed in the Four Kings hotel with her knees drawn up under her chin and her arms wrapped around them. Ravn had been a congenial traveling companion—at least she had acted the part—but not until meeting Gwen had Méarana realized how alone and exposed she had been feeling. Even on her quest into the Wild she had had her own companions around her.

As sector evening came on, Ravn stuck her head in the room and announced that she was returning to the message center in case her earlier calling card had found its mark. "I think maybe noot. Is too soon, but who can say?" She flashed her teeth. "Now you stay here, my sweet. Better you be bored in these room than that you be swept up."

After the Shadow had gone, Méarana hugged her knees tighter. She had not thought on the Shadow War for a long time, so concentrated was she on the task at hand. But that war swirled all around her: silent, deadly, wafting around the un-kenning sheep like a ghostly wind—and Ravn was a player in that war. Even the traitors to the Revolution were yet traitors to the Names. So there was no safety or protection for anyone.

The lights in the suite appeared to grow dim, and the tem-perature fell. Méarana shivered and pulled the blanket from the bed and draped it over her shoulders. But she did not lie down. In the air, she detected a sweetish aroma, something cold and peppermint.

There were no windows in the suite. Ravn had preferred rooms into which none could enter from the outside. Méarana could see the door to the suite from where she sat, and it had not opened since Ravn's departure. Yet Méarana knew there was someone else in the suite. Perhaps in the kitchenette. Per-haps in the common room. But let it not be *in her very room*.

Darkness forgathered in corners and spread wraithlike along the folds of the walls, along the baseboard, along the cornice. The common room grew indistinct, faded into gloom. The tapestry beside her bed billowed, as if there had been a breeze. The needlework featured some ancient battle in which men battled with creatures of fiendish mien, men with the heads of dogs. Heads lolled, fangs showed. The rippling curtain sent them into motion, and at each other's throats.

Hello, Méarana.

Was that a voice? It didn't sound like a voice, not exactly. It sounded like the whisper of the air circulator. It sounded like the thrumming of the habitat's engines deep in the bowels of Tungshen Waising. The ripples in the tapestry seemed to move with purpose.

You have caused us a lot of trouble. We ran considerable risks to come here, and it is not yet clear that we have outrun them.

"I'm sorry."

No, you are not. You would do it again in a metric minute. You went once to rescue your mother; how can you refuse to rescue your father? But the Confederation is not the League; it is not even the Wild. It is something far more deadly than either. You were a fool to step into it, to allow yourself to be taken.

"I know that, but Mother wouldn't go. I had to force her hand. I knew I would be safe again when she caught up with me."

You know a great deal that isn't so. Putting two into danger is not safety.

"You've come with her . . ."

Maybe. We run few and scattered though the coursings of the Confederation. There is no Circuit this side of the Rift. How may our words reach one another's ear? Perhaps she has been caught and pithed—all because of you.

"No. I would know it if it happened. Our hearts are one. As hers stills, mine stops. Who are you?"

The tapestry billowed revealing . . . the empty wall behind it.

There are no names.

This time the voice seemed to come from the darkness of the common room, just outside her doorway.

"Gwen told me her name."

Your mother's daughter cannot be so naïve as that.

"How . . . How many did Mother bring? Or is this a sending and not a bringing?"

Enough and not nearly enough. We have not all come only for you, child. There are other prizes to be plucked. You will not know our numbers or our names, lest these fall out of your memory onto your tongue. Or, worse, be pulled there. Know only that we go to Terra before you and behind you and beside you. But you must tell us one thing. Why has she stopped here?

Méarana hesitated. There were others, not Hounds, who might want to know Ravn's plans.

"How do I know I can trust you? You might be rival Shadows, or even Names!"

The intercom clicked on and the voice whispered over it. "Would Shadows or Names have approached you thus? Let our stealth be our assurance. There have been two close calls already, and we'd not court a third."

"You won't show yourself—"

"—because you cannot describe what you've never seen."

"I wouldn't tell Ravn."

The laughter that greeted this reminded Méarana of the barking of a mastiff. It was short, low, huffing. "I do not underestimate Ravn Olafsdottr. Take grave care that you do not. But let this be a surety. An ancient banner bears a bloodstain that must never be expunged."

That ancient banner hung from the rafters of Clanthompson Hall. Méarana exhaled a long-held breath. "All right. We came here to secure the aid of Domino Tight in our attack on Gidula's stronghold."

"Ah," the intercom breathed. "Domino Tight. *Three* snowballs' chances. Success is now assured."

"Three, plus however many you represent," Méarana retorted with grave assurance. "How do you know that Ravn has no recording devices planted in these rooms?"

A little late to think of that, child. (The voice came again from the common room, and it seemed to Méarana as if that room was growing less dark.) She has, but her recordings will tell her nothing. There is one further boon that we would ask of you, but only if it can be done without arousing suspicions. Learn what you can from Domino Tight about the Vestiges that his paramour guards.

"I'm not sure I can do that, Voice. Voice?"

But there was no answer. The tapestry was still. The sound of the distant machinery, muted. The lights returned slowly to their normal brightness. The sweetness in the air was gone.

Méarana lay back on the bed, fighting tears. They had not come for her at all. They had come for the Vestiges. She had been shown once more her place in the scheme of things.

Later, when Ravn returned to the rooms with Domino Tight's reply, she saw the harper lying in her bed, weeping. Ravn did not ask why. But she did sniff the air and frown at the subtle tang.

VIII. ONE MAN WITH A DREAM, AT PLEASURE

Prizga sits on a long, narrow hill whose blunt end overlooks the gorge of the rushing Qornja River. To the east lies a bowl valley rich with farms. To the west the river snakes across a broad scrubland toward a delta twelve miles distant. Lazarus species roam this plain: go-beeshon and go-camels and the like. A long, graceful bridge spans the gorge. Supported entirely by gravity grids, it hangs faerielike in the air.

Prizga ATC tells Donovan that the local weather is cool today, but from cruising altitude Donovan spies the white of the northlands. In the future, it seems, Prizga will grow cooler still.

After departing the ice cap, Donovan had crossed first a thin, tall-grass prairie and then a polar desert before entering the defiles of immense mountain ranges, dressed in fir and spruce but punctuated also with the quaking golden leaves of aspen. After that, he had headed due west over a temperate semidesert until he struck the coast and turned north into the traffic corridors for Prizga.

In all that time, he had not seen another city.

There had been towns scattered on the grasslands, cheerful lights glowing in the night beneath him. But mountain and desert had been devoid of all signs of human habitation. Glacial pockets in the high mountains had caught the starlight and twinkled false images of house lamps, creating faux cities on the ice fields. Now and then, his general receiver had caught snatches of music, so he supposed that villages or mining towns snuggled unseen in the black crevasses, but never anything even as large as Ketchell until he entered the airspace over the Southwestern Desert.

He passed over great circles of greenery, crops conjured from the arid soil by the constant drip-drip of spidery irrigators that spread like steel webs from the morning-flushed towns at their centers. But the first such installation he had seen after leaving the mountains had been rusting in the fields and the town at its heart abandoned and clatterdown.

It was hard to imagine that this world had once ruled the stars.

But Prizga proved a bustling, friendly city, larger than Ketchell, and, unlike her east coast counterpart, she still squatted upon an anciently urban site. Beneath the modern city lay the broken plasteel and metaloceramic of earlier settlements, and beneath those, fragments of concrete block, broken marble, and the rusty stains of iron rebar. And beneath even that, pieces of wood that scholars felt had once been cut and shaped into boards.

The latter claim was still controversial, and the scholars were limited in their exhumations. Save where happy excavation revealed the bones of the city, the layered ground of Prizga was paved over. To most of the inhabitants, the rubble beneath their feet was a "jinko nuisance," and much of it had long disappeared into ballast, recycle, or scrap sales. The major exception was the ruins poking like iron trees from the soil of the agricultural basin. These were simply too massive to remove, and the farming co-ops had programmed their auto-plows to wind around them. The spars and girders were still known by their ancient Murkanglais name: the *elfwendevaxii* and the basin as a whole was called the *vaxi'prizga*.

Donovan rented a hotel room using the name on one of several ID cards he had prepared for the trip, and spent his first day in town visiting the ruins. Afterward, he took a leisurely dinner on a terrace restaurant overlooking the Qornja gorge. The sound of the rushing water, muted by the mist that rose out of it, soothed him insensibly into sleep.

He hurries down a darkened stairwell. Quietly, because the enemy may have already infiltrated the building. He passes dim and empty offices, long looted of anything of use, littered with casings and sabots and exhausted battery packs, and here and there too the corpses of those who came to seize the offices and those who had defended them.

He pauses at the broadcast studio to beckon to Issa Dzhwanson, the silver-throated actress, idol of millions, who has been for these past few days the clarion voice of their futility. But she shakes her head and like the men and women left behind on the rooftop will not leave her post. "I will maintain the illusion," she tells him. "I will tell the world that reinforcements have come, not that the remnants have left. I will sow doubts in the mind of the Protector."

"I cannot tell you where I'm going," he says. "Any lips can be brought to speak."

"They'll not take me." She laughs. "Go, and go quickly. If you do not escape, it will not matter that we ever fought."

There is not time even for a last kiss. He makes his way into the subbasement, where he scrounges in the maintenance shops for some-thing that can hack and dig and chop. The blocks are ceramic and hard

to break, but once through the surface facing progress is easier. He won-
ders how thick the wall is. Will the Protector's men enter the building
to seize it or simply stand back and bring it down, as they brought
down the Chancellory? Seventeen stories tower above him. There
would be time to realize that it was all coming down to crush him.

Then he is through the wall.

He pulls out the ceramic block and attaches a piton and line to the
back side. He wriggles feetfirst through the space thus opened and hunts
with his boots for a step or platform. Finding one, he drops the short
distance to it and then pulls the block back into the space he had chipped
it from.

Only then does he turn and using his black lamp and goggles view
the space into which he has crawled.

Donovan gasped awake at his dining table. "The steam tunnels!" he cried.

A waiter appeared by his side. "Is something wrong, *snor?*"

"No," Donovan said. "No. Do you have food served on
steam tables?"

"Oh, yes, *snor.* We have steamed perch and sturgeon."

"I'll have some of that."

The waiter hurried off to do as bid, and Donovan rose and
approached the rails along the lip of the gorge. The old steam
tunnels, once used to heat the buildings in the center city. He
remembered now. They had been abandoned in place centuries earlier, when microwave-beamed power had been redis-
covered and ancient technologies had replaced technologies
more ancient still. No one knew they were there—except the
Pedant, who knew everything.

𝔗𝔥𝔞𝔫𝔨𝔰, 𝔇𝔬𝔫𝔬𝔳𝔞𝔫. 𝔅𝔲𝔱 𝔍 𝔡𝔦𝔡𝔫'𝔱 𝔨𝔫𝔬𝔴 𝔍 𝔨𝔫𝔢𝔴.

"The memories were suppressed."

𝔜𝔬𝔲 𝔠𝔞𝔫'𝔱 𝔡𝔢𝔩𝔢𝔱𝔢 𝔪𝔢𝔪𝔬𝔯𝔦𝔢𝔰. 𝔜𝔬𝔲 𝔠𝔞𝔫 𝔬𝔫𝔩𝔶 𝔢𝔯𝔞𝔰𝔢 𝔱𝔥𝔢 𝔪𝔞𝔯𝔨𝔢𝔯𝔰

𝔱𝔥𝔞𝔱 𝔣𝔩𝔞𝔤 𝔱𝔥𝔢𝔪. 𝔅𝔲𝔱 𝔪𝔢𝔪𝔬𝔯𝔦𝔢𝔰 𝔞𝔯𝔢 𝔥𝔬𝔩𝔬𝔤𝔯𝔞𝔭𝔥𝔦𝔠 𝔞𝔫𝔡 𝔢𝔟𝔢𝔫𝔱𝔲𝔞𝔩𝔩𝔶 𝔠𝔞𝔫 𝔟𝔢 𝔯𝔢𝔠𝔞𝔩𝔩𝔢𝔡 "𝔰𝔦𝔡𝔢𝔴𝔞𝔶𝔰."

Oh, wonderful, said the Sleuth. *Another lecture on how Pedant's mind works. Or in this case did not.*

Don't be harsh with him, said the young man in the chlamys.

Besides, added the young girl in the chiton, it was better for us that we did not remember earlier.

"We haven't remembered enough, anyway," the Fudir pointed out. "The idea is not how to get out, but how to get in. We need to remember where those tunnels exited."

Somewhere along the river, obviously.

Sure, Sleuthy, but where? We can't have our little expedition poking around up and down the riverfront. Might have some impact on the surprise factor.

I have a question. Who suppressed those memories?

The Names?

Not the Names. Had they known to do so, they would have already known the way out. And if the Names knew, Gidula would have known—and then what point the secret to inveigle.

Silky! said the Sleuth. *You're becoming logical. The answer is as logical as the question. We did it to ourselves!*

"We . . . ," said Donovan. "Which 'we' would that be?"

His mind fell silent. There had once been a tenth Donovan, but he had gone insane and the others had combined to extinguish him. From time to time, he wondered which aspect of the espionage art that particular persona had been. Ruthlessness, perhaps. An agent needed ruthlessness to kill for expediency, or commit suicide when cornered. It had been the part of man that craved death.

The waiter pushed the steam table over and Donovan selected some choice slices, thanked the waiter, and watched him go. "That was you, Inner Child, wasn't it? Calling for the steam table."

<Someone may have heard us say "steam tunnels," so I sowed doubts with a plausible locution.>

Do you really think someone might be listening?

Ahh, the Kid *always* **thinks someone might be listening.**

"I hate fish," grumbled Donovan.

The Archives of Zăddigah were housed in a building called the Miwellion, dedicated by a minor descendant to a major ancestor who in his day had brought the entire Northern Mark under his sway. Built in a style known locally as Late Imperial and elsewhere not at all, it sported great fluted columns and floating roofs. The live attendant—an old monkey-faced fellow wearing something much like a bathrobe over a plain tunic—blinked astonishment when Donovan strode into the building and confronted him at the desk in the foyer.

The foyer was both narrow and tall, a cylinder, and featured a hemi-dome decorated with holomurals of the great men and women of ancient Terra. The three-dimensional quality of the mural made the dome seem to float in the farthest recesses of the sky. Embedded in the depths of the whirling figures, on the very bottom layer of the hologram, an elderly man with unruly white hair extended his finger to bring all of space and time into being. Evidently, the god Einstein. Across the dome from him, the dark god Maxwell hurled lightning bolts that roiled space and time into superluminal tubes. Overtop of these primeval acts floated more mundane heroes: slaughtering big game, building the first fire, pushing a crude canoe into the sea . . . There were mud-brick cities, marble temples and palaces, and steel laboratories, explorers setting foot on strange shores and on stranger worlds. The whole was in constant motion so that images deeper in the mural could be glimpsed through the parting clouds of later ones overlain atop them.

Donovan wondered why the lobby was not full of people, come for no other reason than to crane their necks at this wonder. But the attendant only shrugged when asked. "Guess everyone seen 'em already." He continued to regard his visitor with tight, beady eyes.

"I've come here to do some research," Donovan told him— and he could feel the warm glow of the Pedant rubbing his hands.

"Research," the attendant said in a voice indicating the novelty of the concept. "You can look at most our holdings on the *mong,* y'know."

Donovan resisted sarcasm. "I don't wish to look at *most* of your holdings, but at the rest. I have already searched the *jan-dak mong,* and those searches led me here—to examine items *not* remotely available."

There is no sigh more lingering and heartfelt than that of a man required to do his job. The wizened creature seemed to shrug within his robe. "And what subjects are those, *snor?*" he asked. "Be aware. There are some that require Nominal permission to view, and these inquiries are noted, logged, and reported."

Donovan already knew from the public *mong* that the interdict included pretty much everything dealing with Commonwealth times. "I am but a poor *zhingo shun* from Old Eighty-two. I search-again through old materials in hope of finding a new understanding."

Eyebrows arched. "Meaning no disrespect, *snor,* but what could you possibly learn from them that hasn't already been learned? The great 'uns of the past . . ." A vague gesture took in the dome above. ". . . have already said everything so perfectly there's nothing more left for the likes of you."

𝕸𝖆𝖞𝖇𝖊 𝖘𝖔, said the Pedant, but there are ofttimes benefits from saying the same thing in a different way, just as one may better appreciate the sight of the 𝕲𝖔-𝕲𝖆𝖙𝖊𝖘 by viewing them from different angles.

The attendant remained unconvinced but escorted him to a room that bore sigils in the ancient Murkanglais proclaiming it a "research room." This amused the Fudir no end, but he did not translate it into "search-again" for the skeptical attendant.

That worthy unlocked a drawer in the wall and handed him a pair of gloves, showed him the commands to copy or scribe selected images or documents, then, with an air of having exhausted himself, withdrew to resume his guardianship of the entrance.

The Pedant was in his milieu. He spent an hour scanning the indicia for anything that seemed relevant to his curiosity and discovered almost immediately that, while there were hundreds of files under the now-expired time lock of the Gran Publicamericana and seven still sequestered under the Audorithadesh Ympriales, there was nothing in the off-line Archive flagged with the Seal of the Great Names.

Yet a wealth of files, documents, and images dated from the time of the Commonwealth's fall, material that on the *mong* was forbidden. There could be but one reason for the oversight.

The Names do not know these files exist! The off-line Archives were visible only to those who came physically to this building, and, to judge by the attendant's reaction, those did not comprise a thundering herd.

The old Ympriale files predated even the Commonwealth, and so were of little interest. Yet they were the only files still under time lock. They were titled *Vyutha 1* through *Vyutha 7,* with no hint of their content. So whatever they were, even the Commonwealth had been unable to read them. *Vyutha,* the

Pedant's memory told him, seemed related to the old Murkan-glais *viuda,* which had meant variously "widow, relict, et cetera."

Both the Fudir and the Sleuth expressed curiosity—if only to learn whether they could pick the lock—so Donovan copied the files on to one of the threads he had brought. Perhaps at further leisure he could break the locks.

As the Pedant became accustomed to the gloves and the various hand motions, he began to wave up information more quickly on the holowall, sweeping documents into piles with a flick of the wrist, opening stacks with the jab of a finger. Embeds linked to other files, shelves, and sections. The Fudir filled several strings with old Commonwealth files for later perusal. Pictures flashed, diaries scrolled, dense mathematical texts unfolded. Pedant soaked it all up at the fastest blink-rate he could manage—even when not one of him could understand what was written. To the slower eye, the infowall grew blurred and smudged.

An agent need not understand the documents he purloins, Donovan thought while he watched the others work. But an eidetic memory was a priceless asset.

The oldest files on the Great Ice bore titles like "An Analysis of Ice Core Data on the Saskatchewan Glacier." Later years contained titles like "Speculations on the Wisconsin Ice." Later documents still: "A Reconsideration of Chathuri's Thesis on the Origin of the El Lenoi Ice." And so they had gone from analysis to speculation to reconsideration. A fossilization of the mind seemed to have set in, the end point of which was the attendant sitting out front, convinced that the great ones of the past had said all that was worth saying.

To Donovan's astonishment, he uncovered ancient documents written in a variant of Brythonic, which discussed other ice ages at the very dawn of human prehistory! Most of the

files from that far back were unreadable. They had been recorded in protocols or on media that could no longer be deci-
phered. Sometime in the ancient past—as media decayed and
the instruments to read them were breaking down—some poor
tech had been faced with the choice of migrating *these* documents or *those* on to fresh media, and decided *those* were not
worth his time. A Dark Age had descended, due less to the
ravages of Kgonzdan the Oppressed or the Scything of the
Beanstalks than to the inevitable decay of substrates over time.
There never would have been enough of a budget or enough
scribes or enough time to migrate every "disk" before it had
passed below the horizon of readability. It was not that people
who lived back then had suddenly turned stupid, but that their
learning had become a blank slate, an inert disk, a broken
thread.

Deep in the Stasis Vault beneath the Miwellion, he learned,
there were physical objects: a "tape," a "thumb drive," an ancient book. Only the book could still be read—by a special
emorái camera that scanned page images at various depths into
what otherwise was a solidly fused block of paper.

Pedant found an image of a barren shoreline recognizably that
of the Bay of Ketchell, but without a city embracing it. A party
of fifteen, bundled in parkas, faced the imager. A few of them
were waving. One was pointing northward, as if to indicate
their destination. The image bore a partly legible caption in
the old Taṇṭamiž: *Capt.(?) Hitchkorn-pandit and his par** **ior
to setting out f** ******. 1* Jun* ****.* The Fudir wondered
where they had been heading to, and whether any had ever
come back.

Donovan used the image as a search term and soon unearthed a dozen similar scenes captured over the centuries
from the same angle. The oldest were flat or, more likely, their

3-D extensions had corrupted. The more recent were holograms. The Sleuth rotated the holograms to match as nearly as possible the viewpoint of the fixed images.

Viewing them in sequence, he could watch the land on which Ketchell was built emerge from the sea. The shoreline receded; harbors became lakes, then farmlands. And Ketchell grew brick by brick. The oldest image of all looked across a broad mudflat on which was cradled a once-sunken ship now careened drunkenly on her side. In the middle distance, beyond the forest that had grown between them and the sea, Donovan could make out the sky-scraping spires of an older city from whose docks and harbors the ocean had retreated.

From the estimated dates of the images, the Sleuth calculated a time lapse of no more than two hundred years from the barren mudflats to the beginnings of Ketchell. Now, according to its residents, Ketchell had "always" been there.

A Farewell to Manitoba, by Henri Sanchez Patel, was the diary of someone purporting to be the last resident of that otherwise-unknown realm before it vanished beneath the ice. He wrote movingly of the empty houses, the silent roadways, the deserted cemeteries, most of all the memories, and how one year the snow that fell in winter failed to melt in the following summer. Even at the speed of Pedant's reading, the lingering love of Patel for his native land came through and reduced the Silky Voice to tears.

But there was one curious passage that caught Donovan's attention.

> *Word came today on the net that the great Kenya Beanstalk has come down at last. It was long expected, but perhaps it would have been wiser to let nature take its course. Its upper reaches were detached and, being at orbital velocity, High Nairobi*

flew off into deep space. But that was the only part that went according to plan. Tragedy was foredoomed. If the world is too poor to maintain those grand old structures, then certainly she is too poor to deconstruct them safely. Different parts of the stalk, they said, had different eastward velocities, and the debris field scattered much farther than officials had so confidently predicted. Tala and Kituni had been wisely evacuated, but the whole structure twisted north and sections separated and screeched over the horizon to fall like flaming shrapnel on Kisimaayo and even as far as Muqdisho. These are places I never heard of before, and now no one will ever hear of them again.

But that could not be right. The Twelve Gates had been scythed down by Dao Chetty in their rebellious attack on Terra during the overthrow of the Commonwealth. The Dao Chettians themselves said so. He wondered if one of them—this "Kenya Beanstalk"—had been brought down earlier for some other reason and the demolition had been tragically mishandled.

<Hush!> said Inner Child. <Someone coming.>

The attendant? asked the Silky Voice.

𝕹𝖔, the Pedant told himselves. 𝕿𝖍𝖊 𝖆𝖙𝖙𝖊𝖓𝖉𝖆𝖓𝖙 𝖜𝖆𝖑𝖐𝖘 𝖜𝖎𝖙𝖍 𝖆 𝖘𝖍𝖚𝖋𝖋𝖑𝖊. 𝕿𝖍𝖊𝖘𝖊 𝖆𝖗𝖊 𝖘𝖔𝖋𝖙, 𝖆𝖓𝖉 𝖘𝖙𝖊𝖆𝖑𝖙𝖍𝖞.

How could They have traced us here? the Sleuth asked. *We had the* niplips *removed.*

"Unless Foo-lin lied," muttered the Fudir.

<But who has found us? Gidula and his people? Or Ekadrina and hers?>

The Brute pulled a teaser from the folds of his garment and in two swift bounds slipped beside the open door. He pressed back against the wall, out of sight from the corridor.

<Close the door!>

No. Then he'd know we heard him.

The faint footfalls approached the entry, and stopped.

There was time for two breaths, then a voice said, "Knock, knock."

Dumbfounded, the scarred man made no reply, and the voice said with some asperity, "You're supposed to say 'Who's there?,' Donovan."

Donovan did not recognize the voice. He shifted his grip on the teaser. "Who's there?"

"Gwillgi."

Donovan did not ask, *Gwillgi who?*

Gwillgi Hound carried a dazer, which more than trumped Donovan's teaser. The scarred man put his weapon away without being asked. Gwillgi did not and was not asked.

The Hound gave the impression of a great deal of energy packed into a small space, like a spring compressed. He was short, dark visaged, and bore a pencil-thin mustache on his lip. His cheeks and chin were a bed of short, sharp bristles. When he smiled, his teeth showed, but not to any comforting effect.

He studied Donovan from topaz eyes that resembled aperture crystals for a laser. "I don't believe we've formally met, Donovan. Or should I say, 'Geshler Padaborn'?"

Donovan retreated to the egg-chair that hung before the holowall and lowered himself into it. He had met his share of Hounds—Bridget ban, Greystroke, Cerberus, and others—but none had inspired the feeling of utter dread as did Gwillgi. If the little man was a compressed spring, he was a spring wound of razor wire.

The Hound gestured and a second egg-chair descended from a recess in the ceiling and hung before the holowall. Gwillgi captured the wall in a glance while he seated himself.

"Did you come here to kill me?" Donovan asked.

Gwillgi's smile showed canines. "If I had, you'd ne'er have

asked that question. Death is best served briskly. Anyone who makes it a play is a fool."

The Fudir relaxed just a little, although he could think of three reasons why Gwillgi might delay an assassination. "I'm on vacation," he said, resurrecting a portion of his bravado. "Come back when I'm on the clock again."

"On the clock . . . ?" Gwillgi considered the phrase, deduced its meaning. "Let's say you're on call, why don't we? I've got some questions. You can answer them, or you *will* answer them."

"Do I have to choose?"

Gwillgi barked. It might have been a laugh. "I can see what she meant. Now, let's start at the top, why don't we. Are you Geshler Padaborn?"

"I . . . don't know." Donovan tensed unwillingly.

The human dynamite pursed his lips. "Well. There goes my script. I expected one of three responses, but that wasn't one of them. How could you not know . . . ? Ah."

"Yes, you must have read the report I gave Zorba three years back."

The Hound nodded. "How many are you, inside that cantaloupe?"

"Nine—that we know of." He grinned nervously. "We've got you outnumbered."

Gwillgi grunted. "Sure. But you're sitting all bunched up. Is Padaborn one of your nine?"

"Might, or might not be. We . . . destroyed one a couple years ago that was, well, dysfunctional."

Gwillgi raised an eyebrow. "Interesting. I've never spoken with the survivor of a successful suicide attempt."

Donovan shrugged. "It might have been Padaborn, but . . ."

"But you don't think so."

"I'm starting to remember things that Padaborn might re-member."

"You think there might be more personas awakening?"

Donovan turned wistful. "Ten was such a nice round number."

"So's twelve. More divisors. Could mean you're still two short."

"Present company planty nuff, sahb."

Gwillgi nodded. "Padaborn or no, how high up in the rev-olutionary cabal are you?" When Donovan hesitated, Gwillgi cocked his head, and the cocking of Gwillgi's head was enough to elicit words from any man.

Donovan took a deep breath. "The Revolution plans to crack me open and suck me dry. They think I know something they want to know. That's why I'm on vacation."

Gwillgi pursed his lips, tilted his head. "That's forthright."

The Fudir spread his hands. "Have I ever lied to you?"

"On Yuts'ga you engaged in battle on the rebel side and fought Sèanmazy to a draw. That was impressive."

"How did you know—"

"I'd been following Domino Tight. He was a coming man among them and bore watching. Then he was killed in a back alley in Cambertown and I switched to my number two target: a loyalist named Pendragon Jones."

"Killed? But he . . ."

"Yes. Tight proved remarkably chipper for being so re-cently and thoroughly deceased. And then, the lagniappe: an unexpected guest appearance by Bridget ban's old lover. Well, one of them. And in the role of the storied Padaborn, no less."

"You were watching—"

"Of course. I arrived late because of an assassination in downtown Cambertown. The mums hit the lyres all over

Yuts'ga and the Confederation cashed out short a minor official. The rebels are trying to maneuver their own people into key offices, aren't they?"

"I'd rather not betray anyone."

Gwillgi waved a hand. His nails were almost like claws. "That would be a neat trick, and I wouldn't mind watching you try. But let me suggest my own name at the top of the list of those you'd not betray. Which side are you working for?"

"I'm working for Donovan buigh."

Gwillgi ran a fingernail along the barrel of his dazer. "Don't try for 'cute,' Donovan buigh. You haven't the dimples for it."

Donovan flapped his arm. "I was out of the Long Game. Out of it! All I wanted was to visit my daughter on Dangchao Waypoint and mend some fences with her mother. That's all. I was kidnapped and brought here against my will." He started to say more but decided not to add any further complications. "I have some debts and obligations now."

"So your promise is suddenly worth something?"

"You're here as the Kennel's observer," countered Donovan.

"It's a big Spiral Arm. We don't want the Confederation to fall unless we know which way it will topple. And that means we need to know what the sides are, who is on which, and how the victory of either would affect the League."

"And now I'm your focus."

"My interests are varied. I still want to know who put Humpty Domino back together again. But why and how you got not only into it but apparently into a leadership position does pique my curiosity somewhat. Old man Gidula picked you up. He's a clever sod. He wins every battle by being late and picking up the pieces. I knew he'd bring you to Terra, so—"

"So you watched the Forks from remote viewers up atop Kojj Hill."

Gwillgi wagged the dazer at him. "I'm impressed."

"You left a footprint."

"Mmm, well. Can't get them all."

"And your lander's skid pressed into the ground when you concealed it in a hidden meadow."

"And from that you knew it was me?"

"I knew it was someone. No offense, I was hoping it would be someone else."

Gwillgi finally made his weapon disappear. "Kidnapped, you say. I could smuggle you back into the League. You could brief Black Shuck personally, then go to Dangchao and learn if Bridget ban will shoot you or not."

"Well . . ."

"Well?"

"It's gotten complicated."

"Oh, good." Gwillgi swung a leg over his knee and clasped his hands over it. "I was afraid it was all too simple. Tell me more."

So Donovan told him more. He just didn't tell him all.

Later, they dined at a restaurant overlooking the Go-Gates from Mount Morn on the northern cliff. The mist from the falls of the Qornja where it passed between the two cliffs created rainbows over the gorge, and it seemed as of the faerie bridge above them were supported on an arch of light.

Donovan noted that as the sun moved lower in the west and cast the cliffs into sharp relief a human figure emerged faintly from the ancient rocks of the southern cliff: a bearded man wearing an expression of unutterable weariness and holding at ease a shoulder-fired weapon of indeterminate type. The outline was much eroded from the water and the stiff wind that scoured the Gates, but Donovan thought it looked sandblasted as well. He wondered how many generations had separated the fulgent praise that had shaped the figure from the obloquy that had sought to obliterate it.

Gwillgi expressed no curiosity about the image; but it wasn't his planet, after all. The headwaiter, when the robot server had summoned him, was equally uninformative.

"We call it the Moment, *snor,* which means 'The Face of Evening.' There is another, a different face, on the cliff below us, but only the finest of lighting calls it from the rock. That is why it is best to patronize this poor place, which *snor* does not forget is called Dinner in the Mist. The view from Prizga is not so fine as from here."

By this the Fudir understood that the two restaurants were rivals. Perhaps there would be something about the cliff faces in the files he had copied at the Miwellion. He wasn't sure why it mattered, or even that it did; but deprived of the Mount of Many Faces, he would settle for the Cliffs of Two Faces.

"I fancy myself a good judge of character," Gwillgi said. "I've seldom been wrong, and never wrong twice. I don't see you working for the Names. Otherwise, you'd be *in* that gorge, not gazing at it. As for the Revolution . . . Are you certain about those apparitions? The ones who appeared from nowhere at the warehouse fight?"

Donovan stroked his chin. His bowl held a steaming heap of vermicelli and rice pilaf, seasoned with a variety of spices, from which he took a forkful. "I can't be entirely certain," he said after he had swallowed. "They may have been lurking somewhere nearby. But Oschous was monitoring the battle through the sensor array, and swore that they simply appeared on his screens."

"I was too late for that part. You think they were Names."

"Oschous wouldn't speak of them directly. That's a common behavior pattern over here."

"Some rebel. And there were a total of . . . How many? Four?"

"I counted four. Two on the rooftop: a woman of surpassing beauty and, after Domino Tight had wounded her, a man enough alike to be her brother. A second man appeared in the old truck apron—he was a walking arsenal—and took out quite a few of our fighters just as we were on the verge of victory. Then, another woman—her beauty was more the hard-as-nails kind—appeared with Domino Tight and Ravn Olafsdottr and helped them take out the *rambo*."

"Which means, if they were Names, the Names are fighting on both sides. Which means the Revolution has sparked a civil war among the rulers themselves."

"It's not unusual," Donovan said, "to find revolutionaries among the rulers. Those who think they can surf the waves of change."

Gwillgi wrinkled his brow. "Surf?"

"Never mind. There's a second interpretation of events."

"No fact explains itself," Gwillgi agreed. "It can always be seen from other angles. I think I see where you're heading."

"The whole Revolution is a sham. The Names have not taken sides in the rebellion. The Names were already at each other's throats—and the Revolution is something they have conjured up to carry on their fight by proxy."

Gwillgi showed his teeth again. "I don't know which would be more discomfited by that, the loyalists or the rebels. Do you think they know?"

Donovan shook his head. "I think Gidula suspects. That may be why he's chosen his own road. I can't answer for the loyalists."

"And you don't know how Domino Tight was resurrected."

"I didn't even know he was dead. When the mums ambushed the lyre, they nearly wiped out his cadre. The survivors who trickled into the warehouse knew only that they had lost contact with their master and his staff. We feared the worst, but when he showed up, we figured he had eluded the trap."

Gwillgi shook his head. "I was there. I saw him. I even waved the knife for him." He blinked, then explained. "'Wave the knife' is what we say in Public Vorhayn, Friesing's World, when we ritually dispatch companions to accompany the dead."

"Umm."

"Don't worry, Donovan. Only for murders. To accompany their victims."

"I never had a chance to talk with Domino Tight," Donovan said. "He teamed up with Ravn Olafsdottr and the two of them attacked Ekadrina Sèanmazy together. That was . . . when I joined the fight."

The eyes of Gwillgi narrowed and his brow grew thoughtful. "When Olafsdottr was killed."

"She wasn't killed. I found that out later. Gidula had her cared for, then dropped her off on Delpaff. If you can track her down . . ."

Gwillgi rose. "It's not good to stay too long in one place. You know what you have to do, right?"

Donovan was not certain he "had" to do anything, let alone the bidding of this spring-loaded ball of razor wire. "I have an idea."

"You'll have to let Gidula find you."

Donovan shrugged. "How do I get in touch with you?"

"You don't. I get in touch with you. But don't expect it too soon or too often. I've been getting calling cards—drone packets entering systems where I've been—but not from anyone I've entrusted with my call-code. I don't know that my network's been compromised, but I won't risk it by answering. Just in case, I've shifted my pattern." He extended a hand, which Donovan found to be rough and calloused. "So think about what you've told me, and where you've used pronouns like 'we,' 'us,' and 'our.' And make sure you're on the right side."

"I told you. I'm on my side; and that's always the right side."

Gwillgi smiled. "I like you, Donovan. I don't like many people, but I like you. That would make it particularly hard if I have to kill you. Betrayal by someone I like is especially galling."

IX. NEVER DO WHAT YOU SAID YOU'D DO

What ploys, o harper, do the Fates dispose
Our timely plans so to disconcert,
Planting their confusions and perplexities
To wriggle wormlike through our minds?
Be we the authors of our own acts?
Belike but froth upon great Ocean's foam,
Teased by winds while darker currents
Down below direct our course.
Our destination's purposed by the breeze
Howe'er we set our sails. Fair dawning brings
What e'er the Fates do weave, until Fate cuts the strings.

That evening, as the sun-lamps dimmed in Sector Seventeen, Ravn escorted Méarana to a nearby restaurant called, in that cozy Confederal fashion, Restaurant *No* 17-04. It was also known, unofficially, as Demvrouq's Place. That it was called this, and called this unofficially, was a flower blossoming through the duroplast of Confederal culture.

It stood a short distance across the concourse from the hotel, but to gain its entrance meant breasting the madding, elsewhere-bent transient streams. The shuttle-fresh starward bound clashed, mixed, and eddied with inbounders intent on the capital. Gray suits, saffron turbans, embroidered gowns, gold and red and black, willowy women, head-scarfed men, skipping children—that last the only spot of humanity not yet humbled and broken.

The harper scanned the faces—masked, veiled, open, wimpled—as she and Ravn swam through them cross-current, thinking she might notice the woman Gwen once more. With rather less anticipation, her eyes also sought out shadows and patches of darkness left by the boulevard-lamps, waiting for one that might come to life and speak.

She thought now that the sweet smell she had perceived in the hotel room had been a gas vented into the air system. She herself knew two ways to accomplish this, which her mother in a fit of whimsy had once taught her. But knowing how the hallucination might have been induced gave her no desire to experience a second time the voice that spoke in the night.

"What *are* you looking for?" Ravn asked her when once they had installed themselves in the restaurant.

"Oh, I like to study faces. Sometimes I see a song in them."

The Shadow leaned across the table. "Well, stop doing it. No one stares directly at another person here, unless they have superior rank. Eyes downcast, please. Draw no attention to self."

Ordinary citizens here were called "the sheep," Méarana remembered. But she had also seen in covert glances that sheep might harbor bitter resentments. "I saw another Shadow the other day," she commented while inspecting the menu, "the first day we were here."

"What!" Ravn seized the harper's wrist and the menu fell to the floor. "Who? Why did you say nothing!"

Méarana tried to pull back, failed. "How would I know who? She was tall, dark skinned—darker than I, but not quite so dark as you—and she carried a thick staff."

"A staff. What mon did she wear?"

"Mon?"

"Her logo, her sign. What was it?"

"Umm . . . Oh! The yin-yang. The taiji."

Ravn hissed. "Ekadrina Sèanmazy! Did she notice you?"

"Why would she notice me? She wouldn't . . ." Then, under Ravn's insistent gaze, "No. She didn't even turn in my direction."

Ravn shook her head. "That is what you must expect should Ekadrina notice you. She knows what Bridget ban looks like, and you resemble your mother passing well."

"She was heading toward the Dao Chetty drop-ports. Probably returning to the Lion's Mouth from some mission."

"I'm sure she was. How many magpies accompanied her?"

"I don't know. I didn't count them." But Ravn squeezed her wrist tighter, and Méarana closed her eyes and tried to conjure the scene in her mind. "One. Two . . . Seven. I think."

Ravn released her. "She should have had eight."

"Maybe I just didn't notice. Or she lost one on her mission, or . . ."

"Or she left one here to watch us. *Kumbe!* I thought I sensed a nearby presence."

Méarana almost said, *Don't worry; it's only a pair of Hounds.* But to a Shadow that would hardly be a comfort. "I'm sure she didn't notice me, let alone mistake me for my mother, or she would have . . ." She fell silent as she considered all the things a Shadow "would have" done if she thought a Hound sat alone on a hotel patio.

"An such a wan sees me wi' ye—"

Ravn's finger touched Méarana's lips. "Hoosh, hoosh, my sweet. Coome with me to the women's comfort station . . ." They rose from the table and wound calmly through the potted shrubbery to the back of the restaurant. "Let no dialect of Gaelactic twist your tongue," Ravn cautioned her. "Search earwig. Become one with it. Empty mind and let Confederal dialect fill it, lest moment of stress betray you. Try dialects of Heller Connat. There is one that resembles Gaelactic—no, out side door—but your kind, the golden-skinned gingers, are found on . . . on Miniforster, Bhaitry, and Wing Bahlo, not on Heller Connat." She looked both ways up the service corridor, then allowed Méarana to follow. "Never do," she whispered, "what you say you will do when your speech may be overheard."

"But Ravn," the harper said in realistic tones. "The likelihood that a detached magpie has been watching us and overheard—"

"Is not zero, and few are the Shadows who have died from an excess of caution." Ravn reached into her shoulder pouch and pulled out something about the size and shape of a dinner napkin. This she pounded several times with her fist and then pressed against her face. It hissed, and steam rose.

"Ravn!" Méarana exclaimed—but in a whisper.

Ravn gasped and pulled the towel from her face, and the harper was shocked to see the Shadow's features sagging like a wax candle. Quick massages raised cheekbones, shortened nose, shaped ears. A close examination in a pocket mirror led to some last-moment touch-ups before her face had once more hardened.

"Ayiyi," she said in a voice Méarana had never heard her use before, "dat hoits like da beaches." She pulled a knife from her sleeve and said to the harper, "Yer mop's too long." A few swipes of the blade sufficed to correct it. "Ah, I missed my vocation, me. Shoulda been a beautician." Then she reached once more into her pouch and from a tube squeezed a dollop of gel, which she rubbed vigorously between her palms. She worked it first into her own bright yellow hair, turning it a dull brown, then into Méarana's now-shortened red hair, turning it dark auburn.

"Now the piece of resistance. A few fasteners pulled loose an' refastened carelessly. A rumplin' o' da clothin'. Wait—while I smear yer lip dye." Before the harper could react, Ravn took Méarana's face in her two hands and kissed her hard on the lips. "Dere," she said, stepping back with satisfaction, "jus' two friends, is all, who stepped up a service corridor fer a quickie."

Ravn put her arm around Méarana's waist and led her out to the plaza. Ravn became another person. She slouched, her eyes searched the walkway, she made way for anyone more colorfully dressed. Méarana perforce did likewise.

The harper thought their dishevelment would attract everyone's attention, but only a few heads turned. A business traveler grinned at them. Beneath one of the boulevard-lamps, a black-clad night-walker in a girdle-skirt and lacquered hair that fit her head like a helmet scowled as if at potential competition. A short man stirring his drink idly at a café table barely glanced at them. Méarana wanted to see whether anyone was watching the restaurant, but Ravn, by body pressure, steered her away onto Corridor 1716-M-2, which led to the Sixteenth Sector.

"I don't know," Méarana said when they were out of the public square and in a narrow walkway lined with anonymous doors. "This may be a lot of trouble for nothing." She pulled away from the Shadow. "How did you do that with your face?" She studied her companion's features closely. "It wouldn't long fool those who know you."

The Ravn took quick glances over her shoulder. "Don't hafta. Jus' enough to get through a tight spot. Wouldn'ta fooled Ekadrina herself for a Bhaitry minute. *Kumbe,* does my face hurt! Subcutaneous implants," she added in a more normal tone. "The hot pad softens them up so I can mold them, but there's a limit to how far I can push and pinch, and after a while it reverts to normal."

An escalator led to the Upper Deck, Level Four, and they backtracked through Seventeen Upper to Sector Eighteen, where they found a seedy residence hotel called Mamma Kitten's. "Mamma," as it developed, was a bewhiskered man who massed at least twenty-one accelerated stones, and his name really was Kitten. He ran everything by word and hand and nothing of his crossed the threshold of Tungshen's information net. His was, in a sense, a hole in the habitat.

Ravn departed for a time, returning later with some fresh clothing and other items that she had secured from an autovendor.

"You leavin' anythin' at th' Kings?" she asked.

Méarana's harp was aboard *Sèan Beta.* "No."

"Good, 'cause I ain't goin' back there."

What Méarana very much feared she had left behind— along with Sèanmazy's hypothetical magpie—were Gwen and the voice that spoke in the night. For a moment, Méarana wondered if Ravn's maneuver had been intended to throw the two Hounds off the scent. But Ravn couldn't know about them. She was not *that* clever. Was she?

Ravn Olafsdottr had known when she had thrown in with the Revolution-within-the-Revolution that she must forswear any vestige of heartfelt comradeship. Every hand might at some time be raised against her, and she could count upon no friends among her friends, and but a handful among her enemies. She had entered the Abattoir in her youth, a gift to the Lion's Mouth from parents forever unknown. Her entire life, she had done the Mouth's bidding, silencing those whose silence was required, aware always of the knife at her back if she failed, until one day she had graduated to second and held the knife herself. She had grown to respect the skill and the craft with which her colleagues maintained the order of the Confederation, but never once did she question the order they maintained. The means were noble, and the means justified the ends.

And now her colleagues stood arrayed against one another for reasons she could barely credit, with herself and too few others standing between them. She could conjure many motives for bringing the Names down, and as many for holding them up. Because Those had laid too heavy a hand upon the sheep. Because Those had saved the Confederation from the chaos that plagued the Periphery. She could understand men who fought for loyalty, for tradition, for justice, or even for raw ambition. But to fight for Kelly Stapellaufer?

The quarrel between Epri Gunjinshow and Manlius Metatxis for the charms of their colleague had provided the trigger. Ekadrina had sided with Epri and Dawshoo with Manlius, and everything followed from that. But she knew that was only the excuse, not the reason. One may as well fight for Jenkins's ear as for Kelly's jade gates. The fault lines had already underlain matters, fracturing the Lion's Mouth into factions before even the factions themselves were aware of it. The rending awaited only some petty conflict to open up.

On the evening of the morning on which the Shadow War had been announced, Ravn Olafsdottr and Domino Tight and two others whose names she must never more remember held a dinner of great beauty and state. The wines had been exquisite; the fare more than fair. Their four banners had hung over the banquet hall in comradeship. One of them—she *must* not think his name—had made a long, tear-driven speech declaring that when all was over this *best foursome* would one day reconvene. At the end of it, all were weeping—Shadows, magpies, even the servants and the banquet-hall staff—and they had embraced and kissed one another and cast many a vow aloft.

And the next morning, Domino Tight had gone to join the rebels and the other two to stand by the loyalists. And now, that "best foursome" could never meet as more than three, and the tally was not yet final.

She had attached herself to Gidula because he had seemed the one steady rock in the tumbling chaos. He could reform the excesses of the decadent Names while providing a brake on the wilder ambitions of Oschous Dee.

But even Dawshoo had known the way was forward, not back into a storybook past.

To what extent, she sometimes now wondered, had her own loyalties been formed by those storybooks, by tales of brightly caparisoned Shadows flying forth to fight and die for duty and honor? Tales in which noble words were spoken in noble company, and in which even an execution could be conducted with pomp and rite. In days of yore, the scaffold erected on Edakass for Mengwa Chertahanseon had been draped with cloth-of-tears and the condemned had been given a red velvet blindfold (which he had of course refused), and his executioner had been his own particular friend, Paphlaq bin Underwood. There had been mournful songs beforehand and playing of such instruments as befitted Mengwa's rank, and no one had touched Paphlaq's right hand afterward for nine and ninety days.

When Shadow Prime—not the present Prime, but an earlier one—had been honored for his services during the Discontentment of the Oatland Sheep at a banquet hosted by the Dreadful Name himself, he had stubbornly refused to wash his hands in the same basin as the Name. The Abattoir had spoken of nothing else for days, and the senior Shadows debated the propriety of the gesture. No one doubted that the gesture was meaningful and beautiful and edifying, and it had now become the custom at any banquet for the guest of honor to three times refuse the basin of his host. The basins themselves had become progressively more ornate.

When the current Prime was a young man, he had received the undershift of Lady Ielnor as prelude to a pasdarm held on Old Eighty-two. He had cradled the garment in his arms the night before, even—so it was said—kissing it, and appeared at the pasdarm the next morning wearing only the shift over his shenmat, no dispersal armor. In consequence of this, he had emerged from the fighting bloody and cut up and with a serious wound in his side. Ah, but what a gesture! It won him the prize despite his scoring only third on points. He had sent the bloody shift back to Lady Ielnor, and she had kissed it and worn it over her gown at the banquet afterward. Ravn Olafsdottr knew that it was all smoke, now wafting away in the new-risen wind, if indeed it had ever been anything more. But she resented that loss and wondered if her determination to go down with the heroic dream of the beautiful life would itself one day be marked as the last in a long line of beautiful, doomed gestures—to bring hot tears to Gidula's eyes and mockery to the lips of Oschous Dee.

Meanwhile, she had her vow to Gidula to consider. The Vow of the Raptor was often sealed by kaowèn—her back twinged where she had been striped—but it was customarily done to underline the keeping of it, not to induce the taking of it. Did Gidula—poor, determined Gidula—even realize that he had crossed a line that he himself had drawn?

Two years past, while Ravn had been hunting Donovan in the Periphery, the Old One had learned . . . *something* . . .

What that something was Ravn did not know, but the learning of it had induced introspection and worry. The man to whom Ravn had delivered Donovan was a very different man than the one who had sent her forth to fetch him. After Donovan had shown himself sane and integrated in his combat with Ekadrina, Ravn had feared Gidula would execute him as no longer suitable for the play. The plan had always been to raise the rebels' hopes with the name of Padaborn, then crush them with the reality of the scarred man. But the plan had shifted—to the invasion of the Secret City—and Donovan's value had changed from brass to gold.

She glanced at foolish, romantic Méarana. Dragging the bait might lure a Hound into the Mouth, even if that were not its main basic function. But the difficulties arose from attracting other hunters beside. She had not wanted to start Ekadrina on this particular scent, and hoped that her suspicions were vain. Yet she had felt herself watched from time to time. If not by Ekadrina's magpie, then by whom?

And there was something else that Ravn could not quite put a finger on. The harper's attitude had changed. Fractionally, to be sure, but it ought not to have changed at all.

Domino Tight was a true believer in the Revolution. It was his strength and his weakness—beyond the obvious weakness of trusting his comrades too greatly. Give him years enough and he might give Oschous a run, a fact of which Oschous was undoubtedly aware. But in the meantime, his zeal burned hot and he imagined a bright day, joy drenched and sunshine filled, if just a trifle vague and rosy, in which every tear would be wiped away. It was a future state worth visioning, and he had not recognized that while all might agree that the present was no longer tolerable, there was no such unanimity on what the future ought to be.

But he and Ravn were gozhiinyaw, blood brothers, and once contact was made it required little to induce him to come with her to Zãddigah-Terra.

"I haff good news," the Ravn announced after returning to Mamma Kitten's from a comm. center in Sector Two Under, one the far side of the cooper body in and around which Tungshen was built. "And bad news."

Méarana, who had spent the better part of the day transcribing notes into the particular code that Clanthompson employed, had delighted to hear the former but worried at the latter. "What is the good news?" she asked.

"My darling Dominoo will be here soon!"

Méarana hesitated only fractionally. "And the bad?"

"My darling Dominoo will be here soon!"

The harper blinked and puckered in thought. "Ah," she said at last. "That isn't good, is it?"

The Ravn threw herself onto the tatty old couch that disgraced the center of the common room they shared. Springs complained, fabric tore.

"Light wants a languid seven hours to make the trip. Shoottles want days. Yet Dominoo will meet me this very afternoon! What cause has Dominoo Tight to shoow light his heels?"

"There are two possibilities."

Ravn cocked an eye at Méarana and planted her chin on her fist. "Which two?"

"One, it's a trap. You're being led to meet someone already on Tungshen. Sèanmazy's magpie, maybe."

"And the timing is unrealistic because . . . ?"

"He doesn't know how long it took you to contact Domino and thinks your friend left Dao Chetty back when you sent your first call-worm."

"Very good. I am assigning that medium probability. And second?"

"Domino Tight came by quondam leap."

"And that means . . ."

". . . one of the Names, likely this Tina Zhi, knows about the rendezvous."

"Yays, and that is the bad news of it. What might Domino Tight have told her in passion of pillow-bed? Or what might she have extracted from him? Your mother did teach you three things, maybe even four. We make you Shadow some-day soon."

"No, thanks. I'll stick with harping."

"This I assign the higher chance. The call-worm I received referenced elliptically in the form of an allegory a bistro in the Fifth Sector that Domino and I know from old. No one but he and I would associate that particular phrase with that particu-lar place. If my enemies know this, they can only have torn it from Domino's lips; and if they have done so, then all is lost in any case."

"Any man might be broken," Méarana agreed. "But if the Technical Name desired to meddle, she would not have so ob-viously transported her lover here, and so announce her par-ticipation."

Ravn Olafsdottr contemplated that wisdom, and reluctantly nodded.

Ravn led Méarana through an intricacy of tunnels and mainte-nance ways halfway around the habitat to enter from an unlikely angle a commercial mezzanine overlooking the plaza where the meeting was to be. And yes, down below was her sweet Dom-ino Tight sitting at a café table and but lightly disguised in the drab, baggy clothing of a sheep.

She turned away from the rail and ushered Méarana into a store. "You stay here," Ravn cautioned the harper. "This shop offers entertainments for transients who must lay over for their connecting flight. There are active and passive sims—*mojies*, they are called here—musics, and suchlike foo-foo. Browse until I come back for you." Then, arranging with the shop-keeper to keep rogue males from bothering the harper and cautioning him on the many undesirable things that would befall him if he failed, she took a circuitous route to the plaza below, so as to approach Domino from another direction.

She came up behind him in his "four," but of course he had positioned a reflective vase to reveal such quadrants and, since they were not at enmity, he rose and turned and held out a weaponless hand in greeting.

The weapon, of course, was in his other hand; but he slipped it into its sheath with an economy of motion. They sat across from each other, and neither said anything for a long moment.

Domino Tight was a changed man from the last time Ravn had seen him. There was a haggard look to him that reminded her of trapped animals. Ravn immediately suspected ka-owèn—or, worse, duxing kaoda. Had he been caught and turned by Ekadrina or her people? Could both of Méarana's scenarios be true? Domino *and* a trap?

Domino Tight spoke first. "You look like your face had an argument with the duroplast."

"Yayss. And the duroplast loost." But her gozhiinyaw did not laugh, and Domino Tight was a man known for his humors. "You do not look well," she told him. "Is the quondam leap so harrowing?"

He shook his head. "Have you ever coupled with a cobra?"

Ravn thought about that, and finally shook her head. "Not to my certain memory."

"That is what it likens to," he said.

"You mean coupling with Ti—"

But Domino hushed her. "If I call her name, she . . . feels

it. Somehow. We're *entangled,* whatever that means; and she would be at my side in an instant. I don't know what might happen if someone else says her name in my presence."

"I had thought her your pleasure."

"As a clerk in the Gayshot Bo, she was sweet and pliable. But now . . . Have you ever seen a cat play with a mouse?"

"Of course. Is part of basic training."

"Well, I'm the mouse. She is insatiable. The things she desires . . . It is as if normal pleasures have long since withered for her, and so she must seek out the novel and the . . . creative. Oh, laugh all you want, Ravn. But it *wears.* And there is always the thought in the back of my mind: What if I cannot perform to her satisfaction? What if I am of no more use to her?" He paused and took the drink that was before him, and it sloshed a little onto the table. "She seems so young, but she is old, old. Eternal youth? You would think it would pall after the first few lifetimes."

"Gidula would find the prospect pleasing. Age does not creep upon him; it races toward him on tiger's feet. He would not mind learning her secret. Ah, but he'll not have the opportunity. Domino, my sweet. Listen to me. There is something I must do—something I have *vowed* to do—but I need you to make the play." And she explained to Domino Tight the nature of her vow.

"Of course I will help. But why move Gidula? He pretends openly to be neutral, but he is one of us."

Ravn picked up a glass of water that her companion had left untasted. "He pretends openly to be neutral, and pretends covertly to be rebel; but that is of no account. My task is outside the Shadow War. He tortured me to extract a vow I was disinclined to give."

"And . . . ?"

"The torture should have come afterward."

"Ah. As when we take the Shadow's Oath . . ."

"Exactly so. So that we know, down in the bone, the penalty for breaking it."

"It seems a delicate point, a matter of mere timing. You would slay Gidula because he missed a beat?"

"If you'll not help me . . ." Ravn made as if to push away from the table.

"I've already said I would. And—hmm—I suppose that tells me all I need to know about why you must do what you must do. A vow extracted by torture ought not be valid. Come the Revolution, all that oathing goes by the board."

Ravn sighed. "I suppose it will. Listen. I will give you back your cloaks and drop you onto the tableland north of the Forks. There will be a ceremonial entry—the Old One keeps the ancient troth—then, while everyone is focused on the Iron Bridge, you will slip though the sensors on Kojj Hill and make your way into the stronghold and go to ground until the moment comes. I have maps, with the key locations pricked off. Study them along the way."

Domino Tight accepted the data slug and it disappeared into his pockets. "Now," he said, "about the woman you left in the *mojy* shop . . ."

Ravn was not surprised he had noticed and apprised the situation. Much could be learned by peering into reflective surfaces. "What about her?"

"Who is that other woman she's talking to?"

Ravn had been watching Méarana with half an eye, and was aware that others had entered the shop and were walking about the displays. Now she saw the harper deep in conversation with a tubby woman in tight, black curls. "Looks like a transient off the liner. Those are traveling clothes."

Domino stared into his reflective vase. "She keeps glancing at us."

"The harper?"

"No, the fat one."

Ravn focused on the strange woman and, as if that infinitesimal shift had been a signal, the strange woman lifted her eyes and stared at her. The moment of contact was brief, because in it Ravn had leapt from her chair and the woman had turned to fly; but it was long enough for a kind of recognition. She was in the Life.

Ekadrina's magpie? Without thinking, Ravn whipped an *étrier* to the balcony and clambered up it. The tubby woman was almost around the corner of the corridor when a spike blossomed from her back and her dull gray coverall began to blacken. A back-glance told Ravn that Domino had been the thrower. Méarana had no trouble blending in with the bleating crowds on the balcony. "Get down and stay down!" Ravn shouted; and the sheep, of course, obeyed. The floorways were carpeted with the backs of transients and shopkeepers.

Blood on the duroplast provided a trail to follow—spinward along the upper level, toward a corner from which all sheep had wisely fled. Ravn halted prudently, then pirouetted across the corner to flatten against the other side. The dance gave her a glimpse of a dim, narrow side corridor where the overhead lamps had failed and had not yet been replaced. The farther recesses of the hallway were shrouded in black, save where the sole surviving lamp spotlighted the body of the fleeing woman, splayed facedown five strides along the corridor.

Never one to take the obvious at face value, Ravn studied the prostrate form until certain it was not moving, and even then approached only by careful incremental steps.

It did no good. An arm from an alcove shoved a dazer to her temple, and the voice behind the arm said, "Don't move."

In that instant, Ravn knew she dealt with a Hound. Only the agents of the League withheld their fire at such moments.

"I am as a stoone," she replied, and kept her hands where her ambusher could see them, and waited her chance. For some reason she trembled. The air held a faint musty scent, as if something had crawled up this passage to die. Not the blocky woman. It was too soon for her aromatic contribution to matter. But Ravn suddenly wanted very badly to leave the narrow confines in which she found herself.

"Who are you?" she asked the unseen voice. Her eyes sought the side of her head, as if by sheer torque they could see through her own ear.

The voice chuckled. "Do you truly wish to know?"

It was the sort of thing a Name would say, but Ravn was morally certain that she confronted a Hound. She tried to turn her head the least bit but found herself unable to do so. *Fool!* she told herself. *It is but a Hound! And when has Ravn Olafsdottr feared puppy dogs?*

"You are off your manor, I am thinking. The Rift is out the other way."

"Do not be afraid," the voice caressed her. "We are not come to your damage. Our interests lie but with one of our citizens whom you have kidnapped. To wit: Méarana Harper. It would please us greatly if you would commit her to us. We will take her home and never more bother you, until some other time."

Ravn was astonished to feel within herself an ardent desire to please this person. "I weep from gratitude at your forbearance."

The voice chuckled. "I see I was not misinformed about Ravn Olafsdottr. I sense you will not turn your hostage over to us . . ."

"What point in bringing her this far if I do not take her a little farther? When she has once served her purpose, you may have her."

She heard hesitation in the silence of the voice.

Then, horrifyingly, the voice spoke again, this time from her other side.

"No, don't turn. It might startle me, and my companion's fate does not fill me with thoughts of rainbows and spun sugar. Let it be a truce, then, and well met between you and I."

"You are no Shadow. How can you call upon the customs of the Abattoir?"

"You would be surprised at what I am, and upon what I can call. Shall it be so? I'd fain take my companion to our ship. There may yet be time to save her. You may keep Méarana for this little while. But be warned. Others are coming for her who will not be so forbearing."

"What stoops me," Ravn hazarded, "from infoorming the Tungshen Riff so that he can interdict your ship?" But she knew the answer in the asking, and knew that the other knew as well.

"Not when you yourself move as the fish that swim in the seas. You'd not draw attention to yourself, nor raise a commotion on the habitat. Your friend's spike was conspicuous enough. We are both best served now by swift and silent departure."

Ravn had never heard dire necessity turned so artfully into negotiated agreement. It was not in the Hounds of the Ardry to stand by while a colleague lay dying. It was one of their great weaknesses. And so the voice must salvage a truce to rescue her companion, and would "allow" Ravn to keep Méarana—*as if her permission had been required.*

Yet there was no denying that the voice had induced in Ravn the desire to agree, to give up Méarana. That Ravn knew it had been *induced* by adroit perfumes and clever pheromones made it no less real an impulse, and she thought that if she had been any less committed to her dangerous course she might have been persuaded. And the voice had made adroit use too of ventriloquism, the darkness, and inattentive blindness to cloud the Shadow's mind and move unseen in her very presence. That solitary overhead lamp should have warned her. It too neatly framed the body of the squat woman, and that meant that the other lamps had been disabled scant moments after the woman had fallen where she had. That one bright spot in the darkened corridor had focused her attention, leaving a penumbra of inattention within which the strange Hound had moved.

"I agree," she said, and then noticed with a sinking heart that the presence beside her had vanished and the body spotlighted by the overhead lamp was gone, with only the blood-trail as evidence that it had ever been there.

Ravn had seldom felt the grip of fear, but she slumped now against the wall of the corridor and trembled. A glance at her timepiece showed that several minutes had passed between the voice's last words and her own agreement, minutes in which she had stood in a trance, prey to any that might have happened along. Of all the Hounds she had ever encountered, even Gwillgi, this one alone frightened Ravn. And she did not even know her name.

Ravn returned to the *mojy* shop to find Méarana sitting on the floor under the watchful guardianship of Domino Tight. The shopkeeper too was there, but the remaining sheep had been allowed to depart.

"I warned you what would happen," Ravn told the shopkeeper, "if you allowed this woman to be bothered!"

The man ducked his head. "But, Deadly One," he said.

"But what?"

Méarana spoke up. "You told him only to keep strange men away. If you meant more than that, he is not responsible for your oversight."

Ravn trembled for a moment, still angry at the fear that had possessed her. She made an abrupt motion with her head, and the shopkeeper scuttled to the back of the store. Deprived thus of one target, she turned to the other.

"And you!" she said to Méarana. "That might have been Ekadrina's magpie! What were you thinking?"

"Is she all right?"

"Who, that woman? Why should you care?"

"Because, as far as I know, she was just a nice lady who stopped and chatted with me for a few moments. And then your friend threw a knife in her back."

Ravn put her face close to Méarana's. "And what did you two chat about?"

The harper waved a hand around the store's displays. "What do strangers normally discuss in such places?"

"The woman was Jugurthan," put in Domino Tight. "Maybe a quarter by blood. That gave her the wide-set body. Their ancestors were genetically modified for some high-gravity planet somewhere in ancient times. The point is: there are no Jugurthans in the Confederation. That 'nice lady' was at least a Pup, maybe even a Hound."

Méarana gasped, but Ravn had the distinct impression that the surprise was feigned and the harper had either guessed or been told the woman's nature. "What did she say to you, Méarana? Did she tell you her name?"

"It wouldn't have been the real name," suggested Domino Tight.

"She called herself Gwen."

Ravn nodded and opened a file on her hand screen. Domino said, "It even sounds Peripheral. Ravn, did you search the body?"

Olafsdottr shook her head absently. "There were two of them. The other suggested a truce and took her away."

Domino Tight grinned. "Walked into a trap. But you're not dead," he added.

"You are ever a keen observer of fact, my darling."

The harper cocked her head in her mother's manner. "And what did the other look like?"

"I never saw her. She remained ever in shadows." Then she found a name in her file. Cŵn Annwn. Close enough, assuming the name was real.

"I've heard of this shadowy Hound," said Domino. "She calls herself Matilda of the Night."

Ravn closed up her hand screen. Then, because the ill-hidden smile of the harper irritated her, she touched Méarana gently on the arm. "I am so sorry, sweet."

The harper withdrew a little. "Sorry? Why?"

"That your mother sent only these others in her place, and did not come herself."

The harper flinched at the thought but then suggested, "Or else she has brought a Pack with her."

Ravn exchanged glances with Domino Tight and both set their faces in grim lines. One more complication in the play. Best they heigh for Terra immediately and conclude their business with Gidula. But Ravn thought it highly likely that the voice that spoke in the dark would be waiting when they landed there.

X. AT THE CAPITAL OF ALL THE WORLDS

The far-lit dawn does night's decay foretell
And in her pitiless glow do future hopes
Pile earth upon the hopes of elder days.
O merciful Night! That thou dost shroud
The ranks of tombs and gravestones proud
Whereunder aspiration now decays,
And clear of buried dreams and tropes
Draws skyward gazes, the which do dwell
Upon far better beacons, more lofty themes.
Today is the wreckage of yesterday's dreams.

Donovan's hajj had taken him halfway around the world and a little more, and what he found was what he didn't find. Desiccated shrublands marched along novel ice-drained coasts, and borders, breeds, and births were all awry. The ancient languages, so carefully learned in Terran Schools around the Periphery, were nowhere evermore spoken, and their offspring sprouted in eccentric places. The great artifacts of the past had seen wind and storm and ice, poverty and neglect, armies and migrations, and—one by one—they had fallen. Even North was not where story had left it. The planetary core was undergoing a phase shift, and the Magnetic Pole had left its icy home to bask now in the golden seas off the isle of Teetee.

Only the oceans themselves and the interminable mountains remained where passed-down tales had placed them. But what of it? If the enclosed portrait is utterly altered, does it matter if the frame is still untouched?

The Wall had been bulldozed by scree pushed down from the northlands in the fore of the Sborski glaciers. Her bastions were stumps, her facades pierced by tumbling rubble. *The Pass of Jelep La,* where the Allies under Marshal Kumar had held off the Cinakar, was choked with mountain glaciers, and the famous Monument of the Lions lay buried beneath centuries of snows. *"Twelve-gated Terra"* had possessed a dozen Beanstalks planted around her girth, but no traces remained of those great sky elevators—at least of those whose locations he passed over. There was no trace even of the Great Fall: wind and rain and jungle and the scavenging of gleaners had eaten them up.

Locals he questioned blinked blank faces—"Marshal Kumar? The Borneo Beanstalk? O *snor,* you speak in riddles."

Only the Wall, in its fragmentary survival, had spawned tales of its origin. It had been built, one old man assured him over a plate of schnitzel in a restaurant in Vayshink, to keep the Ice at bay. Donovan, who knew something of the immense age of the thing, marveled at how legends could supplant even other legends.

In the Archives in Old Jösing, in a close room with a dim monitor, he skimmed through the detritus of records as old as time. A brief video of a sports contest among strangely garbed players. A simulation, experienceable only in part, of something called the Long March. The passenger list of *Krunipak*

Loy, outbound for Megranome, containing tens of thousands of names. In such a swarm, even identity could be anonymous. She may have been one of the Ships of Exile—the time frame was right—but there was nothing in the record that signified desperate flight or banishment, and he found no other like manifests. The proscription list of the Emperor Philip Qangpo—longer even than the passenger list: Emperor Phil had evidently had a lot of enemies. (And had surely missed one in the sweep: he was assassinated after a six-month reign.)

The Pedant soaked up essays, novels, treatises with lightning speed, and heard in their musings "men lonely in a meaningless world." All of their old certainties had been swept away, their gods lost, their philosophies emptied; and they had treasured what remained as a man might shelter from the winds in his cupped hands a small tuft of burning tow rescued from a now-cold fire. They regarded the beauties and great deeds of their past—and the mere technologies were the least among them—as "the last fragile even-glow of a long-set sun." In their mournful and weary cadences he could detect the very themes that had later developed in the Old Planets, on Old 'Saken, on Die Bold, on Kàuntusulfalúghy: the sense that they had been orphaned by forgotten parents.

Is every age, Donovan wondered, *built on the afterglow of another?* What then could history be but the successive devolution of society? Each fire would burn less brightly than the one before. Or was he himself becoming infected with the twilight melancholy of the rotting Commonwealth?

But then he thought: The building was burning, and they ran back in to save what they could. That ought to count for something.

Of those individuals the Fudir had bespoken during his stopover in the Regency of Swak, only five had ever heard of the

Borneo Beanstalk and none recalled that Borneo had been an ancient name for the Greater Swakland Peninsula. Greatly irritated at this amnesia—how could anything so large be so largely forgotten?—the scarred man scoured the Archive for files on the Beanstalk and unearthed a set of five visuals, one of them mobile. Two displayed the Stalk a few years after its fall: the Great Stump, ragged fragments strewn toward the horizon, a then more extensive jungle swallowing up the distance. The topmost pieces, the Pedant told everyone, would have burned up in the atmosphere or splashed far out into the ocean.

The other two static visuals portrayed the Beanstalk before its fall: an immense tower, rising out of sight, dimishing into the eastbound distance to little more than a scratch upon the sky. But it stood already in ruins: Rust had secured hard-won victories, cables dangled from far above, and doorways hung broken and open on a barren departure lounge. An obviously space-tight crawler—the "Jack"—sat out of plumb, jammed on the primary funicular. The tower struts were overgrown with creepers and vines. A monkey with an enormous nose perched on one and seemed to look into the viewer with knowing eyes.

None showed the Beanstalk in its heyday.

It did not seem right that such a colossus had vanished without a trace. It was Commonwealth tech, after all. But perhaps it had been cannibalized for precisely that reason, as folk robbed the battlefield dead.

The mobile image was old and had obviously been migrated onto newer media early on, which may be why it had escaped the Dao Chettian purge of all Late Commonwealth records. The coarse images rastered at times into pixels, and if there had ever been any sound it had not survived the migration. The sequence began with a smiling assembly of dark-skinned blonds. Alabastrines, Donovan thought; but the Pedant told him that Alabaster had not yet been settled at the time of the record, so the physical type had evidently been native to Old Earth! They wore jackets—the climate being already chillier than of yore—and Donovan captured a name on the jacket-backs when they turned. A variety of Old Brythonic but written in the Taṇṭamiž script: *Strine Omnischool.* So this was a university outing of some sort. Perhaps an archeological field trip.

The students explore the old Beanstalk, talking to one another and pointing.

(Donovan wondered if he could have understood them. Brythonic was one of the ancient lingos he had learned in Terran School. But the degraded quality of the images did not allow even lip-reading.)

One of the students strips off his jacket and reveals a bare torso decorated in an intricate pattern of white tattoos that twist down his arms. He beats his chest and laughs and Donovan needs no interpreter. Look at me! I'm one of our ancient ancestors! *The others laugh with him, although some trade skeptical glances with a significant look at the Beanstalk.*

(The builders of the Beanstalk had been no primitive tribesmen. The Commonwealth had not then entirely fallen and Terra never did lose its memory of what it once had been.)

Student laughter is cut short when something plunges into the earth not two feet from the aboriginal pretender. Tree branches whip, leaves dance in a flurry, smoke drifts from a crater wherein sits something white. A frozen moment of surprise, the realization that death has spoken a mere pace away, then heads turn skyward.

And they run.

The images grow chaotic at this point, as the individual with the recorder is running with it and if it has a stabilizer it is turned off. But then, thinking himself safe and perhaps realizing the historical moment, the cameraman stops and begins recording events once more. The sky is filled with tumbling trash. Somewhere far up its trunk, the Beanstalk has buckled and, torn apart by its stresses, has become a rain of metaloceramic confetti. The distant clouds are pierced with contrails, where more lofty segments smoke through the atmosphere farther toward the east. An enormous subassembly strikes the jungle east of the stump, and shattered fragments bounce in all directions. A face appears midscreen and, crappy image or no, the lips are not hard to read. Run, you asshole!

(**Yes, Late Brythonic,** said the Pedant. But the Silky Voice and the others made no reply and the Brute was even more silent than usual.)

But the cameraman holds his ground. He records another impact near the horizon while smaller parts and components strike all around like iron rain. Then the imager pans skyward again and captures a fireball streaking toward the east, breaking up into calves.

And then a mass of mud and vegetation spatters the imager input. Mixed in the slime are streaks of red that might be blood but perhaps only a deeper stratum of mud.

Whatever it was, that was the end of the mobile. Various parts of the scarred man wondered whether the heroic cameraman had been killed at the end by debris from the disintegrating Beanstalk or whether the close call had finally convinced him to join his fellows in flight.

Donovan questioned the appellation. "Heroic? He was a fool to stay."

Maybe, said the Brute, **but it was still a ballsy thing to do.**

"What? To record images that no one would ever look at a hundred years later? Images of an event that most people have now forgotten ever took place?"

But the Fudir, who had been weeping unrestrainedly, wiped the scarred man's eyes with his sleeve. "No," he said. "But he was in at the end of an age and he knew it. He was there when the gates went down."

When Donovan passed over the Roof of the World into the ancient land of the Vraddy, he found no trace of the Taj. Nor did the people of the vast rolling savannah remember that there had ever been such a beautiful thing. They were content to drive their herds from summer to winter pasture and sell the beef in the markets of Gawath. They knew there had been a people on their land before them, and another people before that, but the herdsmen—the *rinnernecks*—were descended from recolonists out of Old Eighty-two and bore names that would have startled the men who had raised the Taj. They had no interest in such things and could indeed tell Donovan more stories of Old Eighty-two passed down in their clans than they could of the prairie over which they now roamed. When Donovan told a group of herdsman at their evening "gaffgläsh" that their plains had once been a jungle and the abode of tigers, they laughed and declared him the greatest liar of them all and kissed him on both cheeks.

The farm town of New Bramburg was an Old Terran settlement, her inhabitants decended of folk who had never left the planet. Donovan decided to spend an evening there, for he was desirous of one night at least among his own people.

It was not a very big town, but then Terra was no longer a very big world. Estimates he had seen in Gidula's library had put the number at just under seven hundred million, planetwide. More than that, there was insufficient arable land to feed. The great farmlands of Terra's past were desiccated steppes or polar deserts now and, while cross-stellar transport of food was not unknown, they would have needed daily armadas to replace their ancient harvests with the bounty of other worlds.

"Zãddigah-of-the-infidels," said the bartender in the

town's only tavern, "is dying. Her primary export is young men and women of twenty."

Another patron of the bar held up a glass. "May they all speedily depart."

Aye, ran the unspoken subtext, *and leave the Earth to those who had always nursed on her breasts.* To these people, even the Terrans of the Periphery were just another sort of outlander, less obnoxious in some ways but more dangerous in others. Such folk attracted the notice of the Names and, by their dreams of resettlement, unsettled the minds of their neighbors. Three generations earlier, there had been a series of pogroms carried out by the hysterical descendants of Eighty-seconds and Bhaitrians on the mere rumor that they were to be expelled and the dispersed Terrans brought back. Thus does one generation's conquest become another generation's birthright. The age when their ancestors had come as conquerors had passed below the horizon of folk memory. Only the Old Terrans remembered, and habitually referred to their neighbors, with some politesse, as "guests," however uninvited the guesting may have been.

The scarred man sat at the bar, feeling unnaturally exposed. He disliked putting his back to an open room, but there was a mirror behind the bar into which was etched the recumbent blue body of Sleeping Bisna, who was here called "Vishnu." It gave him a view of his six. There were few townsmen in the bar. The farmers, the bartender promised him, would return at sunset, and then the joint would get "jumpy."

"Though I wouldn't let on you be from the Diaspora," he was advised; and the others nodded in chorus, offering grave assent. "Most of the clodhoppers are tolerant, but there are a few in every crowd. You know how it goes."

Donovan agreed that he knew how it went. The Terrans of New Bramburg spoke not the Tongue. A few words and phrases of the old Taṇṭamiž peppered their talk but seemed more decorative than substantive. For the most part, the Folk had acquired the clothing and the accents of Old Eighty-two. Blue eyes and fair skin were common among them, and while they were conscious of having lived in this place longer than death, they were less aware that matters now were very different from when their ancestors had flourished.

Donovan bought a round for the house. That custom, at least, had not changed, and for a time he basked in a companionable silence. The shopkeepers and service techs who comprised the daytime population asked him desultory questions. How fare the Terrans of the Periphery? They were not really interested. The Periphery might as well be in the Andromeda Galaxy for all it mattered to them. But they sighed to hear of worlds where Terrans were merely snubbed and not subject to periodic murderous spasms. Life, they thought, must be wonderful in the Terran Corners of Jehovah and Die Bold and Dancing Vrouw.

"Not that we'd speak unfaithfulness to the Names," the bartender reminded everyone, eliciting a chorus of grunts and "of course not."

"Although," the Fudir said, "it was the Names who cleansed Old Terra."

"Mighty are the Names," agreed the bartender. But one or two patrons twisted their lips in skepticism.

"One hears," ventured the Vendor of Approved Pesticides, "other tales."

"That the prehumans—the People of Sand and Iron—wrought the deed?" suggested the Fudir.

"There are stories." The Vendor agreed without actually agreeing.

"Though to say so," added the bartender, "were to disparage the might of the Names."

The Terrans of New Bramburg all looked at Donovan without turning their heads. Who knew how long a tongue a stranger might have that it could lick the ears of others?

"I have seen a mobile, a khinyo, of the fall of the Borneo Beanstalk," the Fudir told them. "And it fell of itself."

"Nonsense," said the bartender. "The Names scythed them down." The Old Terrans, at least, had not forgotten the old lore.

"With monstrous cannon they cut the stalks,
And the roots dried up and the petals fell."

The Vendor shrugged. "Or the People of Sand and Iron did so and the Names reaped where the prehumans had sown. What matter to such as us?"

The others sucked in their breaths. But the Vendor was undeterred.

"Will you inform on me, O Khenrik Jal? Or you?" He turned to the next stool over. "Or you, Jemdar Smidt, my cradle-companion? What do these sword cuts mean . . ." He fingered the scar on his cheek. ". . . if they do not mean we may trust one another? As for this man . . ." He tossed his head at the Fudir. ". . . he has the accents of the Periphery in his breath. He might more fear our tattling than we his."

"Neither was it the prehumans," insisted the Fudir. "The towers were derelict long before they fell, and they fell because they were no longer maintained. The world had grown too poor and too sparsely filled to support them. I know that two fell in this wise—at Kenya and at Borneo—and I think the other ten as well."

"Perhaps the Names knocked down the remnants," said the bartender, salvaging some puissance for the rulers of the Central Worlds. But it occurred suddenly to Donovan buigh that the Old Names may have done so from mercy, dismantling the surviving Beanstalks before they too could topple uncontrolled. It might not be wise to judge the early Names by the decadence of their epigones. If he had learned anything during his hajj, it was that the end of an age might differ vastly from its birth.

"The Commonwealth," said the Keener of Blades, dropping his voice to a habitual whisper when naming the old regime, "would never have permitted such decay."

"Maybe not," the Fudir agreed. "But permission was not in it. The Ice had begun by then, and the farmlands dried up and the growing season shrank. And 'many young men of twenty went away.'"

"There is a song," admitted the Keener.

The Vendor's cradle-companion scratched his cheek. "That one?"

"How runs the lay?" asked the Fudir.

The Keener looked about the room quickly, then lowered his head as the others crowded close to hear. It was a lively, bouncy tune for a matter so poignant.

> "The Ship she lifts in half an hour to cross the starry
>   heavens.
> My friends are left behind me now with grief and sorrow
>   leavened
> I'm just about to slide away in the liner Kat'kutirai
> It's disengaged and the hatch is sealed, I'm leaving dear old
>   Terra."

The others joined in on the chorus.

> "And it's good-bye, Krish, and good-bye, Chang, and
>   good-bye, Mumbai Mary.
> She's disengaged and the hatch is sealed, I'm leaving dear old
>   Terra.

And now the Alfvens' grabbing space, I have no more to say.
I'm bound for the Periph'ry, boys, a thousand lights away.

"Then fare you well, old Terra dear, to part my heart does
*   ache well.*
From old Kamchatka to Cape Fear, I'll never see your equal.
Although to half-formed worlds we're bound where wild beasts
*   may eat us*
We'll ne'er forget the Holy Ground—the daal and beans and
*   taters.*

"And it's good-bye, Krish . . ."

The bar patrons tittered nervously among themselves when
they had finished and two of them glanced once more behind
them in case anyone had entered the bar and heard. But it was
what the Fudir had not heard that interested him. He had
heard no hint of coercion in the song. No indication that the
departure had been anything but voluntary. Yet the legends on
the Old Planets were that the Dao Chettians had defeated
Terra, scythed the Beanstalks, and herded her people onto the
Ships of Exile—to be dumped ill prepared on the barely ter-
raformed worlds of the Periphery.

"What if," he said, as much to himself as the others. "What
if the Cleansing took centuries? What if ships began to leave as
the world dried out, and it was only at the very end that the
Names—or the prehumans—forcibly removed the excess." *An*
excess that the world could no longer support?

"They sent them to the Periphery to die," said the Vendor.

"But if the arable land was shrinking, so was Terra's carrying capacity. To leave them here would leave them to die."

"Then at least they would have died at home," said the bartender, surprising the Fudir with unlooked-for outspokenness.

Jemdar Smidt shook his head. "What matter? Others came, and now they too are leaving. We will not see again Terra as she was: bountiful with green, warmed by hot breaths of zephyrs, when only 'mad dogs and Englishmen went out in the noonday sun.'"

"I've always wondered," the bartender, Khenrik Jal, mused, "what was an Englishman?"

"A native of the Brythonic Isles," the Fudir told them. "Islands now swallowed by the Ice. This land of yours was called Vraddy."

"I have heard this said," the bartender commented as he began washing glasses. "Men from hereabouts went out and settled New Vraddy."

"They were the old Taṇṭamiž, who held the Mandate of Heaven after the Zhõgwó—those you once called the Cinakar."

The others looked uncomfortable. "I've never called anyone Cinakar," said the bartender, and his careful eye assured the others that they had never done so, either.

The Keener of Blades laughed. "It was the Cinakar who filled Dao Chetty. My friends here fear that if they mention certain things too often, the Names will hear and cause them to vanish." He turned on his stool and called out into the empty bar, "Cinakar! Names! Commonwealth!" The others flinched.

The Keener laughed again and faced the bar. The bartender smiled and said in a whisper, "I note that you did not call upon Ulakaratcakan, the Savior of the World."

But the Keener had an answer ready. "So, why push my luck?"

The Fudir said, "Who is Ulaka—" But he was cut off.

"He Who is Not Named is the One Who is to come at the end of days and restore the Commonwealth. But it will be the heavenly Commonwealth, not the earthly one. The Names do not understand that the Nameless One is not a rival Name. He is not even of their aetherial plane. His regency is not of this world. Meanwhile . . ." And the bartender reared back and spoke in a normal voice, "The clack dancers will come through tonight and entertain us. You will stay, of course, O Fudir?"

Of course he would. If only to learn what a clack dancer was.

They arrived just before sundown in a train of booger-vans with enormous tracked wheels, the sides of which were painted with colorful pictures of men like trees: smiling dancers with skin the texture of bark against a background of bright yellow and red. The folk who emerged from the vans wore veiled, ankle-length gowns that concealed even their feet. And they clacked when they walked.

"Clackers cannot wear ordinary shoes, you see," the Keener explained to the Fudir, who did not see at all. Everyone filed into the theater, where the troupe's grounds-crew had already set up the light and sound systems. These were a bad-skinned lot with warts on their faces and hands. "They came from Old Eighty-two," the Keener said, leading the scarred man to a seat front and center of the stage, "along with the *klattriya* and all the other *itarar*."

Klattriya must derive from *kalatiyayttiriya*, which meant "to lead a wandering life." And *itarar* was a disparaging term for outlanders. Donovan wondered why his host was using fragments of the old Taṇṭamiž. To show solidarity? To hint that even here there was a clot of the Terran Brotherhood? Donovan leaned toward him.

"Knowest thou aught of the Shadow War?" he whispered in the Tongue.

The Keener smiled. "May each side slay the other, and the de'il eat the last."

"Hast the Brotherhood chosen sides?"

"Brotherhood? Sahb! What Brotherhood be that?"

Donovan grunted. The Brotherhood was banned across the Confederation and it would be death to admit to membership. But if the Brotherhood had agreed to join the rebellion, as Oschous Dee had claimed, Donovan had yet to find a footprint of that agreement in the words of the Terrans he had bespoken on Zãddigah.

The dancers filed onto the stage and, in unison, dropped their concealing robes.

The farmers clapped with delight, for it is always cheering to look on people more unfortunate than oneself. The clack dancers were naked, though not that one could readily tell. Most of them were covered with warts, but such warts as the scarred man had never seen. They grew in massive clusters—on hands, ankles, torsos, arms, even faces—and indeed endowed the men with the appearance of tree bark. Some of the warts were long and sticklike, others were wide and flat, and all had the appearance of having been carefully shaped and cultured.

𝕮𝖚𝖙𝖆𝖓𝖊𝖔𝖚𝖘 𝖍𝖔𝖗𝖓𝖘, said the Pedant, eager as ever to reveal his fund of knowledge. 𝕿𝖍𝖊𝖞 𝖜𝖊𝖗𝖊 𝖉𝖎𝖘𝖈𝖔𝖛𝖊𝖗𝖊𝖉 𝖇𝖞 𝖆 𝖒𝖆𝖓 𝖓𝖆𝖒𝖊𝖉 𝕻𝖆𝖕𝖕𝖞 𝕷𝖔𝖒𝖆. 𝕬𝖓 𝖎𝖒𝖒𝖚𝖓𝖊 𝖘𝖞𝖘𝖙𝖊𝖒 𝖉𝖊𝖋𝖎𝖈𝖎𝖊𝖓𝖈𝖞 𝖆𝖑𝖑𝖔𝖜𝖘 𝕻𝖆𝖕𝖕𝖞 𝕷𝖔𝖒𝖆'𝖘 𝖛𝖎𝖗𝖚𝖘 𝖙𝖔 𝖙𝖆𝖐𝖊 𝖔𝖛𝖊𝖗 𝖙𝖍𝖊 𝖒𝖆𝖈𝖍𝖎𝖓𝖊𝖗𝖞 𝖔𝖋 𝖙𝖍𝖊 𝖘𝖐𝖎𝖓 𝖙𝖔 𝖕𝖗𝖔𝖉𝖚𝖈𝖊 𝖙𝖍𝖊 𝖍𝖔𝖗𝖓𝖞 𝖌𝖗𝖔𝖜𝖙𝖍𝖘.

The Silky Voice wondered what purpose the old Commonwealth engineers had had in creating a race of such people. Or had they viewed people only as objects, to be experimented upon, and done this simply because they could? The young man in the chlamys winced in pain. How heavy their hands and feet must be!

Then they began to dance. A percussionist used the rodlike growths on his fingers to work a variegated set of drums and cymbals. The dancers picked up the rhythm and began to shake their hands, feet, and bodies. The wide, flat horns on their torsos clapped in tempo; the rodlike horns rattled and rustled, as of shaking a whisk broom. The different timbres and tempos gave the clacking something like a harmony and a counterpoint. It was a wild clattering, a symphony of rhythm. Some dancers wore metallic clips on their horny extrusions, others wore bells, and for variety they would beat on various objects scattered about the stage. Now and then, feet would stomp the stage in unison, and the Sleuth noticed that none of the growths occurred on their soles or palms.

Some of the dancers had only the rods on their hands and ankles and their torsos were otherwise bare, save of moles. When the dance-line parted and let these through for a solo, the farmers in the audience whooped, for these dancers included women.

Donovan was not a man for cringing, and he blamed his discomfort on the young man in the chlamys. He "felt" for the dancers, their discomfort, their embarrassment, their shame at being reduced to making a spectacle of their infirmity.

And yet, said another part of him, they are no more abnormal than sharpies or foxies or Jugurthans. And who are we to tell them they must not make a living as dancers? What other sort of work might they perform, whose hands are as encumbered as these?

And I suppose, said the Silky Voice, that a colony of lepers might form a bell choir for the entertainment of strangers.

But there was something familiar about the rattling of the "drumsticks," something that reminded him of . . .

. . . an old sugar-processing plant gone to seed. The cane has taken root and the wind blowing downriver rattles them like drumsticks. He staggers up on the western bank of the river, and throws himself to the ground among the cane. It is marshy here. He wants nothing more than to lie there and sleep undisturbed until morning. But there is a safe house in the O'erfluss District, if he can reach it.

He looks back the way he has swum and marvels that he had the reserves to cross the river. Flames light the sky over the Secret City, and the hissing of the fires blends with the murmur of the river's current, the creaking of insects. He hears the distant crackle of bolt tanks and thud of buildings.

Not much left of the Revolution, he thinks.

But whatever you rescue from a burning house is a gain.

Motion through the riverside growth! He recedes into the shadows and slips a knife from his belt. A voice whispers his name.

His true name.

It has been years, a lifetime, since he has heard it. And he recognizes the voice.

In relief, he rises from the shadows and whispers urgently, "Over here." He waits to see if he has made one last mistake but recognizes the other when he steps forth. "You made it out of the Chancellery, then."

The other rebel steps forward and embraces him. "Glad to see you got free, chief. Are there any more with you?"

"No. I . . . I thought for a while there were, but . . ."

"I understand." He kisses him once on each cheek. "I hope you do, too."

And with that the Protector's Special Security forces close in and pin his arms to his side and take the knife from his hands. They are not gentle. The goggles are yanked from his head. One of them punches him in the belly and he doubles over. Looking up, he catches the eye of the man who had been his friend, and asks him, "Why?"

And that man shrugs and will not look at him. "Close fits my shirt," he answers, "but closer far my skin."

Donovan gasped and sat bolt upright in his seat in the theater. The Keener turned to him in solicitude. "Are you all right?"

"Yes. No." He rose and hurried up the aisle to the exit. The dancers did not falter at his apparent rudeness. Their rhythmic clacking followed him until cut off by the theater doors. In the lobby, Donovan bent over, hands on knees, huffing.

The Keener of Blades had followed behind him. "You *are* ill," he said. "I would take you to the doctor, but he's in there." He waggled a thumb at the theater.

Donovan sucked in a deep breath and stood upright. "Is the bartender in there, too?"

Nowhere in the official accounts Donovan had read or resimulated on Oschous's *Black Horse* or Gidula's *White Comet* had there been any mention of the internal organization of the Rising. But he remembered now. Padaborn had had four section chiefs for the assault on the Secret City. Rajasekaran had died in the first rush. Lai Showan had been lost trying to hold the Security Police Center. O'Farrell had gone down with the Chancellery Building. And from the ruins of the Education Ministry—from the Lion's Mouth itself—the fourth chief had escaped unseen: Tomas Krishna Murphy.

Only to be betrayed on the far side of the river by Geshler Padaborn himself, who, having been captured earlier, had broken under duxing kaoda.

He was a great man, said the Sleuth. *But it is not given even to great men to endure the third degree of torture.*

𝔥𝔢 𝔰𝔢𝔢𝔪𝔢𝔡 𝔥𝔞𝔩𝔢 𝔢𝔫𝔬𝔲𝔤𝔥 𝔴𝔥𝔢𝔫 𝔩𝔞𝔰𝔱 𝔴𝔢 𝔰𝔞𝔴 𝔥𝔦𝔪, the Pedant retorted

"Not all scars show," said Donovan.

"What?" said the Keener, who had accompanied him to the tavern.

The scarred man shook his head. He thought that Padaborn had buckled under the Threat and not the Tools. Before the Shadows of the Names employed the Tools, they would first tell you in great detail about them. Then the Shadows would show them to you. Then they would demonstrate the Tools on another prisoner. It often saved considerable time.

I wonder what became of him?

Who cares? He turned traitor!

Consider what Those did to us, said the young man, *and he was the greater threat. He had the charism that O'Farrell and we lacked. He could inspire men to die. He may have been harvested, or pithed, or—*

"Or they did to him what they did to us."

That might explain why the rebel Shadows confused the two of us. The simulations and reports named no other rebels but Padaborn. Part of a deliberate strategy, Donovan supposed, to minimize the Rising by minimizing the participants.

"Something still does not feel right."

"I knew it," said the Keener. "You stay here. Take care of our guest, Khenrik Jal, and I will fetch the Dispenser of Efficacious Medicines." The Keener then ran off, leaving Donovan in the tavern.

Donovan turned to the bartender. "You heard him. Give me some of that 'efficacious medicine.'"

And so, following a night of sleepless turmoil, Tomas Krishna Murphy came at last to the last site of all: Iracatanam Antapakirantamthe, the Capital of All the Worlds. If the Commonwealth had had a center, if it could have been said to be in any one place, that place was here, in this great sprawling metropolis, in the Hall of Suns.

"She's a creeping place," the earnest Terrans of New Bramburg had warned him before he had departed. "There are ghosts among the ruins."

From the air, the site of Antapak had shown clearly. As the rain forest had dried out and withered, it had stripped the cloak from the Capital of All the Worlds and exposed her bones to the eyes of strangers. Donovan parked his rented hopper in a broad plaza near the center of town. Perhaps it had once been an outdoor theater, or a sporting venue, or perhaps it had actually been a hopper-park. Now, it was simply an open space littered with a spill of white blocks.

More remained of Antapak than of any of the other sites he had visited, but that is not to say that very much remained. Layered upon the neglect and decay of years was evidence of more deliberate destruction. Those portions of the capital that had sat on the shoreline bluffs had been tumbled into the waters below, where the proud towers of other days could yet be spied gleaming through the crystalline sea. The Names of Dao Chetty had vented a certain measure of spleen on this place, Donovan decided, because it was a reminder to them that they had merely built on the bones of others. Yet by reducing Antapak to ruins they may only have underscored that very fact.

Perhaps they had given up. Some parts of the sprawling city seemed untouched. The old Commonwealth had built for the ages; and, though an age had come and gone, a portion of their work remained. Donovan remembered how parts of the Commonwealth Ark that he and Méarana had found scant years before had remained in working condition.

After an hour or so of wandering, Donovan stopped for a drink of water and a bit of a mustard-and-cheese combination known locally as "music." He sat upon one of the overturned blocks that had once foundationed a building, and tried to imagine what the street before him had been like when this had been a lively capital and crowds of people had thronged its busy avenues.

In the silence, though, he heard a faint sound—a skritch-skratch, a chattering as if by gravel upon stone. He turned and looked behind him and saw nothing. An insect? But it was like no insect-sound he had ever heard before.

The block was uncomfortable. A crack as wide as his little finger ran diagonally across its top surface. He stood and wrapped the remainder of his snack in a kerchief, stuffed it in his scrip. Inner Child had a sudden desire to run from this place. <Something is following us.>

The Brute sniffed the air, listened, took both eyes and searched carefully in all directions. The onetime streets were choked with grass and formed yellow-green rivers around the islands of broken buildings. Bundles of tumbleweed rolled along them. He watched for ripples that disobeyed the wind, a sign that something moved through the grass. **Nuthin'**, he decided. **But . . .**

But you feel it, too . . . , said the Silky Voice.

<Pedant, do you know where we left the hopper?>

"I came here," said the Fudir, "to find the Hall of Suns, and I will not leave until I have set my eyes upon it."

The natural sound of his footfalls and his own breathing covered the faint cracklings, and so he began to walk more briskly. He pushed his way through the grass, hunting for one of the five broad avenues that tradition claimed led to the Hall. From the air, he had marked three likely locations; but landscapes looked different on the weed-grown ground.

He had expected the crackling to fade behind him, but he soon learned that they whispered from all directions. <They're surrounding us.>

"Who is?" demanded the Fudir. "There is nothing out there. Step up to any vantage point and you can see for leagues across the savannahs."

<Oh, surely. But we can't see around the next corner. The genemasters in their heyday did not hesitate to alter men. What might they have done with tigers or other beasts?>

𝔐𝔞𝔡𝔢 𝔱𝔞𝔰𝔱𝔶 𝔞𝔫𝔡 𝔡𝔬𝔠𝔦𝔩𝔢 𝔪𝔢𝔞𝔱 𝔞𝔫𝔦𝔪𝔞𝔩𝔰 𝔬𝔣 𝔱𝔥𝔢𝔪, suggested the Pedant.

<That would be the sensible thing to do—sable tiger is delicious—but might they have prepared beasts to await the

arrival of the Dao Chettians? Might that not be the reason the Names abandoned the demolition of this place? Perhaps something stands guard here . . . >

Donovan came to one of the five grand concourses and turned right toward the city center. From left and from right he heard the buzzing like cicadas on a hot summer's day. He kept one hand on the butt of his teaser.

It's not following us, the Sleuth decided. *It's in situ. We're only walking through their midst.*

<Through whose midst?>

Before him, though the savannah grasses that partially skirted it, Donovan saw a broad, low building in white marble. It sat on a stone platform, through the blocks of which grasses struggled toward the sun. The platform was reached by a series of shallow ramps alternating with short stairways, and the building façade was lined by pillars in a variety of styles: plain, fluted, intricately decorated, with capitals scrolled, palmate, or historiate. The array ought to have clashed, but it did not. The stylistic cacophony somehow achieved harmony.

In the entablature was in inscription in the old Taṇṭamiž: *Here Are All At Home.*

"Do you think it is . . . ?" the Fudir asked himself.

I'm sure it is, sang the young girl in the chiton.

As he rushed up the stair to the patio, Inner Child wondered. <Why was this building, of all buildings, not reduced to rubble by the Names?>

It woulda made more sense, the Brute agreed, **to demolish this 'un and leave the rest of the city be.**

The snap-crackle-pop seemed louder as he entered the Hall of Suns and found himself on the top tier of a semicircular amphitheater dug into the farther hillside. Seats and desks lined the concentric tiers facing a dais on the floor below. Columns rimmed the theater, and between them stood bases for statues. Above, a dome extended toward the center, where a gaping hole spoiled its wholeness.

So there had been an attack, but one that had succeeded in no more than smashing through the dome.

Where is the rubble from the dome? the Sleuth asked. *It should litter the floor below the hole.*

"Scavanged, most likely," said the Fudir. "There may be villages nearby with hovels built of stone."

Most of the niches lining the walls were empty, but a few held the stubs of statues and one held a statue entire. Drawn to it, Donovan looked into the smiling and delighted countenance of a man wearing a bulky environment suit. He cradled his helmet in his arm and seemed to have just taken a very deep breath. On the base beneath, Donovan read: *Tau Ceti Two: Yang huang-ti,* and below that a single line: *"We have a second home!"*

No other statues were intact, but most of the bases were. A nearby plinth read: *New Mumbai: Chettiwan Mahadevan.* "*Then we have never been alone!*"

Donovan hastened to the far left of the semicircle.

Cevvay: Jacinta Rosario. "So this is Barsoom!"

Donovan had always thought Rosario a figure out of myth; but the Commonwealth would have known—unless she had become myth even by then. The first two plinths bore names he did not recognize, even from myth.

Cantiraṉ: Neil Armstrong. "One Small Step for Man!"

And the first plinth . . .

Akalitamkoṭṭu: Yuri Gagarin. "I see Earth! It is so beautiful!"

These niches, Donovan decided, had once borne the statues of the great captains of old, the first to set foot on the various and sundry worlds of the Commonwealth. Cantiraṉ was the old name of Terra's moon, Luna. Akalitamkoṭṭu he had never heard of and its root meaning seemed to be "globe running-around." 𝕰arth-orbit, thought the Pedant. *The first man to pilot a spaceship,* the Sleuth deduced. But Donovan still wondered how many of the older names were true and how many the crust of legend. You could make a statue of a myth as easily as of a man.

He made his way through the crescent tiers. Each seat had a small white-stone podium and on the fronts of the podia were inscribed the weathered names of worlds. In the back row, he found *Henrietta* on one podium. Farther down, *Ashbanal* graced another; and about midway to the floor *Yuts'ga* was inscribed on two adjacent podia.

But he ignored the rest and hurried toward the cluster of seats on the dais, set behind tiers of long benches and facing out toward the rest of the room.

Behind the first bench he found Beta Hydri, 82 Eridani, and Delta Pavonis. Behind the higher bench sat Alpha Centauri, Tau Ceti, 61 Cygni, and Epsilon Indi. Each of them had three seats. The third bench, adorned on its façade with the great starburst of the Commonwealth of Suns, held the five seats of Terra herself, one set higher and in the center. The presider, he assumed.

Sleuth examined the ancient names. Delta Pavonis was obviously Delpaff and 82 Eridani was Old 82. At the second bench, Tau Ceti must be Dao Chetty. The others puzzled him a while longer, but he decided that Alpha Centauri must be one of the Century Suns and Beta Hydri must be Bhaitry. So one of the other two was undoubtedly New Vraddy and the other New Mumbai, although as to which was which he was unsure.

Everything seemed arranged in order of precedence. The Century Suns had lain nearest to Terra, and so had been settled first, and so her seats stood in the center of the upper bench. That would mean that the two flanking her—"Dao Chetty and Epsilon Indi"—were next settled. The next bench down, a little later; and then the mass of suns in the facing rows all the way up to Henrietta-by-the-Rift in the last row.

Donovan could not resist the lure. He could not come all this distance and fail to climb those last few steps.

He found the stairs behind the dais that went to the highest seat, the presider; and there he eased himself onto the hard quasi-marble chair and gazed over the assembled amphitheater. His first thought was not some grand remembrance of the Commonwealth, not some thrill of ancient spectacle. His first thought was that these hard stone seats must have once had cushions.

Only then did he pick up an imaginary gavel and strike the desktop. *Will the Assembly of the Suns please to be coming to order.* He imagined a cacophony of voices slowly diminishing and the—what had they called them? Grand Senators? Delegates? Representatives?—drifting toward their seats.

What had this assembly done? he wondered. In those days, when communication had been only as swift as the fastest packet ship, disparate stars tended toward self-government. If this assembly passed a law, it would be weeks or even months before other worlds would hear of it. Perhaps it had adjudicated disputes, settled trade agreements, orchestrated the exploration and terraformation of new worlds, directed the struggle against the prehumans.

He remembered what Peacharoo, that fortuitously surviving automaton on the old terraforming Ark, had said: *Tau Ceti is a valued and important member of the Commonwealth. They stand shoulder to shoulder with our comrades against the People of Sand and Iron.*

Symbolism, he decided. This gathering had been mostly symbolic. The rituals of unity mattered. Hence, the array of statues and very likely other more perishable regalia. Banners, medallions, standards, ballads, all now forgotten, all of it geared to say: *We Are One.* A hundred worlds or more, from the old home-planet to the newest hardscrabble colony, were one in mind and resolve and brothers and sisters each to the other.

Patriotism meant love of a place, of the patria, and this of a place no larger than one could embrace as whole. But in the new world of the Commonwealth, men had gone from world to world, weakening ties, forging new fortunes, forming a new allegiance to a broader empire, while the stay-at-homes would have preserved their own particularities and celebrated their own festivals. And this would have been most true on the longest-settled worlds, and in particular on Terra herself. Was that why the Exiles, scattered to the Periphery, had so diligently re-created lost particularities?

He looked again at the worlds arrayed before him. Most of them with one seat—one vote? A few—more populous?—with two. The Old Home-Stars with three and Terra alone with five. Had that been in rough proportion to population? Or had the Home-Stars been loathe to dilute their power? He recalled also that Peacharoo had sounded slightly condescending: *This dormitory is reserved for Terrans. Colonists from the Lesser Worlds are housed elsewhere.*

So as Terra cooled and dried and its population grew sparser, Dao Chetty must have asked why Terra retained five votes when her now-more-populous colonies held but three.

The breeze outside the colonnade freshened and a ball of tumbleweed rolled through the amphitheater, caught on one of the seats, broke loose, and rolled out the other side.

Maybe Gidula was right, Donovan thought. Maybe at the end a desperate Terra had tried to use the Commonwealth to sustain itself, tithing the wealth of the colonies to replace what she could no longer produce, even while her own sons and daughters fled for more prosperous worlds. What had been the blackmail? You owe it to your Mother World? But one day a generation arose who knew no such debt of sentiment, who did not keep St. Patrick's Day or Cinco de Mayo, Navratri or Lunar New Year, and for whom Terra was just another planet.

Donovan stood and made his way down the dais and when he left the Hall of Suns he did not look back.

Quite by instinct, he took a different route back to where he had left the hopper, but the geometry of the ruins forced him through the same intersection where he had earlier stopped for lunch. The sun was lower in the sky and the mysterious crackling had subsided a little, though he could still hear it distantly from across the entire city.

But Inner Child was constantly alert to alterations in his environment and the Brute was keen to all his senses, and between the two of them they brought the scarred man to a halt by the block upon which they had earlier sat.

<The crack is gone.>

The Brute remembered that the crack had made the block uncomfortable to sit on. Donovan went to his knees and the Sleuth studied the stone closely. He ran their fingers across it.

I can feel where it was. Like a scar.

"It's been spackled," said the Fudir.

<Someone is in the city with us!>

He turned suddenly and looked down the empty avenue behind him. The freshening evening wind stirred the grasses.

"Who?" scoffed Donovan. "A stealthy stonemason who creeps through the ruins patching up the cracks?"

The wind drove pebbles and grit before it, stinging Donovan's cheek. They rolled across the surface of the foundation block like a miniature barchan. A grain found the slight groove where the crack had been and nestled within it.

There's your answer. Windblown grit has simply filled in the crack. He reached out to dislodge the grain—to free it, as he thought—and found that it was fused with the stone. When he put pressure on it, he experienced a sudden wave of foreboding, as if the entire city would tumble itself upon him and bury him.

He pulled his hand away, stood, withdrew a pace from the wall.

Certain materials of the Commonwealth, called metamaterials, were said to be self-repairing. Like the self-sealing hulls and pressure suits we have.

"But," said Donovan, "self-repairing *stone?*"

It is not true stone, said the Pedant, **but some sort of Commonwealth material.**

Donovan looked out over the ruins. *The Capital of All the Worlds has been rebuilding itself all these centuries,* the Sleuth decided. *Listen to that sound, that unending rustle.*

The young man in the chlamys thought it sounded like the rustle of leaves on the ground of autumn, and thought how lonely the stones must have been over the ages.

"And after all this time," the Fudir said, "this is as far as it's gotten?"

After all this time, the Sleuth agreed. *One pebble at a time. Starting from rubble. You remarked how well preserved the city is. Imagine what it looked like after the Dao Chettians had finished with it! Do you imagine for a moment that they left the Hall of Suns so nearly intact? No, the whole complex is rebuilding itself, but the Hall came first.*

And when it is finished, said the Silky Voice, *when it stands once more the Capital of All the Worlds, then will the Ulakaratcakan appear.*

"No, Silky," said Donovan buigh. "Then will the fleets of Dao Chetty appear, and flatten the place once more."

"If they know this is happening," said the Fudir. "Terra is a backwater now, and even the Terran natives avoid this place. How much might this place change in the span of a life? If the grandchildren see a city less ruined than their grandparents saw, would they realize it?"

The city will rebuild itself, said the young woman in the chiton, but there will be no one to come live in it.

For Pollyanna, of all of the Donovans, to say a thing like that filled them all with deep sorrow.

Imagine, said the young man, waiting for wind and chance to bring materials to it. Ah, the patience of a stone . . .

A shiver ran through Donovan. Once before, he had dealt with a stone of surpassing patience, and the stone had very nearly won. He stared into the gathering dusk, listened to the busy dust and grit. Had any of them changed their shape? Were they twisting stones? It was too dark to tell, nor did he linger to learn.

He hastened through the deserted streets, guided by the Brute's instinct for directions, haunted by the rustling sounds of the restless ruins, until he came at last to the open field where he had landed with his hopper.

Naturally, Gidula was waiting for him—with five magpies and Khembold Darling.

"Time to come home, Gesh," said the Old One.

The Silky Voice stilled the inchoate fear that had driven Donovan from the city, gathered it, and with a proper mix of enzymes put it aside. He drew a breath. "You always knew I would come here."

Gidula shrugged, as if not to belabor the obvious. "You needed a vacation. I had people at each of the villages hereabouts to tell me when you arrived."

"It doesn't matter," he said. "I was on my way back."

Gidula nodded. "Ah. Then you have remembered? You hoped the trip would clear your mind."

Inner Child grew suddenly cautious. "Some things have become clear, but other matters remain obscure. But I am *this* close to it. I can feel it."

Gidula nodded as if he had expected such an answer. "I believe that when we return to the Forks, your last hesitations will vanish. Two," he called, "run ahead of us in Gesh's hopper and send the packet drones off to Dawshoo and the others. Tell them it is time to gather." He turned with the other magpies to his own coaster, but Donovan called out.

"Two?"

The short woman in the black shenmat did not turn, as she needed but a portion of her attention for Donovan. "What?" that part of her replied.

"Don't forget to turn the hopper in to the State rental consortium. I don't want to pay late charges."

This time, the head did turn to look at him, but the blank, flickering goggles revealed nothing.

When he boarded the coaster with Gidula and Khembold, after a secret wink, had taken the pilot's saddle, Donovan said, "Have you ever come here, Old One?"

The aged Shadow grimaced. "To these old ruins? Of course not. What interest do they hold for me?" He frowned over the grass-grown remnants. "Ancient history, Gesh. What does it matter anymore?" He turned his back on the Capital of All the Worlds and repeated more quietly, "What does it matter anymore?" Then, brusquely, "She must have been lush and verdant once, this world, to support the population she did. But that was a long time ago, and it will not be again."

XI. THE PLAY OF THE CORAL SNAKE

It is in the geometry of spheres that the spanned area outruns the diameter, and even so sparse a world as Terra has more sky to it than can reasonably be patrolled. It wants wealth to maintain a 360 Space Traffic Control net, and wealth was no longer Terra's to have. Whole regions were unscanned. Why would anyone want to land on the Ice? Why indeed would anyone want to land on Terra? And so Ravn, by clever piloting through holes in the coverage, arrived on the meadowlands north of Kojj Hill without appearing on anyone's monitors.

Gidula, of course, maintained a stricter watch around his own compound and, since she could not depend on Eglay Portion's neglect, Ravn remained in the detection-shadow and put *Sèan Beta* down well north of the picket line and close to the low blue ridge that marked the northern edge of the great valley. There Domino Tight jumped from the hovering vessel wearing his shenmat and carrying on his back a rucksack containing a number of useful devices. Méarana watched him set off at a run and marveled that the sedge and the clover barely rustled at his passing. He was not yet out of sight when Ravn raised the ship on its gravitics and banked away to the north-northwest. She circled out and up over the Ablation Mounts and came in on the Forks on the standard southwestward approach, picking up the air corridor at Jasding STC and requesting advance clearance from Gidula's own control tower.

"I understand," Méarana said as they came in to the autoguidance slot and Ravn relinquished control. "You circled all the way around to give Domino time to get to Gidula's stronghold on foot."

Ravn removed her comm. harness and turned in her pilot's seat. "You are mistaken. My sweet Domino awaits the infiltration team in San Jösing on Dao Chetty."

Méarana understood again.

After Ravn had landed at the Mount Lefn pad and the tugs had drawn the monoship into the Cliffside hangars, she dressed in her best finery to stroke Gidula's vanity for spectacle. But instead of Gidula's comet or a noncommittal black, she dressed cap-a-pie in her own colors: coral, a black snake twisted. She donned a coral shenmat and, in place of a brassard, a steel armband in the form of a snake circling her biceps. She unrolled the serpent banner and co-opted a planetfallman to carry it. Her boots were thick and steel shod, and she crowned herself with a black "fisherman's" cap, pinned to the peak of which was a copper ring-badge repeating the snake motif. In the cap's band she inserted a single eagle's feather.

"One must look pretty for Gidula," she told the harper. "Eglay Portion will likely hold the bridge and dare me to pass him. I will draw the fight out as long as I can, then let him think he won."

"Draw it out to give time for—"

"For the physical exercise." Ravn turned and put a finger to Méarana's lips. "The world was fortunate when you followed not your mother's art. Your thoughts too often tumble from your brainpan directly onto your lips."

"Should I wait on board?"

The Shadow clapped her hands together. "Ooh, noo, noo, sweet. Dress to your nines, or even your tens, for you moost make splendid entrance with me. I am a Shadow of the Names and moost have a retinue. One poor planetfallman to carry my banner, and you to sing my praises. How silly I would look doing all three myself!"

"But won't that be dangerous?"

"For you to be in the Confederation at all is dangerous. You will be, as we say, 'in my gift.' No one may act against you without my permitting. Play me a suitable introit on your harp. They do not know the instrument well here, so you may entrance them with my entrance. Soomething booth oominous and playfool."

Méarana gave a half smile. "I suppose I can manage that."

Ravn patted her on the cheek. "Of course you can. I have heard you practicing your saga of Donovan and Ravn. Remember, though, the snake strikes for the heel."

Domino Tight had assumed the guise of a pack peddler. By a combination of suasion, threat, and credit balance, he had acquired wares in a general store. Here, at the mountain's foot, Gidula was only a rumor; the Forks, only a place to avoid. Yet there was some desultory traffic thither.

As Jack-a-Mount Peddler, an identity he had crafted during the hop from Dao Chetty, he secured a courtesy ride from an intercity coaster that dropped him off at a farming village just before turning east onto the Ketchell Guide-rail and shifting off manual. This furnished his pocket with a genuine coaster ticket. He had already altered his face through clever art and, by a small stone in his shoe, had instituted a minor limp.

The limp was the excuse for the exoskeleton, which he had altered to resemble an ordinary prosthesis. He set off at a walk along the foot-road, a broad swath so anciently trod that at times pieces of old asphalt had been revealed by erosion. When he was certain he was unobserved, he kicked into overdrive and proceeded at a blur.

Now that the Shadow War had escalated, Gidula's people might be more wary of who they allowed into the Forks. He had heard that Ekadrina was back on Dao Chetty, and that meant that by now every Shadow in the Triangles must know about the fight on Yuts'ga.

Publicly, the Old One had maintained a façade of neutrality. Some of the loyalists must know, or at least suspect, otherwise, but Gidula had kept clear of overt action. True, he had rescued Geshler Padaborn from Ekadrina, and had the Sèanmazy's testimony for it, but a wise man might say that he had also rescued Ekadrina from Gesh, and had the Sèanmazy's testimony for that, as well. And so, while the Forks was not exactly undefended, its best defense was Gidula's deceit.

This was also Domino Tight's best offense. There would be no expectation of attack, at least not of the sort of attack he proposed to mount. Pack peddlers were a common thing among the farming villages surrounding the Forks, and such a peddler would need a license from the Forks Adminstrative Center. Domino Tight had a series of such licenses in his scrip, as genuine as artful forgery could make them, documenting a journey along the northern tier of settlements. There were no roads up that way. No wonder he limped.

He slowed down as he came to a turn in the foot-road and was surprised to see two men ahead of him. They had stepped off the road into a clearing and were heating some water for tea with an irradiator. They were dressed in brown robes with hoods thrown over their heads. As Domino Tight drew abreast at a normal pace, he saw that the man standing was solidly built, with a square jaw. He had a walking staff but did not lean upon it. Dusty-red hair straggled from beneath his brown cowl. A whitened scar graced his left cheek.

"Bless you, my son," the man said, though he was no older than Domino Tight. "May the grace of Existence Himself be upon you. Is this truly the foot-road to Old Flea?"

Domino Tight recollected the map of the eastern coast of the Northern Mark. "Why, sorely it be, and a sore journey you are having afore yourself, your destiny being some twenty leagues distant."

The man in the cowl shrugged. "What is, is."

"You will find it needful to transit the Forks," Domino Tight told him, as any honest pack peddler might.

"If a village welcome us, someone will open his house and we will be fed, and so will they. But if a village do not, then we shake the dust of her streets from our sandals and proceed."

Domino Tight did not know what to make of that, so he said, "It is the holdfast of a Shadow of the Names."

"Ah! Who then more needful of being fed?"

"You speak in riddles, *snor*. I be but a poor peddler of useful but inexpensive wares, benamed Jack-a-Mount." He held out his right hand, dusted it on his traveler's cloak, and held it out again.

The stranger took it briefly. It seemed a limp grip, though the hand had calluses. "They call me Brother Aum. I am a philosopher by trade."

"A curious trade. Be there much profit in it?"

"A great deal, but the investment is hard. Would you share a cup with us? It is the hour for prayer."

The philosopher's assistant held forth a ceramic cup with steaming tea. A delightful aroma, but . . . Domino checked the sun's position. He had to hurry if he was to reach the Kojj Hill line while the pasdarm was in progress. Ravn had planned to ground an hour before local sunset. "No, *snor.* I be honored for the offer, ah, Brother, but I must be in the Forks before the License Bureau closes or I lose a full day's sales."

"Let your road then be your prayer, and your feet its recitation. Remember, son," and he made a sign over Domino's head, "Existence exists, and cannot not exist. He exists as the whole wide world, of all the stars and all the galaxies and all the flowers and animals. He exists in the history of men from the oldest days, when we first knew the difference between good and evil to the present day, when we pretend that we do not. And He exists here," and he touched Domino lightly on the breast.

The day was cool, but the sun shone with peculiar intensity. It was possible the philosopher was sunstruck. Domino Tight laughed and gathered his backpack to a more comfortable position. "That be a knife cut on your cheek, Brother Aum. You were in the world before you went out of it."

The philosopher smiled and touched the scar. "All wisdom begins with sense experience, Jack-a-Mount, and I learned a great deal from it. It is the custom among some native Terrans to fight with sabers purely for the purpose of exchanging scars."

He had not exactly admitted acquiring the scar in that manner, and he had avoided the claim of being Terran. Domino Tight was an expert on wounds, having both sustained and administered a fair number of them. That was not a saber cut on the cheek of Brother Aum.

But whatever shameful past the philosopher was covering up—a life as a brigand? A cutpurse?—it was none of Domino

Tight's concern; nor would it have been of Jack-a-Mount. So he bid the man a cordial adieu and set off ahead of them while they finished their cup of tea. Once out of sight, he quickened his pace once more.

The delay at the picket line was nominal. The watchman was not even a magpie, all those being gathered at the Iron Bridge for the welcoming pasdarm. Domino Tight inserted his identification stick into the reader's orifice, watched it display green with no sign of inner doubt, chatted with the watchman who inspected the pots, pans, and paraphernalia in his backpack, and made no complaint about repacking everything. He offered up his belt knife, but the watchman waved him off. "A li'l sticker like that won't take you far 'mong the gentry of the Forks," he said. And Jack-a-Mount replied that so long as he could reach the License Bureau in time to start his rounds of the villages in the morning he did not care even to meet any of the gentry.

"There's a hostel at the foot of the Enramdon Cut," the watchman said. "Caters to you folk. Got easy access to Summary Hill and Huonshrid Hill, and you can rent goo-goos there, too."

The Shadow thanked him and stepped through the gate, only to hear the alarum sound. This, he had not counted on, and he wondered what substances he might have on him that would set the system off. He stepped back, but the watchman only asked him to try again.

The second time triggered no alarm, and with a wave back to the watchman Jack-a-Mount Peddler continued down the southern face of the hill, humming a popular walking song. When he turned the corner and passed through a wooded section he was brought up short by a sharp knife. In this he took a keen interest.

Not a Shadow, he thought, for had it been, the distance between the edge and the throat would have been considerably narrower. A cutpurse of the sort the philosopher warned against? If so, the man had made a grave tactical error.

"Silence becomes us both," a voice whispered in Domino Tight's ear. The knife vanished from his throat and he turned to see who had held it. "Well met, Deadly One," the short, bristly man said, "for when last we met, you were not so well." He wore a baggy jacket and shorts with many pockets.

The Shadow recalled the boon this man had done him in Cambertown, when an ambush by the Pendragon's mums had blown away his magpies and shattered his body. Asking no price, this man has given quietus to the informer who had set Domino up and a medical regeneration packet to ease his pain. Apparently, the price was now to be mentioned. "Well met, Hound. Do you have a name?"

The bristly man grinned, and Domino saw that his teeth had been sharpened. "You don't know me? Pity. I am called Gwillgi. And you are called Domino Tight."

"You crossed the picket line when I passed through the gate," said Domino Tight. "So the watchman thought I had triggered the alarm by some malfunction."

"It was a long, lonely time waiting for a traveler to cross through, and I had just about decided to chance a bolder move when fortune presented me with your presence. You are remarkably hale for a man that detonation had reduced to bony rubble."

"I had . . . excellent nursing."

"It is about that which we might talk one day."

"You are bold, to step into Gidula's stronghold, Gwillgi Hound. Why should I not turn you over to Gidula's people? You would not like Number Two, I assure you."

"Why not? Three reasons. Because I gave you aid when you were injured. Because I held a knife to your throat and forbore to slice. Because you no more wish to be noticed here than I." He waved off Domino's answer. "You resort to disguise to enter this place. Yet in the Shadow War, you and Gidula are allies."

"What do you know of—"

"I am the League's unofficial observer. Just now I have an interest in a League citizen who has been co-opted into your squabble."

That surprised Domino Tight and he said, "The harper? But . . ."

Gwillgi hesitated. "Yes, the harper."

But the hesitation had told Domino Tight all that was needful. Gwillgi had not known of the harper, and the list of Peripherals in the affair was rather short. Gwillgi had been following Donovan.

Before Domino could speak, Gwillgi held a palm up to his lips and guided him into the brush behind the trees. "Someone follows."

Up near the crest of the hill, Domino Tight made out the figures of two men in robes. "Oh, an itinerant philosopher. We met earlier on the trail."

"Deadly One, you know I am here and I know I am here. That is already too many for my comfort."

Domino Tight understood and remained concealed while the philosopher passed. He was discussing some point of metaphysics with his acolyte and the Shadow caught only portions of it.

". . . and for that reason we see the towardness of nature. Consider the blossoming of the flowers which attract the insects." The philosopher pointed with his staff. "Or the bristling wild boar that lurks in the brush. Or the birds that eat the seeds and drop them on fertile ground. Therefore, since there is no intellect in nature . . ."

The philosopher passed around the bend in the road and so from sight and sound. Domino Tight shook his head. "I suppose all philosophers are a little mad."

Gwillgi's smile was grim. "Mad perhaps, but not boring. Now tell me that this is not just any harper, but *the* harper, and that you are here to rescue her and not to assassinate her. It may be that you and I can work together for a short time and so prosper both our happinesses."

Domino Tight knew he was not at the top of his game. His experiences with the Gayshot Bo had unnerved him to some small degree, and if he could not have a Shadow at his back a Hound would do. Especially if the Hound believed there was a debt of gratitude between them.

"Agreed, then, Gwillgi Hound." And Domino clasped hands with his sworn enemy.

Méarana was no Hound, not even a Pup, but her mother had taught her a few things. So while she played during the pasdarm she could see that Ravn and Eglay Portion were each pulling their punches. It was not a fight "to the bone," as the Shadow had told her, but only an exhibition intended to display their prowess. Nonetheless, she maintained in her music the fiction of strenuous combat, the harp strings singing of triumph and tragedy and close calls.

Only once did she strike a false note, and that was when she noticed her father among the spectators at the far end of the Iron Bridge. He was dressed in a blue-and-green shenmat and stared at her with a face of stone.

After the mock combat there was a buffet and Méarana moved uneasily among Gidula's staff. She herself wore a coral brassard with the Black Snake on it, and theoretically that meant she was on Ravn's staff. Méarana kept trying to find Donovan in the press, but every time she moved in his direction someone would engage her in conversation or inadvertently block her progress while they plucked food or drink from the tables. Several lesser magpies asked her about the strange instrument she had played and she admitted that it was a Peripheral *clairseach*. They confessed it souded exotic but not unpleasant. But others, with lower numbers on their brassards, stared at her with curious and mocking expressions on their faces.

One large magpie wearing blue and green and a bold numeral 1 on his brassard approached and whispered while they selected fruits from the buffet. "He says to tell you that you are a fool." Then the man was gone.

She knew Donovan had sent the man. No one else called her a fool with quite that nonchalance. But her father now wore the shenmat of a Shadow, and had at least one magpie of his own. What sort of prisoner was he? Had she indeed come on a fool's errand?

Only near the end of the buffet did Donovan manage to reach her side. He spoke without preamble. "How did Ravn snatch you?"

Méarana smiled ruefully. "It was my idea to come rescue you."

Donovan shook his head, as if his hearing had gone awry. "Then you are a bigger fool than I thought." He took her arm. "What made you think you could rescue me?"

"Because I thought *she* would follow."

Donovan stared at her. His lips quirked a little. Then he turned his head and said, "I hope the recording of the pasdarm was satisfactory." His finger moved in *a certain sign* that he had taught her years before on Jehovah. *Be careful what you say aloud.*

Méarana looked around, saw the recorders and the parabolic microphones by which Gidula would eavesdrop. Donovan made the hand-sign for *first-and-last,* and indicated Ravn. "She going to set up a concert for you here? Do you think anyone will come?"

She. Come? Meaning, was her mother in fact following?

"Two concerts, maybe. Here I don't have a following. I've a song series about the Shadow War. And the *clairseach* is an instrument they've not seen." *Two. Following. I've. Seen.*

"Ah," said Donovan buigh, nodding. "Close quarters I suppose, on your trip. I wish Ravn had left you behind."

The harper shrugged. She had neither seen nor heard the voice that spoke in the night since the brawl on Tungshen Habitat. "One never knows how things will turn out."

Unobtrusively, Donovan made a blade of his left hand and ran it across the index finger of his right, much as if he were rubbing an itch. Méarana nodded fractionally. Yes, one of the two Hounds was out.

(Will be here soon?)

(Not known. Ravn protect.)

(Trust no one here.)

"Only you, Father," she said in clear Gaelactic.

"Especially not me," he answered.

After the buffet, Méarana and Ravn were escorted into Gidula's office, and there she saw her father again, standing beside Gidula's chair. Two other Shadows—one wearing a rose on buff, the other wearing a daffodil on blue—flanked them both. Roses and daffodils? Méarana thought Ravn's viper far more candid.

Gidula sat room-center in an egg-chair, looking like a corpse propped in his coffin and ready for his ground sweat. He wore a billowing black robe with the comet on his front, and his cap was of the sort Peripherals called a Tudor bonnet. If there had ever been a desk before him, it was nowhere now in evidence. There was not another chair in the room, and magpies stood scattered about in a pattern Méarana recognized from shaHmat as one of mutual support. They might be pawns or rooks or counselors, poised for either attack or defense.

She wondered if Ravn felt vulnerable with no magpies of her own. Méarana touched her sleeve and the knife scabbard strapped underneath it. Poor support she could render in company like this.

The walls were hung with what she called "the art of impressions." Shapes that suggested without depicting. One hung directly behind Gidula's chair: a blackish-brown massif occupied the left side of the frame, while the right was open to a sky in which floated a yellow orb of indistinct border. It suggested a hill overlooking a river valley. A black twisting shape in midair seemed at first a human silhouette but on closer inspection proved to be a bird flying off into the distance.

Ravn bowed before Gidula, sweeping her right arm out. Méarana half-expected her to come out of the bow with a pantherlike leap upon the Old One. Her desire for vengeance might run deep enough to hold her own life disposable in the bargain. And where would that leave Méarana Harper and her father?

Donovan looked on without expression, but his eyes were everywhere at once and full of pain. Had he been tortured and broken?

Ravn rose from her obeisance. "Puissant Gidula," she said, "let the rift between us heal. Let this unworthy one abase herself and salve the wound of her earlier words with the balm of a gift. Behold! I bring you Méarana Swiftfingers, the daughter of Donovan buigh and of Bridget ban and perhaps—though this I cannot guarantee—her mother following desperately and close behind. Prepare then your nets, my sir, for a large fish swims toward them."

Donovan stiffened and took half a step forward before checking himself. Méarana herself managed little more than a hoarse, "Ravn!" But Olafsdottr did not so much as turn to face her. Two of Gidula's magpies—one of them weirdly goggled and engulfed by a headset—took her firmly by the arms and led her beside the egg-chair on the side opposite Donovan. The Shadow who stood there—the daffodil-on-blue one— turned his head fractionally, and gave her a surreptitious wink.

Gidula spoke. "We thank you with great kindness, Ravn Olafsdottr, for the generosity of your gift. Accept these tokens of our appreciation." He gestured and a young afflicted man stepped forward with a silver tray. "First, the balm for those stripes you carried." The servant proffered a cruet of gold and glass. "Secondly, a signet with the comet upon it." The servant placed the ring on the Shadow's finger. "And thirdly, a mere trifle of credits to your accounts, the sum total of which need not concern us."

Ravn bowed again, thanked Gidula, and stepped back. Tears blazed the cheeks of many of the magpies, astonishing Méarana.

The Old One turned smiling to Donovan buigh. "There. You see, Gesh? There was never any need to torture you."

Donovan faced him, though the rose-on-buff Shadow laid a hand on his arm as if to restrain him. Donovan shook him off. "You turtle's egg," he told Gidula, and the accusation carried all the more weight for the lack of volume in Donovan's voice. "There was no need for this."

"Will you now," said Gidula blandly, "tell us what we need to know?"

"Don't tell him, Father!" Méarana blurted.

The magpie in the goggles tsked and the harper felt a sharp

pain in her side. When she glanced at her, the magpie said, "Shh."

Gidula sighed. "So untrusting, the youth these days. Harper, I have as many reasons for keeping your father alive as there are stars in the heavens. Well, Gesh?"

"I never had intention of holding back. But a certain caution informs me. After twenty years and more, topography may have changed and the image in my memory may not match the reality on the ground. I could describe the scene, but you might not recognize it on sight."

"But *you* would."

"More likely than any other. I will lead you where you need to go. You may trust the word of Geshler Padaborn."

"Into the Lion's Mouth?" Gidula framed his chin in one hand, the elbow for which rested on the arm of the chair.

"Even so. I will need close reconnaissance to specify it precisely. You need not detain the harper, but send her on her way home."

"Ah, Gesh, ever the romantic! You and I are more alike than you would allow. We cannot take her with us whither we fare. The Fates hazard the dice, and collect all bets. She would stand in endless peril. No, best that she remain here, well looked after, until we return—or until her mother arrives to fetch her." He looked about the room. "And which of my Shadows would remain here to welcome Bridget ban Hound?"

The Shadow beside Méarana stepped forward. "I, my lord."

Gidula raised his eyebrows. "You, Khembold Darling? How often has Eglay Portion laid you in the dust?"

Khembold's cheeks flushed and he stood more stiffly. "To fall to Eglay Portion is no man's shame. Many are those who may conn a slider, but you set forth against the Names and their Protectors. If Eglay is the more puissant of us, he is more needed in the streets of the Secret City than here."

Gidula laughed. "Adroitly put. Very well; the boon is yours. Two, stay with him and see to administration of the keep. Khembold, you will take care of the harper?"

Khembold bowed. "Of course. As a rose in a summer garden."

Ravn Olafsdottr laughed. "Take care, Khembold Darling, that you not prick your thumb upon a thorn. She carries a knife or two up her sleeve."

"A hammer does not make a carpenter," he said, "or a pile of stone a house."

Méarana contemplated flinging the dagger into Gidula's right eye, and had unconsciously flexed her elbow when she felt the press of a muzzle in the small of her back. It was the small, insectile magpie with the flickering data goggles and the numeral 2 on her brassard. "Please," the magpie whispered. "Try." And it was a measure of Méarana's anger that she very nearly did, despite the promise of death.

But prudence—and a small scissoring of Donovan's finger—forestalled her. There would be other opportunities perhaps in this nest of adders. She had come to rescue Donovan, but it now appeared that he must rescue her, for it was clear that Gidula had exacted her father's submission by an implied threat to torture her. She was thus leverage over a man Gidula both needed and feared, and he was not inclined to give up such a lever.

As Khembold led her away, past the bleak eyes of her father, Méarana said to Ravn Olafsdottr, "Ravn, how could you?"

But of course it was obvious how she could. Later, it became more obvious still.

Gidula climbed to the crest of the Nose as he did most every Fifthday when he was at the Forks, but this time he went with only the Ravn for company. He had changed his bonnet for a beret and his billowing robe for a more travel-friendly single-ton. Ravn drove the quadwheeler and when she had parked it off the road went to stand near the elder Shadow.

The wind through the pinch of the hills that flanked the river tousled the trees and the struggling wildflowers. Gidula removed his headgear and contemplated the river, white flecked and tumbling as it rolled below the Nose. The sound of the waters seemed muted and distant. Quietly Ravn pulled her teaser from its holster and held it loosely by her side. The setting and the solitude were perfect, and artistically satisfying. She rehearsed her moves once more in her mind.

"It almost sounds like voices," Gidula said without turning. "The river, I mean. I wonder if anyone could decipher them."

"That would depend on the language, I should think," Ravn said. She raised the teaser and aimed it at the small of Gidula's back. Paralyze, then push him over. It was important that he know that he was dead, and why. But it surprised her how heavy the teaser seemed.

Gidula tossed a handful of gravel over the side of the Nose. "My wife went off here," he said. "But that was before your time. Before anyone's time, I think."

It would take only the smallest pressure on the firing stud to set up the neural pulse. Ravn tensed. A command went from the motor neurons down the arm to the finger. She could actually feel it, like a line of fire. But the finger remained frozen. She reminded herself that he deserved to die for torturing her. And perhaps for betraying the Traditions he claimed to love.

But she lowered her arm slowly until the teaser dangled by her side.

Gidula sighed and raised his eyes to the sky. "To die," he said, "might almost be a blessing." Then he turned about. "Why did you not tease me?"

Ravn did not ask how he knew. There were a dozen ways

he might have discerned her actions. And yet he had stood there waiting for her to act.

"I don't know," she answered him. "I have every reason to."

"Do you? *Every* reason?"

"Why would death be a blessing?"

Gidula faced the cliff's edge once more. "You never knew Ielnor. She was a woman to match a man: strong where I was weak; needy where I was strong. Her eyes were coal-black, her mind as clear as diamond. She was not in the Life, but she could have been. She held the Forks for me, and that during a time when the holding wanted wit and fortitude."

"She fell off the cliff here?"

Gidula nodded. "And the baby."

Ravn returned her teaser to its holster and secured it. "You must have cared for her very much."

Gidula said nothing for a moment, then stepped to the edge. "Since that time, I have never loved anything."

"Surely—"

"No, it is not good for a Shadow to love. Duty is the higher calling, and duty may one day call upon us to traduce our love. You saw how love led the harper into our trap, as by a nose-ring, and how love gives us now a handle on Geshler Padaborn himself. What was love to them but a hobble! And yet, I have grown passing fond of you during these years of struggle."

"Of me!"

"As you seem to have grown fond of the harper."

"She sings well."

"And yet you turned her over to me."

"I was oath bound to do so. I could not lure Bridget ban herself. But I think Donovan would have told you what you wanted even without the added spur. His memories were genuinely locked away."

"Perhaps. We leave shortly for Dao Chetty. They are wait-ing for me at Mount Lefn."

Ravn nodded. "Then we had better move."

Gidula smiled briefly. "They won't leave without me." He glanced down the side of the Nose. "It does not look so far, but then it is the speed, not the distance, that matters."

Ravn stepped beside him and looked down at the rushing waters below. It was far enough, she thought.

For an old man, Gidula was remarkably strong. He seized her and tossed her in a hip roll over the edge of the cliff.

She found herself suddenly a bird, though without a bird's authority for flight. She spun, and sky, waters, and Gidula's weeping face passed rapidly before her.

Endless training had taught her body what to do. Her right arm snatched a piton gun from her belt and fired a spike into the cliff face. The cable ran out and she swung at the end of it, striking the rocks with such brutal force that she nearly lost her grip on the gun. She grunted and pulled herself up, found a foothold, and shoved her left fist into a crack in the rock face.

Gidula looked down at her, judged where the piton had struck—well below the lip of the cliff. "It is much harder that way," he said. "You will grow tired and lose your grip and only then complete what has begun. Better far to have con-cluded the business in one fell swoop."

"Why? Because I thought to kill you?"

Gidula appeared to consider that. "Some might count that a reason, but mine is more serious. As I said: I had begun to grow fond of you."

A horrible cold seized Ravn's heart. "And Ielnor?"

Gidula's head bobbed. "It was faster for her. She had no place to seize hold."

"You pushed your wife off the Nose?"

"No! Oh no. She leapt. Trying to grab the baby. It was the baby I threw off."

Ravn refused to let the image focus. "You threw your baby off the cliff?"

"Of course not. It wasn't *my* baby. That was the whole point."

"Ah." Ravn had always thought of duty as a noble beast. But it had fangs. It had fangs.

"In each Shadow's path," said Gidula, "there is some fell deed that empties him out and after which there is no returning. Have you ever . . . ?"

"I killed my gozhiinyaw when we moved the governor of Stratfondle." Once more, she saw that farewell feast, tasted the wine they had toasted with. No one knew which side the others had chosen until one day she found the path to the governor's life running through the body of Anwar Cheston.

"There, you see?" Gidula said in tones of sweet reason. "After that what other deed can be so dire? One may trod the Shadowed Path with a lighter heart." He pointed to the rocky knob that crowned the cliff. "Best if you simply let go, Ravn. The upper face is unclimbable. Many others have tried. Why do you suppose Number One has not returned? You see what affection does to one's instincts. Next time, Ravn, once the gun is aimed, don't hesitate."

"I will keep that in mind. For the next time."

"Well . . ." He stood and dusted himself off. "I'm off to take down the *Committee*. Wish me luck."

"Ooh, my sweet Gidula. I fear I can spare you none. For I need all of it for myself."

XII. HANGING TOUGH

A stealthy knave may in the grave
Lay better men and true,
But treachery vile his hands defile
And honor's not his due.
  There is many a way a man to slay
  With garrote or knife or gun;
  But the best of ways is face to face
  Only thus has the better man won.
With banner high your death defy
And proudly win or fail.
The troubadours your deeds encore
And skalds will chant your tale.

Méarana remained in good cheer, and this for two reasons.
Although Donovan had gone with the kill team and left her
here, she had reasoned that this was for her the safest course.
Had he told Gidula everything and stayed here with her, the
Old One would have had no further need of Donovan, and

thus no further need of her. Until Donovan pointed out the secret entrance, Gidula might still need her to hold over him.

That did not mean she was safe. For so long as she was in the Forks, she walked among cobras, and felt small black eyes tracking her every step. They had not forgotten, in the midst of their civil war, that they had another enemy across the Rift. And if she was a lever over her father, she was also a bait for her mother.

Khembold had established Méarana in a small apartment, plainly furnished and of two rooms, just off Jeshire Street in the transient quarter. The sitting room featured a play deck, large stuffed chairs, and a well-supplied cabinet of sensory intoxicants. The back room had a two-fold bed with multiple pillows and a foldaway dresser and wardrobe. To the side were the usual conveniences for those with use for beds.

She had placed her harp atop the pillows and carefully loosened all the strings—metal strings that she played with the nails. Sometimes, when the music carried her, she would find afterward her fingertips red with blood. She bent over the harp and kissed it. *Cecilia preserve me,* she thought. And she added Jude for good luck.

In the front room, she inventoried the contents of the cabinet. There were several aerosols, but none seemed suitable for her needs. Solids whose smoke might be inhaled. A variety of liquids in bottle or syringe. The bottles were steel, ceramic, plastic—but two were glass, and these she removed from the cabinet. She poured herself a tumbler of each. The green-tinged liquid proved a wine of some sort, quite good. The clear one was a silverplate head-banger. Even a sip set up an ache between her eyes. She made a face and poured the rest of the bottle down the drain, leaving the empty bottle on the sideboard.

Afterward, she turned her attention to the play deck, where she played shaHmat against herself.

Before departure, Donovan had sent a missive by way of Magpie Three Padaborn. It was a list of numbers arranged to resemble an account in Dangchao groats: Gr 844.60 + Gr 288.60 + Gr 311.18 + Gr 109.11 and she immediately recognized it as a Clanthompson code derived from *Rosie's Thesaurus*. The numbers represented a taxonomy of concepts. Donovan had seen the code exactly once, years before on Harpaloon, but the Pedant remembered details.

Méarana was not so lucky. She pretended to refer to a list of accounts, muttered something about overcharging for services, and translated the message. *Anticipate/expect. Cross-grained/rough/unsmooth. Sporting/hunting-dog. Cheerfulness.*

That was clear enough. He knew that one or more Hounds were on their way to her. There would be a rough time between his departure and the Hounds' arrival, but she should maintain hope.

Any fool can hope, her mother had told Méarana once, *when success lies in view. It takes genuine courage to hope when matters seem most hopeless.*

Khembold Shadow Darling—no, Confederals placed office-titles last—Khembold Darling Shadow came to fetch her two days after her father had abandoned her among sullen strangers. He came about midmorn on market day, and the Great Square was bustling with activity. Farmers and craftsmen called out greetings from their booths and pavilions and offered wonderful bargains. One man in a brown robe cried out, "Ho, everyone that desires wisdom, let him draw near and take it at our hands, for it is wisdom that we have for sale! Come to the lecture hall tonight!"

On Dangchao such markets were housed under one roof, carefully proctored by the Wardens for cleanliness, and prices were posted, not chaffered over. Buying and selling here seemed more of a sport, much more like the Starport Sarai on Jehovah than the city markets at Port Kitchener. Of course, this was only a citadel, deliberately remote, sutlered by its own outlying villages, and she supposed that what cities the Earth might possess were better furnished than this.

A little ways to the south and east, on the Great Green, an itinerant theatrical troupe had set up in the amphitheater; and as she and Khembold passed by, a Queen (by her masque and tiara) was excoriating a large warrior as ". . . you great lump, you kraken off the moor . . ." At which the warrior cringed and tripped over himself, to the delight of the audience.

Inside the Administration center, Khembold led her to the communications directorate, where magpies and clerks sat by. "Gidula left instructions that we are to simulate his continued presence here," Khembold explained. "By now, the Names may know his standing in the Revolution, and if they know he has departed for Dao Chetty, they may anticipate the play he is unfolding and take measures against him. For that reason, take care in what you say. We don't know that They listen, but neither do we know otherwise."

"In what I say?"

"Here is the communicator. Sit here and wear this helmet. Be aware that Messages Sendable will monitor the call for quality purposes."

"Meaning, I don't spill the beans."

"Spill the beans?"

"A Terran expression my father taught me."

Khembold shook his head in irritation. "Mention no names at all. Not the Old One, not your own, especially not Padaborn."

When she donned the helmet she found herself in a virtual room with Donovan buigh. His image perched on an ordinary hard chair in a room plain and undecorated. A chronometer

floated in midair behind him, set to zero; and a signboard read:
INBOUND MESSAGE STREAM.

"Fudir!" she cried, using one of his less-public names.

But of course he did not hear her. He was far upsystem on the crawl, near one of the gas giants—known for some unknown but ancient reason as Wood-star. He had started talking some time ago and his words and image were just now reaching the Forks. The image, which had been frozen until she logged in, began to move and speak.

The first thing, Méarana told herself, *is to establish that it is a live image and not a sim.* She waited for him to say something no one else could possibly know.

"I am just calling to tell you everything is fine and the trip is so far without incident. Everyone is excited, of course. But I'm curious to learn how much has changed in the twenty-five years since I've seen the place. I may not be able to find my way around, and I thought, 'That can't be good.' But I hope I do because so many folks are depending on me. By the way, you can begin answering whenever you like. You can't interrupt me, and that way I'll receive your responses that much sooner. So feel free to comment on anything I've been saying. If you talk over me, you can always back up and replay."

That can't be good had been a tagline used by Teddy Nagarajan, a Wildman who had died defending their escape from Oorah Mesa on Enjrun. No one else who had been there had survived. She nodded. It was Donovan.

Méarana chatted as if they were in fact sitting together in a cheerless room. It was a curiously one-sided discourse. Given the time lag, it seemed as if they were talking past each other. Donovan would speak, she would answer, but Donovan did not respond to her answers. It would be hours before he could.

"By the way," Donovan said, "give your escort my special thanks for conducting you safely."

The scarred man was multilayered and few of his sentences had but one nut within its shell. His "special thanks" would be some sort of rebuke to Ravn for dragging his daughter into this peril. The harper had not seen Ravn since she and Gidula had gone to the Nose, but the very fact of the request had to mean that the Shadow was not aboard the slider, either.

And that was Méarana's second reason for good cheer. She had spent the evening trying to reassemble everything that had happened to her; and as was often the case when you took something apart and put it back together there was a piece left over.

Domino Tight.

Donovan talked for an hour straight while saying little, a skill he had learned in the Bar of Jehovah. In the course of the monologue, he conveyed several warnings and bits of advice, couched in Aesopic allusions to various shared experiences. Neither code nor cipher, it was impossible for outsiders to break. Méarana responded in like manner but was not nearly as optimistic in her glosses as Donovan seemed to be.

Yes, if Ravn was not on the slider, then she was somewhere nearby, her twin goals of rescuing Donovan and assassinating Gidula now thwarted by circumstance. And Khembold Darling had spoken of his admiration for Geshler Padaborn and had shown by various gestures and words that he was watching over her. But if Mother was truly close behind, taking care of Méarana might take second place to capturing Bridget ban. The garrison was expecting her. She would walk into a trap. The harper's one consolation was that her mother had walked into traps before and knew how to do so with grace and style.

Afterward Khembold escorted Méarana back to her assigned quarters. On the Great Square, the auditorium announced a

public lecture for the coming evening: "Implications of Po-
tency and Act for Being as Such." A small group of villagers
were chaffering with the philosopher, who stood in sandals
and a long brown robe at the open door. His hood shadowed
his features, but he glanced up as the harper walked past.

"Be of good cheer, sister!" he called. "I hope to see you tonight!"

Good cheer, indeed, she thought, and realized a third reason. Krakens did not come off moors!

"Perhaps," murmured Khembold when they had reached
the door, "I might come in with you for a time. There are things
you need to know about how matters stand here."

The sun had gone down and Ravn's arm had gone numb.
Gidula's shuttles had soared off to rendezvous in orbit at Gidula's
slider. *Good-bye, Donovan,* she thought as they rose. *I suppose we
shall not be such good friends now.*

No one would be coming up to the Nose to look over the
edge in the expectation of a dangling Ravn. Or rather, those
who did expect it would not be disposed to come. She amused
herself for a moment with the list of those who might be in the
Old One's confidence. The list was a curiously short one,
Gidula not being widely known for his trust, and most of those
were to have been left behind to staff the Forks.

With her right foot, Ravn felt out another ledge to relieve
the strain on her left. But the thin shelf crumbled under her
and her arm twisted. The cliff was limestone and sandstone
and unaccustomed to such strenuous duty. Rock fragments
clattered and bounced on their way to the river, where a narrow shelf marked the track of an ancient road. A road paved of
bones now, she supposed, but she did not look down to con-
firm this deduction.

How many others had Gidula tumbled off this cliff? And

what had Magpie One done to earn the Old One's disfavor? Or had it been the Old One who had earned the magpie's disfavor? Perhaps there had been some disagreement over loyalties. Judging by how long One had been on "detached duty," he had been removed about the time Gidula began planning the assault on the Secret City.

Was it true, as she had heard, that Donovan had given Five a name? And did he realize the significance of the act? Likely so. Donovan knew more than he let show and played a deep game, deeper perhaps than even Gidula suspected.

But delivering the harper to the Forks had put Donovan off that game. Dancing nimbly around threats against himself, he had been caught by threats to his daughter. Certainly Donovan had understood Gidula's tacit warning.

Everyone had been underestimating Gidula. Dawshoo had treated him as a wise counselor, but past his prime; Oschous and Manlius had openly mocked him. But there was play in the old limbs yet. It was clear to Ravn now that he had violated the traditions of kaowèn precisely because he had known it would drive her to attempt his assassination and so provide him with a traditional excuse for her summary execution. And free him of an affection that might bind him in the future. That he had allowed her to dangle here rather than daze her and watch her fall was a mark of his cruelty.

And his confidence that she could not climb up.

How justified was that confidence? She was rock bound at three points. The small ledge that supported her left foot; her right fist jammed into a crack in the rock; and the cable whose pistol-end she clenched in her left fist. She thumbed the reel and the cable taughtened as it tried to haul her up. But the piton slipped and a shower of stones pelted her. The rock in which the spike was embedded was no more secure than any other spot on the rotten cliff face. It would hold, but not hold her entire weight.

If she could not climb up, then might she climb down? But the sun was low, casting the face of the cliff in shadow. It was hard to see where hand or foot might nestle.

There was a way down. It was fast and certain, but it was also final.

A face peered over the lip of the Nose silhouetted against the westering sky.

"That was hardly a textbook assassination," it said.

"Gwillgi Hound!" said Ravn. "What game are *you* playing?"

The Hound rubbed his mustache with the side of his finger. "If I lifted you up, it might be only that I was inclined to throw you back down."

"You once gave succor to Domino Tight."

"Domino Tight did not place Méarana ban Bridget into the hands of our sworn enemies."

Domino Tight's face appeared next to Gwillgi's. "Pay him no mind. He is only entertaining you while I finish anchoring the rescue line."

"His wit o'erwhelms me," said Ravn. "Domino Tight, my sweet . . . *What are you doing here!* You were to guard Méarana after I had left with Gidula and the others!"

"You didn't leave with Gidula and the others," the other Shadow pointed out. "Gwillgi Hound was right. I have seen better assassinations. Beside, Khembold Darling has charge of your harper; and Gwillgi tells me that Khembold is a devotee of Geshler Padaborn." A cable with a loop in the end snaked over the cliff and dangled by her free foot. She slid her boot into the stirrup and, pulling her arm from the crack, she wrapped it around the cable with no little relief.

"Who told Gwillgi that?" The two men at the top of the Nose began hauling her up. Ravn started to twist but used her other hand to steady herself against the cliff.

"Donovan himself," said the Hound, "when he and I met in Prizga."

"Ooh, Doonoovan was a busy buoy, I see. But he is deceived. Khembold's father was one of those who betrayed the Rising. And the son has no more scruples. Believe me. When the Old One told him to 'take care of' the harper, Khembold knew what was required of him. Once he had secured Donovan's submission, Gidula had no more use for her. She will live only so long as need be to maintain that submission, which means for so long as Donovan might reasonably expect to contact her from the ship and receive a living answer."

"Then," said Domino Tight with a grunt as he pulled Ravn over the top of the Nose, "we have several days while they crawl up to the coopers."

Ravn staggered to her feet, stumbled a bit from the pain in her left leg. "Maybe. Donovan has too many genuine partisans aboard ship. An open break would mean a large war in a small space. If Donovan suspects the harper harmed, he may sacrifice all for wild vengeance. Oh, Domino, you should have let me dangle—or even fall—and not abandoned the plans we laid."

"Can I let a gozhiinyaw fall to her death if I can stop it? I thought that—"

"Yes, yes, and if I had thought the same, I would have done the same. Come, we can only play the game from where we stand now—and hope that Khembold toys with her first."

The three of them set off at a jog, pacing one another. Gwillgi laughed. "He may find the toys a little sharper than he expects."

But Ravn shook her head. "He knows about the hideout knife she keeps up her sleeve."

———

Méarana was her mother's daughter. *There are no dangerous weapons, little one,* Bridget ban had once told her. *But there are dangerous men. And in the hands of a dangerous man, anything may be a weapon.*

Little Méarana had drunk it all in wide-eyed. Perhaps even so long ago, her mother had esteemed a time when enemies might strike at her through the child.

A glass bottle, smashed across the edge of a countertop, could provide knives enough to cut a throat.

She had but stepped within with Khembold close behind when the insectile Number Two rose from the enveloping chair in the sitting room and said with impatience, "Well, has he made his call?"

Khembold did not answer immediately but gave Méarana a shove in the small of the back, sending her fully into the sitting room. He followed, carefully closing the door. "He did, and his get assured him that all was well."

"That should keep him until Gidula has what he wants. The Old One will find some technical difficulty to prevent a second call, and after that they'll be in the tubes."

Number Two stood between her and the glass bottle. She might not have realized Méarana's intended use of it, but the harper knew she could not go through Two to seize the bottle. Every plan is complicated by the presence of the enemy.

These rooms might be her coffin. She faced Khembold. "You forget that I am in the gift of Ravn Olafsdottr. I do not take orders from you, any more than you take orders from a mere magpie." This with a jerk of her head toward Number Two.

"Oh," said that worthy from behind her scrolling goggles. "I think I will enjoy this."

Khembold took Méarana by the arm and pulled her aside.

"Gidula gave *me* the task," he told Two. "I need no help." Then, to Méarana, "Ravn Olafsdottr has played her role, and has exited stage *down*." He laughed. "I will be glad when the pretense is over. The harvest promises much bounty."

Number Two made a gesture of impatience. "Get on with it. We've no more use for it."

"Ah," said Méarana in a catlike voice she had heard her mother use. "But Khembold might have one more use." She reached out and touched his arm.

The Shadow grinned and winked at Number Two. "It may be right."

"It may simply want you close enough to use those toad-stickers it wears up its sleeve."

Khembold's smile broadened. "I don't think it's foolish enough to try that."

Méarana did not think herself that foolish, either. She had seen Ravn at exercise catch knives thrown at her and did not suppose Khembold any less talented.

Taking the initiative, she unfastened her blouse and let it slide down, revealing that her bare arms bore no arms. "What need have I for blades when Gidula has given me his word?"

Khembold shrugged. "Gidula is not here to break it." He studied her. "The blouse was a good start, but you've promised more than that."

Méarana unfastened her pants and kicked them off. She wore ankle boots but left them on. Khembold Darling licked his lips.

"Get on with it," said Number Two. "And watch out for stupid kicks."

"You heard her," Méarana murmured.

"Don't fret, Six-eyes," the Shadow snapped. "Gidula said

to wait until the call had been finished, but he never put an upper bound on it. Go away. I don't need you for this."

"Oh, but I was looking forward to the pain," the magpie said.

"I promise to hurt it for you." He took Méarana's arm and shoved her into the bedroom.

"It's not the same when someone else does it," Two complained as she followed.

"Then you can have it when I'm done," the Shadow told the magpie. "There's no need to destroy the goods right off, is there? We can maximize utility. See how long it lasts."

Number Two snorted. "That's what the little whore is counting on."

"It thinks it wants to delay things, but soon enough it will wish matters had ended more quickly." Khembold chuckled and turned to Méarana, who had lain out on the bed. His lip curled as he placed his weapons belt beyond Méarana's reach. "Do you really think your body will buy me off?"

Méarana smiled sadly. "No, but it might buy me two more minutes."

Number Two could not contain a burst of laughter. Khembold turned red and climbed atop the harper, and smacked her open palmed across the face. He was not wearing a shenmat, and there were useful flaps in his clothing that he could open. He paused and took himself in hand.

"I'm going to enjoy this."

"Oh. So am I," the harper assured him. She stretched her arms above her head and caressed the strings of her harp.

The door to the apartment chimed.

Number Two scowled. "I left orders," she said.

"Then it may be important," said Khembold. "Go check. Don't worry. I'll leave enough for you to hurt."

The magpie hissed impatiently and returned to the sitting room. She checked the door's security scanner. "It's that wandering philosopher!" she said.

In the bedroom, Khembold frowned and turned his head.

Méarana's mother had taught her a proverb once: *She who would lose her life, the same shall save it.* And it meant that when all was at hazard, the timid would die. Only by risking everything with a wild disregard can one save anything.

But while the disregard must be wild, it must never be witless, she had warned. And then she would teach little Méarana some trick of the trade.

And so the signal from the door had left her momentarily alone with the Shadow.

And the Shadow had turned his head.

And the Shadow had exhaled.

All these things she sensed as in retarded motion, as if she floated in the room above herself. It was a configuration that would not last.

Méarana Harper pulled the loosened cord from her harp and with a single, cross-handed motion wrapped it around the neck of Khembold Darling, pulling on both ends with all her strength. Khembold gagged and the metal strings bit into his flesh. She had waited for the exhale before acting, and a man deprived of breath thinks of little else but drawing one.

But Khembold was a Shadow and Shadows do not die easily, whereas harpers might perish as swiftly as butterflies. His arms were free and he punched Méarana in the face, but the harper took the blow and hung on. To lose hold of the garotte would mean her immediate death—though she might count even that a victory and be glad.

Her chances were small, but in a stand-up fight she would

have none at all. Her strength might fail. Khembold might batter her unconscious. Number Two might rush back at any moment.

But there was always the door-chime to give her hope.

The philosopher rang several times and shook his begging bowl before the Eye. Two sighed in exasperation. The common folk accounted it bad luck to spurn a *chit'hoka's* begging bowl. And while she considered it of no matter whatsoever, she had no desire to attract attention. Not all the magpies on staff were trustworthy.

She opened the door, aiming her money-rod at the receptor in the bowl, and had just opened her mouth to chase him away when the sounds of stuggle erupted from the bedroom. Her first thought was that Khembold Darling was having all the fun. "Go away," she told the philosopher before the second thought struck her. And that was that the robed man held a very unphilosophical dazer.

"Quiet now, *a cushla,*" he said in the Gaelactic.

Her paraperception sensed motion in the room behind her, and her third thought was that Khembold was rushing to her assistance. "A Hound," she cried in warning.

But it was Domino Tight whose hand-spike severed her spine, and she fell to the floor before a fourth thought could even form.

At the same time, Ravn Olafsdottr, in the bedroom, threw off the second cloak and leaped upon Khembold's back. She pulled his head back and, pressing a gun to his temple, fired a small-caliber pellet into his brain.

The pellet had sufficient force to penetrate the skull but not to exit and so neither endangered anyone else in the room nor created unsightly splatter. Instead, it ricocheted about inside Khembold's cranium several times. Not that it mattered after the first.

Méarana had acted on the happy intuition that the door signaled Domino Tight, and while her intuition had been wrong, it had been right enough.

At first outraged by Ravn's betrayal, Méarana had in a cooler moment reasoned that had Olafsdottr meant simply to hand her over to Gidula, she would not have first collected Domino Tight. She chided herself for not realizing that immediately, but Ravn had likely acted deliberately to create the necessary mask of shock and anger in her prisoner.

"Quickly," the harper warned her. "Number Two—"

"Oh, do not worry. Sweet Doominoo will handle the vixen, thanks to the fortuitous door-chime." Ravn looked her over. "I might almost envy Khembold Darling his desires, save only to what a poor end he came because of them. Without your distraction, I doubt I could have taken him so by surprise." She stepped to the doorway, pressed against it, and took a quick blick into the sitting room. "Oho," she said, pulling back, "you have a gentleman caller. Please make yourself decent—or not, as your spirits move you, lest he regret his celibacy."

"Celibacy? The philosopher?"

"Yayss. And it pains me to say that he and my sweet Domino are at dazers drawn. How many Hounds did we draw in your wake, my sweet? Too many, I think. Perhaps we should salve things over. For it would be poor form for your rescuers to slay one another in the epilog."

Little Hugh O Carroll was not so easily salved. He held a hand out to Méarana when she emerged. "To me, *a cushla*." He did not shift his aim from the Shadow. But neither did the harper rush to his side.

"Think, man," Ravn Olafsdottr told him. "Who slew Méarana's attackers? Whatever enmities run between your fellowship and ours, on this matter we are as congruent as triangles."

"And we have a truce," Domino Tight said in a husky voice, "with Gwillgi."

"I saw him in the brush with you," said Little Hugh, "up on the ridge. The bristly boar in the bushes. But where is he now?"

"We could not be certain," Domino Tight explained, "that they would choose Méarana's apartment for the kill space. So Gwillgi tracked them outside while we lurked here. I had expected him at the door, not you."

"We really do have a truce, Rinty," Gwillgi announced from behind Hugh. "So why not be laying your dazer aside."

When everyone had put weapons away and a degree of calm had been restored, the Hounds sat on one side of the room and the Shadows on the other. Méarana took a third seat between them. She looked first to the one, then to the other. "There's a moral in this room, I think." Her voice came out a little shaky, because she had begun to realize how close to death she had danced. But it is better to be close from this side than from the other. She felt almost giddy, all light-headed and her senses heightened. The air seemed fresher and more invigorated; the light and colors, more intense.

The razor's edge.

"It was closer than you think, sweet," Ravn whispered to her. "We had no right to come out of it alive, let alone unscathed."

Gwillgi said to Little Hugh, "Where is Greystroke? And if you tell me he is sitting beside me, I will rip his face off with these very fingernails."

"Another Hound!" said Domino Tight. "And the two on Tungshen—"

"Hush, my sweet. I snatched a cub from Mother Bear. A moderate response was unlikely."

Domino pursed his lips. "I am not sure I like this. The Shadow War is one thing; the Long Game, another."

Méarana said, "And where *is* Mama Bear? Was this rescue nae important enough for her tae tag along?"

"Of course it was," Bridget ban said from the doorway, the Queen from the acting troupe. She strode into the room, took in its contents, the body, the amiably gathered Shadows and Hounds, glanced from the hand-spike in the back of Number Two to the weapons belt of Domino Tight, studied the bruises on her daughter's face. "But there is gae more to a rescue than simply barging in, dazers flashing. We're deep in the Triangles, girl, and getting out will be as tricky as getting in." She turned and slapped Ravn Olafsdottr across the face. "I have waited a good long time to do that," Bridger ban said, bending close to Ravn's face. Domino Tight stiffened, but Ravn took the blow in silence.

"I did my dooty," she said a moment later, "though it took some careful choreography to move all the pieces into place."

"Pieces," said Little Hugh. "What pieces?"

"Ooh, Donovan, Méarana, Bridget ban, sweet Domino. Gidula."

Gwillgi snorted. "Seems to me, was Gidula who almost moved *you* into place."

A wave of the hand. "Why play game with no hazard?"

"Hazard? Ye could hae lost my daughter!" Bridget ban took Méarana's hand and turned it over. "Ye're bleeding."

"I cut it on a harp string."

Bridget ban looked about. "There was another. A man."

The harper flexed her hand, rubbed the back of it across

her cheek. "I played a goltraí for him, a lament, and he choked up."

Ravn tossed her head to indicate the bedroom, and the Red Hound strode into it. She returned a moment later, face as crimson as her hair. "Did he succeed?" she asked her daughter.

"He died unsatisfied." And then, more slyly than she had intended, Méarana added, "I used one of your auld tricks."

Bridget ban said nothing for a moment. "We'll speak of it later. You need to work on your grip so you don't cut yourself next time." She turned to the Banty Hound. "Gwillgi! We have been trying to find you."

The topaz eyes gleamed and the smile showed teeth. "I was not wishful of being found."

"Oh," said Méarana. "That's what Father meant! The cross-grained Hound! He knew Gwillgi was close by."

"Yes. He and I met in Prizga, during his 'hajj.' We—"

Graceful Bintsaif came to the doorway and interrupted. "Cu," she said. "Greystroke and I have sabotaged the comm. center. No warnings will reach Gidula's ship before he has departed Terran space. And Grimpen and Obligado have interdicted the port. The remaining vessels now lack a vital part no longer in stores."

"Very well."

"Cu—" The junior Hound glanced at Ravn and Domino and lowered her voice. "There are a great many magpies and lesser militia, and I doubt we can keep the lid on this for very long."

"Tosh. We will be gone before most of them even know we have come. A theatrical troupe, a wandering philosopher . . . Such folk come and go. And Gwillgi may slip out as silently as he slipped in. My daughter is the problem. She has had too much visibility, and cannot simply leave the stronghold. Who commands here?"

Ravn grinned. "The dead body on the bed."

"And who is second?"

"The dead body by your foot. And before you ask who is third in line, I could suggest myself. Along with Khembold and Eglay, I was Gidula's Shadow-associate. As such, I outrank Four, who is the next magpie in line."

"He took One and Three with him?"

"Well, Three. One is at the bottom of the very cliff over which he threw me. The Old One disposes," Ravn added, "with that which he needs no more. Our kenning was that he would have Méarana removed once his ship was out of contact and we laid our plans accordingly."

Bridget ban considered that. "Ye should ne'er hae needed to lay such plans. Ye should nae hae brought her into the Triangles."

Ravn shrugged. "You would not come to help me rescue Donovan."

"Donovan!" The Red Hound turned to Méarana. "And where be your father in a' this?"

The harper turned her chin up. "He went with Gidula to attack the Secret City."

"And ran out on you again, abandoned you defenseless in the stronghold of our enemy."

Little Hugh coughed. "Sure, it seems that Méarana has an embarrassment of defenders."

"Which Donovan could nae hae kenned!"

"Could he not, then?" Little Hugh cocked his head. "He knew Gwillgi was near, and he nodded to me when we passed on the market square."

"He nodded . . . Oh, now there's proof!"

"Mother! An cuid I ken the safest course, so cuid he. He had to take the chance that you were nigh."

"An cuid he tak a' the chances he mought—*but nae wi' me bairn's life!*"

"It was my idea," Méarana said quietly in Standard Gaelactic, "to come here."

Ravn clapped her hands together and rubbed them. "Excellent. Now family quibbles wrapped away, we discuss your escape. Consider fortress staff. Many loyal to Gidula; many loyal to Padaborn. Many loyal to Gidula because they think him loyal to Padaborn. Everything so crisscross, is hard to plan double cross. Guess which he leaves mostly behind?"

"Padaborn's partisans," said Little Hugh.

"Guess wrong."

Bridget ban's eyes widened and she stared at Ravn. "It's an ambush. He took Padaborn's partisans because he intends that they die in the Secret City."

"Yayss. He needs rebels to perform triage on the Names; but once he need them no longer, he dispose of them, too. So, attend me. This is our play. Night is fully fallen, no? And your sabotage of the comm. center will not look like sabotage?"

Graceful Bintsaif snorted. "Dead rats lie where they gnawed through the circuits. And no one will know the fliers are inoperable until someone actually tries to start one up."

"Not for several days, then, for Gidula ordered the stronghold buttoned up. Good. No one saw you enter; let no one see you leave. 'Philosopher,' you will present your scheduled lecture. In half a Terran hour, yes? The 'theatrical troupe' will retire for the night and leave in the morning as planned."

"And the two dead bodies?" asked Bridget ban.

"Even those magpies loyal to Gidula do not know the depth of his betrayals. I will call them together and tell them that Khembold Darling, ruled by his lust, had tried to violate Méarana Swiftfingers, despite her status as my vassal *and despite*

Gidula's assurance of her safety. Magpie Two Gidula, discovering his plans, tried heroically to stop him, but he stabbed her treacherously in the back, and it was only then that I happened on the scene and slew the traitor." Ravn took in her listeners and smiled. "Those privy to Gidula's thoughts may think this be Denmark and smell something rotten in it, but all others applaud how clayver I lie."

Domino Tight nodded slowly. "The best cozening is that which sails close by the truth. They know Khembold's reputation and Two's fierce loyalty to her master. And those privy to Gidula's intentions will take your reappearance to indicate his change of heart."

Ravn nodded. "Gidula is slave to sentiment."

Bridget ban folded her arms. "And what would make more sense than that you should then depart with Méarana to catch up with Gidula?"

"Precisely."

But the Red Hound leaned forward. "Except *that will nae happen.* Do you think me daft, to entrust my daughter to your care? She will depart with me, and we will heigh directly for the Periphery. One of my costume coffers has been fitted out for just that purpose." She turned. "Have you heard, Graceful Bintsaif?"

"Aye, Cu."

"Tell the others, then."

"Two on Tungshen," the junior Hound suggested.

"Yes, heard and noted. Go, now."

When the door had closed once more, Ravn Olafsdottr said quietly, "There was no truce on Tungshen."

Bridget ban grimaced. "A hazard of the game. Disposition?"

"The one called Matilda of the Night escaped with the body of Cŵn Annwn. No confirmed kill."

"If Matilda got her into a meshinospidal in time . . . ," suggested Little Hugh.

"Ah," said Gwillgi, "but our new friend Domino has access to something even better, do ye not, Domino Tight?" Then, to Bridget ban and Little Hugh, he explained, "I was tagging yon wean as an up-and-comer in the Shadow War. One day I saw him blown to something very much like gelatin. Ah, you never saw a leg bent in more directions than his. And two days later, there he is, hale and feisty enough to turn the tables in a Shadow fight on his very own." He turned to Domino Tight. "Ever since, I have been bursting to ask you how that was done."

The Shadow shifted in discomfit. "This was not in our agreement."

"Sweet Domino!" said Ravn. "Your very appearance so soon after your death spoke more clearly of those Vestiges than any admission you might make."

"You should not tell them of the Vestiges," he said, pointing to the Hounds.

"Dominoo! You should noot have toold *me!*"

"They are secrets guarded by the Technical Name."

"But we are to overthrow the Names, no?"

"Perhaps . . . I have begun to wonder . . ."

"Wonder what, my darling Domino?"

"There is talk of targeting *the Committee* but not the others. And I began to wonder why."

"Sure," said Bridget ban, "and is that not obvious? The whole affair is but a power struggle among the Names."

Both Shadows looked at her. Ravn ran a hand through her stubbly hair. "To me, that became clear at the Pasdarm on Ashbanal."

"Yet you continue to fight?"

"It is something to do."

"What of these Vestiges? There are supposed to be seven," Bridget ban suggested.

Domino Tight bit his lip, shook his head. "Tina Zhi never said what the others were. Only that her college was tasked with maintaining the secrets. I have to wonder now if she revealed what she did as a calculated act."

Ravn sucked in her breath. "You spoke her name aloud."

"Yes," said Domino Tight. "I did. When Gidula and his allies reach Dao Chetty, they will expect to find me there. If I am missing, they will suspect discovery or treason and fold the play. So I knew when you pulled me from my post I might need to return there quickly, and I made arrangements with Tina Zhi."

Ravn sprang to her feet. "Quickly, my sweets. We must leave this place." Méarana had time to say no more than, "Why?" when a pinpoint of light appeared in midair and expanded rapidly into a whole person, dusky complexioned, with a long nose and high cheeks, and garbed in white and silver. Her hair was clipped short and dyed silver to match her jewelry.

She spread her arms and cried, "I have come, my—," but then she saw others in the room. She glanced at shenmat-clad Ravn Olafsdottr and the body of Number Two. She glanced at Bridget ban, Little Hugh, and Gwillgi and said, "Hounds!" Last, she glanced at Méarana and said, "Ah!"

"Worry not, my beloved," she said to Domino Tight. "I will rescue you." And with that she reached out, and with her disappeared Domino Tight.

"Quickly!" cried Ravn. "Out! Out! Out!"

Hounds knew how to retreat as gracefully as attack. Only Bridget ban held back for a moment, scanned the sitting room, and set her mouth in a grim flat line before Ravn Olafsdottr shoved her forcibly from the room. The Shadow slapped the door closed behind them.

A moment later, light streamed from the slit windows and the spaces around the door. The door buckled and the windows bulged and splintered. Then the roof sagged and smoke began to rise.

"A good thing," said Ravn Olafsdottr from her position prone to the ground, "that these buildings are blast fast. Automatics extinguish fires in short order." She rose and brushed herself off. "Gayshot Bo thought to protect her reluctant lover from Hounds, but provide now rationale for your daughter's disappearance. Smuggle-out easy now."

Others were coming, attracted by the noise of the explosion. Little Hugh had faded into the shadows of the night—to return as if part of the curious crowd. Gwillgi had vanished entirely. Only Bridget ban—the actress, Gloriana—had remained.

Ravn looked about. "Where is Méarana?" And then she saw that Bridget ban stared with murderous intensity at the ruined apartment. "No! Say that we did not leave her behind!"

But the Red Hound shook her head. "If it was the Gayshot Bo's intention to get rid of the Hounds, she succeeded only in drawing them onward. She took Lucia with her."

Ravn was not accustomed to the harper's base name and it took a moment for her to recognize it for what it was. "Did she? Or did Méarana grab hold of her?"

Bridget ban turned on her. "And why would she do that?"

"You forget why she came with me to begin with. Now you must follow her to Dao Chetty, and so rescue Donovan buigh before Gidula disposes of him as well."

Bridget ban closed her eyes and sighed. "Och, Donovan. What am I to do with that man?"

XIII. THE RAZOR'S EDGE

Flowing water-murmur of the tumbling river
Fills the cloudless overarching sky with whisper
Most comforting: continuo to contrapuntal
Insect-twitter. Sweet music for the foul refrain
As through the rancid womb of night
Dread slaughter creeps to penetrate
The long-sought cavities of Secret City.
Reveals then the overgazing moon
A score of darkened ghosts for gore engarbed.
Throats already destined for the knife do at
This very toll now guzzle sweet sure wine,
Laugh, or sing lewd songs to lusty flesh.
And many—those that hold the rods of rule—
Their eyes now clogged in wrested slumber
Will not open come the morn.
The dawn will herald red; so much is sure.
All else is hazard "on the razor's edge."
Clocks keep muted hours, luring morning near.

And some, their senses heightened by the two-moon sky,
In terrored sleep do fitful turn, and know not why.

The River Zyu—the River of Pearls—is named for its supposedly milky color, though this far down from the Chalky
Mountains the waters are more tea than milk. The Secret City
sits upon bluffs high on the right bank, pinkish in the afternoon sun, surrounded by massive walls more intimidating
than defensive and by the houses and businesses of those who
bask in the proximity of power. On the left bank, massive
apartment blocks squat in uniform ranks on lowlands more
directly open to the river's whims. One block, named "Sugar
Cane City," rises on a tract formerly given over to industrial
cane processing.

"There it is," said Little Jacques, the pale pigmy who
conned the modest pleasure boat that traveled slowly up the
stream. Donovan and Gidula looked where he pointed. The
magpies with them looked everywhere else. All were dressed
in festive river-garb: broad-brimmed sun-hats, water-singlets,
flotation belts. The river was a favored playground for those
who could afford to play.

"Seems different," Donovan said as he studied the mani-
cured esplanade along the waterfront.

"Not too different, I hope," answered Gidula. Little Jacques
smiled without turning around.

"Put in over there," Donovan suggested. "Take it slow and
watch for underwater obstacles. There were piers here once,
and the pilings might linger underwater."

Little Jacques said to no one in particular, "I love it when
you remember things."

"I love it," said Gidula more privately, "*when* you remember things."

"Sometimes memory needs a stimulus."

"Yes," said Gidula, sitting back once more. "I know."

The sign read: NO PLEASURECRAFT DOCKING. Gidula and Donovan jumped ashore while Little Jacques and the magpies stayed in the boat. Donovan shaded his eyes and peered across the river.

"Well?" said Gidula.

"The old sugar plant stood here, and the bank was overgrown with volunteer cane." He strode north along the esplanade about twenty paces, paused. "Here. I think. When I came ashore, I could still see my point of exit under the bluffs." He turned his powerglasses across the river and upstream. The bank there was an impenetrable thicket of rhododendron, sassafrass, hazelwood, and Chinese elm. Donovan lowered the glasses. He would have to tell them about the steam tunnels sooner or later, and it looked as if later had come.

"They assumed I used my power-zoot to cross the river as quickly as possible, and so searched along the southern side of the Secret City. They never imagined that a man fleeing for his life would drift lazily with the current for a time. But I knew my destination, and there was no point coming ashore upstream of here. My betrayer knew the destination, too, and guessed where I might come ashore. I don't know why they never came back to question me further."

Gidula sighed. "The Names decided that the uprising 'never happened,' so it was an embarrassment to have about those who remembered putting it down."

"Ah. False consciousness." Donovan placed the glasses in the carry-case. "Most of the city center was in ruins. How did they explain that?"

Gidula stepped back into the boat. "Urban renewal."

Gidula and Donovan put on a dumb show in case anyone in the sheep pens was gazing in boredom, awe, or envy toward the gleaming towers of Secret City. They disembarked on the right bank to relieve themselves only to have their boat lose power and drift with the current. They scrambled through the brush to catch it. Haha! The discomfiture of the wealthy is ever a source of amusement to the sheep. No need to inform authorities of anything so droll.

Donovan edged inland as he scrambled downstream; and before too long, he found the crumbling exit of a steam tunnel. Gidula, caught in a tangle of rhododendrons, did not notice; so Donovan pressed on—and came upon a second opening! He had tallied six tunnels before he decided he could not plausibly have overlooked them all, and finally informed Gidula. "I don't know which I came out of," Donovan said. "They must underrun the entire city of Old New Jösing. If I explore each, I should have a good idea which served the Secret City."

"We'll come back later with the others," Gidula said. "We don't want the Protectors to wonder about activity along the riverbank." He was not about to let Donovan roam a warren of tunnels in which he might not be found again. "Steam tunnels . . . Who would have thought it?"

Donovan ignored him. "The system fell into disuse; MHD plants were redeployed. New construction sealed over the accessways. Once the drainage tunnels were out of sight, they soon passed out of mind."

Gidula clicked Little Jacques, who was finally able to restart his boat and pick them up.

"And, Old One? 'Sealed over' means exactly that. I had to chop through a subbasement wall to gain access. You'll need drills, poppers, thermastics . . ."

Gidula patted him gently on the shoulder. "If you could exit, we can enter."

———

Shadows and their magpies gathered that evening in shenmats and wearing the tools of their profession. They had tuned the skins to black in honor of the night. At the entrance of each tunnel, they pinged a fix off the satellite, then inside the tunnels where the positioning network was inaccessible they tracked their pathways by dead reckoning off micro-gyros. By superimposing the D/R traces over ground-level maps, they determined that two of the six tunnels led under the Secret City. Donovan and Pyati scouted up each one. Oschous and his own Number One went with him.

The first one was it. But Donovan withheld judgment until checking the second. Then he went back to double-check the first, proceeding uphill until the party came to an ancient flight of stone steps off the tunnel-side, blocked at the top by a deadfall of rubble. Donovan lowered himself on the second step. Pyati went a little farther up-tunnel while Black Horse One kept watch on their backtrail, creating a bracket within which their masters could talk.

Oschous sat beside him on the step, and stroked the fur on his protruding chin. "So. Is this the place?"

"We broke a hole through a subbasement wall. I suppose when they brought the building down the rubble plugged the hole."

Oschous examined the tumbled avalanche of stone and tile. Then he studied the dead reckoning map. "Officially, there was never a building above here. They leveled the site and in-filled with dirt. If we dug through, we'd emerge in a park and frighten some late-night lovers. But now that we have a second fix we can figure out where the tunnel system abuts the Residences." He clapped Donovan on the shoulder. "Well done, Gesh!"

Donovan shrugged.

"What ho! Why so glum, comrade?"

"Because my usefulness to Gidula is now at an end."

Oschous made a Brotherhood sign with his left hand. "But not thy usefulness to us."

Donovan no longer believed Oschous a Brotherhood member, or that the Brotherhood this side of the Rift was not utterly compromised. But neither did Donovan believe that Oschous was ready to dispose of him. The young man in the chlamys thought "the Fox" planned to use him against Gidula—which was fair enough, considering. Donovan leaned toward Oschous. "Be thou not too sanguine that thy battle plan and the Old One's intentions wend the same path."

Oschous flicked his hand, as against a fly. "Gidula doth hold but one vote of three. Yea, a wise counselor, but Dawshoo's voice and mine count for more."

Was Oschous serious? A dazer could fire twelve pulses between rechargings. Those were votes enough. "Remember that this play did hatch from his egg, and it doth place our leadership in places of Gidula's desiring."

Oschous said nothing for a moment, then tapped his positioner and stood. He dropped the Tongue. "Let's return to the others."

They calibrated their dead reckoners just inside the tunnel entrance and sent teams out to map the tunnel network. "To maintain surprise," Oschous told them, "our kill teams must emerge simultaneously at their strike points. Targets must not be given time to spread word. Find exit points closest to— preferably directly into—the Residences."

"Not the Offices?" asked Domino Tight.

"No," said Gidula, "for in the morning we will have a problem."

"In the morning?" one of the magpies asked.

"Surely. When the Confederation awakes, she will need a government. We do not want to wreck the machinery, only replace the operators. The Names have grown indolent. You will find them at home, wrapped in luxuries, not pulling night shift in the Offices. I've marked the Residences on the overmaps."

"You haven't marked all of them," Manlius Metataxis complained. "Where is the Technical Name? Or the Second Name? Where is *the Masked One?*"

"Yes," said Donovan. "I should have thought the Secret Name would head the list."

"This is the list provided us by Domino Tight's source within the Secret City. Some Names favor our struggle. Those we may spare—and later control. So, stick to your target lists."

Donovan did not miss the silent exchanges among the Shadows. *In for a fenny, in for a yoon.* Why spare *any* Names?

"We will take two hours to expedite target acquisition," said Dawshoo. "Leave repeaters at all tunnel intersections. If you cannot find direct access to a Residence, pick a nearby site with reasonable ground access and we will shift the tempo to give you time to enter your kill zones. Remember: you may encounter Protectors. Is that understood?"

"No, Grandmother," piped Little Jacques. "What was that part about sucking eggs, again?" The others laughed.

"Eglay," said Gidula, "by me. Pyati, do you go with Manlius. Gesh, wait you here. Too valuable you are to hazard on mere reconnaissance."

Pyati glanced at Donovan, who brushed his lips and flashed two fingers for an instant where Gidula could not see. Pyati relayed the signal to the other four Padaborn magpies. Eglay Portion came over to him and embraced him. "Don't kiss me," Donovan warned. "It's been done before."

Gidula, hearing the comment, frowned in incomprehension, but Eglay Portion understood. "Which," he whispered.

"Watch," Donovan replied. "Play Two."

Gidula turned. "Do you, good Domino, sit sentry then with our bold Padaborn. Take care of him, that we shall call on him as needed."

The man with the lyre brassard was the only senior conspirator Donovan had not met before. He nodded. "Yes, Deadly One."

After the recon teams had departed, Donovan and the other Shadow squatted in the dark, visible to one another only as ghostly images on night-vision goggles. By all accounts, Tight had done yeoman's work at the warehouse and was a friend of Ravn Olafsdottr; but right now, Donovan was not feeling especially friendly toward Ravn.

After a long silence, Donovan with his shy-side hand unfastenend the loop on the knife scabbard at the back of his belt. "Do you think you can?" he said.

"Can what?"

"Take care of me?"

"Oh." Domino Tight made a great show of placing both his hands in plain sight. "Let me put it this way. Gidula gave the same instructions to Khembold Darling to 'take care of' your daughter."

Donovan's heart froze over, and he half-rose from his squat. "Khembold would not . . . !"

"Would. Tried. Failed."

Donovan drew a breath and eased back down. "What . . . happened?"

"Your daughter strangled him with a harp string and Ravn Olafsdottr shot him in the head, so he is a twice-dead man."

Donovan smiled as a wolf smiles, but not without a little

relief. "That's my girl . . ." Ravn had been playing her own game. But . . . "How can you know what happened on Terra?"

While Domino Tight summarized the events at the Forks, the scarred man consulted the young man in the chlamys, who responded that while body language was difficult to read in night vision, voice-stress analysis showed sincerity. Of course, pathological liars could also sound sincere. Nevertheless, Donovan refastened the knife-loop. "Your inability to describe the philosopher's assistant convinces me," Donovan said. "I know the Man That No One Sees. And I knew Gwillgi to be nearby— and that the harper's mother would come. I had not thought she would bring friends. So, she is safe now, Méarana is?"

"Well," said Domino Tight, "that is where it begins to grow complicated."

The two of them left the tunnel for the riverbank. It was fully night now and the Minor Moon was rising steadily in the east. In another day it would overtake the Major Moon. A Dao Chettian countryman could tell time with fair precision by the relative positions of the two moons. The north wind smelled of fish and of methane vapors from the mantle subjection wells northeast of the city.

"Do you really think they are walking into a trap?" said Domino Tight.

"I think they will succeed in assassinating just those Names Gidula wishes dead, at which point their luck will sour."

"My . . . special friend . . . thought the purge could be done without undue bloodshed."

"Your friend is that most dangerous of creatures: a ruthless naïf. This fight is among the Names; it is others' blood they meant to shed. Is this the spot where you kill me?"

"Yes, and your body goes into the river over there. The *frawtha*—the 'official truth'—will be that you stepped outside for fresh air, a Protector river patrol spotted you, and, rather than lead them to us, you dove into the river to draw them away."

"Brave and noble to the end."

"Gidula wants *you* dead, not your legend."

The scarred man laughed and tossed his head. "The irony is that Padaborn was not so heroic. He betrayed me."

Domino Tight looked at him. "You're not Padaborn? Ah. Now a few things make sense."

"I am happy for you."

"No. You see, there were rumors that Padaborn had buckled under threat of torture, and then they tortured him anyway in case he had forgotten to tell them anything, and when they were done there was not enough of him left to bother with. He was with the smoke. But I dismissed those stories as propaganda, because other rumors held that he had escaped and was in clever concealment—'in the one place no one will look.' So when Gidula announced he had located you, him in the Periphery . . . It gave us all heart."

"But . . . ," suggested Donovan. A night bird swooped across the face of the river and the moons-light revealed a two-shadowed fish rising in the claws of something large.

"Yes. My 'special friend' took your daughter and me to her Residence; and there, for whatever reason of her own, she told us . . . You see, Padaborn *won*—by proxy. After his Rising, a faction calling themselves the *Committee of Names Renewed* declared that the best way to prevent a future Rising was to address the real abuses that the Paderbornians had complained of. Not everything, understand. They thought they could file and trim around the edges, what they called *fairezdroga*. So there was a . . ."

"Coup d'état."

"Yah. They made a sweep of the Old Guard: forced some

into retirement, imprisoned others, encouraged the remainder to a life of sloth and indolence, and cut deals with those they thought they could deal with. Of course, what the Committee learned was that if you cut and trim around the edges to save what you can, you will trim too much for the Old Guard and not enough for the Reformers."

The Fudir knew astonishment. *"And no one knew this was happening?"*

"Which part of *Secret* City is unclear? I chose the Revolution to expunge the Names entirely. Now I find that I have been fighting the Committee at the behest of the Old Guard."

"Wait! The Revolution is supporting the Old Guard?"

"Why? Is that unprecedented? Gidula has targeted the Committee—and the abdicators among the Old Guard. The abdicators fall first—and this will convince the Protectors that the loyalists have broken the Concord, and may induce them to attack the Committee themselves. Think what a propaganda coup it will be when Gidula reveals that Padaborn himself fought to restore the Old Guard, especially if Padaborn is too dead to deny it."

"Why is Gidula doing this?" said Donovan. "He told me the tapestry must be repaired, not destroyed."

Domino Tight shrugged. "Gidula told many different people many different things. Some of them may have been true. Some of them may have been what Gidula wanted to be true. My special friend does not know."

"Then confusion may be precisely what Gidula is counting on! The Old One has goals of his own and whether the Names fall or rise are small matters to him, so long as there is confusion. This will not stay within bounds; this is not another of your pasdarms. If your special friend has Méarana in her Residence, that puts her in a potential kill space . . . How long before the Hounds arrive?"

Domino Tight looked away. "As soon as we were in her Residence, Tina Zhi dispatched a thermal bomb to the apartment. She had seen Hounds, and acted reflexively before I could brief her. I do not know if any survived."

"How long before the Hounds arrive?" the Fudir insisted.

"If they have a fast ship . . . They would be no more than a day and a half behind Gidula, so . . . by morning. Do you think they will come for you?"

"No. But they'll come for Méarana. Now, I've left the messages for Pyati to find. You can call your lady friend by name the second time. Yes, I figured that part out. I need to disappear from here and I need to rescue Méarana from there, and what better way than that your friend should take me from here to there. Then we need to reach the Offices, clandestinely. We'll be safe there. For a while."

"One thing more." Domino Tight unfastened his locator from his belt and flung it far out across the river. He followed it with Donovan's own. "Being the only person to share a secret with Gidula makes my shoulder blades itch." And then he called upon Tina Zhi.

Pyati wept uncontrollably when he and his team returned to the assembly point. He fell to his knees and beat his chest alternately with each fist while tears streamed down his cheeks. Padaborn's other magpies keened antiphonally. The others found them in this state when they returned two by two.

"Silence, fools!" Gidula hissed. "Sound may echo from this tube as from a trumpet . . ."

"Sir," said Pyati, "our Shadow is perished. Would you the traditional mourning deny us?"

"Perished!" Gidula said. His countenance expressed shock. "How?" The others began to mutter. Manlius said, "Ill omen." Dawshoo looked stunned, "Are we discovered?" Oschous said nothing but watched Gidula carefully. Big Jacques looked into the dark recesses of the tunnel with his lamp, "Where is Domino Tight?"

Gidula gestured them all to silence. "No, Dawshoo, we are not discovered. Or we won't be if we keep our voices down. One Padaborn! How do you know your master is perished?"

Pyati wiped his nose on his sleeve and picked up a roll of cloth and a note screen. He thumbed the note screen and handed it over to the Old One. Eglay Portion peered over one shoulder, Oschous Dee peered over the other. "Lord Domino left this," the magpie said. "He explains how to mislead a Protector patrol Padaborn into the river dove—and drowned. Lord Domino, having failed his charge, committed *spookoo*. He too into the river consigned himself. Oh, if only we had by our master's side remained!" He and his companions began to weep again but, acknowledging earlier advice, shed more quiet tears.

Gidula read the apologia that Domino Tight had left and, when he finished, Oschous took it from him, and it gradually made the rounds of the gathered Shadows.

"I don't like this," Manlius Metataxis said. "Maybe we should fold the play."

Gidula's head whipped round. "No! We have come too far to hesitate now. This chance will not come to us again. We can end this war. We can end it tonight. We can . . ." And he paused for a moment and worked his throat in sorrow. ". . . we can avenge Geshler Padaborn."

"Padaborn!" said Oschous in a hoarse whisper, and a sykes-knife six thumbs long sang from its scabbard.

"Padaborn!" echoed Eglay Portion, matching the gesture. It was well-known that the ancient sykes-knife was never to be used with any thought of mercy in a fight.

Soon enough, a steel forest waved in the air, and whispered

cries of, "Padaborn!" lifted from every pair of lips. Gidula smiled and joined them. Not that they expected an old man like him to participate in the personal mayhem the knife implied. But ever the traditionalist, he added, "Deadly Ones! To the blood, and to the bone!"

Eglay Portion, whose own magpies had been left to stand watch aboard Gidula's slider, volunteered as brevet section leader over Section Padaborn. Then, after the others had dispersed on their assignments, he held a hand out to Pyati. "Let's see it."

Pyati, instantly dry eyed, unrolled the cloth on the floor of the tunnel and found wrapped in it: an ankle bangle, the inner mechanism of a comm. link, three smooth river pebbles, fourteen seeds of some plant, and a green ribbon. Pyati studied the array with pursed lips and said, "Good news. But not entirely clear."

Eglay squatted with them. "What is it?"

"It is what Terrans call 'ñēymōlai' or 'message of objects.' A code Terrans use. He signaled us beforehand that two messages would be left: one public, one private."

"I caught that. But . . . What does it mean?"

Pyati shook his head. "Ñēymōlai are not easily read, but a bangle always means a Terran, and you can see it is whole."

Eglay nodded. "Yes, and . . . ?"

"Well, sir. How many Terrans are in the play? Only one, and this says he is whole."

Eglay Portion sank back on his heels, and his breath hissed out. "I . . . see. Clever. But the objects cannot have fixed meanings. Too much would depend on what objects were available."

"Right, sir. Terrans always have bangles on them, but context changes meaning."

Eglay deduced that since the objects had been jumbled together in the cloth their order did not matter. "What means this board?" He picked up the guts of the communicator and turned it around in his fingers. No enlightenment came. "And the pebbles?"

"Repetition of an object," said Number Two, "strips particular meanings and makes it a mere tally."

"So. Three stones and fourteen seeds are but three and fourteen?"

Number Three picked up the ribbon. "He told us on a field exercise that the Colors of Old Earth had various meanings. In the Red–Yellow–Green scheme, Red means 'stand, stop, hold fast,' or suchlike instruction. Yellow is 'take care, proceed with caution.' Green—"

Eglay Portion finished the leap. "Green means 'go, come, proceed.'"

"You have it, sir." Pyati examined the green ribbon. "He wishes us go somewhere. Proceed to . . . where?"

Number Three said, "Why, to three-fourteen, surely! Is that a code for one of our target sites?"

Eglay shook his head. "And neither is fourteen-three. And why *stones* and *seeds*?"

Pyati said, "Told you, sir. Repetition—"

Number Five cried, "I know!" He had been pacing while the others debated. Now he stood framed in the entance to the tunnel. "Look out there."

Eglay Portion and the other magpies joined him and looked out on the moonlit river. The Major Moon was high overhead now, and the Minor Moon was closing the distance. "What?"

Number Five shook the stalk of a plant, and seeds like those Padaborn had used sprinkled the floor of the tunnel. "There is a line of these plants from here to the river. Now look at the river's edge. The stones run along the edge. So . . ."

"North-south," said Eglay Portion, "versus east-west. The map grid."

They returned to their place and opened the grid on Eglay's tablet. It was populated now with a nearly complete network of tunnels beneath the surface map. "Third grid from the north." Eglay turned to Pyati. "Because the river runs north to south. And . . . fourteen grids from the river. That puts our goal . . . Right there!"

The blue-and-greens overhung the map like so many boughs. Pyati said, "Many buildings there, sir. Which one? We won't get but one chance."

"Office district . . . ," said Eglay. "Only skeletoned at night. The Mayshot Bo . . . The Gayshot Bo . . . That's one thing we'll change when we rectify the regime. No more dilettante government . . . Hai!" He turned and picked up the circuit of the comm. unit. "The Gayshot Bo. The Ministry of Technology. He wants us there tonight."

They stood and Pyati shook the cloth, scattering the objects; but the bangle he put in his left calf-pocket. "One," said Eglay Portion. And the man turned to him with an inquiry on his features. "Padaborn placed much trust in you, and it was not mislaid."

"Thank you, Lord Eglay. I wondered at the time why he drilled us so on these object-messages. He *knew*. Oh, he thought many layers deep. He put some trust too in you, sir."

"In me!" That startled Eglay Portion. "I was ready to maim him in what was supposed to be a fair fight at the Iron Bridge."

"*Nishywah*. I know only what he told me. May he not have mislaid that trust."

Eglay looked into the faces that surrounded him and saw that their loyalties were beyond question. How many others teetered on the brink? He suddenly realized that, had he wanted,

Gesh could have assumed control of the Revolution itself. "Do you have an extra brassard?"

Pyati nodded to Two, who pulled a blue-and-green armband from his scrip. Eglay Portion removed Gidula's comet and replaced it with his own rose-on-tan. He fastened the Padaborn colors just below them but wound the one through the other, there being no time for a proper cantoning. When he had finished, he bobbed his head at the others and without another word set off at the trot down the tunnels that led toward the Gayshot Bo. The others followed, their feet falling in silent unison.

Zanzibar Paff had once been an important man. He had been the Bountiful Name. But the burdens of supply and distribution had proven irksome. He had preferred *being* important to *doing* anything important. More and more of it he had delegated to assistants and minions, until one day the upstarts—he could never bring himself to call them by their own self-important name—had suggested that he delegate the Name along with the duties.

He preferred to roll with the punch and make the best of the deal. And so the Bountiful Name had become the Contemplative Name, a comfortable fig leaf. (He could not possibly become Nameless!) He had moved into a smaller Residence with a smaller staff, hard by the White Gate, perhaps the better to contemplate matters, and bided his time. He saw how others in his situation bided insufficient time and, like quick-burgeoning weeds, were mown down when they sprouted too soon. When his old colleagues fomented the Shadow War, he was content to watch from the sidelines. Time enough to join the winning side when once that side became clear.

The Contemplative Name resumed his contemplation of

his bedmates. Three chubby sheep personally selected from his Estate, cheeks red from repeated usage. The man lay now in exhausted slumber, but the two women were still ready. They had learned early that they had better be. The Contemplative Name took a tablet from the salver by the bedside and swallowed it down with Atwah Spring Water. "Wait for it, darlings," he told the two women, and they giggled most dutifully.

The bed was spacious; the room, elegantly furnished. The moiré-weave carpet was from Onxylon near the Makrass Marsh; two of the paintings were originals by Bayard from the Old Bhaitry Renaissance.

In the middle of his penetrations, he felt a prod in the back, and he rolled off his sweet cushion to condemn to death whichever minion had dared interrupt him.

But it was a horrid dwarf of a man dressed in a Shadow's shenmat. *Someone's clown?* But Zanzibar Paff's mind was befuddled by his brain's ecstasy, and he had no opportunity to speak, for a dart pierced his neck and he lost all feeling.

Little Jacques hushed the two women with a finger to his lips. They crawled aside and huddled together, and he knelt beside Zanzibar Paff and whispered in his ear, "This is the price you pay for neglecting your duties and the traditions of your offices. Blink twice if you understand."

The eyes stared back at him full of hatred, but they did not blink. So Little Jacques shrugged and with a swipe of his sykes-knife opened the man's throat from jaw to jaw and let his life drain across the furrows of the satin sheets onto the fabulous Onxylon carpet.

One of the women began to cry, so Little Jacques shot her in the mouth. The pop awakened the man, and he too opened his mouth to cry out in surprise. He was close enough at hand for the sykes-knife. And that left one.

The second woman had raised no alarum. She closed her

eyes and whispered, "Please . . ." Then, open eyed, "Please, what will the Protectors do if they find me alive and him dead?"

Little Jacques understood and made the mercy shot a quick kill. Then he pulled his comm. and used the clicker feature to transmit the code: "Sixteen." That meant himself. "Target-one moved; three collateral." He checked his to-do list to see who was next, left an incendiary device on timer, and slipped quietly out of Zanzibar Paff's pleasure room.

Alexander Gomes-Park had once been called the Industrious Name. Now, he was simply Gomes-Park once more and his once-trusted underling bore the title. *I do the work,* the man had pointed out the day of the coup, *why not bear the Name?*

Such impertinence might have earned him the same re-ward as it had two of his predecessors, whose stains had never been fully expunged from the marble flooring. But he had not come alone to the office to make his observation. A half dozen of the abominable Committee had accompanied him. Outside the door, Protectors held Protectors at gunpoint while the suc-cession was debated.

Gomes-Park had already heard rumor of the disappearances of Names insufficiently attuned to the Tides of History, and he had no desire to float off with that tide. So he had instead re-moved his medallions and placed them cheerfully around his underling's neck. *The joy in your throat today,* he had murmured, *will one day choke you.*

In any case, managing industrial performance on a thou-sand worlds was beyond any man's ken. Quotas would never be met, no matter how many storm-workers were sent, no matter how many medals and awards celebrated achievements, no matter how many managers were disciplined. All that hap-pened was that books were cooked and awards became as meaningful as the output figures they celebrated. He had learned that the best results came from doing nothing and cutting his pattern to match the cloth. Since doing nothing better suited his temperament, it was easier to postdate the plans and secure success *post facto*.

Industrial output had actually improved, but what did that matter when it was not seen to improve by *his* efforts?

Still, he had enjoyed retirement, which he spent in martial exercise and in oil painting. He was enjoying the perfumes of evening in his rose garden and adding tinctures of colored oils to the pattern he had created on the still surface of his water basin when the ground gave way behind and to his left and a Shadow and two magpies emerged from the hole.

There was a moment of surprise on all parts. But though he had been out of office these past years, Gomes-Park sensed immediately that this was no social call, and whipped with his left hand the metal stylus that he used for finely adjusting the oiled shapes. It pierced the throat of the first magpie, severing the left carotid artery. The remaining two broke to either side of the narrow garden.

Gomes-Park never depended solely on his Protectors. He pulled a flechette gun from his purse and fired a pattern into the darkness where one of the shapes had fled. One moment was sufficient to put the dog-whistle to his lips, a second moment to blow it, but he really needed three and was not granted them.

A spinning star ripped into his left temporal lobe, immobilizing him long enough for the mercy blow, which was delivered with professional competence.

Big Jacques clicked "Eleven" on his comm., then added, "Target-Three moved. Less Magpie Four." The target should not have been up and about at this hour, least of all dallying in the rose garden. A restless night perhaps. The Protectors would be here in a moment, so he hefted the incendiary packet and whicked it high above to land on the roof of the Residence. Then he whispered the wounded Number Seven to him and they retreated to the tunnels. On the way, he paused to admire the colored oils the target had been scribing—because with a squad of Protectors on its way it was a ballsy thing to do. He almost wished the old man had had time to finish it.

He pulled the brassard from Four's arm in passing, and set an explosive charge in the rubble where they had broken through from the tunnels. Damn bad luck. Now the Protectors would learn of the tunnels, though the pocket-bomb might delay matters for a time.

Hayzoos Peter, the Powerful Name, was on his link. "Yes," he said as his striker dressed him, "I can see the fires from my window. All are in the Residences. Do you know which . . . ?" He paused, listened, nodded. "All but two are Old Guard . . . ? Wonderful. The Protectors will think we are breaking the Treaty of Comity. It isn't any of our people who . . . ?" He listened some more. It was because he was good at listening that he had been able to assemble the Names Renewed, remove the decadent Old Guard, and reinvigorate the Confederation. It just takes a while. It takes a while. Steering the CCW was like turning the great pleasure vessel *Gung Höng Hoy*. For a long time, the reef would continue dead ahead.

A Protector opened the door to admit another Protector, a *söng'aa* by rank. The latter was clad in battle dress rather than the ceremonials worn by the door wardens. Not exactly a Shadow, not exactly a boot, but partaking somewhat of the nature of both, the Protector's countenance revealed nothing behind his goggles and comm. mandible. "Sir," he said without preamble, "Shadows on the rooftops, and in the alleyways. All through the Residences."

"Ours or theirs? Chestli," the Powerful Name said to an aide, "warble Prime over at the Abattoir. Find out if Sèanmazy and her people have gone rogue. And let's move away from the terraces and windows, shall we?"

The civilian group moved toward the suite's door.

"Shall I order the bolt tanks warmed up, sir?" asked the *söng'aa.*

"Not yet. I remember the shambles my illustrious and ever-mourned predecessor made of the Official Quarter during Padaborn's Rising." The Committee had kept the man as a sop to the Old Guard, but he had never stopped scheming, and Hayzoos had finally tired of the charade. "If these are Shadows run amok, we may still be able to contain it. *Söng'aa,* are there reports from elsewhere in the city?"

"One stray report, sir, from the Office Quarter, near the Gayshot Bo. Possible Shadows. No confirmation; also no fires or explosions in that quarter. Sir, this was never supposed to touch the boots or the Protectors, let alone the Names."

Hayzoos had warned his brothers and sisters on both sides of the Discontentment to take no hand in the Shadow War, and he himself had worked carefully to maintain neutrality, awkening too late to the awful truth that the entire affair had been instigated by the Old Guard. *It is the habit of power that the fist clenches tighter in rigor mortis.* "Matters do have a way of getting out of hand." If Ngaumin Heer, the Second Name, was behind this, there would be hell to pay. It had been a *wojök,* a peace gesture, to allow her the second office, a sign that the Committee of Names Renewed was merely furthering the will of an Old Guard now honorably retired. Everyone had agreed to believe that.

Though evidentally not everyone. Acceptance-now had been traded for resistance-later. And "later" was "now."

But the initial targets had been Old Guard—and that made no sense.

Hayzoos was fully dressed and armed now, and he pulled his cordon in from the perimeter of the bedchamber. "Quickly now to Central Office," he said. And the *söng'aa* told the other Protectors, "Exit in formation seven."

They opened the door to find one of the door wardens on the floor, his ceremonial uniform chopped to rags by flechettes, and the second warden in a crouch aiming his gun at the official party. Behind him were five magpies in black-and-white diagonal stripes. All of them poured withering fire into the party of the Powerful Name. The *söng'aa* died first, throwing himself in front of his master, and the other Protectors, caught like a cork in a bottle, lacking room for maneuver, were cut down, one by one. The Office minions fell like wheat before a scythe.

Three of the attacking magpies died in the counterfire, for surprise was no longer theirs, and Dawshoo Yishohrann was himself badly wounded. The traitorous door-warden left no more memory than a greasy spot on the marble floor.

Afterward, Dawshoo spoke through clenched jaw over his link. "Four. Collateral only. Target-Six prepared, escaped. Three magpies moved. Awareness spreading; resistance stiffening." The link encoded and squirted the message. Good work, indeed. Dawshoo himself had moved five targets already. Three in their sleep, two in flight. This had been the first return-fire. He hoped that Oschous had not run into similar resistance. The link vibrated and he looked at the query. It was from Oschous. "No," he answered. "I don't know how he escaped. He was in my sights, then he was just . . . gone."

Like at the warehouse, Oschous messaged; but Dawshoo had not been at the warehouse.

The one regret of Paul Feeley, the Radiant Name, was that his aim had not been better when he had intervened on Yuts'ga. But Jimjim Shot had been hurt, her beauty disfigured, and how could anyone so disfigured head up the Ministry of Arts? His sister's mutilation had wrenched him for a moment, and had thrown his game off just a bit, or the whole nonsense might have been ended right there. And if only that *oaf,* Ari Zin, had not intervened so bombastically, only to discover that in war people got hurt! Boo-hoo. Paul had heard later that Padaborn had intervened on the reactionaries' side. *Padaborn!* Had they not settled his case a score of years ago? Or had he truly been in hiding these last twenty-odd years? Hiding where? But if Padaborn fought at all, he ought to have raised arms in support of the Committee! *If even Padaborn has turned against us . . .*

The view from the rooftop of his Residence provided Paul with a panorama of the Secret City. Seventeen Residences were, by his count, already burning and one had collapsed already into glowing ruins. Commotion roiled the streets. Milling sheep, servants and merchants, cadenced Protectors at the double-quick, cries of anguish, shouts of confused ignorance. Silver ribbons cast by the two-moon night shimmered in pools and ponds. Shadows and magpies glided sylphlike through the turmoil. The Red Gate groaned open and a squadron of bolt tanks rolled into the Secret City from the cantonment, and the Radiant Name could see that the disorder had spread on the wings of rumor into San Jösing itself. Or at least, into the Old Town. The sheep pens on the east side of the Pearl were showing lights but no evidence yet of disorder.

By his estimate, the first Residences attacked had been Old Guard, but the assassinations had spread to the Committee now. The Powerful Name had barely escaped, and had named the malcontent Dawshoo Yishohrann as leading his attackers. Word was that Sèanmazy's loyalists had attacked the Old Names for some mad reason—though Sèanmazy was denying this—and now the reactionaries' dogs had responded by attacking the Committee. In either case, dogs must learn not to bite the feeding hand. Both Shadow-factions must be supressed.

"It might be one faction," suggested his captain-Protector when the Radiant Name had voiced his thoughts, "sowing dragons' teeth on both sides of the furrow." Protectors lined the rooftop, guarded the drop-wells, watched the skies, the Residence walls. Who knew from which direction attack would come? Their mouths set in grim, worried lines. *What,* wondered Paul Feeley, *did they suppose they were paid for?*

The first attacks had been stealthy, and word had not spread until dozens had already lain in their own gore. Now the attacks were more open, the targets better prepared. He wondered if the spectacular firebombs were not themselves a form of distraction. Who was clever enough to pull off the Play of the Dragon's Teeth? Gidula? But the Old One was neutral so far as anyone knew, dreaming his mad dreams of a past that would never come again.

"Slinger!" cried the Protector at the monitor station.

Everyone dropped prone except the Radiant Name, who stood gloriously erect in his sparkle armor. It was important to put on a proud show. The slinger, a rigid wire missile, slid off the armor's field and pierced the side of the nearest drop-well.

"Sir," said the captain-Protector. "We should evacuate the rooftop. We are too exposed."

"Nonsense." He did not consider his Protectors' lack of sparkle armor, nor the fact that they could not winkle out at a moment's notice with a quondam leap. Perhaps he should have, for they surely did.

The captain-Protector clicked over the company link to evacuate the rooftop. Then he pulled an incendiary pack from his belt and punched it active. And then, because to turn on his Protected was the most wretched violation of a Protector's oath imaginable, he embraced the Radiant Name.

Paul Feeley knew instantly what the man had done and winkled out; but the captain and—more crucially—the incendiary pack held between them winkled with him. The packet ignited as the pair reemerged from uncertainty into the Residence's Safe Room. The captain-Protector dissipated in a plasma burst. The sparkle armor protected the Radiant Name from the blast, although the compression wave mashed him severely; but the heat, confined within the Safe Room, melted him inside the twinkling energy field. He retained human shape for a time, but only until the field collapsed.

Ari Zin was prepared, and he dispatched with his own dazer the first Shadow to slip into the command center in the Residence. He did not ask how the man had entered. That was for his Protectors to ascertain. He had meanwhile to direct the counterattack. The screen pricked off on a map the Residences and other locations where Names had been attacked. The processors sifted the mode of assassination, the faction of the victim, the location, and the time sequence in hope of conjuring a pattern that made sense of it all, and from which to plan the counterstroke.

The door signaled and the warden checked the monitor. "It's a Shadow," he announced. "Black, a taiji."

"Sèanmazy," muttered the Martial Name. Her faction supposedly supported the Committee. "Admit her, but stay wary."

The Long Tall One strode in with her cape and singular walking stick. She glanced at the War Board and took it in, considered the body of the Shadow in the corner. "Ah. Egg

Mennerhem," she said. "He has for several weeks been in Ne-
ngin City lurking. We were curious for what purpose. We tink
dere are reserves following after da initial infiltration. This one
was not of da first water."

Or you would not have slain him was the unspoken subtext.
"How did they . . ."

"Dere are abandoned tunnels under dis city, from da old
days. Da rebels have been using dem to scurry under our feet.
You search your subbasements, Martial Name, and you find da
loose vent or floor tiles dat da rats wriggle up." The Shadow
gripped her stick with both hands and leaned her cheek against
it. "But tell me dis what I have heard from lips dat were soon
deceased. Was dis war but a shadow cast upon da wall of da
cave by da fires of your enmities? To what exactly have we
been loyal all dese long years?"

"To the Confederation," said Ari Zin without hesitation.

A toothy smile split the Shadow's face. "Now dis is a strange
ting," she said. "I have dis question asked tonight of several
Names, and your answer, I judge, is da first honestly given."
She nodded to the body of Egg Mennerhem. "You plug dose
holes in your basement, Ari Zin, for I tink the Confederation
will have need of you when dawn breaks." Then she turned
and strode to the door. Ari Zin called after her.

"Sèanmazy!"

The Long Tall One cocked her head in question but did
not speak.

"If the Old Guard had stayed in power, you would be
fighting for them, wouldn't you?"

A grin split her black face. "Of course!" Then she swept
out of the command room, her cloak billowing behind her.
Her long staff rapped twice on the floor and a dozen magpies
seemed to appear from nowhere and followed her out.

The captain-Protector closed and sealed the door once

more. "She scares me," he admitted to the Martial Name. "I'm glad she's on our side."

Or that we're on hers, Ari Zin thought.

The Abattoir was dark and empty, its recesses barely visible even in night vision. A red glow from the fires outside eased through the slit windows, casting uneven and capering shadows on the Cöng Sung, the great long wall with memorials to Shadows past. Manlius Metataxis slipped though the darkness, becoming one with it. He was down to a single magpie now, and he had left her in the Rose Garden to ward the entrance.

There was fell work this evening, but Manlius did not think that many of those involved would be mounted on the Wall. He came to the end of the Wall and passed through the portal to the proving ground, the place of blood and sand. For a moment he could hear the roar of the candidates in the surrounding grandstands, see the examinees struggling with the obstacles that emerged from floor, ceiling, sidelines, while Prime—or perhaps Dawshoo or Ekadrina—sat in the Judgment Seat and passed or failed the candidates. And afterward, for those who passed, the parties, the laughter, the numbing liquors and smokes. *We were all one, then,* he thought.

He glanced above, where a thousand banners hung listless in the unstirred air. Even in the dark, he could make out some of them, and sought out his own: sky-blue, a dove. But it was too dim and the light of the burning city played strange games with the colors.

Some, he saw, had fallen. The sight took him aback. A banner was cut down only when its Shadow died. He picked one up and saw that it was Egg Mennerhem. Another, it shocked him to notice, was the red swallowtail pennant of Little Jacques. There were a dozen or so, some loyalist, some rebel, rumpled on the ground. Someone, it seemed, was keeping score.

The black silk banner of Prime lay beneath the Judgment Seat, and when he looked up Manlius saw Prime himself sitting in the Seat, as if ruling on all that transpired this night. He flinched under that stern disapproval.

But Prime's gaze was too far and too fixed and looked now upon another world. Perhaps he had grown too melancholy as he cut down banner after banner, as word came to him that his children slaughtered his children. Perhaps he had willed his heart to stop.

The building shook slightly as somewhere outside a bolt tank fired. Just like boots, he thought with contempt, to use an ax when a scalpel was wanted. He did not think Dawshoo had counted on this, or at least not this soon. The click–link had gone down, and he knew not the current status of the struggle. *Who is winning?* Big Jacques had clicked just before. It was hard to imagine the Large One as frantic, or to read that into a series of click codes. *Who is winning?* Manlius looked around the floor, at the crumpled banners. *No one,* he thought.

Time to withdraw, maybe. He heard the rush of a ground-support craft outside. A window rattled. Yes, time to withdraw. Find a nice quiet planet somewhere. Just one last errand.

"You old fool," he scolded the corpse of Shadow Prime. It was the duty of the Lion's Mouth to stay loyal, the old man had said. But loyal to whom? To the self-appointed Committee of Names Renewed? Or to the truly anointed Names? "Old fool," he said again, and he heard the whisper of his own words and knew the world had come to an end. He had called his father a fool. He paused one moment more to savor the pang of sorrow at memories forever lost, at brotherhood irreparably broken; then he cantered on cat's feet up the maintenance ladder of the drop-well into the transient apartments.

He found Epri Gunjinshow in the apartment of Kelly Stapellaufer, as he had known all along he would. An hour's wait
in a closet was the only cost to his revenge. He watched them
through the crack in the door. Somehow, all the fire had gone
out of the hate and it had become just another wearisome task
to finish before he could quit for the day. He was simply tired
of eating erect. Seeing her drawn and haggard face, he wondered that he had ever found Stapellaufer attractive and thought
that he had clung to her only because the skalds would expect
him to.

He knew that in a sense this woman and he and Epri had
been the proximate cause of the conflagration now raging outside. He was not so foolish as to believe they had been the real
cause, and he was not so foolish as to suppose this would somehow set everything right.

That both Epri and Kelly bore burns and scars pleased him
in some indefinable fashion. He would have detested the thought
that they had ridden out the turmoil here in her bower, the one
thrusting repeatedly between the thighs of the other. But they
had retreated here, perhaps to rest and clean up before returning to their fates.

But their proper fate was not to die anonymously in the
confusion of the Secret City. The troubadours would not like
that. The Beautiful Life demanded that Epri Gunjinshow die
in singular combat with Manlius Metataxis while Kelly Stapellaufer looked on with coupled sorrow and love. Life must be
corralled and tamed to the strictures of drama. And so he
waited in the darkened closet until they had disarmed and
were half-undressed, when they were at the awkward state in
which swift action is difficult. Perhaps they did have some
thrusting in mind. Then he stepped forward and shoved the
door closed.

"Prime!" shouted Epri, then saw his mistake, though he did not yet realize that it was the penultimate mistake of his life. "Ah." And his eyes instantly inventoried the weaponry within his reach.

But Kelly Stapellaufer stepped between the two men. She held both hands clenched into fists. "Stop!" she said.

"I mean to end it," said Manlius. Then, to Epri, he said, "Prime is dead. He killed himself." He didn't know why he told Epri that, only that he thought Epri should know.

"And so you have destroyed the Lion's Mouth rather than submit to the ruling of the Courts d'Umbrae?" Epri demanded.

He made it sound like Manlius was in the wrong. Manlius shook his head. "None of it matters anymore."

Epri stepped behind Kelly and laid both hands on her shoulders. This would prove the last mistake of his life. Manlius wondered if Epri thought he would not shoot him through Kelly's body. And then Manlius wondered if he could actually bear to do so.

"Did you ever ask yourself, Epri Gunjinshow," Kelly asked without turning, "whether I welcomed your attentions?" And with that she thrust backward with her right fist.

In her fist she had held the hilt of a variable knife. The blade snapped out and pierced Epri's abdomen. The shock froze him and she stepped to the side, ripping horizontally, then down. His body opened up and his bowels dumped forth onto the floor. Epri lived long enough to contemplate this sight before he collapsed atop it.

Manlius Metataxis watched in astonishment and not a little gratification. So, Kelly had loved him all along. She opened her arms and Manlius stepped into her embrace.

"Or yours," she murmured, and Manlius learned that the hilt had two extensions. Kelly Stapellaufer thrust forward and the second blade launched itself into his body. The pain messages had not even time to reach his brain before his mind shut down.

Kelly Stapellaufer, whose charms had pretexted the Shadow War, stood naked between the two corpses that had once been her lovers. "Oh, the Abattoir!" she cried. "Oh, the Lion's Mouth!"

There was only one other target left in the room, and so Kelly used her knife one final time.

XIV. THREE, WITH A NEW SONG'S MEASURE

In desperate grapple the sides contend.
Ambush and sudden death unleashed:
Friends turned foul, the hidden fist descends,
The goblet tinctured, the knife unsheathed.
The long night creeps now toward the dawn
Midst riot, betrayal, and siege.
While death that now her leash lies loose
Runs wild and knows no liege.

They kept the lights low lest attention be drawn to the Official Quarter, and through the windows of the Gayshot Bo watched the Secret City burn. The flames rolled across the skyline like the waves of a molten ocean and provided the only light from the now otherwise darkened Residencies. Suppressor drones hovered in the air, bright yellow, blinkers flashing, drenching the hopeless structures with foam and water. By strange and tacit agreement, no one had targeted the fire wardens, whether from residual respect for civic order or because the wardens' activities were futile in any case.

"We should be out there fighting with the others," said Magpie Three Padaborn.

"It's what we trained for," Four explained.

Domino Tight had been sitting at table with Eglay Portion pursuing a desultory game of Aches and Pains on a play deck. The room was a sort of conference lounge, with tables, chairs, racks of reference media, a holostage. In the corner, well away from the windows, Méarana sat with curled fingers playing imaginary harp strings, conjuring a grand goltraí from the depths of her being. She had always thought the Confederation irremediably evil; but there was ever a yin within the yang, and the tears on magpie cheeks were genuine.

"We never trained for *this*," Domino Tight said, by which he meant *that*, the chaos outside the window.

Eglay Portion pressed a button on his game console. "Aches!" he declared. Then, to Domino Tight, "Of course we did. Treachery and betrayal were our stock-in-trade."

"No. I don't mean . . . on the job. I mean against one another. Guard your Keep."

Eglay Portion grunted and bent over the holodisplay. Some pieces were immobile once placed; others moved to various rules. The rules could change. He studied his options.

"There goes another one," said Three.

A heretofore-darkened portion of the skyline lit up from the flash of a bolt tank. Domino Tight sighed. "That was Tina Zhi's Residence."

At that, the Technical Name appeared from a bright spark in the center of the room, her milky skin smoke smudged, her arms bundled with small objects that she tumbled onto an empty table, where they clattered and rolled. Méarana imagined a single sharp pluck on the highest string. The Name took short, gasping breaths. "But Gidula assured me . . ."

"Gidula assured many people of many things," Donovan said. "But what he assures and what he can actually deliver are two different things. He bridled the tiger; now he must ride it. What did you learn out there?"

Tina Zhi ran a hand through her hair, leaving a streak of soot in its silver. "This is all I saved." She spoke as if to the scattered bric-a-brac on the table. "This is all." Then, to Donovan she said, "The boots are in it now. The district swoswai has overruled the Lord Protector and ordered all Protectors into the military cadre. Obdurate Protectors have been fired upon, and some have joined the Shadows." She shook her head, her whole body. "Rumor claims that Ekadrina and Oschous have combined against Dawshoo and Gidula."

"I knew the Fox would catch on sooner or later," Donovan said.

"The fight proceeds at right angles," Tina Zhi reported. "Loyalist and rebel fight rebel and loyalist."

"Apparently, neither side much liked being manipulated," the harper suggested.

The Name turned on her and for a moment the old terror blazed in her eyes, so that they seemed almost violet. But she could not maintain the fury, and sat heavily in a nearby chair.

Eglay Portion shook his head. "What price rebellion? What worth loyalty? It has reached the point of unreason. They fight because they have been fighting."

"We really ought to do something," insisted Three.

"What would you suggest?" asked Donovan, ostentatiously counting the room. Himself, a Name, two Shadows, five magpies, and a harper.

"I might play a suantraí and put them all to sleep," said Méarana when his finger came to her.

Donovan grunted and turned back to the window, "When morning breaks, the world might be glad that there were those who stayed out of it."

"I don't know," said Three. "My knife longs for a throat. What will I say when my apprentices ask what I did in the Great Rising? 'I sat in a lounge and played Aches and Pains with Domino Tight.'"

"And lost," said Domino Tight, placing a new Keep on a key locus. "What makes you think there will be apprentices? The Order is finished. The walls of the Lion's Mouth are breached."

The Fudir turned to Three. "Whose throat?"

Three waved his arm across the window view. "Whoever was responsible for *this!*"

"Why, then, that would be Gidula; and there is this one thing you must know about Gidula. If you don't go to him, then somehow he will come to you. This night's battle has not yet begun."

Pyati looked up in surprise. "You can't mean *that*—" And he encompassed all that transpired outside the Official Quarter. "—is no more than a diversion!"

Magpie Two was monitoring the building's security. "Motion on the roof," he announced. "Wait one. False positive. No further signal."

Donovan tossed his head, and Number Four left the room so silently that Méarana had to check to make sure he was gone.

"I don't understand," said Domino Tight, "why the Names have not winkled to other worlds."

"With what guarantee?" asked Méarana. "The Old Home-Stars may be as happy with Dao Chetty's fall as they once were with Terra's. Leap for help and this fight may yet spread."

Domino Tight shook his head. "Too many stayed to be killed. It cannot all be for love of death."

The Fudir nodded to Tina Zhi. "Tell them."

"It's Technical. They would not understand."

Méarana, listening from the corner, decided that Tina Zhi did not understand, either. She had learned certain things by rote, nothing more. "You only have a few such devices," the harper guessed, "and you don't know how to make more."

Pyati turned from the window. "I'm afraid," he announced, and clapped his arms around his body. "I cannot explain it. But a deep, unreasoning fear grips me."

Magpie Five nodded. "I feel it, too."

None of the others were brave enough to admit this, but Méarana noted how the Shadows stirred and even Donovan buigh appeared uneasy. She felt it herself: a vague disquiet verging on flight. She shivered and crossed her arms over her shoulders. The air held a cold whiff of peppermint.

She smiled. "Company is coming."

Oh, indeed, it was. Inner Child noticed that some shadows in the darkling steets below were moving. <Deadly Ones,> he told the others.

"Coming *here?*" said the Technical Name. "To assassinate *me?* But I *supported* the Revolution!"

"How would they know you were here," the Fudir asked, "and not in a greasy pall of smoke in the air above your Residence? No. Yon Shadows are not coming for you, but for the Vestiges."

"Well," said the Technical Name in a stern voice, "they cannot have them. The Gayshot Bo regulates their use."

"I don't think they intend to ask your consent."

Three made an exasperated sound. "Four left the hallway door open when he went to check the roof."

But the Pedant knew that Four had done so such thing. He flashed the headcount . . . Still nine. But that meant . . .

The Fudir sighed. "Greystroke, my old friend. How long have you been standing here?"

The ninth man, garbed in a nondescript shenmat, shrugged. "Long enough to know you may be glad to have me. Rinty?"

Little Hugh emerged from a corner of the room. Like Greystroke, he held a teaser, pointing down. Both stood with their backs to solid walls out of respect for Tina Zhi. Even so, every magpie's hand dropped to his weapons belt. But Donovan held his hand out to his side with fingers splayed and they froze. Domino Tight, who alone had made no overt move, took advantage of the pause to move a piece in his game with Eglay Portion. His eyes shifted to Little Hugh. "Is Gwillgi with you?"

The answer came with the man as more Hounds entered the room, spacing themselves. Four was with them—not a prisoner, but not looking very happy, either. Bridget ban entered last of all. She always knew how to make an entrance.

The Fudir grinned at her. "What kept you?"

The Red Hound glanced past him, found Tina Zhi. "We are not here as your enemy. We have come for two things only. My daughter—and a glance at your Vestiges."

"The daughter you may have," said Tina Zhi. "It was not I who needed her. But to look on the Vestiges is not permitted. The sacred is not for the gawping eyes of the profane; and if I will not permit the approaching Shadows to see them, why would I permit the Hounds?"

"Red Hound," said Greystroke, with a nod toward the widow. "This may not be the proper time to quarrel."

Ravn Olafsdottr danced into the room. "Doonoovan, my sweet! How *perfect* to see you once more! How is your heads holding up?" She crossed to the window, peered out from a corner. "Enemy reach Spring Garden Street," she said in Manjrin. "Best prepare welcome. Helloo, Doominoo! I kiss you later." She turned to Bridget ban. "And might I suggest," she added, "we bury hatchets for time being? Time enough afterward, we bury each other."

"Who is coming?" the Hound asked.

"Gidula," said the Fudir, earning Bridget ban's attention at last. "He has been playing factions against one another. Shadow against Shadow, Shadows against Names. He has a mad dream of restoring the ancient aristocracy of the Lion's Mouth."

"Is it so mad as all that?" asked Eglay Portion with a gesture toward the flames. "Better dreams past than nightmares present."

"How many with him?" the Fudir asked Ravn. "Did you get a count?"

"Did I not tale you that we would be great friends soomday? Today is that happy day! We celebrate later. Gidula has three Shadows with him: Big Jacques, who was with the rebels, and Aynia Farer, and Phoythaw Bhatvik, who was Ekadrina's adviser. A score of magpies escort them: comets, tridents, lions, and crows. Oh, and they have a Name."

Donovan looked up. "Which?"

"Secret Name. He who give you bad haircut."

Despite nine resolutions to the contrary, the Fudir's hand went to his scalp. "You recognized him?"

"I recognize his golden masque: the all-concealing Sun. He alone is never seen, even by other Names, so he is recognized by not being recognized." She leaned toward Donovan and added in a stage whisper, "Is why they call him 'Secret'."

Donovan turned to the Technical Name. "Could he leap directly into the building?"

Tina Zhi vanished, startling some of the Hounds. An unlooked-for answer, but the Sleuth understood immediately her purpose.

Meanwhile, Donovan had been revising their defensive strategy. Certain things problematical with nine became more achievable with eighteen. "Can we count on you?" he asked Bridget ban. "They will think the building abandoned. The staff minions have fled out through the Red Gate into the Lower City, and the building's Protectors have been drawn into the fighting. We can take them unaware when they enter."

"Our orders are to avoid involvement."

"Yes, but involvement has not avoided you. To stay out of it, you must withdraw; and if you withdraw, you get no glimpse of the Vestiges."

Bridget ban drew a great breath. "Lackaday. I came for my daughter, an' I'll nae place her in danger for the sake of a few prehuman geegaws and baubles. Come wi' me, Méarana. I'll summon Grimpen down to the rooftop. He is masqued as an Information Ministry skycar. No one has fired upon them yet, but I'll nae wait until they do so. Tilly, Greystroke, we're pulling out."

The other Hounds hesitated. The harper put on her stubborn look. "I came to rescue Father. I'll not run off and leave him."

"The way he ran off and left you on Terra? Show some sense, lassie."

"Listen to your mother," Donovan told her. "It's unlikely all of us will emerge from this fight; less so if the Hounds won't help."

Méarana stuck her chin out. "I'm not inexperienced in a fight," she reminded him.

"This is not a mob of 'Loons or tribesmen from the boonies of Enjrun."

But the harper crossed her arms and sat back in her chair. "Then you come with me."

The silence of the Shadows and magpies filled the room. The Fudir glanced at his followers and shrugged. "I have my own duties." Behind him, Pyati brushed a tear from his cheek.

"Well," said Matilda of the Night. "Come to that, I came for the geegaws, which is how Black Shuck secured our Kennel authorization. So I ought to stay and hazard the chance."

Gwillgi shrugged. "And my posted duty is to observe the Shadow War. This seems as reasonable an observation post as any."

Little Hugh said, "The Fudir an' I, we started out together, on the hunt for January's Dancer. I don't see why we shouldn't end it together."

Greystroke rolled his eyes, said nothing, but did not move toward the door.

"Graceful Bintsaif?" said Bridget ban.

"Aye, Cu?"

"An' I gave the order, would ye be throwin' my thick-headed bairn o'er yer shoulder an' cart her tae the roof?"

"Aye, Cu. If you gave the order."

Bridget ban turned to the door just as Tina Zhi returned, entering in the normal fashion from the hallway. "I have damped the field," the Technical Name said. "Even those with tokens can no longer leap."

"Oh. Well," said Bridget ban, "that makes all the difference in the world."

Eglay and Domino had shut down their game and the Fudir used the play deck to project an image of the kill space. "I've highlighted the Cache, where the Vestiges are kept," he said. "We have to assume that Gidula and the Secret Name know the location, and will go straight there. We don't know which entry they will take—"

"They will take each entry," said Ravn. "They will come as water comes, through every channel."

Donovan studied the building plan, though he and the Sleuth and Inner Child had been considering options ever since the Child had spotted the approaching party. He pointed. "Three, Four, and Five, disable the drop-wells, force them onto the stairs. Plant traps to rake the stairwells, but with the triggers near the top so we catch as many as possible. Greystroke, take Little Hugh, and Matilda. You three are the most accomplished at camouflage. Wait near the main entrance, allow the enemy to pass, then follow behind, picking off stragglers. Matilda, salt the lobby and stairwells with fear. Shadows and Names will not run, but they might advance less boldly."

"What of me?" asked Pyati.

"The enemy will gather at these two points," the Fudir said, "and converge on the Cache from both ends of the building. Eglay, you take the east wing; Pyati, take the west. Domino, you take this choke point, where the main stairs come up. Take one magpie apiece. Pluck some fruit, then withdraw to this line. Draw them in as far as possible before pruning. Once they trigger the stairwell traps, they will know the building is defended and will act accordingly. Keep them complacent as long as you can. Our advantage is that we know their destination."

"Little good will it do them," said the Technical Name. "The Cache is unbreakable."

The Fudir shook his head. "They will not have come all this way under these circumstances without some plan to effect entrance."

"Likely, the Secret Name intended to *leap* into the Cache; but that way is now blocked, thanks to my timely *technical* action."

"Gidula leaves no contingency unplanned. Is there a hidden way into the Cache?"

"If there were," said Tina Zhi, "neither Gidula nor the Secret Name would know of it."

In other words, said the young man in the chlamys, there *is* a hidden way. *Right,* agreed the Sleuth. *If the Cache is sealed and she went in to deactivate the leaping tokens, how did she get out? So:*

If Gidula knows the way, he must have learned of it from one of the College. The Virgins were sworn to secrecy. And two years ago he began to urge the attack on the Secret City and—perhaps, plan the decimation of Names and Shadows alike.

"Gidula kidnapped one of your Virgins about two years ago," Donovan said, "and tortured her into revealing the hidden entrance." Once again, Tina Zhi's body language was louder than her denial.

"We only know that Beata disappeared," she admitted, "not that Gidula was behind it."

Together, Donovan and Bridget ban bent over the holomap of the building.

"This room above the Cache . . . ," the Hound said, pointing.

"A fane," Donovan told her, "dedicated to the Daemon Muse."

"Where the College conducts its private rites," said Tina Zhi. "None else may enter."

Then that is where the hidden entrance is concealed, said the Sleuth.

"And Gidula kept it in his pocket until he could use it," said Bridget ban. "Do you mean he instigated this entire battle as a cover?"

The Fudir nodded. "You have tantalized the other Names," he said to Tina Zhi, "with dribs and drabs: the leaping tokens, the sparkle armor, the accelerated healing. You can understand how a certain cupidity might overcome them. They tire of golden eggs and would have the goose entire."

"Who!" Tina Zhi demanded. "Who else is in it?"

"Beside Gidula and the Secret Name? No one meant to survive this night. People, when you surrender your positions, fall back to here, covering the fane. Five, to the Security Room on the top floor. Keep us apprised of movements within the building. No argument. Your role is vital, and once Gidula realizes we are are tracking him, he will send magpies to search you out. Ravn—"

"I have my oon target, sweet. There is a man who left me to dangle on a cliff when he could have killed me. Such kindness demands reciprocity."

"And you," said Bridget ban to Donovan buigh. "I suppose you will hunt down the Secret Name and take your long revenge."

But Donovan shook his head. "Revenge is for fools. If the past is to have a hold over me, I would prefer it to be the good times and not the bad. Should he and I meet, only one of us will leave, but I'll not seek him out. Let Fate decide whether we encounter each other. Defense of the Cache is foremost. Méarana, the point of least immediate danger is with Five and the system monitors. Stay with him. Bridget—"

"Ochone! 'Tis an ill fork ye hoist me on," the Red Hound said. "I know where my heart tells me to be. I know where my head tells me I must be. Graceful Bintsaif, go with my daughter and Five Padaborn. Her life is your life."

"Aye, Cu."

Donovan completed the dispositions. "Remember: active measures, fluid defense. Find long shots and go for the snipe when you can. Booby a few traps. Plant diversions. Hit and run . . ." He stopped and scanned his small army. "And all the other elementary instructions which none of you need hear." He held a hand out. "To the blood and to the bone," he said. The Shadows and the magpies slapped his hand and departed silently to their posts.

Gwillgi allowed his sharpened teeth to show. "We're your ace, Donovan. They won't know that Hounds are on the scene."

"Act insofar as you hold that secret as long as possible," Donovan told the Hounds. "Just remember: whatever ruthlessness you may think you own, the Shadows own ten times more. Their skills are no greater, but their hesitations are less. And of them all, Gidula is the most treacherous. He smiles."

Greystroke wore coveralls of anycloth. In the lobby, he altered them to resemble a shenmat. Little Hugh watched in dismay. "Ye cannot be serious."

But Greystroke showed his teeth. "Easier to blend into a crowd." He detailed a brassard on his left arm with a symbol hard to discern.

Matilda of the Night joined them. "Stairwells prepared. Put these filters in your noses to block the effects."

Greystroke complied. "You reveal your secrets."

"Don't be a fool. You have no idea what my secrets are. There are four stairwells they can take and only three of us. Let us not all trundle up the same one."

"East wing," said Greystroke.

"East main," said Hugh.

"And I'll follow whichever west-side team needs pruning most."

The three of them were silent for a moment. Then Hugh thrust his hand out. "We'll meet at the fane." The other two, after a moment's hesitation, took it. "Or on the farther shore," said Matilda of the Night before she faded into the darkness.

"She's good," said Greystroke. Then, to Hugh, "We'll make it."

"As long as *she* makes it." He meant Bridget ban.

"It's an awful box he's put her in this time."

"It isn't the Fudir who put her in it, Grey One. Sure, 'tis bad cases all around, but hush now." And Little Hugh too faded into the darkness of the deserted building to wait. He knew as well as Greystroke and Matilda the risks of operating in the enemy's rear.

The power is out, Lord Gidula. No lights. The drop-wells are dead.

The hazards of war, eh, Old One?

It is that, sire. But a darkened building will attract no attention from elsewhere in the city. Stairs and ladders, then. Comets, with me up the left-hand stairs. Tridents, up the right hand. Lions, odd numbers, the stairs at the east end; even numbers up the ladders in the first drop-well. Crows, odd numbers, west end; even numbers, second drop-well. Clear? Go.

Little Hugh emerged from concealment after the intruders had swarmed up. Every plan of battle was complicated by the presence of the other side. He whispered into his throat mike, "Three magpies climbing maintenance ladders in each drop-well." He hoped that Five Padaborn would relay that to whoever needed to know. Otherwise, assets would be inserted behind Domino Tight and Eglay Portion. Then he set off after the ascending tridents. He felt again as he had felt during the guerilla on New Eireann: terribly alive.

Magpie Seven Bhatvik had thought himself third from the rear, but when he glanced over his shoulder on the stairwell he saw no one behind him. This was not a good thing to see, and he shivered a bit with unreasoning fear. He climbed a few more steps, then quickly looked back. He still saw nothing.

Which was too bad.

"Maintain queue discipline," murmured Magpie Three Farer to the shenmat-clad figure who had come up beside him on the stairwell. It was the last thing he said.

Four to Double Crow. Gravity grids reactivated in the drop-wells. Featherlight. We can leap the rest of the way up easy.

Negative, my pretty. Power is intermittent. Do not rely. Repeat: do not rely.

Good call. Gravity is cycling. Getting heavier . . . Lighter now . . . Heavier . . . Six, Ten, vacate, now! Oh, by the Fates!

Report, Four. Report.

Double Crow, this is Ten. Gravity peaked at three ji. Four and Six lost hold of the laddering. They're jam at the bottom. I'm out of the shaft on the third floor. Dislocated shoulder.

Something was wrong. Big Jacques sensed it before he knew it. A quick gesture, propagated down the line of tridents, brought them all to a halt on the stairwell. Malfunctioning gravity grids in a city in chaos he could understand. But the crows and lions were both reporting missing magpies, and he could not imagine that the unoccasioned dread that had gripped them all on entry to this building had impelled them to run. Some of the Names had the means of inducing such trepidation, although the Secret Name had not thought the Technical Name to be one of them.

"Count off," he said, and listened as the numbers ran down the stairs. He did not need One to tell him that the count came up short. Interesting. Every flock but Gidula's was coming up short. Was the Old One trimming his allies already? He had needed an escort-in-strength to cross the burning city. Did he suppose he needed them no longer?

A glimmer in Big Jacques's goggles captured his attention. Something on the wall along the railing. A line of somethings. He recognized pasties—antipersonnel mines—on a wire ignition.

"Down the well!" he ordered his flock. "It's a trap!"

The trident magpies flew down the stairs, rappeling over banisters, trading grace for speed, and a moment later the pasties ignited, sending a sheet of shrapnel across the stairwell. Big

Jacques heard grunts of pain, then, below him, a different sort of cry. Flashes of light and the acrid smell of electrical sparks told of a brief, intense firefight two floors below.

Big Jacques hurried to the scene, found Two down and Five aiming fire systematically into the dark at the bottom of the stairs. "Stalked, Trident," said Five.

"How many?"

"Saw one, but must have been others. Moved Two, Seven, and Twelve."

Big Jacques considered that. "Gidula assured us the building would be unguarded. Either Gidula is an optimist or Sèanmazy followed us here after that tussle on Big Fish Street. Could you read the brassard?"

"No shenmat. Coverall. Protector, maybe? Whoever he was I potted him good. Gone doggo, though. Hunt him down?"

"Let him bleed out." Big Jacques contacted Aynia Farer and Phoythaw Bhatvik and told them the building was being defended, numbers unknown. But he did not contact Gidula, who could figure that out for himself.

The explosions in the east end stairwell took out a goodly number of lions, which evened the odds very nearly to six-to-one. Eglay Portion and Four Padaborn had positioned themselves to cover the exit and waited until three lions were through before opening the dance. The invaders were aware now that they were being opposed and returned fire. Dazers. A bad hit, but short range. A thrown knife was silent and did not betray its origin. Hard to reload, though. One of the three went down; a second reached an office and burst into it. The door had been triggered and the explosion caught her in the doorway. The third magpie ducked back into the stairwell, and a momentary silence ensued. Eglay Portion tried to think what Aynia Farer would do next.

"Maybe the trap on the stairway got everyone," said Four.

Eglay Portion did not think so, and a moment later a series of explosions suggested that the lions had made their own exit from the stairwell at an unconventional point. They could outflank Eglay's position now. "Pull back to the second line," he said.

But Four pointed, "Here comes one!"

A shenmat-clad figure slid from the doorway into the corridor and made a sign with his left hand. Eglay blocked Four's shot. "That's the pass-sign. It's that Greystroke fellow."

They left cover and retreated up the corridor. Aynia and two magpies came around an unexpected corner. Four stepped between Eglay and the lions and took the brunt of the dazer blast. Return fire drove the lions behind the corner again. Greystroke and Eglay sprinted toward the fane.

Tina Zhi came to the side of Domino Tight as softly as a dream and bearing the same strange weapon that she had brought to the Battle of the Warehouse. "The Secret Name, Big Jacques, five tridents, and a lion who survived Three's little game with the drop-wells."

The magpie with them smiled at the compliment, though he was vexed that one had survived.

"Big Jacques," said Domino Tight. "I always liked the Large One."

"Like him a little less," suggested the Technical Name.

Domino Tight sighed. "He could just as easily be fighting on our side, if he had thought it more fun."

"He *was* fighting on our side."

"Don't remind me," said Domino Tight.

Tina Zhi turned the curious U-shaped weapon in her hand. "The Secret Name is wearing sparkle armor. This will deactivate it and leave him vulnerable."

Domino Tight nodded. He remembered that from the Battle of the Warehouse. It also meant that, unlike the jump tokens, the sparkle armor was not controlled by a central field. What other secrets had the Technical Name been withholding from the Confederation, even from most of the other Names? Youth, perhaps.

And why was she now so willing to help ambush one of the leaders of the Old Guard, given that she had been supporting them through the Revolution? Because these intended to violate the sanctity of the Gayshot Bo? He did not believe it was for love of himself. Given how long Tina Zhi must have lived, what novelty could one more mayfly lover provide?

The Shadows believed the war had started because Shadow Prime had dispatched Epri Gunjinshow to rectify matters after Manlius Metataxis had incestuously coupled with his comrade-in-arms, Kelly Stappelaufer, and which task Epri had accomplished by seducing Kelly himself. It was the sort of story Shadows liked to tell themselves. But when they had wiped the tear away, they also knew that they were fighting to overthrow Names grown overbold. So what they *believed* and what they *knew* were at odds, and all that was left was laughter.

He focused on the darkness of the stairwell. Most of the tridents had escaped the trap. Big Jacques had been too keenly observant. The main stairwell opened on a function space. There was a reception desk, waiting chairs, and several small tables with inquiry portals. Large pots bore broad leafy plants. There were any number of hiding places, all of them far too obvious. "When they sortie from the stairwell," he told Three and Tina Zhi, "they will scatter in all directions, accepting casualties. They will almost certainly direct fire on the receptionist's desk, since that is the obvious place for defenders to cover the stairwell."

Three had strewn crispies on the steps. He listened now to

the sounds from the stairwell. "Time to take our places," he said. He shot a climbing grapple to the decorative, painted ceiling. Once there, he removed a panel that he had previously prepared, and insinuated himself into the duct space. Shortly, small gunports appeared in the moulding.

Tina Zhi placed a hand on Domino Tight's wrist. "It's too dangerous," she said.

Domino Tight finished snapping the titanium exoskeleton into place. He shook out the gossamer cloak that would make him invisible. "What better place to hide than the one place they will not expect—in plain sight?"

"They are no fools. Someone will realize."

"If anyone is left. At short range, I can use my dazer. And Rinty will be coming up behind them. We have them trapped! Hurry, cloak yourself."

The reception area became apparently vacant. This might lull Big Jacques—or raise his suspicions.

The tridents emerged in a fan, shielding both Big Jacques and the Secret Name. Domino counted eight and began to drop magpies with his dazer. Three fired flechettes from above. The Secret Name's sparkle armor died and he spun about looking for the weapon that had done it. Domino Tight numbed him in the thigh, and he nearly toppled. But Big Jacques maintained his calm.

"Is that you, old friend? What price this treachery?"

Domino Tight did not answer. The best way to locate an invisible man is from the sounds he makes.

"Never did think you jumped in the river. I guess that means Padaborn is here, too." Big Jacques fired pellets into various quarters of the lobby, on the likely assumption that Domino was in at least one of them. He wasn't.

"If the Name was your target, too late. He's crawled off down the hall until his leg heals."

A shower of flechettes rained on the tridents from the ceiling and Big Jacques and the remaining tridents returned fire, bracketing the likely source. A thud in the ductwork signaled success or a ruse. "Boys," said Jacques, "let's shift. Pattern G."

Only two magpies rose with Big Jacques and they scattered in three directions. One drew a shot from the apparently still-active Three, another, a dazzle from Domino Tight. But Big Jacques learned the power of chance in the affairs of men, for he had taken a serpentine run toward the farther hallway that intersected with Domino Tight.

The two of them toppled to the floor with the bigger man on top. Dazers flew higgledy-piggledy. Hands punched and poked; knees pistoned. The cloak was ripped aside. Domino Tight wrapped arms around his foe as tight as iron bands.

But iron bands were nothing to Big Jacques, and he broke free and rolled to his feet. Padaborn Three abandoned silence as he scrambled along the ductwork and punched a hole in the plaster to fire a wire gun at Big Jacques. In his anxiety not to strike Domino Tight, he shot wide; but Jacques took it as an invitation to leave. He kicked Domino in the head and, as he ran into the main hallway, pulled a throwing knife from a scabbard and in a single fluid pirouette pinned Domino Tight through the chest.

Méarana Harper listened to the dim sounds of battle from the floors below, wondering whether she had lured her mother to her death. But Bridget ban was a fixture of the universe, like the mountains and the rivers, like the Rift of Stars that separated the Perseus Arm from its Orion spur. Her mother was very like that Rift, too; her very absence was a sort of presence. And how could an absence ever be lost?

"This is all my fault," Méarana said.

Neither Graceful Bintsaif, who watched and listened to the

front hallway, nor Padaborn Five, who sat before the console of view screens and detectors that occupied the middle of the Security Center, turned to answer her.

"I would say it is the Ravn's fault," said the junior Hound. "It was she who maneuvered you into going with her into the Triangles. Your mother followed, and the rest of us followed her."

"I could not leave my father without succor."

Graceful Bintsaif shook her head. "There is a niggling in the back of my mind that our arrival rather upset the plans of Donovan buigh. The scarred man is like Mary's lambs. Leave him be and he'll return."

"Listen to the two of you," said Five. "None of this involved the Periphery at all. What is happening out there grew in our own gardens, not your *fayzukeq* personal lives. I see now that Padaborn did his best to delay this day of wrath, and only Gidula's threat to torture you . . ." He paused.

"There," said the harper. "It is my fault, after all." But she wasted no time wishing it had all never happened. The time for that wish was a long time ago.

"Fates!" said Five, rapping a monitor with his knuckle. "We've lost Domino Tight as well as the Hound Rinty."

Méarana brushed a cheek with her sleeve. As long ago as she could remember, Little Hugh had been a friend of the family. A lover once of her mother, which made him a relative of some sort. And Méarana had lured him here to his wyrd. It was supposed to be simple. She and Ravn and her mother would pluck Donovan as neatly from Gidula's fortress as a pickpocket removes a purse from an unwary tourista. *How* they would do this Méarana had had no idea, but she had owned the fantasy so long she had come to believe it.

It is the young who catch the gliding snake. A Terran proverb her father had once told her. The young do dangerous things from innocence. Well, she was young no longer. Although she might never become any older than she was this night.

Gidula's force would not come through the doorway she guarded: the hallway led deeper into the building. If Gidula did assault the control center his Shadows would come through the junior Hound and the Padaborn magpie and so give her a chance to escape. That was why Graceful Bintsaif had posted her here. She already had the escape route marked out in her mind. Down this hall, down a back stairway, across, and . . . she'd be at the fane. With her father and mother. All of them together at last, if only at the last.

"Well played!" Five exclaimed, and without turning from her vigilance Graceful Bintsaif said, "How now?"

"Big Jacques is down. Pyati ambushed him. Oh, he was the best they had. He was good. And Aynia Farer is wounded. I wonder that Gidula does not back off. Over half his force is down."

"He can't back down," Méarana said. "This isn't one of your duels. He has bet everything on this one throw. If he backs down, there is no second chance."

"Wait one. Padaborn!" Five spoke urgently into the comm. "Gidula has hung back from the fighting and has peeled off with two of his comets. Ravn, Eglay, and, uh, Greystroke, you are facing Aynia, five lions, and one comet. But Pyati is falling back from the west wing, followed by Phoythaw and four double-crows. No, I don't track Matilda Hound. She doesn't show anywhere on my screens. But there were five double-crows two minutes ago, so I assume she is . . ." He paused and listened. "Gidula is going up the three-four corridor toward the rear of the building. Yes, he is knocking out as many eyes as he and his two wingmen identify. So are the others. They know we're watching now."

There was only one way into the control center from the front side of the building and it was likely booby-trapped, so Gidula did as he often did and created another way. Explosive packs blew holes in the walls on either side of the entrance Graceful Bintsaif guarded, one on the west wall, one on the south. The eyes had been blinded across that whole row of offices and Five had no indication beforehand.

Both he and Graceful Bintsaif had fine reflexes, and it was just bad luck that they both turned to the same breach. That was bad luck for the comet who leapt through the west wall, as he was thus slain twice; but it gave the comet coming through the south wall a clear shot. She cut down Five where he stood behind the console, and Graceful Bintsaif spun about in time to see Méarana's thrown dagger embed itself in the comet's throat. Graceful Bintsaif's grace shot was superfluous and put her back to the west wall, and it was through this crumpled breach that Gidula stepped to stab her in the back.

Graceful Bintsaif collapsed and Méarana hurled her second knife straight toward Gidula, but the Old One merely grabbed it from the air by the handle and would have flung it back on the instant had he not seen that it was Méarana who had thrown it.

"You!" he cried. "How . . . ?" Then his eyes dropped once more to the body at his feet. In the flick of that eye, the harper fled down the back hallway. Gidula pursed his lips, but before pursuing he leaned over Graceful Bintsaif. "Does it hurt?" he asked.

"No," said the junior Hound through clenched teeth.

Gidula reached down and adjusted the knife. "How about now?"

Satisfied, Gidula set off in a brisk but unhurried pursuit of the harper.

The fane was a wide oval room encircled by seven statues of women in various poses: one in a grand jeté, another holding a caduceus on high, still others holding a sheaf of wheat, wearing stars over her naked body, and so forth. Green and white drapes dressed the walls, and a red-stained altar squatted in the center. The absence of benches or knee pads meant the initiates stood during their ceremonies. There seemed no separate adytum, though an iconostasis inlaid with emeralds and pearls stood folded against the wall. Below the altar was a drain hole for the blood and offal of the sacrifices. Bridget ban decided it was too narrow and too obvious to be the hidden entrance to the floor below. The walls and doors were not blast proof, and there were no firing ports.

Ravn Olafsdottr laughed. "And why should there be, Red Hound? This is a temple, a place of ritual. Who among the builders expected that one day it must be defended?"

Bridget ban snorted. "Have they even the slightest inkling of what they worship?"

"Of course not, Hound. More inkling, less worship."

"One set of doors," Gwillgi said. "They open on the mezzanine. That means we cannot see from inside what the Gidulans are about on the other three sides."

"Other five sides, Bristly Hound," Ravn told him.

"Four," said Donovan. "To attack the fane from below, they must enter the Cache, and if they can do that, they need not capture the fane. We can't defend from the inside. Limited field of fire through the doors, and a death trap if they lob explosives inside."

"So we interdict the corridors leading here. Spread mighty thin, Donovan."

"Defenders have an advantage."

Gwillgi barked. "Not *that* much an advantage."

"The others will converge here; and if they can't, they'll be a worry up our attackers' butts."

We can do this, said the girl in the chiton.

𝕴 𝖜𝖆𝖘 𝖙𝖍𝖎𝖓𝖐𝖎𝖓𝖌, said the Pedant, raising groans from half of Donovan's mind. 𝕿𝖍𝖊 𝖇𝖊𝖘𝖙 𝖉𝖊𝖋𝖊𝖓𝖘𝖊 𝖔𝖋 𝖆 𝖌𝖔𝖔𝖉 𝖔𝖋𝖋𝖊𝖓𝖘𝖊.

"We'll throw the defense forward. Along the mezzanine there and there. The crows are likely to come from the west side; the lions from the east. But some might come along the hallway behind the fane. And they may as easily travel through the ducts or even straight through the offices. If they have enough poppers they can open doors where there are no doors. Go forward, find likely spots for improvised devices, then plant the devices a little past them. Gwillgi, take the west mezzanine; Ravn, the east. Bridget, the back hallway, east. I'll prepare the back hall, west."

Ravn hissed—stealthy footfalls from the east—and the four of them folded to the floor, blending in with the décor, weapons pulled and aimed. A moment of quiet descended during which Donovan could wonder how badly he had miscalculated.

A voice whispered the password: *kuwatnim,* which meant "liberty" in the old Taṇṭamiž lingua franca. But passwords could be learned and voices imitated. And so the voice added, "When the banner snaps, the fight begins."

"It's Eglay," Donovan told the others, and he told the Shadow to come forth.

Eglay Portion had brought Greystroke and Three Padaborn. "That Technical Name," said Three, "she wouldn't leave Domino Tight."

Shortly, Pyati came in from the other direction with One and Two. "Where is Matilda?" asked Bridget ban.

"Didn't see her," Pyati answered.

"That is what you may expect to see in my case," said

Matilda of the Night. "Your man, Pyati, took out Big Jacques. But the crows were nipping hard at his heels."

"Rinty should have reached my position, coming up behind Big Jacques," said Three. "But Jacques twigged to the trap and they reversed direction. I think they caught your Pup coming up behind them."

Greystroke, if it was possible, became a little grayer. And the Fudir remembered old days in Amir Naith's Gulli. On to the Hadramoo! *Och, Hugh!* he thought, and the rest of him left him momentarily in peace. But there was little time for peace in a time of war, and the Silky Voice embraced the sorrow and sequestered it.

The Sleuth calculated from the intelligence the Pedant had tabulated from Five that they faced fourteen magpies, three Shadows—one wounded—and a Name. Seven bogies were approaching along the mezzanine from each direction, but Gidula, the Secret Name, and two of Gidula's comets were missing. Uncounted casualties?

No, Donovan decided. Gidula would not perish as anonymously as that. A flanking movement was more probable. Around the back of the fane or . . . above it.

That would bring him too close to the Security Center for the comfort of Donovan's minds. He redispositioned everyone, placing himself and Bridget ban behind the fane, since that was where he expected the flank attack. Everyone vanished into offices, into ceilings, or—in Matilda's case—simply vanishing.

I have a theory about Matilda of the Night, said the Sleuth.

You gotta theory about everything. Shaddap an' get outta my way here.

Inner Child set himself to watch and listen to the approaches. The scarred man's eyes took on that peculiar wandering characteristic that meant each eye was watching independently. Each ear was listening independently. It was not a state that he had ever tried to describe to others, but it seemed to him that he stood in four different places that were somehow the same place. Donovan and the Fudir peered out through the eyes; Sleuth and the Pedant listened. The Silky Voice fell back to the hypothalamus and began regulating the flow of adrenaline and other enzymes, heightening his senses, broadening his time-sense.

Five burst in on his attention. "Security Center. Attack imminent!" This was followed by two low-intensity thumps and the snap of weapons fired. Then the comm. went silent.

Donovan did not wait but was already on the run. "Gwillgi," he said over the link. "Take my post!" He heard Bridget ban say, "Ravn, take mine," then he shot a tzan-wire to the ceiling and climbed up it.

The shortest distance to Méarana was straight up.

Méarana found her carefully laid plan foiled and barely escaped the escape route. While Gidula had come in the front, the Secret Name had been circling around the rear. She saw the man in the golden masque hesitate at a distant intersection, and she sidestepped quickly down another hall. Behind her, she heard Gidula call to the Name in a language her earwig did not recognize.

If you hide, she told herself, *they will find you.* The problem with hidey-holes was a lack of exits. Safety, should any quality so elusive be had, lay in distance. She reached into her scrip and pressed the detonator, and the corridor she had intended to use blew in from shaped charges. She did not go back to see if her pursuers had been caught in the blast. If they had, she ran for no reason. If they hadn't . . .

The hallways formed a rectangular grid with nearly identical office spaces along each; but there were a few diagonal corridors, too—for shortcuts, she supposed—and foyers at the multi-way intersections. Panic fought the calm she needed. Her mother had trained her in a variety of arts, but she was by no means their master.

"There's no need to run," she heard Gidula say. How far behind her? Did he see her, or was he talking to the night? "I only want to know how you got off Terra. I have no reason to do you harm."

Did he take her for a fool? Would she suppose he *needed* a reason?

They were all sick, the Shadows were, even those like Ravn and Domino. There was something empty deep inside them. Like a shadow cast by the light, they were all form and no substance. Somewhere back along the pathways of their lives they had turned the wrong way and had become irretrievably lost, even to themselves.

"Who are the others with you? Renegade Shadows? You can't trust them, you know. Remember how my own dear Ravn betrayed you. Some are wearing coveralls instead of shenmats. Are they Protectors? They do not fight like mere boots."

Méarana saw a partly open door on her right and, without breaking stride, stooped as she passed and leaned her flashlight against it. Then, pirouetting up a side hallway, she threw her ground voice, "Am I a fool?" just as the tilted flashlight pushed the door slightly open. To Gidula, the visual and auditory cues would make it seem as if she had cracked the door to speak.

"I think," said Gidula, "that the question carries its own answer." And he shot a gas canister into the barely cracked doorway. "Sleep awhile. Later, we will speak."

Méarana had not awaited the outcome, but, as the old stories ran, she "plied swift heels" down the side hall, then cut right again.

Straight into the arms of the Secret Name.

———

The Secret Name had never been too certain of Gidula. The Old One was without doubt a useful tool. But a tool with a mind of its own could turn on its user. That the ancient Shadow and he had different plans once the Committee had been purged was a certainty, but the Secret Name had overseen the Bureau of Shadows for many years since his predecessor's untimely demise and there was little in their thinking that he did not grasp.

Yet Gidula's plan to seize the Seven Widows had shocked even the Secret Name. The nature of the objects had never been too clear to him, save that they were sacred and ancient. But new technology was destabilizing. You never knew who might rise and who fall when something new appeared. Carefully controlled, allowed to a few, their secrets guarded by a sworn college, the dangerous servant could be kept in its place. The Gayshot Bo was among the least of the ministries, and the feckless Tina Zhi had been left in place largely because no one else wanted her post.

The leaping tokens had allowed selected Names to oversee Confederal affairs directly. But this had not been an unalloyed gift. Some of the token-holders had aligned with the Committee. Now Gidula had begun to wonder about eternal youth, the one thing that might tempt the Old One off the pure path of tradition. He was so afraid of dying that he had let his fears become the master of his acts, and so a quiet coup had become a blazing city. But every blessing is a curse, and the Secret Name wondered if Tina Zhi had found eternal boredom instead.

While one part of his mind was thus engaged, another part kept watch on the darkened hallways he traveled. That reminded him of another miscalculation. Gidula had not expected the building to be defended and they had walked into a well-laid trap. That seemed appropriate to the Secret Name. No prize so great should be won without a struggle.

Circle around behind her, Gidula had told him. There would be a reckoning for that casual inversion of status. Shadows did not give orders to Names. Why this girl—obviously no magpie—was of such interest the Old One had not bothered to explain. That told the Secret Name everything he wanted to know about Gidula.

The girl had seen him, the Ever-Vigilant part of his mind knew, and so would seek to evade. And so, the Planning part of his mind concluded, he must circle out farther still. His Vigilance heard soft footfalls, distant snaps and explosions, Gidula's muttered curses.

The Secret Name smiled. Apparently, the girl had managed to fool the Old One in some manner. The Secret Name dipped into the Memory Well and found the floor plan he needed. The Calculator examined all the possible routes the fleeing girl could have taken and computed her likely present positions on each route. He allowed his Body to light-foot to the maximum likelihood spot.

And was gratified when, turning a corner, he found his arms full of a beautiful woman.

Beautiful, but not domesticated.

Méarana found her every mother-taught move blocked with contemptuous ease by the man in the maniacally smiling sun-mask. However she struggled, his grip on her tightened, squeezing her against him. "La, *snortcha,*" he said, his sweetened breath filling her with unreasoning fear. "Tell me why the Old One is so interested in you." Sun-rays framed him like a lion's mane, his lips moved behind the fatuous smile like something wet and slimy lurking in a cave.

Méarana remembered her father's advice. *Never tell them*

what they want to know, in case, learning all they wish, they might then dispose of you.

"I don't know," she said. "I was just working in my office and all these people came rushing in and they started fighting."

Her captor studied her for a moment, and Méarana saw with horror the way his eyes wandered, and that under his graying hair a myriad of scars ran every which way.

"No," he said. "You struggled too long for a sheep. You are golden skinned. But not from Miniforster. You did not recognize my rank. You are Peripheral. A Hound? No, insufficiently skilled. Just what has old Gidula been up to?"

"Are you the Sleuth?" the harper asked.

The Secret Name cocked his head in puzzlement. "I ask the questions. You supply the answers. That is the order of nature."

Méarana threw her sky-voice—"I'm coming!"—but she was too close and the old man was not fooled. And so, arms pinned, legs pinned, hugged close to her captor, she employed her only remaining weapon.

She kissed him, thrusting her tongue through the mouth-opening and between his lips.

The golden man had not been kissed in a great many years, and possibly never at all. He did not transform into a Prince, but he did recoil in sheer surprise.

And the floor gave way beneath him.

He fell to waist-height among the piping and ducts that underlay the floor, and like truth rising from hell, Donovan buigh emerged from below. The Secret Name struggled against the imprisoning hardware, but one of his eyes looked on Donovan.

"La, Tom," he said.

The scarred man pried the mask from the face, tossed it aside. "La, Gesh," he replied. "Hold still, please." He pointed a dazer at the man's head. "I like you better pinned than loose."

"He didn't hurt me, Father."

Donovan did not turn. "That would have come later."

"So, you've remembered," said the Secret Name.

"Some. Enough. I guess if you can't beat them, join them."

"It was actually the Lord Protector's idea. He wanted a spy among the Shadows. Tom, *you don't know what they would have done to me otherwise.*"

"Given you a worse haircut?"

"But the operation worked! I'm completely integrated. I can perfect you, teach you to become fully yourself. You cannot imagine what it is like!"

"Who else?"

"Does it matter?"

"Who else!"

"Lai Showan. She was the first. But . . . She couldn't integrate, she . . . flew apart. We had to put her to sleep. Can I move my arms now? This pose grows discomforting. And I fear my ankle is twisted in these pipes."

Donovan did not answer such a transparent ruse. He remembered that he had been already tenfold in the Rising. Had all the chiefs been? Rajasekaran and O'Farrell, too? The Sleuth leapt from the ruse to the half-truth that underlay it. *The Lion's Mouth had created five of us . . . Five who might not be missed. And we rose up. Not for liberty, but for Geshler Padaborn's ambitions. And afterward, he would not tolerate any other like himself.*

He could have killed us outright, the Silky Voice pointed out. *He must have retained some feeling for our brotherhood.*

Yes, said the young man in the chlamys. He thought he could still use us, if only we were a little less than himself. But only two of us survived the Rising, and the operation failed. And Lai Showan went mad and we . . .

"Spent a time on the edge of madness." The scarred man's finger nearly depressed the button on the dazer.

The Secret Name started at the apparently random utterance and a moment later nodded, as if he had followed Donovan's chain of reasoning. "And now, there are only the two of us. Imagine what we could achieve together! We have pulled down the Nomenklatura at last! We have wrecked the Lion's Mouth! What we could not accomplish by direct assault we have accomplished by burrowing within. Now, we have the opportunity to build something new, something better, *something worthy of our goals.* Do you understand? We are the new men. We are something beyond the merely human."

Bridget ban skidded to a halt behind Geshler Padaborn. Her eyes danced one to the other, took in the scene, understood it. She held her teaser on the Secret Name. *A teaser,* thought Donovan, with a tinge of the contempt that Shadows felt. The Hounds would always be one notch less deadly.

"To me, Méarana," said Bridget ban.

"Father rescued me . . ."

"That was nice, considering he was the whole reason you needed rescuing."

Geshler Padaborn cocked an eyebrow. He hadn't known that part, Donovan saw. He was thinking now how he might use this new fact.

Padaborn smiled. Inner Child started. <Behind us!>

Padaborn spasmed and collapsed where he stood. Donovan swung to the new target.

And saw Gidula with dazer in hand.

"Oh!" said Gidula with sentimental affect. "The whole loving family." He twisted the aperture to wide sweep, fatal range. The recharger hummed.

Donovan stepped in front of Méarana Harper, but Gidula's aim was spoiled and the beam went wide.

What spoiled Gidula's aim was the abrupt drop of Ravn Olafsdottr through the ceiling and onto his back. She rode him for a moment as a man might ride an unbroken horse. But she pulled on the reins and his head reared back and he choked. The Old One threw himself back against the wall to crush Ravn, but she maintained a hard grip.

Gidula began to bleed from the neck and the garotte bit into his flesh. He fell backward to the floor, pinning Ravn beneath him, and still her choke hold did not slacken. His legs began to kick spasmodically, increasing in tempo. Then they were still.

The corridor remained prone for a time; the acrid odors of electrical discharge, hanging in a thin, smoky fume, tinctured the air. The silence grew loud.

Gidula was the first to move.

His chest heaved with the sound of a pellet-gun discharge, and something emerged from the rib cage to embed itself in the corridor wall. He rolled aside.

"Ooh," said Ravn Olafsdottr. "That was joost to make sure." Then the perpetual smile faded and she struggled to her knees beside the corpse of the Old One, and she wept uncontrollably into her hands.

The fighting around the fane had started well enough, with death flitting through corridors on the run, emerging from unexpected corners, exploding where least expected; but the attackers had rallied and had driven the defenders back on the fane itself and matters had devolved into a gunfight.

Gwillgi, Eglay, and Three were wounded. Two Padaborn was dead. But the attackers had been pruned very nicely. The last two trident magpies were dead, and Phoythaw had only two crows and one comet remaining in his force. Aynia, wounded to begin with, had withdrawn from the fight, though three of his four magpies continued to fire on the defenders. Pyati and One defended the door of the fane and Matilda and Greystroke were in isolated siege at their two corners unable to reach them.

"Low on pellets," One reported, "and my recharger is almost dead."

"Knife never runs dry," Pyati told him.

"Yes," the magpie responded, "but it lacks something in range."

"Here." Gwillgi tossed his own gun to One Padaborn. "You point the barrel at what you want to hit, and press that button twice in quick succession."

The magpie's lips quirked, and Gwillgi said to Pyati, "Ay! I wish I hadn't used my medipack on Domino Tight that time in Cambertown, because I certainly could use it now."

Pyati spared him a glance. "Maybe so, but had you not saved him we might not be fighting here together."

"Was that supposed to convince me I'd done the right thing? Never mind. I would do it again, for the same reasons I gave Domino."

A flurry of discharges sounded down the hallway. "Bad aim," said Pyati. "No hits here."

"Maybe they shifted their strength to Greystroke or Matilda," Gwillgi suggested. "Keep us pinned down while they overwhelm those two."

"This fane had better be worth defending," said Pyati.

"Donovan has not come back," Gwillgi pointed out. "Nor Bridget ban. And where's your Ravn? They could double our strength."

"Then, bigger massacre," said Pyati. "Nice. Lord Padaborn did not 'bug out' on me, so I stand where he told me to stand."

One, listening, nodded. "We are not like Hounds. We can defend a hopeless position."

"Braggart," grunted Gwillgi. He pulled himself up to the barricade they had made of the office furniture. They had built such barricades in several offices on the approaches to the fane, at points that might interdict an attacking party, forcing Phoythaw and Aynia to pause and check each one, lest ambush lurk behind it. What normally lurked was an explosive device, but they had quickly learned to detonate those remotely.

"Someone's coming!" said One.

They all heard it. A regular thumping from the west hall-way, where Phoythaw's force lurked. The snap of a teaser interrupted the thumping briefly, then it continued. A darker figure loomed in the dark hallway and struck the floor three times with a tall wooden staff. Taijis swarmed in the background.

"Cease and desist!" the Long Tall One said. "This pasdarm is suspended!"

Pyati groaned. "Is Ekadrina Sèanmazy with reinforcements."

"More coming from the east," said Gwillgi.

"Black horses," said One. "And us caught in between."

Ekadrina stepped aside and Tina Zhi passed through the ranks of taijis, bearing the body of Domino Tight on a gravity cart. "I would enter the fane as high priestess of the Seven Widows," she said.

"What she means," said Oschous Dee Karnatika, "is don't shoot. The Riff of District Twenty-seven has declared a Peace. The Secret City is under martial law, and all are to lay down their arms. Where is Geshler Padaborn?"

A portion of the ceiling fell onto the mezzanine and two dozen guns—taijis, black horses, and Padaborn's defenders—were instantly leveled at the spot. Ravn Olafsdottr's face appeared in the gap.

"Peekaboo!" she said.

AN CRÍOCH

I heard the forester cut a tree, giving thanks for his
security.
"What need," said he, "for pillars, or for pommels bright,
Or walls festooned with art? Why should I fear betrayal hid
Behind flash-friendly teeth? Why fear the goblet tinctured
With a comrade's venom? I need not bow nor bend the knee
Because no gift beguiles me; but work holds me in liberty.
Dressed not in robes or shenmat grim, I gain the greater joy
From what my hands and mind employ.
By night, do I sleep well content
While lords see all their powers end."

In the first place, they gathered in the fane on furniture scav-
enged from the nearby offices. Ekadrina Sèanmazy and Oschous Dee Karnatika sat side by side on float-chairs obviously
intended to demonstrate their collegial rule. Their magpies,
staged alternately, encircled the room. One of the black horses
had proven to be Greystroke, who had used his anycloth to

blend in with them up to point when they counted noses. Of Matilda of the Night there was no sign.

Three more chairs, ground propped, had been set facing the two senior Shadows, and in these sat Donovan buigh, Bridget ban, and Méarana Harper, still twitching a little from the penumbra of Gidula's dazer. Méarana had been shielded from the worst of it by Donovan's body. He lolled in the seat, but his open left eye showed that some part of him was active.

Gwillgi, Three, and the other wounded lay on pallets with medipacs or their Confederal equivalent, at least until they could be transported to an autoclinic. Two of Ekadrina's magpies had brought in Little Hugh on a gravity cart. He was white from loss of blood but still clinging to the edge of life. On another pallet lay Graceful Bintsaif. A Riff's magpie with the death's-head brassard of a medic attended to them.

"So," said Ekadrina, taking the lead. "What mess have we here? Hounds in da Secret City! Not just one, but fife, and I suspect udders left to guard your line of retreat. Dat is not good. A violation of de Treaty, I t'ink."

Bridget ban tried to answer, but her tongue would not cooperate and all that emerged were "aws" and "ahs." Ekadrina nodded and said, "Cogently argued."

Greystroke spoke up. "We came to rescue her daughter—who had been kidnapped on the orders of your renegade Gidula."

"Ack, he was not *my* renegade." Ekadrina turned to Oschous. "Yours, I tink."

The Fox smiled. "I have never seen a play of so many sides against so many others. Had I not been one of the sides being played, I would have admired the Old One's balance. He played both you and me for fools, Tall One. We both wanted the same thing, but fought on different sides to achieve it."

"Ya, I luff you, too. I fought from loyalty to da Names. It's

what we are: da Shadows of da Names. Don't suppose de re-
forms of da Committee had anyt'ing to do widdit." She turned
to face the captives. "So dis is our problem. What do we do
wid you? Normally, dose like Padaborn and his magpies and
his allies would be moved, as traitors to da Names. Except
none of you assassinated any Names tonight. But den, for con-
sistency, I would need to move my pardner, too." She tossed
her head toward Oschous Dee. "And dat would be an inauspi-
cious beginning of our pardnership. And if I moved you Peripheral dogs, dat might make problems wid de League, and as
you might guess, we are not well positioned to deal wid de
League just now. And you, poor lamb . . ." She addressed the
harper. "You are da innocent caught up in madders beyond
your ken. For people like you, we have da folk saying: 'Too
stupid to live,' and normally we would accommodate dat, too.
But nuttin' today is normal."

"We start today with a clean slate," said Oschous Dee. "We'll
build a new world, more efficient than the old, better shep-
herds to the sheep. I own some responsibility for dragging the
former agent Donovan buigh from his retirement and forcing
him into the Shadow War. All that he did after was for his own
survival, and I can't blame a man for that."

"So we are agreed," said Ekadrina in a tone that indicated
agreement ran not very deep. She, at least, her earlier glance
had shown, was not about to build a new world. She intended
to rebuild the old. But that meant restoring the surviving
Committee to their offices, and so while their motives might
differ, she and Oschous for the time shared a common purpose.

Donovan struggled toward the surface of his body. The
Silky Voice sent soothing molecules to stroke his unhappy
nerves, to calm his agitated muscles. "An easy comfort, no?" he
said, and all eyes turned to him in surprise.

"I take no comfort in what lies outside dese walls," said Ekadrina. "Nor in what lies inside."

"You think the old system will collapse at last, and all the abuses, all the flouted traditions, all the small imperial impositions, they'll all be swept away. You'll build something new."

Oschous Dee nodded—so did Pyati and the wounded Eglay Portion. Ekadrina sat still but said, "We will purge da corruptions. Dat was Gidula's dream, too, before his fears seduced him."

"But if everyone has become so habitually wolves or sheep that the collapse must come, you will carry those same habits into the new world, too. People whose most forgotten ancestors were sheep will not become on the instant self-reliant beavers. Your new world will be built by those who have known only the old. You've been given a clean slate, you say? But what you have just erased was written by you, or people like you. What makes you think the new script will be any different?"

"That is why," whispered Eglay Portion, "we need you to lead us."

Rolling boulders uphill was not high on Donovan's list of priorities. By the looks on their faces, neither were Ekadrina and Oschous delighted by the suggestion.

"My needs are simple; my wants are few," the Fudir said. "When I bought my ticket a year and a half ago, I intended to visit friends on Dangchao Waypoint. That is still my goal, and has always been."

Ekadrina Sèanmazy struck the floor with her staff. "Den hear our ruling as joint custodians of whatever it is dat we are joint custodians of. Da agents of de League will be repatriated wid our t'anks for defending da Gayshot Bo from de renegade Gidula. Dis was above and beyond your call to duty—is dat how you say it? Call to duty?—which was merely to rescue a kidnapped citizen. Eglay, Ravn, and da magpies Padaborn. You cast your lot wid Donovan buigh. So be it. You will be

exiled wid him into de League. Aynia, you should have remained loyal to me. But unlike da late Phoythaw Bhatvik, you
surrendered when called upon. I will grant da confusion of da
past day. So your motion is remitted to exile Coreside. You
will be sent to a new world, dere to found a new colony.
Dere." She brushed her hands. "All cleared up. All set right."

"Deadly One," said Gwillgi, whose strength was returning. "What of Domino Tight? He and I are gozhiinyaw. Will
he come with us?"

"From my point of view," said Oschous, "he remained loyal
to the Revolution when even Big Jacques was seduced by the
renegade Gidula."

"Is dat a recommendation?" said Ekadrina.

"You could name him liaison between the Lion's Mouth
and the Kennel," Gwillgi pointed out. "If you are to begin
anew, that is a new thing you may try."

"Deadly Ones," said the scarred man, "the fate of Domino
Tight may be out of your hands. The Technical Name took him
below for healing. And she has been down there a long time."

"Yes," said Bridget ban, who rose unsteadily from her chair.
"How long for this accelerated healer to restore someone?"

"My sweet Domino," said Ravn, "was closer to death than
any man on this side of it."

Gwillgi shook his head. "He was closer in Cambertown—
yet fought at the warehouse."

Ekadrina pulled her chin. "If de reins of da Confederation
are in our hands now, we ought to know what is down dere."

The Fudir said, "She swore that no one outside the College
would ever see them."

Oschous rose from his seat. "There is a new order in the
world."

An intuition struck Bridget ban and she seized her daughter's hand and went swiftly to the fane's door. Donovan followed

her, pausing to activate Little Hugh's pallet and pull it with him. Ravn and Greystroke did the same with Gwillgi and Graceful Bintsaif. Pyati and One pulled Three outside to the mezzanine. Ekadrina watched them, glanced at the colored tile that Tina Zhi had used to open the secret entrance, and within moments the fane had cleared.

Oschous exited last. "We will all feel foolish if nothing happens."

The floor of the fane buckled and sagged, and a moment later the sound of an explosion reached them.

Ekadrina leaned on her staff and contemplated the wreckage. "Dat's good," she said. "I hate to feel foolish."

In the second place, they gathered in the Cache.

The room was a shambles; the seven vaults, empty. In one, they found Matilda of the Night. No one asked how she had followed Tina Zhi into the Cache while everyone had been watching. Ekadrina rolled her eyes. "Am I to find a Hound behind every potted plant and curtain?"

Matilda was bleeding from her nose and ears. Though the vault had sheltered her somewhat, the concussion of the explosion had thrown her against the back wall. "Recognized me," she gasped. "Should . . . have expected. Took . . . Vestiges. Leapt."

Ekadrina looked to the scarred man and Bridget ban. "Da Amnesty holds. Take her up." Donovan called up to Pyati and his magpies to bring down yet another gravity pallet. Ekadrina took Bridget ban by the arm. "So, de Vestiges are gone; and you have seen all dere is to see, which is nutting. I would not take da fruits from da laborer's mouth; but whatever your Matilda recorded, a copy would be appreciated." When Bridget ban hesitated, Ekadrina added, "Dey were ours to begin wit.'"

"Is justice now one of your watchwords?"

Ekadrina shrugged. "I always t'ought it one of yours."

"I doubt there be muckle useful even in full-spectrum scans. But if she took any records, you will have them. Call it a gesture of amity for this day."

Donovan had been so preternaturally silent that Bridget ban glanced in his direction. "Why not round up the Vestigial Virgins for a cup of coffee? Even some of the office sheep may know something."

Ekadrina tilted her head back. "You t'ink any of dem are coming back after dis? Dey will vanish into de sheep pens. Too many records destroyed dis day. We will search for de Virgins; but I t'ink Tina Zhi will pluck dem to her personal planet long before we find dem, and what man knows where dat is?"

"It's a big Spiral Arm," agreed Donovan buigh.

In the third place, they gathered in Grimpen's ship. The cutter had been left in Dao Chetty orbit in charge of Obligado, marked with suitably official-looking Confederal identifiers. Matilda of the Night had been using a small two-man craft expropriated somewhere in the Confederation. They left it behind, taking from it only its medical supplies, food stock, and the body of Cŵn Annwn. The old *Sèan Beta* still lay under Mount Lefn.

The ship was more crowded than she was wont, but Little Hugh, Graceful Bintsaif, and Matilda of the Night took up very little room. They occupied three of the four autoclinics. Gwillgi and Three Padaborn, less seriously wounded, took turns in the fourth.

The scarred man went to the clinic and sat with Little Hugh for a while, carrying on a one-sided conversation. "You didn't have to stay," he told the comatose man. "You could have taken Méarana forcibly and departed before Gidula entered the building." He remembered how he had cold-conked Hugh on the front stoop of a Chel'veckistad tenement and run off alone to secure January's Dancer. "I'm sorry I got you into any of this." He hesitated. "Do you remember when you told me of your childhood, and I never answered?" Little Hugh said nothing and the machine continued to breathe for him. "I wasn't being secretive. I had no memories of it, none at all. But now that I remember my name, other scraps may follow."

Tomas Krishna Murphy. It was the name of a stranger; but it was a Terran name, so that much was true. Donovan had been a code name, assigned by the Lion's Mouth.

So, you are no more the "original" than any of the rest of us, said the Sleuth.

He did not know Graceful Bintsaif so well, but he stopped at her tank and paid his respects. She had given her life—or at least nine-tenths of it—to buy Méarana a little time. For that he would always love her.

Matilda of the Night he did not know at all. He didn't think anyone did. *What is your secret?* he asked her sleeping form. There was something odd about her, like a jigsaw piece that did not fit anywhere in the scene.

When Donovan visited with Three, he brought Pyati and One with him, and he told both magpies that he would give them names for their services rendered in the defense of the Gayshot Bo. "Choose your own names, and tell me, and we'll have the baptism." This reduced One and Three to tears, which in Three's case upset the autoclinic until he calmed down. Pyati said, "And our brothers, Two, Four, and Five?"

Donovan agreed to a posthumous naming and thereby unleashed another torrent of weeping and profligate thanks and praise. The easy and extravagant emotions to which the Shadows were subject continued to amaze him. Yet they could hate as easily as love, and torture with the same intensity as caress, all the while believing they could bind such things with rules and rituals.

———

Despite the crowding on Grimpen's ship, the scarred man contrived to be alone. There was a bubble he grew around himself, a sealed-off sphere of space and time within which, whatever crowds hubbubbed about outside, loneliness was the sole resident. Patrons of the Bar of Jehovah knew it well. One would not think a mind that was nine could ever be alone, but there was a certain degree of introspection such a condition imposed, and in a certain sense he could and did turn his back on the world.

It was especially so when matters had drawn to a close, when he had accomplished whatever he had accomplished, and it seemed that there was nothing more left to do. He had felt this after he had consigned the Twisting Stone to the subspatial void, after he had watched the sun dawn inside *A. K. Prabhakaran,* and on a dozen lesser occasions before he and Bridget ban had ever crossed paths.

Grimpen spoke to him briefly and some of the scarred man must have answered, for he went away. Gwillgi sat across the mess table from him, but while most men took keen interest when Gwillgi sat down by them, the scarred man devoted only a portion of his attention to the now-healed Hound. Inner Child, of course, heard the Alfven warning—short-long, short-long—and the Brute braced for the moment of physical discomfort when they leapt the bar; but the rest of the scarred man was astonished to realize later that they were already in the tubes and headed toward Sapphire Point.

The young man in the chlamys was as good at reading himselves as at reading others, and so he knew that he had once admired Geshler Padaborn above all men and it distressed him seven times seven to see what Gesh had become.

Had the Leader seriously believed that he was continuing the Rising by stealth from within the ranks of the Names? Had that been his goal, he would have *led* the Committee of Names Renewed, not conducted the resistance against it. Unless the last thing a revolutionary wants is another man's revolution. He drank an imaginary toast to the Padaborn-that-was, and a second to his brothers who had also been multiplexed.

Ravn Olafsdottr sat for a time just outside the scarred man's bubble and talked at him. If at any time in his life he had wondered what it would be like to have a sociopath for a friend, his hypothetical curiosities had been answered. They had saved each other's life, which made them closer than any two people could be. She had saved his daughter's life—twice. But she had also dragged his daughter into a place where the saving became necessary. Méarana could take care of herself in a wide range of circumstances; but the Shadow War had been beyond that range, and even Hounds and Pups had not come out whole. Ravn was the sort who would rid a dog of fleas by throwing it into the fire—on the calmly rational grounds that fleas could not survive elevated temperatures.

It had all been because of him. Méarana's kidnapping, her near death. The death of Cŵn Annwn, the terrible injuries to Little Hugh, who had been a friend before the scarred man had known he could have friends. He hadn't asked for them to come; he hadn't counted on them coming. But they had come nonetheless, and if they had not come precisely for him, they had stayed and fought precisely for him.

She had come for him. The harper, who had urged him out of his niche in the Bar of Jehovah. The mere thought of the kitten braving a fight among tigers brought tears to his eyes. He had never done anything to deserve such loyalty.

As Bridget ban could easily attest.

The people aboard *Great Moor* had taken to sleeping in shifts, and were calling one another the night hawks and the morning larks. Bridget ban, of course, had contrived to place herself at the opposite time of the day to the scarred man. Perhaps this was a sign that he should not have bought the ticket to Dangchao Waypoint in the first place. But what foiled her of this intention was that the scarred man knew no night or day and he in his own self could split his shifts. A part of him was always awake; and Inner Child, of all of him, never slept.

So it was Inner Child who saw Méarana and Bridget ban enter the refectory and who heard the daughter say to the mother, "He wants only a bowl of uiscebeatha to be as I found him on Jehovah."

"Perhaps," said the Red Hound, "you should have left him there."

"Ah, no, Mother, for then I would have lost *you,* out in the Wild. Remember that, I pray. He came for you when no one else could."

"And now I have come for him, so the score is paid. He has lived too long in the Shadows and has learned their lawless ways."

Inner Child had aroused the rest of the scarred man, and the Silky Voice took the tongue to answer. *No, not lawless, my dear. They have their codes and laws, just as you do. Different laws and different codes, it's true. They are more flamboyant; you are more considered. You both dance with death, but you dance at decorous arm's length while they dance in passionate embrace.*

Bridget ban came to the table and sat across from the scarred man. The harper stood a little behind her. The Fudir could see how closely they resembled each other, but he could see the differences, too. In the chin, and in the ears. Those Méarana had gotten from him.

"Do you admire the Shadows, then?" asked the Hound.

Donovan grinned through the scarred man's lips. "I admire them—and pity them. I have seen them laugh, and seen them weep. And while they laugh and weep for different reasons than you, the tears themselves are genuine."

Bridget ban leaned forward. "You killed Padaborn in cold blood. He was helpless; he was our prisoner."

"Ah. My old Leader. He was far from helpless, and he was not our prisoner. I dared not turn my back on him to fight Gidula. But . . . It was not I who shot him."

"No?"

"It was Gidula."

"But, they were allies. They had entered the Gayshot Bo together."

"Oh, yes," said Donovan. "But you underestimate the levels of deception and treachery at work. Gidula would never have shot the Secret Name—until the masque came off and he saw Geshler Padaborn."

"How do you know that?"

"I don't, and we cannot ask Gidula; but that's how the smart money bets. The Secret Name always wears a masque and is the only Name who is nameless. Poor Gesh. His mind was what mine should have been, working in perfect harmony."

"Is it so good then," Méarana asked, "to brook no dissent?"

Ha! said the Sleuth. *She got you there!*

The Fudir grinned crookedly. "Maybe not, but it is quieter."

Bridget ban spoke up and her voice was not as harsh as it might have been. "What is it you want, Donovan? Or should I call you Tom?"

The scarred man shook their head. "No. Tomas Krishna Murphy died in the siege of the old Education Ministry. What was left of him died in a bed on Gatmander. He had been betrayed by the man he loved and trusted most. He wanted to die and nearly took the rest of us with him. What do *I* want? Most of all?" He thought about the question. "I want to sit under my own vine and fig tree and not be afraid. I would like to visit Clanthompson Hall, if you would permit."

Inner Child noticed how Méarana's hand, laid casually on her mother's shoulder, tightened its grip.

"Oh, you would? Donovan, *ye keep breaking things.* The Dancer, the old Commonwealth Ark, now ye've broken the entire Confederation!"

"Well," said the Fudir, "the Confederation stood between you and me. It seemed the fastest way to reach you."

"Love, is it? Why, we hae barely spoken in twenty years!"

"Aye, there is something cruel about love. Otherwise, it wouldn't hurt so."

Bridget ban did not smile, but her countenance grew more serious. "Maybe it is time for you to come home."

The scarred man looked up. The young girl in the chiton sang, but her song did not reach his lips. "Why? Does your estate need a vine-dresser?"

"No. Because you stepped between my daughter and the gun of Gidula."

" 'Our' daughter. Mine was a desperate gesture. If Gidula had not wasted a charge on Padaborn . . . If not for Ravn, once I'd dropped, he would have had a clear shot."

"Not right away."

The Fudir looked at Bridget ban and nodded. "Yes. Who said we have nothing in common."

"And Méarana had two more knives. Given such a pause, she might have . . ." Bridget ban visibly tore herself from the world that might have been. "Ye won't gang scootin' off agin, wi' nary a word?"

Donovan nodded. "Fig tree. Vine. And I'll leave word."

Bridget ban could hardly complain, as she herself was often absent on Hound's Business and the word she left was ofttimes cryptic. "We'll see. Don't think it will be like twenty years ago."

Twenty years ago, Bridget ban had used her charms to seduce Greystroke and Little Hugh, as well as the Fudir, as a way of binding their loyalties to herself. Even two years ago, the Fudir might have thrown that in her face before the Silky Voice could stop him. But Bridget ban was not now who she had been, and neither was he. "I know," was all he said; and Méarana, of all of them, showed relief on her face.

Donovan rose and pulled open his coverall pants. "That reminds me. I have a present for you." Before Bridget ban could raise a brow or Méarana blush, he plucked a thread from his undergarment and pulled it free.

"I hope that's not what's holding it all together," said Bridget ban. But she recognized it for a data thread.

"I wove it into my undergarment," the Fudir explained. "It seemed the safest place, and I haven't changed the garment since."

Bridget ban hesitated before taking the proferred thread, and then held it between her fingertips. "What is it ye have for me, Donovan buigh?"

"Old files I copied in the Miwellion in Prizga. They are titled *Vyutha 1* through *Vyutha 7*. 'Vyutha' is a term related to the old Murkanglais *viuda,* which meant variously 'widow,' 'relict,' or 'vestige.'"

Bridget ban's head jerked up. "Vestiges? Oh, well played, Donovan buigh! Well played. Imagine caching the artifacts, then leaving the documentation out where anyone could find it. Where is Prizga?"

"On Old Earth, on the western shore of the Northern Mark, just south of the glaciers."

"You knew about the Vestiges even then?"

"No, I copied the files because they were the only sealed files in the Miwellion. Briddy, they're *old*. They were sealed by the Audorithadesh Ympriales—and they were still sealed when I found them. It will take tender work to break them open."

"The Ympriales?" Bridget ban and her daughter alike showed bewilderment. "I've never heard of it."

"It was an empire on Old Earth shortly after star sliding had begun, after the fall of the Gran Publicamericana but before the formation of the Commonwealth of Suns. It included most of the Northern Mark and parts of Yurp and a place called Strine."

The Red Hound shook her head. "But then . . ."

"Aye. The files were time-locked all during the Commonwealth."

"Then the Vestiges cannae be Commonwealth work?"

"No. And that means they are not prehuman, either. Otherwise, there would not have been so much fuss when Mahadevan found the ruins on New Mumbai. It would have been old news."

Bridget ban shook her heads. "Then . . . If not the Commonwealth and not the prehumans . . . Who made the Vestiges? Where were they found?"

Donovan flicked the dangling thread with his finger. "That depends on how good your decrypters and seal-breakers are. But it does make you wonder why those early expeditions were so keen on finding alien intelligences."

Bridget ban nodded slowly. "They believed they were out there to be found. Do you think the Confederals know?"

"I doubt it. It was all superstition with them. One problem with hiding things away—it becomes too easy to forget what they were." Donovan sat back on the bench. "They might be something worth looking for, though."

"Why, so you can break them, too? I thought you were retiring under your fig tree?"

"Ah, what can it hurt?"

"You, above all men, ask that? You finally *deign* to show up at Clanthompson Hall, old man, and right away you want to run off again?"

"Old man? I've barely a century in my scrip as yet. I'm just hitting my stride. Beside, *you* should talk about haring off."

Méarana had left her mother and father, and joined Ravn Olafsdottr, who stood a little distance away. She was eating one of Donovan's noisome dishes, something called Chicken Joe Freezing. To all appearances, she had just woken up and set to breakfast, but Méarana had no doubt the Shadow had listened to every word her parents had exchanged.

The Shadow wore coveralls now, and she reached into one of their commodious pockets. She pulled out a metal wire and handed it to Méarana. The harper studied it. "A harp string."

Ravn nodded. "Used to strangle Khembold, later to strangle Gidula. Achieve artistic closure. You use that, my sweet one, to string your new harp." Then she waved her spoon in the direction of the other table. "They quarrel," she said around a mouthful of chicken.

"Yes."

"But you smile."

"It marks an improvement over twenty years of silence."

Ravn put down her spoon. "Are you satisfied, then? I told you in your Hall that I had promised to give Donovan a gift." She hugged herself. "Ooh! I am soo clayver!"

Méarana crossed her arms and studied the Shadow. She still had not made her mind up about the woman. She suspected that Ravn had transported her into danger precisely so that she could rescue her from it. "And what gift was that?"

The teeth were impossibly white against her coal-black face. "Ooh, I am sooch a sentimental oold fool. I gave him Bridget ban."

NOTES FOR THE CURIOUS

It's a big Spiral Arm and the technology of thousands of years from now is about as imaginable as airliners would be to Assyrians. It helps that there were intervening Dark Ages, lost technologies, and deliberate suppression of innovation. That lets us get away with over-the-horizon science and technology of here and now. Take some stuff that we maybe almost know how to do, and then suppose that we can do it really well. Techne that makes an appearance in *On the Razor's Edge* includes:

1. **"Subway tunnels" through space.** Just a gleam in the physicists' eyes, for now: http://www.npl.washington.edu /AV/altvw86.html.
2. **Domino Tight's exoskeleton.** We're already making their precursors: http://www.technovelgy.com/ct/Science -Fiction-News.asp?NewsNum=2174.
3. **Invisibility cloaks.** We can't make them yet, but see here:

http://www.cnn.com/2010/TECH/innovation/11/16/
space.time.cloak/index.html?hpt=T2.

After this manuscript was written but prior to publication
"researchers led by the University of Texas at Austin have
cloaked a three-dimensional object standing in free space,
bringing the invisibility cloak one step closer to reality":
http://www.kurzweilai.net/scientists-create-first-free
-standing-3d-cloak?utm_source=KurzweilAI+Daily+News
letter&utm_campaign=778bb63bfe-UA-946742-1&utm_
medium=email.

4. **Self-assembling ruins of the Hall of Suns.** Researchers at
the University of Michigan have developed a concrete
material that self-heals cracks and recovers most of the
original strength. Now project it way into the future:
http://ns.umich.edu/podcast/video.php?id=804.

5. **More self-assembly and self-repair of shenmats,
equipment, and systems.** Self-healing polymer mixtures
from Oak Ridge National Lab and the University of
Tennessee: http://www.ornl.gov/info/ornlreview/v42_3
_09/article15.shtml.

Nanoparticles assembling into complex arrays at Lawrence
Berkeley National Laboratory: http://newscenter.lbl.gov/
press-releases/2009/10/22/new-route-to-nano-self
-assembly/.

A University of Illinois polymer with self-sensing
properties that can react to mechanical stress: http://news
.illinois.edu/news/09/0506polymers.html.

Raytheon HEALICS Technology incorporates self-
healing into a complex system-on-chip (SoC) design,
providing the capability for the chip to sense undesired
circuit behaviors and correct them automatically: http://
raytheon.mediaroom.com/index.php?s=43&item=1410&
pagetemplate=release.

6. **Teasers and dazers.** At Old Dominion University, nanosecond-long high-voltage pulses that punch holes in cell membranes could be used for a Taser-like weapon that stuns targets because the pulse temporarily disables human muscles: http://www.newscientist.com/article/dn16706 -shocking-cancer-treatment-may-also-yield-weapon.html.

Shadow culture is based loosely on the decadent Franco-Burgundian knighthood of the fifteenth century, the main source for which is Johan Huizinga, *The Autumn of the Middle Ages.* Many of the anecdotes, events, and poems in the novel are based on actual anecdotes, events, and poems of that era, including the sudden passions of cruelty and sentiment. The story of Prime and Lady Ielnor's chemise is adapted from the poem "Des trois chevaliers et del chainse." The song Ravn listens to in Chapter 2, while shepherding Méarana into the Confederation, is adapted from Alain Chartier's "Ballade de Fougères." The introductory poem to chapter 7 is adapted from a prose passage in *Le Jouvencel,* the autobiography of Jean de Bueil. The introductory poem to chapter 14 is a mash-up of "Le Dit de Franc Gontier" by Philippe de Vitry and Eustache Deschamps, no. 184.

Descriptions of **the society of the late Commonwealth** and certain twilight attitudes attributed to its writers and thinkers were adapted from Peter Brown's *The World of Late Antiquity* concerning the outlook of fourth-century pagan rhetors.